PERDITION, U.S.A.

BOOKS BY GARY PHILLIPS

NOVELS

The Jook
The Perpetrators
Bangers
Freedom's Fight
The Underbelly
Kings of Vice (as Mal Radcliff)
Warlord of Willow Ridge
Three the Hard Way (collected novellas)
Beat, Slay, Love: One Chef's Hunger for Delicious Revenge (written collectively as Thalia Filbert)
The Killing Joke (co-written with Christa Faust)
Matthew Henson and the Ice Temple of Harlem

SHORT STORY COLLECTIONS

Monkology: 15 Stories from the World of Private Eye Ivan Monk
Astonishing Heroes: Shades of Justice
Treacherous: Grifters, Ruffians and Killers
The Unvarnished Gary Phillips: A Mondo Pulp Collection

ONE-SHOT HARRY NOVELS

One-Shot Harry
Ash Dark as Night

IVAN MONK NOVELS

Violent Spring
Perdition, U.S.A.
Bad Night Is Falling
Only the Wicked

MARTHA CHAINEY NOVELS

High Hand
Shooter's Point

GRAPHIC NOVELS

Shot Callerz
Midnight Mover

GRAPHIC NOVELS CONT.

South Central Rhapsody
Cowboys
Danger A-Go-Go
Angeltown: The Nate Hollis Investigations
High Rollers
Big Water
The Rinse
Peepland (co-written with Christa Faust)
Vigilante: Southland
The Be-Bop Barbarians
Cold Hard Cash: A Martha Chainey Escapade

ANTHOLOGIES AS EDITOR

The Cocaine Chronicles (co-edited with Jervey Tervalon)
Orange County Noir
Politics Noir: Dark Tales from the Corridors of Power
The Darker Mask: Heroes from the Shadows (co-edited with Christopher Chambers)
Scoundrels: Tales of Greed, Murder and Financial Crimes
Black Pulp (co-edited with Tommy Hancock and Morgan Minor)
Black Pulp II (co-edited with Tommy Hancock, Ernest Russell, Gordon Dymowski & H. David Blalock)
Day of the Destroyers
Hollis for Hire
Hollis, P.I.
Culprits: The Heist Was Only the Beginning (co-edited with Richard Brewer)
The Obama Inheritance: Fifteen Stories of Conspiracy Noir
South Central Noir
Witnesses for the Dead: Stories (co-edited with Gar Anthony Haywood)
Get Up Off That Thing: Crime Fiction Inspired by the Songs of James Brown

PERDITION, U.S.A.

GARY PHILLIPS

This edition first published in 2024 by
Soho Press
227 W 17th Street
New York, NY 10011

Library of Congress Cataloging-in-Publication Data

Names: Phillips, Gary, 1955- author.
Title: Perdition, U.S.A. / Gary Phillips.
Description: New York, NY : Soho Crime, 2024.
Series: The Ivan Monk mysteries ; 2
Identifiers: LCCN 2023056129

ISBN 978-1-64129-441-6
eISBN 978-1-64129-442-3

Subjects: LCGFT: Detective and mystery fiction. | Novels.
Classification: LCC PS3566.H4783 P47 2024 | DDC 813/.54—dc23/
eng/20231206
LC record available at https://lccn.loc.gov/2023056129

Interior design by Janine Agro, Soho Press, Inc.

Printed in the United States of America

10 9 8 7 6 5 4 3 2 1

For my mother, Leonelle,
who knew the power of words
and tried mightily to impart
their secrets.

"Who knows what happens to a human being from one moment to the next? These things are incidents. There is more to life."

—Ray Arcel

PERDITION, U.S.A.

CHAPTER 1

"Say, brother, I ain't runnin' no newsstand where you stop and browse for hours. You gonna buy or what?"

The other man, an older gentleman in a plaid vest and a pair of doubleknit slacks in dire need of a hot iron, massaged his chin between thumb and index finger.

Scatterboy Williams let out an exasperated growl. "This is a genuine Cartier chronometer, my man. Stainless steel band with gold trim and a two-carat movement."

The man chewed his lip and looked at Scatterboy, then back to the watch in his outstretched palm. "Two carats, huh?"

Scatterboy nodded. "That's right. You go to any one of them stores where them Jews and them Iranians shop up in Beverly Hills and you see this fine timepiece goin' for no less than three thousand dollars."

"How'd you get one?"

"You really want to know, or you want a good deal on a handsome watch?" The salesman grinned, because he knew the answer. People were so predictable.

"Two-fifty," the man mumbled as he grasped the watch, turning it this way and that to determine its authenticity.

That was okay with Scatterboy. He doubted if the man had ever seen another Cartier to compare it to. "It's gonna be three hundred in a minute, reverend, if you don't make up your mind."

"Very well, brother Williams. I wouldn't be doing this, only the beautiful Omega my dear wife bought me some twenty years ago is just too beat to be fixed again."

He droned on about the need for a preacher to keep up appearances before his congregation and what not. But Williams wasn't paying much attention save for the twenties the baritone-voiced healer extracted from his cracked-leather wallet. The money and watch were exchanged, and the holy man strapped the timepiece around his bony wrist.

"Is this band alligator skin?"

"That's illegal, reverend," Scatterboy said without a trace of irony. "It's snake, dyed to look like that."

"Yes, of course," the other man responded as he rose from the booth in the King Lion barbecue restaurant. "Well, thank you, Mr. Williams. I hope I see you in church soon."

He didn't wait for an answer and exited the establishment. Scatterboy leisurely finished his order of links, greens and potato salad. He also downed another can of Shasta cola, and sat working particles of gristle from his back teeth with a toothpick. The booth was next to a window which afforded a view of Ludlow Street, the main drag of Pacific Shores, and Scatterboy gazed out as the sun set.

Once upon a time, or so the old-timers would tell you, Pacific Shores was a going concern. Chiefly a town erected around the shipyards, the Shores enjoyed a solid, if limited, economic base for decades. Following Pearl Harbor, there were ships needed for the war. Following the war, there were ships needed to stem the red tide. By the '60s, a steel plant and a GM factory supplemented the shipyards. The working-class residents of the Shores—Blacks, whites and Latinos thrived.

In those days, most everyone owned their own home and worked twenty to thirty years at the same job, got a pension, and hung out at the VFW or B.P.O.E. hall when it wasn't bowling night. Not that the Shores was a model of an ethnic utopia. Like most of America, the various races tended to congregate in their own churches and shop in their own stores. But a standard of civic harmony prevailed.

By the tail end of the '70s, harsh changes came to this city located some thirty miles south of Los Angeles. Ship orders were down, "outsourcing" became the new corporate buzzword, and the GM plant moved to Mexico to cut costs. The outmoded steel plant closed for good. The two shipyards reduced two shifts to one, forced some workers into early retirements and laid others off. Eventually one moved to a "right-to-work" state whose legislature believed things like employees' rights originated in *The Communist Manifesto*.

By the mid-'80s, the only heavy industry left in Pacific Shores was one shipyard operating with a skeletal crew. The smaller businesses, dependent on a healthy workforce, withered and blew away in the recessionary winds sweeping the Southland.

Robert "Scatterboy" Williams, who had once worked as a shipyard welder, watched his second prostitute saunter by the King Lion. With a deft thrust, he freed the last piece of meat between his teeth. He rose, burped, and left the barbecue place.

A cool breeze coming off the ocean greeted him as he made his way along the street. Walking aimlessly, he turned over several options in his mind. All in all, he was about seven hundred dollars richer than he'd been two weeks ago.

The seven hundred was the net from what he'd paid the sly Swede for several of the questionable Cartiers.

Whether they were genuine or not didn't matter to him. That they'd been stolen was a certainty. What really mattered was that others wanted them.

Problem was Swede wasn't the most easygoing guy to deal with. He was always cautious, always wondering if you'd slipped up and would lead the cops to him. But, Scatterboy allowed, there was a lesson to be learned from that sort of thinking. Which was why Swede'd never done time when guys like him found themselves marking the days in Deuel, Folsom or—the Lord help his homeboys—Pelican Bay.

Scatterboy drifted along a residential street with rundown Craftsmen and Spanish bungalows in need of paint and patching. A few of the lawns were trimmed but most were brown and shaggy. A tired street in a worn town.

Passing by an old Riviera parked at the curb, he noticed shapes moving in its darkened interior. He tensed, considering how fast he could gain some distance. Fortunately, the barrel of an Uzi wasn't suddenly erupting in his direction. Peering closer in the fading light, Scatterboy was relieved to see the windows were up in the vehicle.

He was no gangbanger, but given the vagaries of drug turfs, one never knew what real or imagined line of demarcation you were crossing. As he got closer, he could see two teenagers inside the Buick. The boy was sitting in the driver's seat, and had his arm around a girl next to him. The youngster gave Scatterboy a challenging look, and the girl sipped on a beer.

A thin trail of vapor was rising from between the two of them, down where the boy had his other hand. Scatterboy grinned wolfishly and walked on. Weed and pussy were about all a man could ask for these days. He got to the corner of Creedmore and Osage and stood there, thinking.

The watches were a good hustle but they took a lot of time to sell and required a lot of exposure. The seven hundred wouldn't last forever and he'd promised the mother of his baby girl he'd do better at supporting the kid. Slangin' product was not his forte. He could never score enough crack on his own to make any real money. And if he wanted to be big, he'd have to be beholden to a gang lord. The thought of being in the pocket of some kid with a 9mm tucked in his belt, and malt liquor fueling his thoughts, was not his idea of upward mobility.

Well, he reasoned, something would turn up. He crossed the street and started in the direction of his apartment several blocks over. As he got mid-block on Creedmore, an open-air Jeep rounded the far corner.

The driver crept at a slow pace then pulled to the curb. A light came on under the dashboard. Scatterboy could see that the man at the wheel was dressed casually, and he studied a map spread out on his knees.

"Maybe something's turned up already," Scatterboy happily intoned to himself.

He got closer, rehearsing how his next moves might go. Slip close while the lost chump looked for his route. The man wasn't wearing a seat belt. Perfect. Just ease up, yank the square out of the car by the elbow and slip an arm around his throat. Grab the wallet and run off before the mark could react.

The other man wasn't too big and Scatterboy, standing over six feet, had worked out daily on the prison iron yard. He gloated inwardly and drew closer, trying to control his hurried breathing.

"Do you know how I can find Terminal Street?"

"Wha?" The man's head had come up so suddenly it caught Scatterboy off-guard. Shit, now this punk could ID him. He turned sideways and pointed back the way he'd just come. Scatterboy figured to give him his directions, then as he looked that way, jump him. Fuck it, he needed the money. He better not resist. "Yeah, man. Go to the end of this block, make a left and go down another four or five blocks, you can't miss it."

"I don't plan to."

"Huh?" Scatterboy said as he pivoted back around.

The bullet entered his head on the right side of the bridge of his nose. It angled up and left the rear of his skull near the top of his close shaved head. The Jeep did a vicious U-turn and sped off as Robert Williams, aka Scatterboy, fell dead to the pavement.

—

CHAPTER 2

The small single-family house was the second from the end of the block. The grass was brown, and a low hedge bordered the driveway. A baby swing rested on the enclosed concrete porch. A cat leapt onto the balustrade and curled out on the warm stone railing.

"Are you Ivan Monk? Are you the man I need?"

Assuming the questions weren't meant to be existential, the private eye said, "Yes. Are you Clarice Moore?"

The screen door opened outward to reveal a teenaged girl with long strands of thick cornrowed hair. She was holding onto a baby. The kid had three of its fingers jammed in its mouth and drooled as it eyed the stranger. "Do you have some kind of identification? Mom says I should ask to see that."

It occurred to Monk that Clarice Moore should have listened to her mother when she'd told her about boys. He produced his photostat and the young woman took it from his hand.

She consumed it with a fierce glare. The baby began to cry and Clarice bounced the child gently and continued to peruse the private investigator license. Finally she handed it back. "Come on in."

He entered a room that reminded him of his mother's house. The home was lived in but cared for like a favorite shirt. Hanging from the walls were prints—a Charles White, a Rome Bearden, and an artist Monk didn't recognize.

"Come on in the kitchen. I've got to get Shawndell's formula."

Monk followed Clarice Moore into the back of the house. She retrieved a baby bottle warming in a saucepan and leaked a few drops from the nipple onto her slender forearm. "Can't give this child cold formula, no sir. Little Shawndell wants it toasty." She held up the child and giggled at her. "Isn't that right?"

She gave the baby her nutrition, and put her in a highchair. She sat at the kitchen table but didn't offer Monk a seat.

He remained standing in the doorway, his arms crossed. The young woman looked at him, then down at a few letters and a folded newspaper on the table. She shifted the letters around but didn't speak.

Monk broke the silence. "You said over the phone that your boyfriend had been murdered."

For an answer she unfolded the newspaper. Monk got closer to read it. The paper was the *Press-Telegram* from two days ago. Clarice's thin finger hovered over a five-paragraph article relating the street shooting of twenty-six-year-old Robert Williams. Who, the report stated, had been on parole for assault and robbery from Solano State Prison. It went on to say that he'd previously done time at the California Youth Authority for second-degree manslaughter. Police sources said the investigation was continuing.

"Do you think someone he knew from Solano did him in?" Monk took a seat at the table and watched her face and body movements.

She looked at him and for the first time Monk noticed her light-caramel eyes and the tiny freckles that dotted her fine boned coppery face. "I don't know anything about that. I just want you to find out who killed Scatterboy."

"Scatterboy?"

"Yeah."

She didn't seem inclined to explain the root of the nickname so Monk said, "How'd you find out about me?"

The baby threw her bottle on the floor and smiled a toothless grin at her mother. Clarice put the child over her shoulder, and walked out of the room patting her back gently. Several minutes later she returned alone.

"My mother remembered hearing about you on the radio. Something to do with the mayor of L.A. killing Koreans," she said earnestly.

Monk blinked. "It wasn't the mayor, Clarice. Was it your mother's idea to have me look for Robert's killer?"

"No, that was my idea. Matter of fact, I kept on about Scatterboy's death until finally she said if I wanted to do something so bad, I ought to get a detective. I told her I didn't know no detective and that's when she got smart like she do and said if I listened to more than Ice Cube and Yo Yo I'd know about you and how you was a Black private eye and famous and all."

In the face of unassailable logic. Monk moved onward. "This is not a game, Clarice. The father of your child wasn't a candidate for a Nobel Prize."

"That mean he deserved to get killed like he did?" There was a sternness in her voice but the eyes were calm as they locked on him.

Monk tapped the paper. "This seems to infer your Robert was out doing something he shouldn't have been doing at that time of night."

Her lip curled upward but she fought to get it under control. "I know he wasn't out seein' no other woman. I know Scatterboy was loyal."

"That's not what I'm talking about, Clarice. Anyway, how do you plan to pay me?"

Peeved, she leaned close to Monk. "I ain't on welfare, man. I work part-time at a Radio Shack. I can pay you for your time and effort."

Monk continued to humor the headstrong girl. "Fine. Do you have a list of Robert's friends and acquaintances?"

"I told you, none of them had anything to do with this."

"The investigation has to start somewhere."

Her brows bunched in that absorbing countenance she'd used on Monk's license. Abruptly, she got up from the table and left the kitchen again. The sound of a drawer opening and shutting forcefully filled the empty moments as Monk waited.

Clarice returned and put a single piece of white lined paper on the table. She sat and began to laboriously write on the sheet. At various intervals she would pause and study her output. Then she would resume in her slow, steady pace. Finally she slid it across to Monk.

Listed in compact block letters were individuals with names like Li'l Bone, Two Dog, and an Angel Z. There were no addresses for these and the others written down. But she had indicated where a particular individual might hang out. A Junior's Liquors, a place called the King Lion, and so on. Lines were drawn from the names to the places.

Monk said as evenly as he could, "I could spend a lot of time looking for these people you put down here just so I could talk to them. Don't any of them live somewhere? Didn't Robert have a mother or father, some relative somewhere?"

Clarice snatched the paper from Monk's hand. "Why you got to be askin' so many smart questions? Look, that's how I know where to find them. Ain't none of them got an office, man." She began to jiggle her left leg and slap the table quietly with the back of her hand. "I mean you acting like you don't want to help and all."

"Come on, Clarice," Monk said, allowing exasperation to color his voice. "Robert, Scatterboy, or whatever you want to call him probably got done in by a homey he'd stiffed."

She pointed at the doorway. "Then why don't you leave, Mr. Headlines."

"All I'm trying to say, Clarice, is that you know perfectly well what kind of dude Robert Williams was. Be realistic. I bet if you thought about it, you could come up with one or two people on this list who might have done him harm."

She was having none of it. The determined teenager cocked her head and bounced her leg again. He waited for a few minutes, but all he got was the sound of her foot tapping against the patterned linoleum.

Monk got up and headed for the front door. He looked back at her sitting in the kitchen, head cradled in her hand, fuming. He clucked his tongue, feeling like he was casting her adrift. Slowly, the big bad detective went back into the afternoon air.

RONNY AARON sold his next-to-last dub of crack to a blonde woman whose license plate frame read: I only tan in Newport Beach. The Infiniti roared away and Aaron took his lanky frame along Ludlow. He was tired and he walked without much of a destination in mind.

It had been a long night of mostly haggling with money-poor crack heads. But the two or three sales to upscale clientele—Pacific Shores was less than a half hour drive due north from the Orange County border—who paid the rate and split, made up for the hassles.

Aaron adjusted his Fila so it rested more fashionably on his head and drifted into the Zacharias corner market on Osage.

"Give me a half pint of Seagrams," he said to the middle-aged Latina behind the counter. Hefting his purchase, he walked back outside and ran into one of his customers, an addict named Herbert who was always short of cash.

"My man," Herbert effused.

Aaron kept walking but Herbert wouldn't take the hint.

"Say, bro', how 'bout a little something on credit?"

Aaron gritted his teeth and marched on.

"You can't speak, motherfuckah? Can't say shit to one of your best customers?" Herbert shoved Aaron from behind and the drug seller stopped, then turned to back-hand the man.

"What the fuck's your problem, Herbie? You don't want me to get in your ass right here in the street, do you?" Though he knew Herbert could be violent, Aaron also sensed he was too strung out to cause him much damage.

Self-contempt or anger contorted the crack head's face. He spat red on the pavement between them. The contempt overtook the anger, tightening the slack skin around the pin-prick eyes. "I got to have some, man. I've got to."

"Fuck you, punk." Aaron strode off, triumphant. He left Osage and went east along Kenmore. He felt good having stood down Herbert. Word would spread and those that inhabited the depths of Pacific Shores would know he was not a man to be fucked with. Hell, he was a man of respect.

"Yo," a voice said from somewhere behind him.

Feeling immortal, Aaron turned. "Yeah," he said, Napoleon addressing a lesser. He grinned crookedly. "What?"

The first bullet tore into his left kneecap and he sunk to the sidewalk on his good leg. "Motherfuckah," Aaron screamed, grabbing for the .32 tucked in his back pocket. The second bullet entered his open mouth, busted out his new fillings, and continued to travel downward. The slug exited his back below the shoulder blades. Ronny Aaron was already dead when his body gently crumpled to the earth.

CHAPTER 3

There was no mention of Ronny Aaron's shooting in the *L.A. Times*, nor any coverage of it on the nightly news. There were three paragraphs in the lesser-circulated *Press-Telegram* out of Long Beach, but it was a dry summing-up of an insignificant life. He was just one more penny-ante drug dealer the sheriff's deputies in Pacific Shores were glad to be shut of.

Even if there had been banner headlines about Aaron's killing, it probably wouldn't have been the topic *du jour* at the reception for California's new Senator, Grainger Wu, at the Sunset Orchid Hotel in L.A.'s Chinatown.

Jill Kodama stepped out of the ladies room just as Walter Kane was placing an empty glass on a table in the foyer. "Jill, I saw you come in earlier. I meant to say hi but you know how it is when you get cornered by ass-kissers."

"Not that you're opposed to that in certain circumstances."

"Yeow." Kane did a Groucho Marx with his eyebrows. He was over six-two and rapier sharp in a grey double-breasted suit. Underneath the jacket was an aqua-hued shirt with a spear-point collar and a black tie. A crimson pocket square completed the look. His auburn hair was cut modishly long, and he sprouted a thin, Errol Flynn mustache.

Standing close to him, Kodama was greeted with the aroma of vodka mixed with Obsession for Men. "Yeah, it's a tough job being the senator's chief aide, running interference with the oil lobbyists, the aerospace industry, and the tourist bureaus. Helping them figure out which political action committee to dump their next ten thousand on."

Kane grinned and the two walked back toward the room where the reception was taking place. "What a cynic, and you're not even old enough to drink."

"You can quit the flattery, Walter. I've already voted."

They crossed the threshold into the reception area, called the Autumn Lounge. A jazz sextet played a low samba from the raised stage off to one side. Kodama plucked a white wine from the hosted bar and took a sip. "Seriously, Walter, Grainger's got a hard row to hoe and we both know it. A freshman senator from California who won in a tight race."

"And standing on liberal legs," Kane added. "'Course it didn't hurt he has sound fiscal programs that appealed to the older, whiter electorate."

"Despite a campaign where the racial mud-slinging flew fast and furious in the last weeks."

They both turned to the new voice as Ursala Brock walked up. She was a large-hipped, small-waisted, handsome Black woman who handled urban affairs for Senator Wu. The two women kissed one another on the cheek.

"Yeah, the mailer Jankowsky put out in the last month ran with the headline, 'A Peril from the East,'" Kane said. "So of course he gets a lot of attention for it. Then the old cocksucker goes on talk shows and claims it referred to the fact that Grainger had been an assemblyman from the East Bay—Oakland." Kane winked broadly.

The band began a version of a Cedar Walton tune called "Midnight Waltz." Kodama asked rhetorically, "So with less than a three-percent margin of victory, does our favorite son have a chance to do anything in the Senate?"

A toupeed white man in a pin-striped three-piece suit, his vest straining against an ample belly, grabbed Brock aggressively from behind. "Ursala, when the hell are you going to forget about politics and come work for me?" He quaffed a healthy amount of the drink he was holding.

Brock smirked. "I lay awake nights thinking about the good the advertising council does, Harry." She removed the ad man's hand from her body, giving Kodama a sidelong glance.

"Fuckin' A," Harry agreed and wandered off to cop a feel on some other woman.

Momentarily a silence descended on the trio. A reflection on the forces that created men like Harry, and an understanding it was his universe they were operating in, not the other way around.

Eventually, Kane spoke. "You're right, Jill, we ain't got shit in the way of a mandate, but I'll be damned if we won't fight for the high ground." Somehow the aide had obtained another vodka tonic and was sampling it steadily.

Brock put her hand around Kodama's waist. "Before we take Pork Chop Hill, sarge, I want to know how's that brutally handsome Black man of yours?"

Kodama bared her uppers. "How come every time I see you, you got to be asking about my man, honey?"

"Girls," Kane intoned. He leaned into them like a schoolyard leech, "I'm serious, you guys," he pointed the rim of the glass at Brock. "Tell Jill about the kind of mail we've been getting."

She eyed him curiously. "Well, what else do you expect to get in the office of the first Chinese-American, hell, the first Asian from the mainland to become a member of the U.S. Senate?"

"Meaning there's a certain level of racism and intolerance we must accommodate," Kane said, baiting her as the sextet swung into a rendition of Herbie Hancock's "Cantaloupe Island." Several people bobbed their heads to the jaunty beat.

"Meaning we have to push to accomplish some goals," Brock responded testily, "'cause we may not get a second go-round."

"All of us are well aware of the limits of politics," Kane slurred.

"My point, Walter, is that we need to do something about these groups," Ursala replied aggressively.

It seemed to Kodama this was getting to be an old argument among her two friends. "How do you mean, Ursala?"

"I mean, your honor, that I don't think the goddamn nazis, the Posse Comitatus, gangsta rappers calling for bashin' their hoes, the Jewish Defense League, or the fuckin' War Reich have a right to exist, let alone exercise their poisonous free speech."

Kodama was used to being grilled for being a cardcarrying member of the American Civil Liberties Union. "I suppose I don't need to remind you our chapter broke with the national and didn't go along with the nazis' march that year in Skokie, Illinois."

"I'll give you that," Brock conceded.

Kodama said, "Now before you expect me to go into my patented 'The Constitution is nothing if it's not for all of us,' who the hell is the War Reich?"

"A group of skinheads who started in the Pacific Northwest," Kane contributed.

"An all-too-typical group of young disaffected whites who see it as their Aryan destiny to create a homeland for their race." Brock waved a silent hello to a passerby.

Kane said, "They're connected to that fire bombing of a Puerto Rican family in Port Huron."

"No question these are serious times, Walter. This state passed the anti-immigrant 187 and that goddamn three-strikes 184."

"Which takes even more discretion away from judges," Brock observed. "Further demonizing Black and Brown youth."

"Which," Kane said, sipping more vodka, "is right in line with the thinking behind Colorado's gay-bashing Proposition M measure. The lines are being drawn in this country just like in Bosnia."

"I hope you're wrong, Walter," Kodama said.

Wu called to Kane from the stage and the chief aide polished off the last of his vodka tonic. He placed the glass in the dirt of an urn next to a twisted thick-trunked cactus. "But we can only do what we can to make the system work," he said, his breath heavy with drink. He jogged to the stage.

"Enough of this depressing shit" Brock took Kodama by the arm, leading her to one side. "So what's going on with you and Ivan?" Her eyes glittered mischievously.

"Cool, cool. How about you and Terry?"

"We spent last weekend up in Monterey. Got away to talk about the future. You know Terry, he had champagne sent up to the room and took me on a balloon ride."

Brock took delight in her stock broker boyfriend and his doting on her. "And what does the future hold, Kreskin?"

"Love or ruin, baby. But Terry and I will face it together."

"Ivan and I have a good thing," she said defensively. And surprised that she felt the need to blurt it out like that.

Brock perceived it as a challenge. "Four years is enough time to make up one's mind."

"We're comfortable, Ursala."

"My shoes are comfortable, girl. But I walk on them."

Kodama got hot. "Ivan doesn't take me or our relationship for granted. We both have careers."

"So do a lot of us. Maybe it's you who likes the status quo."

"What if I do?" Kodama replied tersely.

Brock drew close. "Jill, if you're happy with where you're at, so am I. We've known each other too long to fall out over some silly men." They hugged and Brock went off toward the stage where Wu beckoned her.

The wine glass was in her hand, but Kodama had suddenly lost the taste for the stuff.

CHAPTER 4

"Yo, home, you getting' it steady from Tracy?"

Jimmy Henderson took another swig of his cranberry juice. "A man doesn't go around saying he is, or he ain't. A man has to be circumspect about such matters."

His cousin, Malik Bradford, gave him a light sock on the shoulder. He downshifted, and guided the VW beetle around the corner. "Well if it was me going out with one of the finest hammers in our poli-sci class, I'd be showboatin' to every jealous brother I knew." He regaled Henderson with an oblique glance. "You are using the hat?"

Henderson didn't reply. He chewed a handful of his fries and pointed at the market on the corner. "Pull over, man."

"What for? We just got some grub at the King Lion."

"Don't be cute," Henderson chided. "Let me have a five, will you?"

"Next time don't be leaving your wallet at home," Bradford replied as the Volkswagen coasted to the curb in front of the Zacharias store. The young man in the passenger seat got out and entered the small market. He emerged moments later holding a small brown bag and got back in the car.

"What's in the sack?" Bradford inquired with mock innocence.

Henderson showed him the two packs of Sheik rubbers and reclosed the bag. "Satisfied, doctor?"

"Uh-huh," his cousin said. Both of them burst into laughter.

The Beetle did a U-turn in the street and presently stopped directly in front of the Neptune Manor, the plain apartment house where Henderson lived with his mother and two younger sisters.

"Okay, Jimmy, don't forget to be at the library at two. We'll go over your chemistry assignment."

"Bet, Malik." They performed an elaborate handshake which ended with them lightly knocking their fists together. The bug took off into the gathering evening.

Henderson walked toward the rear of the building. Something disturbed the thatch of shrubbery to his right and he expected to see one of the neighborhood cats dart across his path. But he didn't panic as the figure of a man suddenly filled the space in front of him.

"What can I do for you, my man?" The muscles in Henderson's calves tensed.

The form didn't talk. One of the arms started to come up perpendicular to its body. "You gotta give it up," the darkened shape finally said.

Henderson was already reacting. His angular body was in the air and latching onto his attacker. The two went down on the hard surface of the walkway, even as the pistol went off.

"Shit." Henderson grimaced as an unfamiliar sensation speared his left thigh. He choked back a stab of nausea and aimed his fist in the direction of the other man's head. He connected with the jaw underneath the blur of white hair. He was about to follow up with another blow when the man slapped him alongside the head with the flat of the gun. A white thug in the Shores was unusual, but Henderson had little time to reflect on the oddity of the situation.

"Little coward pussy bitch," Henderson cursed through the pain. He was on his side, facing the apartment building when several lights went on in the three-story structure. "Help me," the young man yelled. Just then the warm muzzle of the gun was pressed against his neck and he could feel his wallet being lifted from his back pocket.

"Hey, what's going on down there?" a woman's voice queried hesitantly from above.

There was a slight movement of the weapon against his flesh and Henderson reared up. He wrapped his hands around the arm with the gun at the end of it.

"Fucker," the other man snarled. "Let go."

Henderson tried to stand but his bleeding leg wouldn't support him. A fist crashed into his side and he sagged, letting the arm loose. But he knew what would happen next if he didn't act. From somewhere he tapped into a reserve and lurched toward the figure which was backing up.

"Goddamnit," the other man said.

Henderson clung to the man because his life depended on it.

"I'm going to give you what's coming to you," the attacker promised.

A door opened somewhere and Henderson punched the robber in the gut. There was a rush of wind from the man and Henderson grinned weakly with satisfaction.

"I called the police on you crack fools," a grandmotherly voice said from above. "I'm tired of you misfits cornin' here and getting high and doing all that devilment you always doin'."

Henderson gasped, "Help me, please."

The attacker's body straightened and there was a flash

that temporarily blinded Henderson. He fell to the ground again and could hear the man running off. He fought to clear his vision and became aware that he was having trouble breathing. It felt as if jagged chunks of his lung were swimming in his mouth and he coughed up some thick liquid. Jimmy Henderson prayed it wasn't one of his nine lives.

CHAPTER 5

Delilah Carnes was sitting at her desk in the rotunda, entering data into her reliable 486, when Monk got to his office at seventeen minutes after nine. Monk and the architectural firm of Ross and Hendricks shared office expenses and the salary of the all-purpose Delilah.

"Good morning."

"Mademoiselle." He picked up her empty coffee cup and filled it from the steaming carafe. Adding milk, but no sugar, he replaced it near her.

"Thanks. You have somebody waiting for you in your office."

"Look like money?" He chuckled, heading for his closed door.

"The kind you're used to."

As he opened his office door, he caught a glimpse of a baby crawling on top of his colonial desk. The kid picked up a paperweight and brought it down forcefully onto the desk's polished surface. Then she rolled the glass orb until it dropped off the edge, thumping dully onto the carpet.

Monk stifled a comment and entered. Clarice was reaching for Shawndell on the desk. She then proceeded to change her daughter's disposable diaper. He remained standing near the entrance.

"I'll bet you'll believe me now," the young mother said as she finished cleaning up her daughter. She folded the weighty thing and dropped it in the wastebasket.

"How do you mean, Clarice?" Monk got a kick out of her pit bull attitude. It seemed that once she set her mind to it, damned if she wasn't going to get satisfaction. He picked up the paperweight and placed it back on a small pile of letters.

Clarice pointed at a folded newspaper beside the squirming Shawndell.

He retrieved it and pulled one of his Eastlakes away from her and the smell of fresh baby feces. Monk sat down near the window and read the item she'd circled in red in yesterday's *Press-Telegram*. It was an account of a robbery and shooting of a college student named Jimmy Henderson. The young man was in critical condition at Long Beach Memorial. The article went on to point out that Henderson was the third young man shot in the same general area in less than a month.

Monk looked at Clarice who was dancing with her baby. "All right," he said.

"That boy got shot less than four blocks from where Scatterboy got killed." Shawndell swept a flabby hand across her mother's cheek.

"Pacific Shores has seen better days, Clarice." Even as he said it, he wondered if he wasn't trying to rationalize his own inaction. "Unfortunately, it's not too unusual for a number of robberies and shootings to take place in a given area. Especially if a gang figures it's easy pickings for them."

"Scatterboy had over two hundred dollars in his pocket when he was shot." She set Shawndell loose to roam on all fours across the office rug. Occasionally the baby would make an effort to stand, stumble along a foot or so, then go back to crawling around.

"But Henderson was robbed," Monk emphasized. "That could mean more than one person doing these shootings. Once there's a smell of blood, the pack comes out."

"If it's gangsta shit, then why wasn't Scatterboy's roll taken? And if you read that article better, you'll see that the one they talk about didn't have a wallet on him so they ain't sure about the robbery thing."

Clarice's single-mindedness got on Monk's nerves, but he had to concede her point. "I don't have an answer for that."

"You act like such a wheel and all, why don't you find out?"

"There's a future waiting for you in international diplomacy."

"See how you do?" Shawndell was squealing delightfully at the sound of her mother's raised voice. "You always got a come back, but you think 'oh she's just a youngster,' so what I got to say don't mean anything." Clarice picked Shawndell up and bounced her daughter on her slim hip. The child giggled quietly, her amber eyes locked on the paperweight.

The young mother went on. "But I know plenty, Mr. Monk. I know I got to raise this child, and that I got to stay in school and I got to get out of the Shores." She stopped, adjusted something on the baby's overalls, then spoke again. "It took me an hour and a half on the bus and blue line to get down here, and all you can do is be a smart ass." She struck a defiant pose.

Monk leaned back in his chair, alternately annoyed and bemused by the young woman. Finally he said, "What do you want to know, Clarice? Do you want to know that the father of your child owed money to some hustler and got his reward for being late in payments? Is that how you want your daughter to know about him?"

Clarice stopped bouncing her child, and stared at Monk. "That's my concern. As it is, she'll never get to meet him."

Monk felt ashamed. "You got heart, Clarice."

"You sayin' you'll look for his killer now," she said hopefully.

"Yeah, I'll try. But"—he wagged a finger at her—"you gotta come clean about some things. How is it that Scatterboy had that money on him?"

"He did odd jobs." She set the child down.

"It's not like I'm not going to pull his record, Clarice. Save us a little time, dig?" He leaned forward expectantly.

Shawndell squirmed loose and set off for the desk. She did her best to reach the sought-after paperweight. She gave up and went off in the direction of the brass coat rack Monk kept in the corner.

"He used to sell watches and rings and things like that, you know," Clarice finally offered.

"He steal these items?" Monk asked matter-of-factly.

"Sometimes," she admitted. "Sometimes he got them from some others who made them."

"Knock-offs."

Clarice's eyebrows and shoulders lifted.

"Who was his supplier?" Monk watched Shawndell as she tried to shake the coat rack. But her hands weren't big enough or strong enough to get a good grasp. Content to make the effort, she'd periodically push her forehead into the center pole.

Clarice folded her arms and sat on the edge of Monk's desk, her neck pulled inward like a turtle's. She spoke with her head cocked downward. "I was with him one time when we went to pick up some of these watches. I don't remember the address but it was a place near downtown."

"You mean Long Beach?"

The head swung quickly from side-to-side. "No, it was

L.A. One of those places where they sew clothes near the Sports Arena."

There were numerous such garment operations on Grand, Hope, and the other streets east of the Arena and Coliseum, sweatshops that paid low wages or piece rates to Central American immigrants and carried perky names like Little Miss Casuals or California Burst.

"Do you remember what street it was on, what the name was on the building?" Monk was up once more, pulling a note pad out of his desk drawer. "And what was the name of the cat you two went to see?"

Monk could almost see the neurons connecting in her head, the look of concentration was so intense on Clarice's face.

"Swiss . . . no, Dutch." She paused, rubbing the side of her head. "Swede. That was it. Swede is what Scatterboy called him."

Monk was writing it down. "And the place."

Shawndell was crying but Clarice ignored her. "I wasn't driving."

"So that means you don't remember where it was?"

The baby was on her back, her legs and arms working circles in the air as she gave her lungs a workout. "I'm not sure," the young mother said as she picked up her child to comfort her. "I had Shawndell with me and that took all my attention. 'Sides, I waited in the car while Scatterboy went in to take care of business."

Casually, Monk stroked the ends of his goatee. No rush, no sweat.

Presently, having quieted down the baby with a bottle, Clarice said. "Oh yeah. The building was brown with yellow stripes running around the top." She rocked back and forth with Shawndell. "It was near Broadway."

"Broadway and what?" Monk was sitting in the Eastlake, looking out the window at a seagull doing a loop-the-loop in the morning sky.

"Broadway after downtown," came the terse reply.

Monk checked any sarcasm he was considering. "Like around Twenty-Ninth Street? Thirty-Fourth Street? Adams?"

"Before Adams. 'Cause we drove up Adams afterward and got something to eat at a pastrami place."

"Making progress," Monk mumbled to himself as he made notes. "Did you see the one called Swede?"

"Nope. Scatterboy came back out of the building with his watches and we took off."

Monk said, "Did you bring the sheet you wrote those names on the other night?"

She produced it from the diaper bag and handed it to him.

He brushed talcum powder off the sheet and read it. Several notations were now included next to two of the names Clarice had originally written down. There was a street address for the one called Li'l Bone and another hang-out for Two Dog.

"How much do you want me to pay you?" Clarice asked guilelessly.

Monk looked up from the writing. The teenager and her daughter were playing silly face with one another. He figured to give it a go for a few days, reach a dead end, then inform his client it was hopeless. But if he didn't charge her something, she'd be pissed and suspicious.

"Give me a hundred as an advance and I'll have Delilah give you our standard contract. You are old enough to sign, aren't you?"

"I'll be eighteen in three months, Mr. Monk."

"Okay. I'll get Delilah to draw it up now." He was going to add, "send it home with her," but he felt bad about putting

Clarice and Shawndell back on what passed for public transportation in L.A. "Then let me give you a lift, so you and your mother can read it. She'll have to sign the contract."

"You can take me to my aunt's place in Wilmington. She'll watch the baby while I go to work. Now are you gonna do your best to find out who killed Scatterboy?" She gazed unblinkingly into Monk's face.

"You really loved him," Monk concluded.

"Just realizing that, huh, detective man?"

"I'm slow, but I'm thorough."

"I hope so," she said seriously.

MONK ENTERED the automatic double doors to the intensive care ward and asked which room Jimmy Henderson was in. Behind him, a man was being wheeled in by two paramedics. The elderly gentlemen was covered in a blood-stained blanket, his body rigid, the resigned look of certain death composing his face.

Monk's mother was a nurse and he'd seen more than one dead body, had even been in on autopsies, but the I.C.U. of a hospital always gave him an ill feeling. The beeping machines they plugged the near-dead into, the respirators for the lung-impaired, and the infusion of drugs to fool failing organs were bad enough. But the worst was the morphine tap, reserved for the greatest pain, a zombitizing technique that family and friends were grateful for, and that caused the patient to slip numbly away like a rudderless boat bobbing on waves of a chemical sea, soon to disappear over the horizon forever.

But while they tapped and jabbed and inserted, they let you know, in their taciturn way, that everything was going to be just fine. And as the staff went about their tasks, they joked and carried on about what they were going to do after work or who was sleeping with whom. How else could someone deal with decaying bodies and weeping relatives in this constant parade of sorrow, amid the stench of body waste and Lysol?

"Are you family?" a young doctor asked irritably. Off to his side, a nurse was attending to the man they'd just brought in.

"I'm a good friend," he lied.

The intern looked over at one of the rooms that surrounded the nurses' station. Each intensive care room had a large window in the wall and a large pane set in every door.

In one of these rooms, Monk could see three Black people. One was a thin, handsome woman in her forties. The other was a heavier man, a little older, in a pullover knit shirt. The third was a studious and serious younger man. They were gathered around a figure in the bed, the focus of numerous tubes and wires leading from equipment and monitors. It was there the doctor had directed his gaze.

"As you can see, Mr. Henderson's family is already in there," the young intern unnecessarily informed Monk. He was busy filling out information on a chart. "You'll have to wait until they're gone and then we'll see about letting you in." He kept writing.

The woman had begun to weep, placing her head on the older man's shoulder. The younger one had a determined bearing about him, his hands gripping the bed's railing. Monk walked away from the station toward the room. If the young doctor noticed, he didn't say anything.

The door was cracked and Monk could hear the sobs of the woman and the man saying the things people always say to comfort another's misery. Now was not the time to ask questions, but it was opportune.

In the bed, Henderson's chest barely rose and fell. The

young man's face was obscured by an oxygen mask and there was a catheter trailing from beneath the heavy blanket. Both of his arms had solutions flowing into them as the monitor droned over the bed.

Placing himself halfway into the room, Monk quietly said, "Excuse me—"

Suddenly the body convulsed, the monitor sounding a high-pitched wail, and all eyes fastened on the wounded man. A nurse and the young intern rushed in. Monk felt like a reporter from a supermarket tabloid, a ghoul slobbering for the next body to expire.

Another nurse wheeled in a machine on noisy casters and the family was ushered out. Unaware of Monk, they were looking through the window as the new machine was hooked up to Henderson. Like a pariah, Monk drew back from them, trying to will himself invisible. The staff feverishly worked over the body for some moments, then stopped. The doctor looked at one of the nurses, then at the family. He came outside.

The mother shook her head as if to ward off the evil of finality the doctor brought with him. He touched the older man's arm, whose face was ashen. The younger man looked away, noticing Monk. He walked over to him.

"You a cop?" he asked belligerently.

"No." He told him who he was and why he'd come.

The other one digested this in silence, touching his glasses. "I see. Can I have one of your cards?"

Monk handed him one. "How's Jimmy?"

"My cousin's in a coma." He turned and went back to his aunt and uncle.

There they hovered over the almost still body, the father's head tilted upward, possibly hoping to invoke the intercession of a deity.

Riding down in the elevator, Monk had a pang of conscience. If he'd taken Clarice seriously the first time, would Jimmy Henderson still be whole? Probably not. To thwart this outcome would have taken a lot of insight and more than the usual amount of luck. Still, his inaction had been inexcusable.

It strained credulity to believe that it wasn't the same gunman who'd cut down all three victims—he'd learned about the killing of Aaron after a call to the *Press-Telegram*—in so short a time. A serial killer targeting young African American men was not too far-fetched. A new kind of Night Stalker. The Black Stalker. Jesus.

He'd have to check to see about the caliber of the bullets used. And whether the sheriff's department out in the Shores was looking at these killings as related.

In the car, he reviewed other possibilities, for example, gangbangers exacting their own payback. Williams and Aaron were bad actors destined to meet bad ends, while, on the surface, Henderson seemed legit, but if not, he wouldn't be the first college kid to walk between two worlds.

By the time he got to his apartment, he'd developed more theories. But he kept coming back to the similarities among the three shootings. The more he went over it, the more he knew he was stretching it. Making excuses for the guilt he couldn't shake.

Monk got a glass from the cupboard, put some cubes in it, and poured a desensitizing dose of Ron Montusalem rum. He was on his third go-round when there was a tap at the door.

"Yeah."

"Ivan, it's me."

"Come on in, baby."

Jill Kodama used her key and entered the apartment. She

looked at the bottle and his feet up on the dining room table. "Long day, honey?" She made no attempt to hide her displeasure at his drinking alone.

Monk let it go. At this point, he was letting a lot go by.

Kodama sat at the table. "You want to talk about it?"

"Eventually." He had some more rum.

A drawn out, "Okay," issued from her. She got up and went into the kitchen. Drawers were opened and shut, bottles on the refrigerator door rattled, the butcher block slid out, a bottle cap was twisted off. Kodama returned with half a sandwich, three olives, a quarter of a pickle, and a tall glass of sparkling water.

Monk drank, she ate. He finally said, "'Member I told you about the goofy kid with the baby who came to see me?"

"Um," she said over a mouthful.

"Well, a third young Black man has been shot in Pacific Shores. He's alive, but just so."

"Critical?" Kodama finished.

"Coma." Monk had another taste.

"So you're celebrating the fact he's not dead," Kodama stated sarcastically.

"Something like that." He placed the glass heavily on the table.

Kodama chewed and studied him. "Do you think we've settled into a routine?"

"Maybe this booze gave me a fever, but did we just segue in our conversation here?"

She picked at a space between her teeth with a clear nail. "You heard, bub."

Monk patted her leg. "I was trying to unload my troubles on you. See that means we're communicating."

"Did you know I was coming over tonight?"

"No, not exactly."

"But you're not surprised either?"

"Jill, you have a key to this place like I have a key to your house. I mean, we're a couple, right?"

"Absolutely." She tipped her glass up and bit down on a piece of ice. "But you still haven't answered my question." Kodama ground the chunk up on her back teeth.

"If you're implying are we tired of one another, I can without reservation say I ain't bored in this thing we got going." He paused, considering whether he wanted another drink. Monk decided the buzz he had on was best left unstoked. "Can you say the same?"

Her dark eyes were unwavering. "Of course."

"But . . ."

"Don't be so fuckin' fast. The fact is we both have careers that require too many extra hours and too much emotional drain."

"We're always there for each other, Jill."

"I know, doll." She leaned over and kissed him passionately. "Maybe I'm getting possessive in my advancing years and want some more of your time."

"Hey, I'm the one that suggested we move in together awhile back," Monk pointed out.

"And I said I'd think about it. But I don't want us having a home together and it's just some place to shower and change clothes. I know too many professional couples doing that bit."

"Well just like dominoes, you gotta work at it to get good." Monk winked at her.

She scratched his goatee. "Sure you're right. So why are you so worked up over these Pacific Shores shootings?

Monk had to search around in his head for the answer he wanted. "Really, I guess I feel funny that I was all too willing to write off Scatterboy's murder as just another street death."

"And what made you change your mind?"

"I'm not sure I have. Only seeing how Jimmy Henderson's family is shaken by his condition reminded me that even the bad deaths deserve an answer."

Kodama calmly took a bite of her pickle. "A hustler gets killed, the cops don't care, the man don't care. But Ivan Monk, the people's detective is supposed to be different."

"You goddamn right," he said, smiling.

Kodama got up, standing over him. "Come on, let's get some rest. Then we'll get you back on your horse in the morning, Tex."

Exhausted, Monk grumbled, "Yee-hah."

CHAPTER 6

Monk raised his arm in time to block the ballpeen hammer coming at his head. He caught the shank across his forearm and yelled. Monk tensed his leg muscles, lowered his shoulder, and drove into his opponent's mid-section, pinning him against the wall of the loading dock, air escaping in a bleat from the man's lungs.

Quickly, Monk rammed his knee into the smaller man's groin.

"*Pinche mayate*," the man wheezed as he sat heavily on the floor.

Monk plucked the tool from the man's limp grip. From behind, he heard several loud gasps. He turned toward the shop floor while still watching the man propped against the wall.

Three long rows of compact work tables filled the factory. Sitting at them were women, mostly Latinas with a few Asians sprinkled about. Each table contained a sewing machine, bolted in place, spools of thread, scissors, thimbles, and assorted pieces of fabric. Behind each seamstress was a large cardboard box containing an explosion of silks, rayons, and cottons. On the floor in front of the tables were smaller boxes that contained their finished product. Today's job seemed to be ensembles for the upwardly mobile working woman.

Monk grinned. "Relax, ladies, I'm just going to hit him once or twice at most." He devoted his attention to the man at his feet. "Give me a good reason why I shouldn't split your head open?"

"Fuck you," the other man spat in clear English.

Without missing a beat, Monk took a vicious swipe with the hammer, pulling loose a chunk of plaster less than an inch above the belligerent man's head.

His eyes got wide and Monk could hear chairs crashing to the floor as several of the seamstresses got to their feet, excited and scared. "Crazy *gavacho*," the man rasped at Monk.

"I come in here asking a couple of innocent questions and you got to go be unfriendly." Monk took a twenty-dollar bill from the pocket of his Levi 501s and placed it on the floor between them. "Have you rethought your answers?"

The man, Monk presumed he was either Salvadoran or Guatemalan, looked at the bill, then looked back at his interrogator. "I told you, no fuckin' Swede works around here."

Monk had asked his cop friend—the only friend he had on the LAPD—Detective Lieutenant Marasco Seguin, whether he'd heard about a man called Swede who sold watches out of the garment district. Making discreet inquiries, his pal had turned up two possible sites for Monk's quarry. This place, called Casual Life, on East Thirty-Fourth Street, was the second stop.

"Well, I hate to contradict you, my friend," Monk began. "But I'd have to conclude from this greeting of yours"—he jiggled the hammer—"that you know differently."

Several of the sewing machines were humming and Monk had the impression his pulse was keeping time with them. "What would you say to another twenty joining that one?"

The other man sneered. "I say you don't have the *cojones* to use the *martillo* like I do." A defiant cast settled on the man's face.

"Yeah, you called my bluff, all right." Calmly, Monk drew his .45 automatic from underneath the sport coat he wore. The sewing stopped, the man's expression took on an icy pallor. Monk walked over to one of the stations as all the women rose, their heads darting here and there looking for the quickest exit.

"Now," Monk said, addressing the man who was now standing, "you're some kind of supervisor around here, I gather."

The statement required no reply.

"And I bet whoever the boss is expects these jobs"—he kicked one of the smaller cardboard boxes—"to be done on time. After all, we can't have these off-the-shoulder outfits selling for, what, $200, $300, getting to the stores late, now can we? Especially when you're paying the workers such fantastic salaries like $4.85 an hour."

Several of the woman who understood English nodded to one another. The other man edged nervously away from the wall. "Now wait a minute, homes."

"Ah, now we're communicating," Monk disingenuously retorted. He was standing over one of the production tables, the muzzle of the gun inches away from the heavy-duty, high-tech sewing machine. "Where can I find Swede?"

Nothing.

Monk shot the motor.

The other man's mouth tightened into a hard line of despair. "Look man, Swede is the owner, okay?"

"Uh-huh." Monk moved over to another table and leveled

the gun, the executioner come to call. "So when is the good gentlemen around?"

"He don't have regular times, man. He comes, he goes, you know?"

For an answer, Monk killed another Brother-computerized sewing wonder. Some of the women clapped.

The man on the loading dock rushed over. "Shit, them *maquinas* cost thousands, man."

"And what happens to productivity if there's not enough of these rascals around?" Monk strolled to another station.

"I'll call the police," the man said, pointing.

"Go ahead." The automatic barked and its slug ripped past the thick casing into the grimy floorboards.

The other man clutched his head as if the top were coming unhinged.

"Hey," Monk said, "look at it this way, if you just give me a hint of when and where I can find Swede, he don't have to know I got it from you. But how many more sewing machines can you afford to replace before Swede comes back and blames it on you?"

The man held a hand out in front of his body as if he were pushing off a tremendous weight. "I give you a, *como se diese*, a clue, yeah?"

"Yep." The gun rested by Monk's side.

"Maybe I know where he gets his car washed 'cause I take it there a time or two."

"He gets it done regular."

"Maybe."

The gun wavered.

Both hands pushed in front of him. "Yes, all the time. That car he treats better than a woman."

"What does this car look like, and where is this car wash?"

IT WAS a 1955 Lincoln Capri hardtop with fender skirts, painted in a hue GM used to call Palomino Buff, accented with white for the roof. It had dual exhausts and the engine was 341 cubic centimeters with a stroke of 3.5 inches. In its time, it sold for a whopping $3,910, $28 more than a Series sixty-two hardtop Cadillac. Now, it was priceless. Until today, walking across the street to the Flying V car wash on Figueroa near Venice Boulevard, Monk had only read about this particular model.

He got a good look at the man getting out of the beautifully restored vehicle. Swede was a white man in his late fifties, tanned, fit, and wearing a grey sharkskin suit and black cap-toed shoes. His hair was white and combed meticulously to the nape of his neck. He carried a folded edition of *USA Today* in his smallish, thin hands.

He entered the glassed-in walkway that provided a view of the cars as they went through the brushes and rollers. Monk stepped from the hot smoggy day into the air conditioned interior. Sitting on a plastic chair was an elderly Black woman studying a religious tract. Her lips moved as she read. Monk and the other man were the only other two inside the waiting area.

Swede was standing at the rail, his Lincoln emerging from a mass of soap as he read the sports page. Monk came up beside him.

"Mind if I have a word with you. Swede?"

The other man didn't look up from his paper. "I don't know you, trooper."

"But you know a friend of mine. You know Scatterboy Williams."

Swede turned to the next page in the newspaper. Though he didn't seem to be watching the Lincoln, he shifted his body in accordance with its position in the car wash. "Scatterboy send you to see me?"

"Let's just say I want to move some of the items he used to. Only I want a franchise."

The burnished eyes flitted over Monk briefly. The delicate hands refolded the paper, and he marched outside. His Lincoln was just coming onto the detailing lot. Monk trotted after him, noticing the car of the elderly woman, a late-model, lowered Mustang, also emerging.

"You so set you can turn down business, Swede?" Monk said, gaining the shade of the canopied waiting area where the dapper man sat, watching the workers wipe down and vacuum his car.

He glowered at Monk. "Sit down." He indicated the space next to him on the wood bench. Monk did so. "So you're more ambitious than our friend Scatterboy."

"Damned skippy, I am. Matter of fact—"

The butterfly knife was pressed against Monk's side so quickly, it took several moments for his brain to process the sensation. Swede had the paper over it, but Monk could see as well as feel its sharp tip against him. The older man had turned his body so that if anyone was paying attention they were just two friends having a conversation. "Now who the fuck are you?"

"I told you, man, Scatterboy said to look you up."

"Scatterboy is dead."

"So?"

"So how'd you find me?"

Monk was angry for letting Swede get the upper hand. He had underestimated the man, but he should have known you don't get to be a fixer, middle-aged or otherwise, by being soft. "Scatterboy told me where he met you to get the watches. I been watching after you for some time, I knew you come here on Thursdays."

The perfectly coiffured gentleman rose. "I don't know what you're up to, mister, but I know you weren't Scatterboy's friend." He started for his car then stopped. Swede didn't turn around but spoke, "Don't let me see you around again, hear? Next time I won't wait for an answer."

With that the man in the shiny suit enjoyed a leisured walk to his clean, smooth '55 Lincoln, Monk no more a bother to him than a bug on his windshield.

Sitting on the bench, Monk choked down an urge to tackle Swede and beat the living shit out of him. Other than proving he could do it—and he had his doubts that he'd get that far before the other man opened him up like Sunday catfish—it probably wouldn't do anything to advance his investigation, not to mention putting his license in jeopardy. No, Monk told himself rising, if necessary, he'd take another run at Swede. From his blind side.

Simmering, Monk drove over to West Forty-Eighth Street and the Tiger's Den. It was a combination gym, training facility, and sauna, owned and operated by the Zen ghetto master of the four-cornered world, Tiger Flowers. A one-time Golden Gloves champ and ranking middleweight, Tiger was a compact man on the far side of sixty who could still do five miles of road work to start the day.

Pushing himself through a workout of weights, abdomen crunches and jumping rope, Monk found he couldn't sweat enough to chase the bitter taste Swede had left with him. He hated for anyone to get the upper hand on him. No. What really bothered him was his attitude. He was cruising through the case, figuring to be done with it soon. He was slipping, and that made him worry.

Bap. Damn, the right arm was still tender from that hammer blow in the garment factory. Bap. Monk dipped his left shoulder and drove straight into the heavy bag.

"Like a lot of fellas your size, Monk, you rely too much on your upper body strength." The voice was a quiet rasp, a file dragged across shards of glass. "Get up on your feet, make your legs do some work."

"Thank you, Tiger." Bap. The bag swung back. Bap.

"It's not often you work out on the heavy bag," Tiger observed. "Somethin' must be up your craw."

Bap. Bap.

"Very well." Tiger wandered off.

Rivulets of sweat peppered Monk's eyes and his left side began to ache. Bap. Fuck Swede and his mamma. Bap. Why the fuck was he going to all this trouble for some knucklehead girl and a kid in a coma? Hell, Clarice was much better off without some no-talent, third-rater like Scatterboy Williams.

Bap. Kiss my black ass, Swede. Bap. Bap. Bap.

CHAPTER 7

Warren Depriest, whose street name was Li'l Bone, was busy head whipping an ese from South Gate with a chair leg he'd broken off at the time Scatterboy was shot and killed. He was two months into his lockdown waiting to go to trial on an armed robbery charge. Because his opponent had been coming after him with the sharpened end of a spoon at the time, DePriest wasn't put into segregation after the incident.

He was being held at the Metropolitan Detention Center on Alameda. It was south of the old main annex of the Post Office, near the edge of historic Olvera Street and its touristy shops. It was ten stories of hard linear function designed by one of those Brie-and-bottled-water architectural firms. In this era of down-turned economies, the upscale architects had abandoned skyscrapers for the booming field of prison construction.

California and Texas were vying for incarceration capital of the free world. Each state had more than twenty prisons on the drawing board, and enough abused, out-of-work, and under-educated bastards to fill them. Though mainland China still had more prisons, America was locking up more people.

The MDC was a concrete wonder of trellises and balconies, every tier enclosed by bars done in large *X*s with rows of concertina wire entwining them. No one moved on the balconies, no bird alighted on the roof.

While tagged with a state crime, Li'l Bone and other similarly charged prisoners had been placed in this sterile, well-kept federal facility due to the massive overcrowding at the Robben Island of L.A., the County Jail a few blocks away.

Monk had learned DePriest was awaiting trial from the friendly waitress he'd slid the twenty across to at the King Lion barbecue joint in Pacific Shores. It meant turning right around and heading back to L.A., but since he'd yet to run down any of the other names of Scatterboy's social club, it seemed worth the gas.

"Naw, man, I can't tell you nothin' about what happened to my man Scatterboy." Li'l Bone yawned and scratched himself on his side of the bullet-proof glass. "Since I caught this case, my mind's been kind'a wrapped up, know what I'm sayin?"

Monk bargained, "If you help me on this, Bone, and I find the joker who killed Scatterboy, that might look good when it comes time for your sentencing." He wasn't really sure about that, but it sounded right.

Bone stretched again. "I'm bein' square with you, Monk. Clarice and me went to grade school together. I wouldn't dis her or my dead ace boon by not telling you straight." He leaned forward, suddenly showing some interest. "Don't you think I asked around in here when I got the 411?"

"And did you find out anything?"

"Nothing. But I'd a been surprised if I did. Scatterboy wasn't down with no set. He didn't try no game on nobody in the life."

"He did sell knock-offs," Monk reminded him.

Li'l Bone regarded him contemptuously with a wave of his hand. "Only to the squares. And what sucker really believe that he gonna get a legit Rolex fo' two bills? Ain't no square done the boy."

"So you think it was just a random thing?"

Bone seemed to give it serious consideration. "That's weird to imagine, detective man. Scatterboy knew them streets and knew the ones who packed in the Shores. He had his eyes open, know what I'm sayin'?"

"An outsider then," Monk said, thinking aloud.

"Could be."

A light went off over Monk's head signaling time was up for the interview. A guard in a tailored blazer appeared. On the breast pocket of his jacket was the logo of the contract firm the feds hired for the security services. It seemed to Monk privatizing to the cheapest bidder was the sick mantra too many bean counters ommed to. Politicians eager to talk tough on crime and three-strike every fool whose final felony was stealing a six-pack from a store sought to balance budgets by abdicating governmental oversight.

The guard was a bespectacled clean-cut young Black man who looked more like a mathematician. He gave Li'l Bone a nod and the prisoner rose. "Or it could be that crazy-ass Herbie did all three of 'em."

"Who?"

"Herbie," Li'l Bone said as he walked away. "I heard he shot another player I know."

DePriest walked through a peach-colored door which swung shut behind him. Monk wrote down a notation and left the Center. He made his way over to Continental Donuts on Vernon near Eleventh Avenue in the Crenshaw District. He parked on the lot the place shared with Alton Brothers

Automotive Repair and Service. Curtis Armstrong, co-owner of the garage, was bent over the engine of a pitiful-looking twenty-year-old Datsun 510.

"Curtis," Monk blurted as he walked past, "how's the carriage trade?"

Armstrong, an overweight man with a tiny voice, unlimbered himself from his task. "Well, my ebony Nick Carter, I'm just fulfilling my mission in life to try and keep on the road these sorry-assed vehicles our people are forced to drive 'cause that's all they can afford workin' at some sorry-ass slave job."

Not missing a beat, Monk said, "You the man for this job, my brother."

Curtis Armstrong grunted something and returned to his labors. There was a sign announcing Alton Brothers over the maw of the garage's grease bay. The brothers had long since died, but Curtis, far-sighted as well as frugal, saw no need to spend unnecessary money in getting a new sign. Monk shook his head in admiration and went into the donut shop.

"What it bees, chief," Elrod, the six-foot-eight, mobile mountain, ex-con manager, greeted. His voice was a bass fiddle at the bottom of a deep well.

"Like this and like that."

They shook hands. Sitting at the counter in the restored '40s decor of the donut shop was a man named Andrade, part-time accountant, full-time alcoholic. With the precise calm of a sniper, he sipped his large coffee and stared at something way beyond the shop's walls. Two glazed donuts, like pop art sculpture, lay untouched on a napkin before him.

In one of the booths two other regulars played a game of chess. Monk moved toward the back again. "I've got something I want to check on, and then we'll do that inventory."

"Right on," the big man rumbled as he changed the filter in the coffee maker.

Monk had bought the donut shop several years ago with money he'd saved from his tenure in the merchant marines. The exact wisdom of the purchase still eluded him. He certainly didn't clear much money from the enterprise. And it didn't give him entree into the higher echelons of the business world. But it was nice having some place all his own. A totem of mediocre coffee and fried dough against a hostile world.

The building was in the shape of an ell and Monk took the passageway down the short shank. Opening a steel-sheered door, he thumbed the overhead fluorescents to life, and entered a room done up with cheap wood paneling, containing a free-standing safe tucked in one corner, a cot, two industrial-green file cabinets, and a folding chair in front of a small table where an IBM clone rested. Two other folding chairs leaned against the safe. There was a phone jack but no phone.

Monk uncoiled a phone cord from the PC and inserted it into the jack. He sat down and powered up the computer. He tapped out commands and the modem in his computer dialed and then connected with one of the online services he subscribed to. A few more strokes on the keyboard and Monk got into the database he was seeking—the morgue of the *L.A. Times.*

He punched in "Pacific Shores" and got an item recounting the shooting death of known crack dealer Ronny Aaron and the subsequent arrest of one Herbert Gaylord Jones. This article was written after the Henderson incident, and speculated about a tie-in among the three shootings.

Monk compared the facts, dates, locations. Aaron was shot a week and a half after Scatterboy, on a street named

Kenmore, while his client's boyfriend was killed on Creedmore. Monk typed Williams' name in but nothing came up. He printed the article, exited the service and turned the machine off.

He looked up the streets in his *Thomas Guide*. They were eerily close. The shootings, though all of them took place in the Shores' Black section, seemed to have no other pattern connecting the three.

He quit the room and spent the next two and a quarter hours doing the career-enhancing, mind-expanding task of shop inventory with Elrod. As a petty bourgeois capitalist, Monk was pleased to discover that the price of sugar had dropped, owing to a glut in the Third World. But as an international citizen, he had to wonder what that meant for the common folk in those countries. Elrod snapped him out of his reverie with evidence that their flour salesman may have been overcharging them.

"I'll have a sit-down with him and appraise him of our discovery," Elrod said implacably. "I'm sure we can reconcile the matter and receive the proper credit."

"Talking means, talking, yeah?" Monk beamed at the big man, not bothering to correct his malapropism.

"Of course, chief."

Monk tried to reach Clarice but no one answered at her home.

"I'm gone, blood." Monk wound his car up onto the Harbor Freeway heading south. Taking the Broadway exit off the 710, Monk entered downtown Long Beach a little past three in the afternoon.

Once referred to as Iowa-By-The-Sea, Long Beach had started out as a subdivided tract of rolling land leased to an Englishman named William Willmore. He promptly christened it Willmore City, and decreed it alcohol-free. This and other factors contributed to its economic failure and he had to deed it back to the land-rich Bixbys.

Eventually the town took on the name Long Beach, and for several decades it became a haven for residents—many from Iowa—whose idea of fun was a rocking chair and a pitcher of lemonade on the porch. But the discovery of oil, and the laying of tracks for the Red Car trolley line changed all that. When Monk was a kid, his mother and father occasionally brought the family here to the Pike, a now-defunct amusement pier modeled after Coney Island.

Standing in the parking lot of the *Press-Telegram*, Monk was swept with a powerful memory of one such excursion when he won a teddy bear for his mother at a ring toss game. As he pridefully showed his mother the prize, several drunk, laughing sailors, reeling from a roller coaster ride, sloshed by. When one of them mumbled something about "niggers," his dad was going to take off after the crew but his mother restrained him. She reminded him that if the police were called, it would be him—not the sailors—arrested.

On the way home that day, Monk and his sister Odessa sat in the back seat of the family's Chrysler staring at the stuffed animal on the seat between them, somehow hoping the inanimate bear could explain a harsh reality they'd just barely started to grasp. That night, Monk was so troubled by the incident he couldn't sleep. Wandering to the kitchen for a glass of milk, he found his dad sitting at the table, silent and brooding.

Before him was his favorite whiskey, Crown Royal, and a chipped coffee cup half full of the liquor and ice.

Josiah Monk's chair was propped back against the wall, a hand held to his temple, his eyes closed. Sensing another's presence, he stirred, focused, and snatched a stiff piece of paper next to the bottle.

"You see that, Ivan?" Josiah Monk asked his son, shaking the paper at him.

"What is it, pop?"

"My honorable discharge from the Army. After Korea, son."

His father's bleary gaze bore down on him. For the first time in his young life, his dad was making him scared. "Uh-huh."

"The white man said go fight them red gooks. Said we had to keep the world free from being put in chains by Mao and Moscow. Well I did. I even made three stripes, and got some shrapnel in my side for the trouble." He grabbed the boy by the shoulder, his callused mechanic's hands digging into the young muscle, hurting him. The father drew him closer, the alcohol emanating from him like a backed-up sewer.

"But what about ours, boy? What about ours?"

The demographics of Long Beach, along with its economic base, had shifted since his dad had first asked that question. But no answers, from father or son, had come in the meantime.

About the size of San Francisco, Long Beach was now a vibrant, sometimes volatile, co-mingling of Samoans, whites, African Americans, Latinos, Filipinos, and Cambodians. The last were arrivals whose lives had been forever transformed by their survival and escape from the kill-happy Khmer Rouge in the mid-'70s. Little Phnom Penh was now a thriving community in dramatic juxtaposition to the conventional but moribund "attractions" of the landlocked Queen Mary and the empty dome that once housed the Spruce Goose.

Monk entered the quiet offices of the newspaper and asked for the morgue. He was directed to a well-lit space on the second floor where a middle-aged Black woman in a chiffon dress sat at a desk, writing on an pad of unlined paper. She looked up as Monk approached.

"Can I help you, sir?" She had high-boned cheeks and an even tan coloring. Her lined eyes were oblong, and her face, framed by black hair piled high and streaked intermittently with grey, made an arresting impression. Her gaze lingered on Monk. "You've come to look up your old college record."

"Pardon?" Monk suddenly felt flush at the collar.

The woman rose, and by doing so demonstrated how well she kept herself in shape. "You look like you used to play some ball, Mr. . . . ?"

"Monk. I played back in college, linebacker, but that was a long time ago."

"How long, Monk?"

Jill sentencing him to the torture of a thousand sharp knives flashed in his mind and he revealed to the back-issue bombshell only his card. "I'd like to see the last two weeks of the *Telegram*, please."

"Sure." She moved from around the desk and smothered him with a look that made him nervous somewhere below the thorax. Monk followed her to some shelving behind a row of file cabinets. She pointed at a particular stack. "After a month, we photograph the issues onto microfiche, but these cover the period you're looking for."

She extended her hand and Monk shook it. "I'm Gloria, Monk. If I can help you in any other part of your investigation, don't hesitate to let me know."

"I'd be a fool not to."

She was about to comment when a new customer appeared at her desk. "Excuse me," Gloria said, and went over to talk with the woman, a short-haired Latina in a business suit holding a slim attache case.

Monk took the pile to a nearby desk and went through the stack. He found the accounts of Scatterboy's death and the recent shooting of Jimmy Henderson, the kid whose name he'd never forget. With the issues in hand, Monk walked back to the magnificent Gloria.

"Where can I make copies of the articles I want?"

"Oh, you can have those, we can get more from circulation. Just let me make a note of the volume and number."

As she wrote the information down, Monk was aware that the woman in the business suit was standing to one side, appearing to browse through a bunch of back issues. But he had the distinct impression she was eavesdropping on his conversation with Gloria. "There you go," the tidy woman said. She handed Monk the issues with her business card.

Monk pocketed the card. "Thanks for your help, Gloria."

"Of course."

On his way out, Monk caught a glimpse of the short-haired woman walking briskly toward the shelves with the back issues. He left the newspaper and drove over to Clarice Moore's house in the Shores to pick up the contract. His knock produced no answer. There was a car in the driveway but that didn't necessarily mean anything. He knocked again, waiting and listening. After the third attempt, he left a note and drove away. Back into Long Beach, he discovered a Norm's, a bowl of soup, a turkey melt, and a side of coleslaw.

Sitting at the counter, Monk read the afternoon edition of the *LA. Times* while working on his second cup of coffee and puffing on a thin Cuesta-Rey. Presently, he got up and dialed a number on the pay phone situated between the men's and women's lavatories.

"Hello," the honey-dipped voiced murmured.

"Hi, Gloria, this is Monk."

"Well, well, couldn't stay away, huh?" The voice went down a notch for a throaty effect.

"'Fraid I'm still on the client's time, my dear."

"Shoot."

"And since I am, would you mind telling me who that woman was sneaking around when I was there?"

The voice went up two octaves. "You call me up to ask about another woman?"

Monk chided, "Come on."

"She wouldn't tell me, Shaft. Though she was a little put off by the fact that you took those two particular issues of the newspaper."

"How do you mean?"

"Oh"—Monk could almost see her cocking her head—"she went through the pile and then nonchalantly asked if I could get her copies of those issues. I said sure, no problem. Then she tried with the small talk, asking me if you were a friend, had you come there before, that kind of thing."

"What'd you tell her?" Out of the corner of his eye, Monk could see a young man with long hair suddenly retch and throw up on the counter.

"You'll have to buy me a drink to find out."

That wasn't too hard a request. "Sure. Where?"

She told him and Monk hung up. A waiter had retrieved a bucket and mop and was cleaning up the mess as the kid watched him glassy-eyed. Walking to the cashier to pay his bill, Monk reminded himself how innocent this all was, just doing his work, he'd buy the lady a drink and get his information. It wasn't as if he and Jill weren't solid. Then why, Monk rolled over in his mind as he sat in his Ford, did he allow himself to be put in a potentially compromising situation? Could it be the relationship was reaching the same ol' same ol' stage? Was it her own growing ambivalence toward him that made Jill hesitant to move in together?

He fired up the car, its carburetor gulping air and fuel like a hungry cheetah, the motor growling in a basso-profundo confidence. Maybe, he smirked to himself, he was just trying to rationalize an excuse to take a tumble with Gloria.

To kill some time, Monk went to a favorite used bookstore called Acres of Books. More than an hour later, he left with several volumes including a second edition of Chester Himes' *The Real Cool Killers* and drove to his rendezvous at the Hideaway, as Gloria had instructed him.

He entered a dim-lit affair replete with hanging plants and a guy in a tux at a piano with an oversized brandy snifter on it.

Monk bought Gloria Traylor two Manhattans while he dueled with a Cuba Libre. She ran through the highlights of her life story. A term as a pit boss in Atlantic City. Trips to Africa. Sunsets off the pier in Hermosa Beach.

Traylor told him the woman with the tomboy haircut hadn't given her name, nor had she, Gloria, given the woman his name. But Traylor definitely had the impression the woman was a professional of some kind from her clothes and the authentic Louis Vuitton attache case she was carrying. The woman got copies of the same two back issues he'd obtained.

"She say anything else after receiving the copies?" Three-quarters into his drink, Monk was beginning to feel mellow. The kind of looseness that in combination to sitting and talking with a good-looking woman could lead to other things beside sitting and talking. He banished tempting images from his mind and zeroed in on her words.

"She put them in that fancy case of hers, which by the

way had the initials XY and C in gold Gothic English letters embossed on it."

"Huh?"

She winked at Monk over the rim of her glass. "You heard me, handsome. An X, Y, hyphen C. She tried to think up more stuff to talk to me about, but really she was just trying to get your name." She paused. "But that would ruin the spell you're putting on me, or is it the other way around?"

Anticipation and anxiety fought for control of Monk. As his libido wrestled with his conscience, he tried to keep his voice neutral. "You observe anything else about Ms. X?"

The older woman placed a hand on Monk's forearm. "Is business all we're going to talk about tonight?"

Monk smiled awkwardly. "Before this leads us somewhere, maybe I better be straight with you—"

"You're married," she interrupted.

Lying was a good way out, but he relied on the truth. "No. But I do have a girlfriend and we're committed to each other." At least he believed they were.

"How committed, Monk?" she said too sweetly, allowing him to twist the knife he'd put in himself.

"Shit," he exhaled after more rum and coke. "You know you're fine, Gloria, and you damn well know I find you attractive."

"And pleasant company."

"Yes, that too." He placed his hand flat on the bar and fixed her with a look. "I'm not saying I'm a candidate to take over when Mother Theresa steps aside, but I want to try and walk the line, dig?"

"You got the shoulders to bear the burden, honey." She leaned over and kissed him full on the mouth. Monk didn't make much of an effort to pull back.

"I'm not waiting by the phone, or any of that other

romance novel bullshit, baby. I got a life too, dig?" She got up from her seat and turned for the door, then held a hand up in the air.

"I think she was a lawyer," Gloria said, swiveling her head in Monk's direction.

As if emerging from a trance. Monk said, "What makes you say that?"

"When she opened her briefcase, I got a glimpse of a letterhead that said something like Fuler, one *L*, Evans, I think, and another name."

"Sister, you're a real gone chick, as my dad used to say."

"Ha." She bent down and kissed him on the cheek and walked out of the Hideaway as the piano man played a Duke Ellington number, "I Let a Song Go Out of my Heart."

Monk ordered some water. He downed it, and left to the sounds of clinking glasses and laughter. The sexual energy shot through the place like lightning waiting to strike. He got in his Galaxie, turned the motor over, then clicked it off.

An epiphany had suddenly descended on him. He was going through the motions, but what the hell for? What, if anything, was he really going to discover concerning the murder of Scatterboy Williams?

All right, three young brothers had been shot, two of them were dead. But those two weren't exactly sterling characters, and Henderson may have been an isolated incident. He was the one that broke the pattern. His case seemed like an out-and-out robbery attempt.

Clarice's hundred was spent, and even if he had the inclination to ask, there wasn't going to be any more scratch from her. He was operating on his own funds. Altruism was fine, but that didn't keep gas in the Ford.

Had he really wanted to meet with back-issue Gloria to learn more? Or was it just the handsome woman's attention he desired? Out on the parking lot, a man and woman were arguing.

The woman started to walk away, the man grabbing at her arm. Monk had his hand on the door handle, but the man missed and slid down against the fender of a wine-colored Mercury. The drunk man laughed uproariously, sitting against the tire. The woman gave him the finger as she raced away in her car.

Monk also left. Driving past dilapidated buildings held together with memories of better times, he felt an anger rise in him. It emerged from vague questions which stabbed like an ice pick at his psyche. Was there anything to this case? And why was he involved in it? He had empathy for Clarice, but so what? She was naive, wanting to believe there was a profound truth behind her boyfriend's death. But there wouldn't be. The tragic demise of youths like Williams, caught in a web of uncertain origin, would never have meaning.

He headed for Clarice's house. He'd refund her money if need be, and move on to more profitable ventures. There, he finally admitted it to himself. That's what was lurking behind his anxieties. He had to come up with his end of the ducats for him and Jill to even consider playing house together. Jill was too diplomatic to say it but maybe his position further down on the economic scale was one of the reasons for her hesitancy. She didn't go around flashing her pay stub, but Monk knew a superior court judge's annual salary was $99 grand plus some change, on top of which she earned more through speaking engagements and writing assignments for various publications. Monk did well to make forty or fifty percent of that in a year, including his small income from the donut shop. Goddamn. His foot accelerated the Ford through the evening streets even as he neared Clarice's neighborhood.

The anger at himself and his situation was smoldering by

the time he got to Clarice's house. He rang the bell, waiting. There were lights on inside, and the same powder blue Cressida in the driveway. A shade moved in the window next to the front door. Another moment passed, then someone said. "Yes?" through the door.

Monk identified himself.

Another silence then the female voice spoke again. "What do you want?"

"I'd like to see Clarice."

"She ain't your client," the voice he knew must be Clarice's mother retorted.

"I'd still like to talk to her. It's about what she wanted me to look into." Monk raised his voice. If nothing else, she'd have to open the door to make him be quiet. He heard the mother talking to someone else. The porch light came on and the door opened slightly.

"Clarice don't want your services anymore," the mother's disembodied voice said from the black aperture.

"Let him in, Mom," Clarice all but shouted from inside the house.

"Girl, I told you to watch that tone with me."

The door closed but didn't shut, and Monk could hear them talking heatedly with each other. He pushed on the door, and it gave way to his touch. He stepped inside.

The mother, a good-sized, light-skinned woman in a jogging suit and curlers, was talking hurriedly with her daughter. The mother's hands were on her hips, her back to Monk. She whirled around upon noticing the reaction in Clarice's face.

"Now I don't know who the hell you think you are, but you can take your private peepin' ass back out of my house."

Monk barely heard her. It was Clarice's face that got his attention. In the light of the living room's lamps, the fresh bruises on the chin and side of her face were as stark as lit flares along a midnight highway.

"What happened, Clarice?"

The mother morphed in front of him. "She ain't got to tell you a goddamn thing 'cept bye. It was all this foolishness that brought this on her, and I'm gonna put a stop to it."

"I'm grown, mama, I can—"

"Shut up," the mother commanded.

"I won't," Clarice said, a grunt breaking ranks. "This is my house too."

The mother narrowed her eyes at her daughter. "Look, Clarice, don't you realize you need to get on with raising your daughter. What's done can't be undone." Her voice had softened, the underlying worry breaking through. "You just have to leave it alone, baby."

"Would you please tell me who beat on you, Clarice?" Monk had positioned himself between the two.

"She can't tell you nothin', mister," the mother said, gaping resolutely at him. "Go away."

"I want to help."

"It's your help that done this to my baby girl."

"No, that's not so," Clarice interjected. "I'm the one that messed up."

"How?" Monk asked.

The mother warned the both of them with deadly looks but Clarice didn't balk.

"I wanted to do something in finding Scatterboy's killer," the young mother said in a low tone.

The mother shook a large finger at Monk. "She got out in them streets among them dope heads and chippies. You know that's no place for my girl to be."

"What the hell were you thinking, Clarice?" Monk said, also feeling protective of her.

Unconsciously, the teenager touched the purplish stain spread across the side of her face. "I just wanted to do something, they all said he wasn't worth it."

"They?" Monk asked.

The mother chewed her bottom lip. "The school where she goes," she answered. "It's a high school designed for pregnant and parenting girls." She moved over to her child, and gently placed her hands on the back of her neck, massaging the area. "She's trying so hard."

"You're talking about your friends at school?" Monk asked.

Clarice shook her head in the affirmative. "They be goin' on 'bout how me and Shawndell was better off without him. Just 'cause the fathers of their babies are dogs don't mean mine was." She looked at her mother for confirmation, but even her love didn't go that far.

Tears glistened on the young woman's cheek, and she shook loose from her mother's hands. "I don't care what anybody thinks anymore. I know I got to make my way for me and my baby. So what if I can't go partyin' or cruisin' like I used to." The energy seemed to leave her suddenly, and she sagged against the wall.

"I got to think of my child now. I can't do childish things anymore, I know that. But all the time you hear on the radio and TV 'bout how unwed mothers ain't nothin' but a burden on society. How the politicians want to make examples of us as just wantin' to have children, get on welfare, and do nothin' with our lives. Well, maybe I made a mistake having Shawndell, but that don't mean I don't love her and want to do right by her."

"But why you got to be so set on knowing who killed Scatterboy?" the mother pleaded. "If you do find out, that ain't gonna bring us no help." She didn't finish it, but Monk knew she meant if it was gangs, then they might retaliate if one of their homies was nailed for the deed.

"Because in Newport Beach or Sherman Oaks, the police would try a little harder if it was three nice white kids cut down in the streets. Because everybody thinks it's just one of those things when it's us. We're Americans too, Mom."

"You stay off the streets and in school, and I'll do my part, Clarice," Monk promised. "I'll do my best to find the one who killed Scatterboy."

"Mister Monk," the mother said, "you know we don't have much money."

"I know that, Mrs.—"

"Call me Helen."

"Don't sweat the money, Helen. This one's for the future."

Well, Monk concluded on the way home, he was really on the high road to shoring up his finances. But what the hell could he do? Write Clarice off even before she got into the race? The kid was trying her best in a game where the playing field was mined.

On the drive home, his father kept whispering to him. "And when we do get a peek at the rule book, them cracker bastards are laughin', 'cause they ain't even goin' by one."

CHAPTER 8

The law offices of Fuller, Evans, and Woznyak were located in a smoked-glass and brushed-steel high-rise on Wilshire near Normandie. The boulevard was in the finishing throes of having the Metro line installed.

It was all part of the Metropolitan Transit Authority's aluminum- and fiber optic–lined traveling road show and tax boondoggle. The rail system the huge agency was constructing was supposed to accommodate 365,000 daily passengers.

Half of the damned thing had already been constructed throughout the city. But save for some City Hall workers who took a short hop to the venerable Langer's Deli on Alvarado, and immigrant women who used it to get to the Grand Central Market downtown, most days its pristine underground halls were virtually empty.

Still, one had to marvel at the hubris of an agency which had already spent $330 million a mile with its attended payoffs and kickbacks; had cut back bus services where most of its riders could be found to subsidize further construction; and had used wood shunts in a tunnel beneath Hollywood Boulevard to save money—thus causing a huge sinkhole in the famous avenue. There had to be a board who believed in chaos theory guiding the work.

It was like a plan that had been set in motion so long ago, nobody could remember what they were building, but they damn sure were efficient about it.

Riding up to the twenty-fifth floor, Monk mused on what his dad would say about all this if he were alive. When he'd come to live in L.A. after the war, the red and yellow trolley cars were still running in some parts of town. Indeed, once upon a time, L.A. had the most extensive rail system in the country. But post World War II, people on the coast bought into the Detroit manufactured idea that a car was guaranteed in the Constitution. And the combine of rubber, oil and gas, with General Motors at the helm, maneuvered to buy up the trolley cars and their rights-of-way from L.A. and the growing suburban spokes.

Now, decades later, the MTA had already gone broke laying down tracks in virtually the same routes the city used to own.

The elevator stopped smoothly and opened onto an anteroom done in rococo Italian furniture. Prints by Orozco, Homer and Tanner graced the ginger-hued walls. Monk ambled over to the receptionist who sat behind an ornate desk with spindly legs. The thing looked like it was going to collapse under its own weight if you breathed on it.

The woman was an eastern Indian with a complexion nearly as dark as Monk's. "My name's Shayne, and I was looking for one of your attorneys." He handed her one of his several fake business cards.

The card identified Monk as an adjuster for the Helm Insurance Company headquartered in East St. Louis, Illinois. "Which one?" She asked, placing the card face down on the polished desk.

"Well, that's the problem. You see I inherited this assignment from someone who just up and left the company. Can you imagine that? He just up and left the company and took his files with him."

Apparently the woman at the desk couldn't as she gave no indication.

Monk twitched his leg impatiently. "Can you believe the gall? He's going to try and build up his business on the back of our company."

An impenetrable wall began to rise between them.

Monk continued his spiel. "This is a claim involving a Mr. Kinsolving who was in an incident at the intersection of Painter and Summit in Pasadena."

"If you're from Illinois, then what have you got to do with it?"

Monk did his best to look put upon. "He was insured with us and we have an affiliate office out here in Culver City. Only as I said, our agent left and I had to come out here to do the company audit, and fill in until we get a new person for the slot. We are not big, but we are thorough."

"Wonderful."

"The lawyer I'm looking for is, I believe, a Hispanic—oh I'm sorry, I believe you say Latina out here—a woman whose first name starts with a *Z* or *X*." Monk revolved a hand in he air. "That much I was able to reconstruct from our secretary who talked with our agent—sorry, our ex-agent—last." He put a hand on his hip, waiting.

The woman considered Monk for several moments, seemingly hoping he would disappear. He didn't and she tapped the desk with her palm. "Insurance case."

"Insurance case."

"I think I know who you mean."

Monk tilted his head but remained silent.

"I'll have to take your card and pass it along to the proper attorney."

"And who would that be, ma'am?"

"I'm sorry, Mr. Shayne, but I can't give that out until I've cleared it with the attorney."

"I have a lot of things to do while I'm here. Are you trying to tell me you can't give me her card or buzz her so that I can discuss this matter with her?"

"She's not in the office right now, and since you are not on her calendar, I prefer giving the attorney your card. She can call you." With that, she rose and started to leave.

Monk said, "Don't you need a local number for me?"

Exasperation slumped her body and she pushed the card toward him across the desk's shiny surface.

In bold marker, Monk wrote out a phone number in the 310 area code on the back of the card's pebble finish.

The receptionist picked it up and entered the door to the inner suites. She closed it behind her.

Monk lingered for a time but no one returned. He took the elevator back down to the street and retrieved his car from the distant, overpriced parking lot. He stopped at his donut shop and entered through the front.

"Honest" Abe Carson the carpenter was sitting at the counter, sipping coffee. Abe was a raw-boned brown-skinned man with knuckles the size of quarters and tapered forearms that looked as if they were carved from walnut. He possessed an even-tempered disposition, and was meticulous about doing his job right, and for the price he'd quoted. Hence his nickname.

Monk patted Carson on the shoulder, and moved behind the counter to pour himself a cup. "What's going on, Cool Breeze?"

"Most of the same, a few things different," the deep-voiced

craftsman said. He pulled a folded sheet of paper from the center pocket of his overalls and placed it on the counter. He continued to sip his coffee thoughtfully.

It was Elrod's day off and Lonny, the part-time worker and full-time musician appeared from the back. He was dressed in faded jeans and an oversized work shirt, tail out, and he carried a tray of fresh, deep-fried, devil's-food donuts, sliding them into place in the display case.

"The Monk," he exclaimed.

"What's up with the Exiles, Lonny?"

The Exiles were his current group, three other men and one woman, all of them in their twenties. Their political repertoire of songs and rap attack against the State was glossed with the sensibilities of Hendrix, Cameo. Art Tatum and Dean Martin. At least that's how Lonny explained it to Monk.

"Got a gig cornin' up at the Dread Room in East Hollywood, chief. You oughta bring the judgie judge by, we gonna premiere some new cuts."

"Is that right," Monk said less than enthusiastically.

Lonny huffed. "You can't hold that other time against me when you showed up at one of our sets and those Rolling Daltons and East Side Furys decided to blast it out."

Monk sighed audibly. "Maybe it's just me, Lonny, but I don't consider part of my concertgoing experience to be ducking bullets and bottles."

"It'll be copasetic, I assure you. You won't even have to bust no heads like you did last time." Lonny wheeled around and headed into the back.

Monk spoke briefly to Josette, a single mother who worked the counter three days a week, and then sat down next to Carson at the counter. "How's work?" Monk poured a sizable volume of milk into his coffee and stirred in a small amount of sugar.

"Well, you know, being self-employed ain't all they said it would be on that home study course I subscribed to off a book of matches," Carson laconically drawled. "But I've been working on a house extension over on Cimarron near Manchester." Carson picked up his cup and tipped it toward the folded piece of paper on the counter. "I had to go over to the hardware store on Western to get a few things and encountered this when I came out."

Monk picked up the white sheet of paper and unfolded it. The thing was a bad photocopy of a typewritten original which had been blown up. It read:

> "Brothers and Sistahs: don't be fooled by our supposed leaders telling us that Mexicans are in the same leaky boat as us and we must work together. Illegals are crossing our borders at rates too fast to mention. They are taking our jobs and now want to take us out, and not just in the election ring. We must stand strong, we must close the border and unite for Black self-improvement. Don't listen to the sell-outs who go begging hat in hand for foundation grants and dollars from big white corporations so they can drive around with a white woman on their arm in their Jap cars made in Korea. Stand up for your rights."

There was nothing else on the paper.

"Somebody gave this to you?" Monk asked, tapping the flyer with the back of his hand.

"It was stapled to a phone pole outside the store."

Even though the flyer looked as if it were done on somebody's kitchen table with a beat-to-hell Underwood, it seemed to Monk the spelling errors in it were deliberate. The message was clear and concise and subtle, implying

Blacks should use violence against Latinos before they moved against Blacks.

"You take this thing seriously?" Monk asked Carson. "I mean, do you think this is the work of just a couple of disgruntled brothers, or a real organization?"

"I was at the lumber yard last week and I heard a couple of guys talking about seeing these, or similar ones around town." Carson indicated the paper with a nod of his head and took a long drink of his coffee. "That's why it caught my eye and I took it down."

Monk observed, "This is like those weeks after everything jumped off in '92, and all of a sudden people started to see stuff coming over their faxes. My sister at her school got one which was supposed to be from the Swans claiming that they were going to start killing police officers after sundown."

"I remember," Carson said. "Some folks said the cops' dirty-tricks boys put those warnings out themselves as a way of undermining the truce the Swans and the Daltons were getting under way."

"Or recently another flyer was going around," Monk added. "This one from some unnamed gang stating that on the upcoming weekend there would be a lot of drive-bys as a way of gang initiations."

"My ex-wife in Oakland even saw some of those," Carson added.

"But you think there's something more to this one?"

"I'm just a student of life, Monk," Carson articulated.

"This is true, Abe. You are the only man I know who's been able to explain to me Dadaism and the fellas down at Kelvon's." Monk referred to the Abyssinia Barber Shop and Shine Parlor on Broadway in South Central.

It was a constant source of amazement to him that Kelvon Little, the co-owner and head barber of the establishment, made a living at barbering. Considering how many characters Monk always found hanging around the place—from Old Man Spears who came in to listen to the ball games on the decrepit Philco to the retired postman, the hairless Willie Brant—who came to gab but hardly use, or need, Little's services.

"There are worlds within worlds. Sometimes they orbit independently of one another, and sometimes they collide."

"Meaning?"

"Meaning I suspect more of these are going to be showing up." Carson turned his head as the bell over the door jangled. A teenaged Latino couple who were holding each other so close they looked joined at the hips, entered and approached the counter. Josette filled their order, Monk and Carson drank in silence. The two departed and Josette leaned over the counter.

"One of those flyers was in the wash house where I do my laundry." She opened the paper that Monk had refolded when the couple had entered. "It was kind'a like this one," she began, scanning the paper, "but it talked about illegals being the source of AIDS. That if you looked at when the U.S. started getting a lot of people coming here from Central America that was when the disease was starting to spread."

"Damn," Monk declared.

Josette looked perplexed. "AIDS came from someplace, didn't it?"

"So you believe what the flyer was talking about?" Carson inquired.

"No, not really," Josette said defensively. "But it is true we're seeing more tuberculosis because of immigrants and people with the virus who can't shake the TB."

Monk frowned at her. "That's because of the fucked-up

health conditions on top of the fucked-up economic conditions in other countries."

"Several of whom enjoy the dubious benefits of interference by the supposed intelligence community of the U.S. of A. in its eternal search for red agitators and other troublemakers, such intervention contributing to the movement of these unfortunate immigrants," Carson illuminated in his erudite fashion.

Josette put her hands in the air. "Hey, I'm just telling you two how some people see this out there in the streets. And I don't just mean this is a totally Black thing," she emphasized. "There were two older Mexican women in there who were nodding their heads when they read that flyer, too."

With that, she bagged two crumb donuts for the next customer. Carson and Monk discussed whether the Oakland Raiders would blow it again this year or would Hostetler, Brown and Williams help pull them out of the basement. Later, Monk called his office to catch up on his messages with Delilah.

"Ms. Scarn called from the Bureau of Consumer Affairs."

Monk grimaced. "What did the bureaucrat from hell want? Somebody make another complaint about my license?"

"No, nothing like that," Delilah began in a measured tone, aware that the delightful Ms. Scarn always got under Monk's skin. "She wanted to know if you'd be on a panel Consumer Affairs is putting on."

Monk stared at the receiver, working his jaw muscles. "She say what kind of panel?"

"Something about a presentation at the Kiwanis Club of Agoura Hills on the benefits and privileges of being a licensed representative of the State of California."

"Tell her I'll think about it."

"She'd like an answer by Friday."

"Anything of a little more relevance," Monk said flatly.

"A Mrs. Urbanski called and would like to hire your services."

"She say what the job was?"

"No, but she said she'd call back," Delilah said.

"Okay. Anybody else."

"Yeah, Dexter. He said he'd be in town tomorrow and might drop by. Only—" She stopped talking, seemingly deliberating on whether to continue.

"What?"

"He sounded kind of distracted, Ivan. Not the usual Dex, you know?"

"If he's got something on his mind, he'll speak it. See you when I see you." Monk rang off and headed for the door. Abe Carson was now engaged in a game of chess in one of the booths. His partner was a woman named Mindy. She was half Chinese, half Puerto Rican, a former drug addict and hooker who kicked both habits and now worked as a counselor for runaways.

"I'll keep you abreast of my forays," Carson said, moving his bishop into position to take her pawn.

"Right on, Red Rider."

Monk took the freeway back toward Pacific Shores, stopping off in Gardena to get a late lunch in an out-of-the-way cafe called the Onyx. He liked the Egyptian motif of the place. On either side of the main door were plaster reliefs shaped to look like standing sarcophaguses. Male and female. The arms of the two were crossed in front of them in the familiar burial fashion, but in their hands were knives and forks rather than the customary mystic implements or harvest tools.

Monk relished his Nile burger with mint and a side of the spicy Tutankhamen salad. Afterward, he got to the Shores. Cruising by the record shop Clarice had listed as a hangout for Maurice "Two Dog" Rexford, he spotted a trio of men lounging in front of the Beneficent Paternal Order of Elks Lodge a few doors down.

When last in town, he'd stopped at the record shop and asked about Two Dog, but the young clerks weren't inclined to give him an answer. The detective parked and walked back to the group.

The Black men were in their late fifties to early sixties. One of them had on a worn Kangol cap and another sat on the long end of a plastic milk crate, leaning forward on an expensive cane.

"Any of you gentlemen know a young man who goes by the name of Two Dog?" Monk said as an introduction.

The man with the cap adjusted it on his head and leered at the one sitting on the crate. The other man, a large individual with arthritically curled hands and thick glasses propped himself against the wall of the Masonic Lodge. "You the heat?" he demanded.

Monk gave the man one of his business cards and the other two crowded around to peer at it. The one in the cap adjusted it again and he looked suspiciously at Monk. "He in trouble of some kind?"

Warily, Monk responded. "I just need to talk to him."

As one, the trio gave Monk the cold treatment.

"It's nothing that concerns him directly," Monk said, wondering if that was true, "it's about his friend who was murdered, Scatterboy Williams."

That got a pulse as the man on the milk crate lifted his cane and pointed it at Monk. "You sayin' this boy might have information 'bout who killed Scatterboy?"

"I don't think so. But he might be able to tell me when he saw Scatterboy last, maybe what Scatterboy was working on."

"Hustle you mean," the heavyset man amended. Cynical

laughs went up from all three. "Who you workin' for, man? Scatterboy didn't have no folks, leastways none he ever made mention of."

"His old lady."

The man on the crate pinched his nose with his thumb and index finger, massaging the bridge. "That's a goddamn shame that child got to raise that girl without the father 'round." The pronouncement got a bobbing of heads from the other two. "Yeah, mister, we know Two Dog. That boy grew up around here same as my boy did." He paused, an unfocused memory fogging his vision.

Presently, the man with the cane spoke again. "Two Dog works part-time at the record shop there. He'll be around day after tomorrow 'bout one or so."

Monk reached into his coat and plucked out his wallet. "I appreciate this."

The tip of the cane touched Monk's hand. "Keep your bread, man. If he done wrong, then you do your job. But if he didn't, don't you be one of those helping him along the crooked road."

The heavyset man put his hand on the shoulder of the man on the crate and Monk said nothing. He turned, waved off, and left the trio. Wise men whose counsel was no longer heeded in a world traveling by too fast, and burning out too quick.

By the shank end of the afternoon, Monk again drove past Junior's Liquors on Ludlow. He was working on the assumption that Two Dog, Angel Z, or any of Scatterboy's other running partners, were more likely to be around in the evening hours.

Clarice had given him an anemic description of Angel Z: he was half-Black and half-Filipino and was inclined to wearing tank tops to show off his prison-formed pecs. What she told him about Two Dog was a biography by comparison.

He was short, black as shoe leather, and inclined to felt-covered Borsolinos. There was another one called Hugo, but Clarice wasn't sure what he looked like.

There were only two people in front of Junior's. A woman in cutoff jeans, knee-length boots and a head topped by an obvious weave. She was arguing with a man in a plaid vest and flooding double knits. Monk slowed and put the car in neutral at the curb. The woman approached his car on the passenger side and he rolled down the window. The man in the vest walked away.

"Wanna date?" she smacked, leaning down to talk.

"Where can I find Angel Z or Two Dog?"

"You a cop, baby?"

"No, but I got business with them."

"This sure is a nice hoopty." She beamed, admiring the restored Ford. "You gonna buy me one if I be good to you?"

"How about I let you start your own Christmas Club account?" He produced a twenty and held it up for her.

"Shit, you must be a cop to be that cheap." She straightened up and strolled back toward Junior's. A man came out of the liquor store holding a bottle in a brown paper bag. The working girl clamped a hand around his arm, showed some teeth, and they walked off together.

Monk spent the next hour cruising the Shores. His occasional stops consisted of asking pot-bellied prostitutes and gentlemen with practiced hard stares about the objects of his quest. The exercise produced nothing except four "fuck offs," two "fuck off, motherfuckahs," and one "say, nig-gah, step on away from here 'fore you get hurt."

Eventually, the 500 was brought to rest at a burger stand on Creedmore. He sat on the outdoor bench and joylessly ate a double cheeseburger and large fries, with an extra large root beer to help ease the mediocre food down his throat.

Across the street, an interesting group of young men gathered.

The small crowd stopped and stood talking in front of a 7-Eleven. The inside store lights back-lit their bodies to give the tableau a painterly, impressionistic quality. A couple of them looked like typical street rovers replete with bandannas wrapped around their heads and over-sized shirts buttoned up to the collar.

But what caught Monk's eye was the one who dressed like a frat brother lost on his way to a kegger party, a young man decked out in pressed chinos and a sport coat with patches on the elbows. Looking closely, he was pretty sure it was the cousin he'd met the other night at Jimmy Henderson's bedside.

Another one of the crew was dressed in jeans, T-shirt, and a bright colored vest. Still another, with longish straight black hair and brown-olive skin, was a good candidate to be Angel Z.

The members of the band talked for several minutes, then split up into two divisions. Monk got up and ambled to the order window of the stand.

"Let me have a coffee, will you?" he said to the man with the receding hairline behind the screen.

"Sure." The proprietor poured it, handed it through the gap, and then shoved a crusty sugar server and a styrofoam cup of milk through.

Monk put change on the metal counter top and mixed the ingredients into his coffee while standing at the window. Seeking to sound disinterested, he said, "Those youngsters who were across the street, they supposed to be some kind of prep school gang?"

The man with the high forehead was pouring himself a cup of coffee also. "I've seen that group out now for the last two, three evenings. I heard over to the Elks Lodge the other night they're supposed to be looking for the Shoreline Killer."

Monk took a sip of his coffee. It was as bad as it was weak. "What's that all about?"

A shoulder lifted. "There's a rumor going around that a serial killer has been stalking young bloods in the Shores. Now the way I hear it, one of his victims lived long enough to tell his mother that he heard the killer say he wasn't going to rest until every brother under twenty-five was dead and buried.

"But you know how shit like that gets started. Some drugged-out crack head probably's been hallucinating and told one of his crazy buddies, and before you know it, motherfuckahs see conspiracy behind every doorway. I tell you what it is"—he leaned close for emphasis—"some hard working guy like you or me got tired of them drug slangers makin' the streets unsafe for our wives and girlfriends." He drank some of his brew, seemingly enjoying the taste.

"See, the law can't do it, can't clean up our community, and this dude has said enough is enough, I gotta do for self. Ain't that what Farrakhan was talking about in the Million Man March? And I say more power to him if we can take back the streets." The man left the window and began to clean his grill by scrapping a spatula back and forth across its surface.

Monk sat down at the bench again and slowly finished his coffee, staring at the 7-Eleven across the street. He stayed that way even after the proprietor extinguished the overhead lights.

Doggedly, the tired detective spent the next several hours driving and walking around the streets of the Shores. At one point, a sheriff's car put its spotlight on him. The two deputies inside the vehicle, murky shapes in their military brown shirts, conversed with one another, the probe steady on Monk in his car.

The deputy in the passenger seat swung the incandescent beam away from Monk's immobile face. The car, its dark outline prominent for several expectant moments against the descending evening, idled like a sleeping rhino. A beast operating on whim and caprice, which at any moment could be an agent of destruction on Neptune Avenue. Monk tensed, and breathed through his mouth to remain calm.

Slowly the patrol car drove off, and Monk could feel the muscles relax in the back of his neck. After another hour he found himself on a side street off Neptune, the main drag. He spied the group of young men, now rejoined as one, as they crossed in mid-block, heading in his direction. He pulled to the curb and shut the motor off. They walked past where he was parked and Monk got a better look at them.

The college kid, Jimmy Henderson's cousin, was present and so was the one with the long black hair Monk typed as Angel Z. As they passed by, Monk made mental notes of what they looked like. The cousin, in elbow patches, was about Monk's complexion and height, though thinner in the arms and torso. His horn-rimmed glasses gave him a bookish appearance. Also in their gathering were two Monk characterized as the rough and ready sort; a slight swagger to their gait, a certain practiced detachment that hung over them like overdue child support payments.

Another one was iron-buffed in the upper body and had on a ridiculously over-sized surfer-style T-shirt. Several other mismatched types rounded out the odd troop. They moved on and turned south at the end of the block. He let the posse get along, determined to talk with the cousin, alone, later.

Monk waited several beats then got out of his car. An

earlier contact had given him what purported to be a lead. Another prospect from Clarice's list was somebody named Midnight who, his teenaged client had informed him, wasn't a do-rag wearin' Uncle Tom, but an albino Black man. Supposedly Midnight's forte was being able to boost a car stereo no matter what the alarm system.

According to Monk's source, there had been a healthy dose of stereo and radio thefts on the opposite side of town last week. The source, a heavily moussed transsexual named Roxanne, told Monk she knew it was Midnight and further surmised that the master thief would now strike on this side of town, now that the focus of the heat was across town.

In fact, the busty Roxanne had added, placing a hand on Monk's thigh, she was pretty sure this was where Midnight would be tonight He had a date with a woman who Roxanne also had a relationship with, only the stereo thief didn't know that. She also asked Monk if he was going to be busy, say around three-thirty in the morning. Monk had graciously begged off until some other time.

It wasn't much of a lead but Monk couldn't be picky. At least it gave him a direction, like a swimmer making for a buoy in the morning fog. For the moment, it was important to get to know the streets of Pacific Shores, learn its byways like Scatterboy had known them. Walking along, Monk pondered the mind of the Shoreline Killer. Was he a racist murderer waiting in the shadow of the moon for some twisted inner trigger to go off so he could kill another Black man? Though he hadn't dismissed the gang option, he now leaned more toward some kind of sicker mind at work.

Why, he wasn't exactly sure. But maybe, he allowed, he hoped to make a splash for himself by tracking down and bringing to justice a headline murderer. By the media compass, an isolated gang killing is just business as usual in the ghetto. But serial slayings, according to some weird inner motive, like the Hillside Strangler, got a lot of play. And money deals, too.

Maybe that was it. In all his time as a P.I., he'd never worried about money. Like any working stiff, he had to scuffle now and then to keep the landlord happy. But now, edging close to forty, living by his wits was starting to fray at the edges. He tried to convince himself that these ruminations only sprang from his confusion over Jill and his new-found need to move up the economic ladder.

But, as he meandered along Osage, there was a unexamined part of him that hid a dusty mirror. Tentatively, he picked it up and brushed away the dirt. He could see his face, much like his father's. Like any Black man, his dad had had his share of disappointments. But when things looked up, when the old man angled and borrowed fifteen grand from a gambler friend, he'd been able to open his own car repair place on Hooper. But pops was a better mechanic than he was a businessman, and seemed to always be only two steps ahead of his lenders.

Monk had left the residential streets and was now moving along a series of one-story shop fronts. Roxanne had mentioned, actually whispered in his ear, that this might be Midnight's territory tonight. With some active night life, it attracted people and cars from out of town—easy prey for Midnight's skills.

In the reflection of the window of an auto parts store, Monk saw a fleeting blob merge with the cars parked across the street. He walked on to an all-night adult book shop two doors down and entered. Monk paid the dollar browsing charge—good toward your purchase—and positioned himself so he could look out the front window.

A late model Ford Bronco stood out among the older

makes parked across the street. Leafing through an issue of Big Tops and Tails, he watched. Presently a figure, a flash of white stark against the upturned collar of a ebon leather jacket, walked past the rear fender of the Bronco. Monk tossed the magazine back on the shelf and exited the establishment.

The thief glided briskly along Osage, passing momentarily in front of the neon sign of a tavern. The milky white skin of the man with the fade cut was an artist's contrast to the dark ensemble he was clad in. Monk trailed Midnight with the notion of confronting him. If he knew something about Scatterboy's death, he might be happy to talk if Monk made a deal not to bust him.

Situational ethics justified making this kind of approach, Monk had concluded some time ago. If a petty thief could lead him to a murderer, fine. But there was the greater likelihood Midnight didn't know jack and would tell Monk any old lie just to get away. Or maybe he was the one who iced Scatterboy. There was only one way to find out.

They were now moving along Creedmore. There were a few people out, some leaving a second-run movie house, so Monk didn't feel too exposed. Midnight was on the other side of the street and he suddenly cut through an alley. Monk cursed himself for being spotted, and ran diagonally across the street toward the alley. He stopped at its gloomy mouth, but could hear nothing.

Cautiously, he went down the murky passageway. On one side of the narrow alley were dumpsters overflowing with garbage. A heady stench wafted through the air. A noise made Monk halt. His throat constricted and his hand went toward the .45 in the belt holster beneath his sweatshirt. There it was again and Monk strived desperately to place it. He inched forward, his heart beating a syncopated rhythm in his head. His foot collided with something and the automatic filled his hand before he could think.

A groan emerged from the ground. Monk bent forward and strained his eyes. A homeless man lay on a pallet of old blankets and flattened-out cardboard. He rolled toward the wall and continued to sleep. Monk went on.

Midway, Monk stopped again to listen and look. The alley cut through to another street. A lamppost on the far street spilled light into the causeway. From where he stood, Monk could make out a recess in the wall up ahead. Gun forward, he approached the area. He found a wood door with a grimy pane set in it. Using a discarded newspaper, Monk wiped at the pane with little result.

His hand on the knob, he pressed his shoulder to the door and was surprised when it gave in easily. It hadn't been locked. He stepped into a dark space with looming masses on all sides. Moving further inside, his face encountered a spider's web. Reaching out to brush it away, Monk found it was a cord and tugged on it. An overhead bare bulb came to life, emitting a weak light. Good enough to see, low enough not to be noticed through the opaque glass of the door.

The room was filled floor to ceiling with debris of all sorts. Part of an old platen press was buried underneath a doorless refrigerator. Mounds of shoes, handbags, and clothing were scattered all over like a leather moss. Several engine blocks and truck tires also took up positions around the room along with portions of old radio sets, parts of discarded TVs, and a huge open crate of gears the size of cup saucers.

To his light was the one uncluttered area in the room. There was a chair and table, and three car stereo units of recent vintage upon its surface. A screwdriver and a pair of needle-nosed pliers were also on the table. A tool box rested on the floor near the table. Brother Midnight's work shop.

Monk peered around the rest of the room, but could discern no other way out. Midnight must have lit in here and dumped his cargo. If he'd spotted Monk, then he'd no doubt unloaded his goods and taken off toward the other street. Probably long gone by now. On the other hand, maybe he hadn't seen Monk and he'd dropped off the unit while he went about the business of swiping others.

The detective left, extinguishing the light before he opened the door back onto the alley. He continued in the direction of the next street and found himself on another commercial avenue of low-slung brick buildings. A large junkyard fenced in by a combination of corrugated metal and chainlink was at one end. The junkyard was directly to his right, blocking a portion of the street from his view.

Two Doberman pinschers slunk across the junkyard's dirt lot, their black short hairs glistening under the pale glow of the street lamps. They rose behind the fence and pointed their wet snouts at Monk. Anticipation dripped off their slightly parted mouths but they didn't bark. A burst of laughter punctuated the scene, and Monk clawed for his reholstered weapon even as he flattened against the junkyard's wall.

Another set of laughter punctuated the air, and Monk could now discern two sets of lungs at work. He got up, the strangely silent guard dogs panting and watching him with felonious eyes. He went around a corner of the junkyard, followed by his two shit-grinning, four-legged pals. On that block, there was no curbing and a lowered '64 Impala, a six-four as the youths say, was parked. It was at the edge of a grass lot down toward the other end of the junkyard.

The Impala was under a street light and Midnight in his black leather jacket and colorless face was prominent standing near the front of the vehicle. Perched on the hood was a shapely woman in fringed orange hot pants and a knitted halter top, her dark skin like beautiful varnished maple. Midnight threw his head back and laughed again. A forty-ounce bottle of malt liquor was also perched on the car.

From his vantage point he watched the couple as they nuzzled and drank and told each other private little jokes. He was about to call it quits and go home. He wasn't a voyeur, just a snoop, and a blind man could see where all this foreplay by light post was heading. Besides, now he knew why Midnight was in a rush. Monk would come back tomorrow, stake out his workshop, and brace him then.

Turning to retrace his route, Monk heard an engine downshift and looked back to see a red Jeep whip around the corner near Midnight and his lady friend. The colorless Black man was pulling on the woman's arm as the driver of the sport vehicle shouted something. The unmistakable retort of a gun pealed above the now barking dogs. Monk was running forward, the .45 in his hand when he heard the sound of rushing feet from behind him. A glance to the rear revealed the young men on Shoreline Killer patrol. They were running fast, yelling as they got closer.

Shifting his attention back to Midnight, Monk saw the Jeep screech into a vicious U-Turn. The vehicle's heavy bumper sideswiped the '64. Midnight was down on his knees, grasping the Impala's front fender as if it were a life preserver. The young woman was screaming and Monk drew a bead on the shooter. He pumped a shot out on the ran, managing only to wound the car's rollbar. The driver turned his head at the loud metallic twang. And for a nanosecond, Monk felt as if he were viewing Midnight's other dimension image.

The face in the Jeep was bone-white, the mouth a jagged line of disgust, the hair as ash-white as innocence betrayed. Only this man was Caucasian, his incredible whiteness gave his square-jawed face a ghost-like quality, as if he maintained his physical presence by will alone. The barrel of a revolver extended forward from his shoulder, and he cranked off two shots which flew over Monk who was already prone on the ground.

From that position, Monk cradled the butt of the automatic in his left hand and squeezed off two more rounds at the retreating vehicle and its off-road, muddy tires. It took the corner at a sharp angle and escaped in a prolonged squeal. Monk got up and started to where the woman was latched onto Midnight.

"Oh, goddamn," somebody hollered from behind and Monk pivoted. One of the young men in the roving patrol was also on the ground, holding his hand over his side.

"He's been hit, man," the cousin with the Ivy League look said to no one in particular. "Goddamnit, somebody do something." Everybody crowded around the injured youth, the collegiate kid propping his wounded comrade on one knee.

"Let him lie flat," Monk warned, walking closer. "If he's bleeding internally, you'll do more damage than good."

As one the young men stared at Monk, all of a sudden two other guns were pointed in his general direction.

"Just who the fuck are you?" one of them demanded.

The cousin was going to answer when two patrol cars plowed around the same corner where the Jeep had disappeared. The official blue lights revolved wildly, in eerie silence.

Monk became acutely aware he was still holding his gun. He threw it away from his body and clasped his hands on top of his head. "I suggest you gents do the same," he said, not daring to take his eyes off the onrushing law.

Several thuds behind him indicated the young men had heeded his words. Or maybe it was the four deputies and their automatic shotguns that had convinced them.

A big Latino deputy, a sergeant, whose biceps strained his short-sleeved shirt, leveled his shotgun directly at Monk's head. "All you motherlovers drop to the ground on your knees. Now."

Monk did as ordered.

"Hey, call an ambulance, man, my friend's hurt," he heard the cousin shout.

"Fuck you." The shotgun shifted off of Monk and onto the young man. "Everyone of you sonsabitches get on your knees and face me, now, while I'm still in a good mood," the sergeant bellowed.

Apparently everyone did. Two other cops came up to join the sergeant while the fourth went over to the Impala. The sergeant ordered, "Everyone prone out." He pantomimed with the shotgun by jerking it toward the ground.

"Look man—" elbow patches began.

"Look man, my shit-stained skivvies. Kiss the ground."

Monk and the others did so. Having the dubious honor of being in front in this horizontal parade, Monk was handcuffed with metal bracelets. A few of the others were too and the rest were manacled with the plastic, more uncomfortable versions. Each man was patted down and one of the deputies handed Monk's permit to the sergeant. He saw this because his head was turned to one side. The sergeant stood back, keeping his gun at the ready.

The sergeant thumbed a flashlight on and carefully read the photostat. He looked from it to Monk, then walked off. No doubt to verify its authenticity by radio. Presently he returned and approached Monk.

"All right, Mr. Monk, why don't you tell me what happened." It wasn't a question, it was a royal order.

"Let me sit up first."

A space of time dragged before the muscular sergeant

said, "Okay. Turn over slowly and get into a sitting position. Anything else I will infer as a hostile action."

"I'm sure you will," Monk said under his breath. He sat up, and was greeted with the deadly serious look of a man who didn't take no shit and had heard it all before. "Before we get started, I want you to call an ambulance for that kid."

"I believe I'm in charge here."

"Yeah, you damn sure are." Momentarily, his mouth went slack as he imagined what it might feel like to have the stock of a shotgun rammed against his teeth and nose. In a measured tone he said, "So make a decision and get an ambulance for that kid."

Time stretched again and Monk could only guess what was happening behind the sergeant's face which was as stern as a Tolmec statue.

"There's one on its way, hot shot. Now let's get to my questions."

It was Monk's natural inclination to hold back information, particularly when he dealt with authority. He told the sergeant how he happened to be following the one called Midnight this evening. Monk omitted the parts about the young man's line of work.

"A white man with dead white skin." Again, the sergeant spoke without inflection. He looked over at the other deputies—another car had arrived with three more—as they went about securing the crime scene, sorting out stories, and so on. The boxish head swung back. "Okay Monk, we'll go over it again until we get it right."

With that he marched away and for the next hour and a half, Monk, Midnight—unhurt but shaken—the young woman, and the group of young men sat on the ground against the sides of two cruisers. Their hands remained cuffed. True to the sergeant's word, the one who was injured had been taken away in a red and white Schaefer ambulance.

The leader of the roving band was Henderson's cousin. His occasional comments gave Monk the impression that he might be pre-law. He would ask the deputies what they were being charged with, what about the Miranda rights, and so forth. Each remark was met with stony silence as the deputies walked to and fro. They joked with one another or sporadically threw a look in Monk's direction.

Eventually, everyone was carted off to the sub-station in nearby Wilmington. Monk was placed on a padded chair in an interrogation room and spent the remainder of the night and early morning having his story dissected by the sergeant, Verrano, and a Captain Olson, a scrawny white man in his mid-fifties with a rolling gait, an initialed belt buckle, and bad breath. The last fact Monk surmised was intentional, just part of the arsenal of interrogation.

Monk's license was threatened, his manhood was questioned, and his lack of brains underscored several times. He was also pointedly told that private eyes and criminal defense lawyers weren't fit to be shark chum. Through it all Monk stuck to the truth, more or less. At one point the captain was called out of the room.

When he returned, they took up the usual line of questioning but Olson was more interested in details about the killer than he had been before. Monk figured Midnight had also repeated his story over and over of how he remembered the killer looking like Casper the Unfriendly Ghost. And since there were no stolen goods on him, and presumably the Impala was clean, they might be more inclined to believe him. He also knew Olson had to be thinking how he was going to handle the press once the Shoreline Killer story hit the papers.

Around six in the morning, Monk was allowed to wash up and was asked to step into the captain's office. He entered a claustrophobic cubicle that had a speed bag rig bolted into one corner of the room and several bowling trophies on a lopsided shelf.

"Have a seat, Monk."

Olson sat behind a desk which contained among other items a stapler and two neat piles of file folders. A lone file was before him on his tattered blotter and it didn't take somebody with a detective's degree to figure out who was the subject in the folder. An oversized, stuffed envelope was next to the file.

Two covered styrofoam cups were also on the desk alongside a box of donuts precariously perched on a stuffed vertical file organizer. Monk slumped into the offered seat.

"Go ahead, help yourself." Olson opened the folder and pretended to read it for the first time.

Monk devoured a glazed donut and began working on a crumb before prying the lid off the coffee and taking a swallow of the hot bitter brew. It was like drinking steamed donkey sweat, but it was invigorating.

Olson leafed through several pages in the folder, closed it, and looked solemnly at Monk. "We might have a situation on our hands."

All of a sudden it was "we." Monk said, "You mean the dead-faced killer."

Olson rubbed his hands together, reminding Monk of a character in an old movie playing a money-grubbing banker. He talked as he rubbed. "You know these kind of things can escalate uncomfortably if they aren't handled responsibly."

"I have no intention of talking to any reporters, if that's

what's got you worried, captain." Which was the singular most truthful statement he'd given all night. He polished off the second donut and lusted for a third.

"I know you've got some seasoning, Monk," the captain said, buttering him up. "It's the wild cards in this deal that I'm worried about."

"You mean Midnight? Why the hell would he talk to the papers, he's not one for over-exposure," Monk countered.

"I agree, Mr. Lake's activities require a certain anonymity. I'm much more concerned about Bradford and his bunch. He seems too willing to put his campaign in the court of the media." Olson finally took the lid off his coffee.

"What exactly is Bradford's connection to all this?" He took Bradford to mean the leader of the crew.

"He's a cousin of a kid named Henderson who was shot about a week ago."

"He's in a coma." Monk put the third donut down, uneaten.

"I know. Anyway, Bradford's one of these campus radical types. He's of the notion that the LAPD and us won't do justice to the Black man and catch the Shoreline Killer," Olson said as neutrally as he could. He tried to look indifferent as he tasted his coffee, but Monk knew he was gauging his reaction.

"So you think he's trying to build himself a reputation?"

Olson lifted a brow. "Everybody has different perspectives, Mr. Monk."

"So as one pro to the next, captain, what do you want from me?"

Olson reared back in his swivel then leaned forward, his long fingers grasping the coffee cup like a hawk capturing its prey. "Maybe you could have a chat with Mister Bradford and at least try to get him from making so big a noise in the press. I'm not so much worried about the *Press-Telegram*, after all, who the hell reads it? But if the fucking *Times* picks it up, then the copycat TV news will get it. And sure as God made little green apples the Shores will be crawling with Sally Jesse, Montel and every fuckin' body else fuckin' up our investigation."

The captain took a pull on his coffee then added, "It means messing up your action too, Monk. How long will your client pay you once she knows somebody else is looking for the killer for free?"

He'd told Olson about Clarice but not how little she was paying him. Could be Olson thought Scatterboy left a little something under the mattress from his wheeling and dealing. Monk said, "You got a point there, captain. I'll be happy to have a little talk with Bradford."

As if he were a U.N. ambassador negotiating a difficult treaty, Olson slapped his hand on the file on his desk. "Good. Ah, of course you'll still have to fill out a weapons discharge report."

"I always do it by the book. I take it you're not holding Bradford?"

"No, the other two guns at the scene besides yours belonged to two of the brothers with him but he wasn't packing."

"You planning to come down on them with both feet?"

Olson sucked something out of a back tooth, then responded.

"We don't tolerate vigilantism round here."

"I'm not saying you do, captain. But if you want to cool Bradford out, and if the guns are registered to the owners, a misdemeanor goes down smoother than a felony concealed weapons charge."

"I'll give it some thought." He bit off half of a sprinkled.

Monk got up and stretched. "I'll fill out the report before I go. Can you give me an address for Bradford?"

"Yeah," Olson mumbled over his donut. He produced a 3x5 index card and tossed it in Monk's direction. "Also, I'd like you to give a description of the shooter to our artist. I already have your statement that the vehicle the alleged crook was driving was a bright red Chrysler Wrangler Jeep, open-air, late model, with mud caked on the big tires. Anyway, she'll be here at eight-thirty."

"Aw hell. I suppose I can get a ride back to my car after that, right?" He picked up the card and tucked it in his back pocket.

"Anything for a pro." Olson grinned. It was like looking at a cottonmouth before it struck. He touched the envelope. "Don't forget your goods."

Monk was delivered to his car by ten and crawled into his bed in Mar Vista a little before eleven. He hadn't been this tired in a long time and he slept the sleep of the just until twenty past four when the ringing phone awoke him.

He plucked the receiver off the nightstand and slurred into it. "*Que?*"

"Chief," Delilah's velvet voice floated to him through the wire. "I know you said not to bother you because of your long night, but I've got two messages I thought you might want to hear."

Monk yawned. "From who, D?"

"Dexter says he'll meet you at the Satellite at seven tonight. And a woman named"—and there was a pause—"Xylina Ysaguirre-Chacon called."

"Hot damn."

CHAPTER 9

Ysaguirre-Chacon was indeed one of the lawyers at the firm where Monk had left his fake card. She'd only left her number, but it matched the one on the card Monk had pilfered from the snotty receptionist's desk. He wanted to talk with her but more immediate concerns pressed him.

After a long shower and a meal at the Chinese-Mexican cafe called the Picante Eggroll on National, Monk got over to his office after six. Delilah had gone home but Hendricks, of Ross and Hendricks, was working at a draft table as Monk knocked on her door.

"Ivan, how're things?" the stately architect asked.

"Getting interesting. What are you working on?"

"We're in the running for a series of virtual reality arcades from Mid-City to Oxnard."

"The brave new electronic age dawns."

"So it would seem." The edge of her number two pencil followed the side of her T-square in a precise, even stroke. "By the way, some woman just left here looking for you."

"Did she leave a name?"

"Urbanski. I told her you'd be in tomorrow and that bent her whistle somewhat. She mentioned you never seem to be around, and she's not used to being held up on important matters."

"She say what she want?"

"No."

"What did she look like?"

Hendricks made some notations on her work then looked over at Monk. "Mid-forties white woman, natural blonde, a little touch-up I think. Good dresser. Stylish but not ostentatious." She went back to her work. "Her handbag was a DKNY, genuine, not a swap meet special."

"Well, if it's important, she'll call back I guess."

"She left a note for you, slid it under your door, made a point of telling me so."

"Thanks."

"Mmm." She was engrossed in her work again.

Monk entered his office and picked up the envelope. It was the color of lilac and smelled like it too. In a feminine script his name was spelled out on its cover. Hitching a hip onto his desk, he opened the perfumed envelope and removed a similarly hued sheet. In the same feminine script, it read: "My dear Mr. Monk, it is quite possible I shall be in dire need of your services within the next two weeks. Please consider this a formal offer."

It was signed Tassia Urbanski. There was no phone number nor address on the note or envelope. He refolded the sheet and placed it on his desk. He dug out the index card Captain Olson had given him and dialed the number for Malik Bradford. After three rings an answering machine came on the line and Monk left a detailed message, including his office and home numbers.

He checked his watch and left his own note clipped to Urbanski's for Delilah. He said goodnight to Hendricks and drove over to the Satellite bar on Adams Boulevard. It was a cozy neighborhood kind of place whose mostly Black working class patrons included bus drivers, phone operators and Chief auto parts clerks. And it seemed, a school teacher or two.

His sister Odessa was sitting at a table with Dexter Grant.

"Please don't tell me you two have started dating," Monk said seriously. He kissed his sister on the cheek, and sat at the table.

"Even pious public school teachers can come in for a beer now and then at a family watering hole."

Grant winked broadly at Monk. "Yeah, you can't have all the fun."

Odessa said, "What's happening on this case of yours down in Pacific Shores?"

Monk ordered a beer from a passing waitress. "It's coming along."

"I got news for you, Black Eye," his sister shot back, "it's busting out all over."

"Huh?"

"The story was going around my school today about the Shoreline Killer."

The beer had come up and stopped midway to his mouth. "What?"

"Mrs. Waterson, the math teacher lives in Wilmington and she'd heard about it at the market she shops at."

"It figures." The beer made it to his mouth.

His mentor scratched the side of his chin with a weather-tanned hand. "Now that you don't have to protect your sister's delicate sensibilities, why don't you tell us what's going on?"

"But first," Monk said to his sister, "what are you doing here?"

Odessa answered. "I think that's none of your business, brother dear. Now what about this serial killer rumor?"

Monk filled them in on his progress including his spotting of the white-haired man in the fire-engine red Jeep.

Odessa placed a hand on his arm. "Ivan, this sounds like it could be some kind of Klan thing."

A pained look screwed up Grant's face. "We got to be careful about what we say. That sort of talk starts going around up here in L.A. and we'll never get the cats back in the bag."

"That's certainly Olson's take on it, Dex. But if it's already going around a school in South Central L.A., then how long before everything ratchets up?"

"But that's just the point, Ivan," Grant responded, "if the big media starts sniffing a story, then you can be damn sure the killer will move on."

"If it's a serial killer, he may welcome a game with the authorities," Odessa observed.

Monk spread his hands in the air. "So which is it, Odessa? Is he a serial killer who just happens to be playing out a racist fantasy, or is it some kind of supremacist plot?"

"If it is a serial killer," Grant began, "then maybe he'll stick to playing hide and seek with the cops. But there's plenty of examples of these guys splitting for easier pickings once the temperature heats up."

"And thinking more about it, I'm not so sure about the supremacist angle," Monk said. "So far, there's nothing to tie the dead-faced man to Scatterboy's killing, and there's already been someone else arrested for the second murder."

"So you think there's some other connection between the attempted killing of Henderson and the attack on this Midnight?" Grant had some more beer. "That could mean Bradford's up to more than he's let on."

As if on cue, a man entered the bar and sauntered over to their table. He was over six feet, broad in the shoulders and wore sharp-toed boots. His tight-fitting jeans revealed an athletic build. He bent and kissed Odessa on the mouth.

"Frank, this is my brother, Ivan."

Frank extended a corded hand and shook Monk's. "Odessa's mentioned you. I'm pleased we finally meet." His brown eyes hovered on Monk then went over to Grant.

"I'm the family's trusted manservant." Grant also shook hands with the man.

"I didn't realize I'd have to run the gauntlet tonight," Frank joked.

Odessa rose from her seat. "I didn't realize Ivan and Dexter were going to be here either. Let's get going." She put on the jacket that had been draped on the back of her chair, then placed a hand on Monk's shoulder. "Now I know you know how to handle yourself, but don't do anything foolish." She kissed him on the forehead, waved goodbye to Grant and left with her date.

Grant chided, "How old would you say Frank is?"

Monk was still staring at the door his sister had gone through. "Dude can't be more than thirty, thirty-one."

"Yep."

"Shit." Monk raked down some more beer.

"Relax. Anyway, you ain't got much room to talk considering you're younger than Jill." Grant guffawed softly.

"There's not but a few years difference," Monk said, pointing at Grant. "Not like this boyfriend who'll have to take a nap during the day."

"He won't be taking it alone, slick," Grant needled.

"Shit," Monk swore again and ordered another round of beer. "So what brought you to town today?"

Grant tipped the waitress after she'd set down the fresh brews. "A funeral, Ivan. Father Time come a'knockin."

"Somebody from the force." Monk knew it without stating it.

A sharp "Yeah" escaped from Grant. "Perry Jakes and me

went a long way back, Ivan. Back to the days of Black Mariahs and twenty-cent roast beef sandwiches at Cargo's on Alameda.

"He was the first one in the door, the guy at your back going down a blind alley." Grant trailed off, trying to get his voice under control. "Don't get old, Ivan," he said, looking up. "You gotta keep burying your friends."

Monk knocked the rim of his glass against Grant's. "I'm going to get you busy, enough of this maudlin jive."

Grant smiled faintly, raising his beer to the hand of the specter at the table.

"MIDNIGHT, MY main man."

He stood there, one hand holding a car stereo unit, the other one around the light cord. He blinked at Monk who was sitting on top of one of the pieces of machinery in the thief's workshop.

"Glad you finally made it. Sitting around in this unheated room for two days and these cold nights y'all have out near the ocean here sure isn't good for my rheumatism." Grant shifted uncomfortably.

Midnight ogled the ex-cop, who was resting on a folding chair with a Dunkin' Donuts coffee cup in his hand, his legs crossed and his upper body tightly encased in a flannel shirt and an armless parka. "What?" he began and suddenly jerked on the light's string.

Darkness enveloped the room but Monk was already on his feet, having anticipated the thief's action. He bent his body forward, arms extended before him in a sweeping motion. Monk caught Midnight around the lower legs and they both slammed against something solid and heavy. The radio he was holding went skittering across the cement floor like a big metal rat. Grant pulled the light back on. Grabbing the kid around the collar of his leather jacket, the larger man hauled him to his feet.

"Young brother, we just want to have a few words with you. Okay?" Monk said forcefully, shoving Midnight into the chair Grant had vacated.

The colorless Black man exhaled a lung full of air and pointed a pale hand at the detective. "I know you, you with them other dudes who was down at the sheriff's station."

"I'm not with Bradford and his group. He's looking to avenge the shooting of his cousin, Jimmy Henderson. I'm the one looking for Scatterboy's killer."

What passed for a sly look slitted Midnight's lids and he folded his arms. "What kind of reward are they giving to find the guy who hit Scatterboy?"

Grant hooted, "And I suppose for the right price you'll tell us what you know."

"I might," Midnight shot back.

Monk said, "I doubt if you know jack about who killed Scatterboy."

Indignantly, Midnight retorted, "If you think that, then what the hell are you doing here?"

Grant was about to speak but Monk held up his hand and he stopped. "When was Scatterboy killed?"

"Huh?"

"What, are the acoustics bad in here?" Monk bellowed. "When was Scatterboy killed?"

"Why should I tell you?"

"Because I'm authorized to share half the reward with you if your information leads me to the murderer."

Midnight looked from Monk to Grant, each giving him the poker face. "You're lying."

"Don't forget, Shadrach, I'm the one who pulled his piece the other night taking shots at the man who tried to cap you."

"I'm supposed to be grateful?"

Monk knew it would be easier for him to scale City Hall with an ice pick. "The sheriff didn't hold me, did he? We're in your place, right?"

Midnight considered the information, looking from Monk to Grant, each one giving him nothing in the way of body language. Finally he said, "How much is the reward?"

"More than you make selling these tinker toys." Grant flicked a hand at one of the radios on Midnight's workbench.

Midnight rolled his tongue around his closed mouth, poking out his cheek as he did. "I ain't tellin' you nothin' for free."

"But you gotta convince me you know what you're talking about," Monk countered.

Midnight all but stuck out his lip like an obstinate child. A begrudging "all right" issued from him softly.

"What day was Scatterboy killed on?" Grant said.

"I don't remember," he mumbled.

"What was he killed with?" Monk asked.

"A gun," Midnight blurted triumphantly.

Grant asked him. "What kind?"

"Don't know."

"How many shots?" Monk tested.

"I wasn't there, man." He kicked at the floor.

"Then you're just dickin' us," Grant said angrily.

"Yeah," Monk drawled, "Let's go call Olson."

Midnight stood up furiously, upending the chair as he did. "You two cold-eyed bastards are trying to fuck with me."

Monk looked at Grant for mock solace. "I gave him every chance."

"Chance my ass." Midnight started for Monk.

"Whoa, champ." Grant said, his well-traveled .38 Police Special popping into his fist. He waved the piece and

Midnight righted the chair and sat heavily onto it. His entire frame seemed to sink in on itself as if he were wasting away from the expenditure of energy, his slick moves not fast enough to outdistance fate. "Why don't you two sorry-assed Amos and Andy leave me the fuck alone."

"We like you too much." Monk patted him on the knee. "Besides, you may know something of value."

"Yeah? like what?"

Monk didn't have a specific answer, but Grant said. "What did the man in the red jeep say to you before he took a shot?"

Midnight said nothing.

"You want me to tell Captain Olson about this Santa's workshop of yours?" Monk indicated the room.

A glum "no" escaped. Midnight's lower face clamped together. "I guess you didn't say anything or he wouldn't have let me go."

"So did the man say something?" Grant reiterated. Monk gave him a questioning look but went along with the flow.

Midnight rubbed the back of his neck with his hand, then dropped it flaccidly into his lap. "You're right. I remember I was kissin' on Jackie, rubbin' all up on her when we hear the burnin' rubber. I look up and see this candy red Jeep speedin' for us." Midnight talked like a man in a trance, his hands clasped together and his body erect in the chair.

"Coming closer I'm thinking, 'aw shit,' here I am a sittin' fuckin' duck and without my rod."

"Did you recognize the driver?" Grant said.

"No. And I'd remember somebody who looked like him."

Ignoring the irony, Monk proceeded. "So he's coming closer."

"Yeah, I can tell by the way he's startin' to slow up he's gonna try a drive-by."

"Could you tell what kind of gun it was?" Monk asked him.

Midnight stared straight ahead again, visualizing his close call. "Automatic of some kind. Didn't really get that good a look 'cause I was tryin' to pull Jackie off the hood and down to the ground." In a fast motion Midnight slapped his hands together loudly. "I swear I could see the bullet leavin' the chamber and feel the wind as it whipped past my head."

He paused and looked over his shoulder, possibly looking for the Grim Reaper. "I don't know why I wasn't killed."

Monk was tempted to say something profound about Midnight being given a second chance in life so that he could do better. Instead, he asked, "What did he say, man?"

Midnight's head tilted toward the floor for several moments then he said, "It sounded like he was clearing his throat."

Grant inched closer to the young thief. "Think hard."

Several moments elapsed. The left side of Midnight's face bunched itself up in his concentration. "Shit, I never got past intro Spanish in school."

Grant declared, "It was Spanish?"

"No, I just meant I don't know nothing about words that ain't American. It wasn't Spanish, I hear that enough from the eses. The shooter said something like 'dad, dod' or something. It was quick, like he was spitting it out from his throat."

Monk frowned at Midnight then watched Grant as he advanced before the seated radio booster.

"*Fur die herrlichkeit*," the ex-cop said.

Midnight's jaw hinged open. "Yeah. I mean I don't know if those were the exact words but the sound was like you just did, like that."

"What did you say, Dex?"

"I had a hunch if it was a neo-nazi type he'd be versed in

National Socialist history. I imagine our friend might have said something like, '*Fur die herrlichkeit und die ehre.*' For glory and honor." Grant translated. "It was one of the slogans used by German foot soldiers during the war. Something they might say over drinks before a bloody campaign."

CHAPTER 10

Kodama's short-nailed fingers rubbed Monk's close-cropped hair. Her back arched as she lay on the kitchen table, moaning with pleasure. She pushed on the rear of his head, the muscles in her upper thighs tightening.

After a fashion, Monk, wearing only a shirt, rose from where he'd been kneeling between her spread legs. He leaned his perspiring form over hers and Kodama latched onto him, pressing her clothed body against his. "Hey, baby," he rushed out heavily. He started nibbling on her neck.

Kodama fondled him and whispered, "Come on, Ivan."

Monk pushed up her skirt and entered her. Kodama wrapped her feet around his back, the shirt wet from perspiration. "Naima" on vinyl by John Coltrane throbbed even through the scratches with a low, strong intensity from the beat-up but dependable stereo. Their own sounds blended with Coltrane's sax as the master bore notes into the timeless ether.

"Thank you," Monk said after Kodama handed him a glass of pineapple juice. He took a drink and put the tumbler on his nightstand where a candle burned, spiked in a hunched-over gargoyle of patinaed iron. Monk watched

Kodama get in on the other side of the bed. She eased toward him and they kissed for a while.

"That was quite something tonight," she enthused, running her hand through his pubic hair. "Not that I'm complaining, but what brought all that on?"

Monk feigned indignation to mask any guilt he might display from his escapade with Gloria in the bar. "I'm not sure where you're going with that line of questioning, your honor. I believe you were the one showing up on my doorstep at eleven-thirty tonight. Dressed seductively in your Sag Harbor matching coat and skirt."

Kodama retorted, "It's about as sexy an outfit as what Janet Reno wears."

"Can I help it if you severe-looking broads make me hard as a calculus test?"

Kodama, clad solely in an azure pair of panties Monk had bought her on one of their weekends away, snuggled next to his nude form. She studied him, and said, "Okay, the bench will rest for the evening. But it retains the right to exercise its option of revisiting this item."

Monk caressed her round, solid buttocks. Kodama's body and general physique belied her forty-plus years of living. She hit the gym at least two times a week and did a full regime of cals, weights, and those goddamn step aerobics. Plus some jogging on the weekends around the Silverlake Reservoir down from her house. He slipped his hand between the crack of her cheeks, her tongue carrouseling with his.

"What's been happening in the docket?" he asked, returning to rubbing her buttocks.

There was a barely audible sigh. "Too much of the same, Ivan. Just the usual sad spectacle of kids with big guns and small brains. The jury came back yesterday and sentenced a sixteen-year-old, tried as an adult, to fifteen years for second degree. Seems he and his homey had a falling out and they had to pop a cap on each other."

Monk moved his hand up to the center of her back, the topic shifting both of their moods. "Over?"

Kodama shook her head slightly from side to side. "Bullshit. One accused the other of ripping off his rap lyrics."

"Kids who have nothing attach a lot of meaning to whatever it is they can hold onto for themselves. Whatever it is they can call their own."

"Now who sounds like a feminazi, fag-loving liberal," she snorted playfully. She got on top of Monk and rocked easily. "How's your case going?"

Monk told her, omitting his scene with Gloria of the back issues department.

"Have you looked around in Scatterboy's pad?" Kodama leaned close and took a bite on a particular spot on Monk's chest. It was on an old wound he'd received from a ricocheting .38 slug.

"Yeah, he had a little hovel down in the Shores, which contained nothing in the way of a clue. He was killed not too far from it, though." Monk's words triggered the image of the odd assortment of young men he'd encountered earlier.

"What?" Kodama said, noticing his drift.

Monk mentioned the young men and what the man at the hamburger stand had said to him.

Kodama reared back contemplatively. "If one of them was this Angel Z, then could be he was with Scatterboy that night. Maybe these young men know something no one else does about the Shoreline Killer."

"Could be," Monk conceded. "Or it maybe it's just one more urban folktale started by bored men sitting on crates at Junior's Liquors."

"Hey, how about some kind of vigilante, someone who's had it with incompetent cops, and knee-jerk liberal judges."

Genuine surprise animated Monk's face. "You joined the fuckin' NRA?"

"The only thing I'm fucking"—she reached back and tenderly grabbed his testicles—"is between you and me, honey." She let go and folded her arms, giving her a supercilious look astride the naked detective. "People don't want to try anymore. It's not by accident we're building twenty-two new prisons in this state."

Monk placed his hand on her muscled brown thigh. "But that's the easy answer. The Great Society didn't work, it's 'cause them dark folks ain't got the intelligence to raise themselves out of the ghetto."

"What's the real answer then, Ivan?"

"We learn from the past, Jill. Don't create more poverty pimps, and take a few lessons in ruthlessness from our enemies."

Kodama stopped rocking and got very serious. "How ruthless?"

"Enough."

"You're taking this case kind'a personal, aren't you?"

"I'm cool." He said, trying to sound detached.

"All right."

Testily he replied. "If you got something to say, your honor, say it."

She got off, eyeing him. "Do you want to make this killer pay for every wrong done to African Americans? Wrongs done to you?"

"Apparently it's okay if the killer wants all Black men to pay for some wrong done to him or some other white person." That sounded worse than he'd intended.

"That's not what I meant."

"Then what are you asking?"

"Look, if it was JAs or other Asians I might not be so objective either."

Monk sat up. "But I'm supposed to be. I'm just supposed to go about finding this white-haired motherfuckah like looking for a guy bouncing checks."

There was a silence while Kodama seemed to collect her temper. "The other night you got drunk because of what this alleged white killer had done to Jimmy Henderson. And now you feel all protective of Clarice and her daughter."

"That make me a bad person, Jill?"

"Of course it doesn't. Your caring is one of the qualities I love you for, darling. But I'm concerned that you have this thing wrapped around your brain, Ivan. It's squeezing too tight. This killer, or killers, can't stand-in for every racist and bigot in America, baby."

Monk got his arms and hands working. "I'm a professional, Jill, I know what the hell I'm doing."

She touched him. "I just don't want you getting so deep in this you can't see straight. Or you do something so—"

"What?" he challenged.

"You should see the look on your face," she said hoarsely.

Indignantly, he said, "I have feelings involved, I admit that. It ain't like any Black man with any good sense wouldn't. But I'm not out of control, dig?"

"The very fact my advice makes you so defensive, is an indication—"

His voice raising, "Hey, stall me out on the indication, all right?"

"Fine, shithead." Her temper finally gave way to his unreasonableness. Kodama got out of bed, put on her robe, and stalked out of the bedroom.

Monk hit the headboard and turned on the portable TV.

David Letterman was playing the dozens with Madonna. Just as well, he rationalized. He was having too much doubt about them moving in together to bring it up tonight anyway. From the medicine cabinet he got the clippers and cut his toenails.

CHAPTER 11

Walter Kane's hand was on the man's upper thigh, rubbing and kneading the conditioned muscles encased in the light blue faded jeans. The other man, Chip, nuzzled the senator's aide on the neck as the hand moved upwards. A bottle shattered on the floor. Kane was inclined to ignore it but then somebody screamed and he was forced to look around.

"Fire, fire!" a voice in the cozy dimly lit bar yelled out.

Chip's eyes flashed open and he almost fell off the bar stool. "Jesus, look, Walter."

Kane spun around and saw a bright glow creeping into the room from the doorway. Reflexively, he leapt off his stool and started for the door, removing the jean waist jacket he was wearing. Two others were also running toward the door, one of them holding a fire extinguisher.

Foam shot from the device's nozzle in a spray of snowy mist. There was another crash and instantly Kane turned to the source. To his left another fire blossomed on top of a lacquered table, like a baked Alaska gone awry. Wind billowed the curtains above the table and over the broken window. They caught fire even as Kane made it to the spot.

He yanked the curtains free from the rod and threw the

burning cloth to the floor. He slapped at the table with his jacket again and again. A smell of gas permeated the room and Kane could see the remnants of the bottle all about him, the vestiges of the home-made Molotov cocktail which had come in through the window.

A lick of flame tongued at his shirt but he kept beating at the fire with his jacket. Gas eddied off the table onto the floor and he was certain the fire would spread. Fortunately, Kane was soon joined by the man with the extinguisher who swept at the flaming currents on the floor.

"Eat me, faggots."

Through the broken window Kane could see a pick-up truck, riding high on lifts and big tires, roar past the window. He tore away from the table and made for the entranceway.

"Where do you think you're going?" Chip demanded, grabbing at him.

"Come on," Kane said through gritted teeth. He went through the now-tattered curtain and out onto the street in time to see the truck zoom past.

"Crack-lickin' low life mutants." A white teenager was leaning half out of the passenger window gesticulating and shouting at them. "The War Reich will kick you ass-reaming pigs off this earth." With that he let out a rebel yell and the truck hauled east along Larrabee, swallowed by the nebula of 1 A.M. West Hollywood.

"Fuck you, redneck," one of the denizens who was out at this hour bellowed.

Several people gathered around the Spike, the firebombed bar. They comforted those who came stumbling out into the cool early hours. Chip put his arm around Kane. "Are you all right? You're shivering, let's get home."

Kane was focused on the end of the street and what lay

beyond it. "I'm not cold, Chip. I'm shaking because I want to tear someone's head off."

"Let's go home," the other man emphasized.

Kane kissed him and said, "And in the morning, let's buy a gun for the apartment."

Chip mumbled a lame "sure" to avoid an argument, but knew he would talk sense into him later. Shortly, as they sweated by the heat from the fireplace, Kane entered his lover from behind. He drove hard as his powerful hands clutched the other's slim legs. The larger-built man was hissing with pleasure as Chip matched the rhythm of his body.

"I can smell blood in the air," Kane said later in a voice belonging to a stranger. "There's going to be a new day, a new way of doing things."

Chip was fascinated by the ragged emotion Kane expressed. He found a sensual new quality to embrace about his man. It only occurred to him later that it also frightened him.

CHAPTER 12

"Whoomp, there it is." Lieutenant Detective Marasco Seguin, Wilshire Division LAPD, gently tossed the folded newspaper onto the tabletop.

Monk, sitting with Grant, nodded at his friend. "You won the lottery and your picture is on the front page."

Seguin eased out of the charcoal Hugo Boss double-breasted jacket. He draped the coat around the back of the chair and took a seat opposite. "I wish I was, 'cause I could have told the captain to go F himself when he told me to find you this morning."

Over a mouthful of grits, Grant said, "What gives?"

Seguin unfolded the paper. It was a copy of the *Los Angeles Sentinel*, the venerable Black weekly. He pointed at a headline slugged below and to the left of the masthead. "My captain gets a call from a sheriff's captain named Olson very early this morning. Seems this Olson had an understanding with a certain private eye known for playing the angles."

"Stop, you'll turn my head," Monk teased. The headline read: "Black Men Targets in Pacific Shores." Monk skimmed through the first few paragraphs then looked up. "This isn't my fault, Marasco. Bradford's been ducking my calls for the last couple of days."

Grant moved the paper so he could read it. While he did, he mixed some of his scrambled eggs with his grits, and forked in a healthy portion. He then picked up the paper and opened it to where the article continued on the inside.

The waitress came over and Seguin placed his order. She went away and the plainclothesman made a brief survey of those gathered for breakfast at Dulan's. The restaurant was located on the southern end of the Crenshaw Strip, a major thoroughfare of the Black business district. Stores along this section of the boulevard ranged from the three Bs, the staples of Black businesses—beauty shops, barber shops and barbecues—to banks and major chains like Sears in the Baldwin Hills Crenshaw Mall.

Even the avant-garde was served via Leimert and Degnan Streets that veered off Crenshaw. Located there was a cafe where jazz could be heard on its upper floor until early into the morning on weekends. Another place offered live theater. And a writer's workshop with an open mike session was at yet another location.

Dulan's was where the shakers and breakers, the preachers and back sliders in the African American community had their power confabs over such fare as hot links and biscuits or trenchers of meat loaf savored with peppers and herbs.

Seguin waved at a city councilman who the other week had been on local TV shaking a finger at the Chief of Police. He said to Monk, "So lay it on me, bro', make me look good to the brass."

Monk slavered jelly across his buttered wheat toast. "There must be something more than Olson being pissed off for your boy to send you out to talk to me, Marasco." He took a big bite.

The city cop leaned back in his chair and rubbed an index

finger along one side of his drooping mustache. "We'd like to know just what are your interests in the murders down in the Shores."

Monk asked, "Is Harbor Division officially investigating these murders?"

"Yes, and coordinating with a contingent in Orange County."

Grant spoke up. "Then the official line is the killer is coming across the border to do his dirty work."

"There's nothing that organized, Dex, aside from coordinating the sharing of information at this point."

Monk proceeded to tell his friend of the events that led to his encounter with the weight-lifting sergeant and the mediawise Captain Olson.

Seguin's order arrived and he thanked the waitress. He ate in silence and listened, then said, "So this Malik Bradford, the one quoted in this article, has a personal and political agenda?"

"Like I said, I haven't talked with him yet but from what Grant found out over at Long Beach State, it would seem my man has got something going on."

Seguin turned his head in Grant's direction.

"The kid is a campus activist and does a weekly opinion column in the school paper. He imparts his views on such issues as the homeless, police abuse, Black self-development and the need for national health care." Grant polished off his grits and gravy by sopping up the remains with a biscuit. "Even I have to admit the kid's not all hot air."

"Then he's the next coming of Farrakhan?" Seguin asked genuinely.

"I read the copies Dex made of Bradford's stuff, he's for real," Monk interjected.

"What do you make of his excursions into the Shores on these patrols of his?" Seguin stirred milk into his coffee.

"You mean do I think he's just grandstanding to get headlines?"

"Whatever," Seguin replied.

"Probably like any dissident worth his copy of *Let Them Call Me Rebel*, he's got to get out amongst them, Marasco."

"Part opportunist and part idealist," Grant said.

"Nothing wrong with that as long as you can keep the balance," Monk concluded.

"Sure you right." Seguin ate more of his breakfast.

"Now that I've been so forthcoming, how about a little something from your end?" Monk finally asked.

Seguin made a big production of looking at his watch. "Gosh, can you believe it?"

"Oh, what a fucking comic you are," Monk deadpanned.

"Don't you know I have to keep alive the myth of the antagonism between PI's and cops?" his friend teased.

Monk went on. "You guys are talking with your counterparts in the Orange wasteland. Even if it's not official, what's the operating theory?"

"Several scenarios are being considered, including white supremacists on a mission. Suburban revenge for specific crimes. Vigilante justice. We're not ruling anything out. There's also the angle about white bikers in Calipatria Prison trying to corner a piece of the crack market. Several of these guys are from the San Pedro-Wilmington area."

Seguin added, "The drug dealer who was killed, Ronny Aaron, seems he had a run-in with one of these boys about half a year ago."

"Over turf?" Grant asked.

"Yeah," Seguin responded. "And the one called Midnight, Brian Lake, he's been known to help launder drug money."

"Have you heard if any of the civil rights groups or other

Black organizations have received letters or calls lately?" Monk said.

Seguin gave him an even-tempered look. "Southwest reports that the Southern Christian Leadership Council has received several hate calls since this business started. But they seem generic, you know, the usual stuff like the jigaboos got what was coming to them and so forth."

"Were all the shootings done with the same gun?" Grant broke in.

"No. Each shooting involved a different caliber weapon. And we're supposed to get the report today from Olson on the rounds fired at Ivan."

Seguin took another bite of his unfinished omelet, rose, and threw some money onto the table. "I really gotta book, gents. Officially, Ivan, I'm to remind you as a licensed investigator the authorities would like to be kept informed of your progress." He winked broadly. "The reality is ain't nobody got a good solid lead to follow up. Give me something down the road, all right?"

Monk held up two fingers pressed together. "You know me and the police, ocifer."

"Thanks, brougham." Seguin slipped his fluidly muscled frame into his jacket then said, "You two take it slow."

Grant snorted, "At my age, I'll take it any way I can get it."

"I know you will." Seguin saluted and marched out of Dulan's.

Monk said, "The different kinds of guns could just mean our killer has more than one piece at his disposal."

"Yeah. Between the two of us we've got six or seven gats. Look, I've still got a couple of contacts down in Anaheim. What about I take a run out there and see what I can see?" Grant slurped at some orange juice.

"Sure, as long as you feel up to it." Concern tinged Monk's

comment. He recalled an incident in a warehouse where he'd let Grant talk him into going along. The older man got shot and Monk spent sleepless nights second-guessing his decision.

Grant tensed. "Now listen up, number one son, I know I'm not going to be the first through the door any more. I realize my limitations. But I can do some of the leg work."

"Nobody said you couldn't, Dex."

"You fuckin' right. If I sit around on my fat ass counting the days to my next pension check I'll be dead for sure. I've been some kind of cop damn near since I was out of knee pants. Let an old man have his fun."

"Whatever you find out, you let me know, dig? No one-man shows."

"Okay, grandma."

They finished their breakfast making small talk. Afterward, Grant drove off in his cherry 1967 Buick Electra 225. Monk headed over to his office where he found a woman waiting.

She was sitting in one of the Paris chairs in the rotunda, reading some pages stapled together. Her slim attache case with gold leaf Gothic initials rested against the side of her nyloned leg.

"Ms. Ysaguirre-Chacon."

"Mr. Monk." She offered a manicured hand sans polish. "How'd you find out my name?"

He shook it. "You tracked me down as well. Once I found your office, I worked backwards through the court records."

"Can we talk inside?"

"Of course."

Delilah tuned the radio on her desk to the all-news station and said, "Mrs. Urbanski called. She'll be here at eleven. And she sounded like she expected to see you."

Monk snarled playfully at her. The attorney rose and Monk was greeted with a fragrance he couldn't identify. It was strong but not overpowering. The counselor was wearing a tailored Anne Klein II burgundy slacks suit and low heels. Her black hair was cut short and stylishly framed her angular brown face. He opened the door for her and she entered his office.

Ysaguirre-Chacon took a seat in one of the Eastlakes and crossed her legs. Monk plopped down opposite her in his padded swivel and said, "How is it that you came to represent Herbert Jones, Ms. Ysaguirre-Chacon?"

"Chacon will do, my married name can be a bit much I know." Her voice was pleasant but not powdery. It seemed to Monk that Ms. Chacon had perfected the image she wanted to project.

"The law firm I work for, as you may have guessed, does its fair share of *pro bono* work and we drew the case of Mr. Jones."

Her gaze never left Monk's face. "And of course that's what brought me to the back issue department of the *PressTelegram*."

"What did you expect to find?"

A kind of crease appeared on one side of her mouth. She seemed to be humoring Monk's request. "My client maintains his innocence. Yes, he knew Aaron. He did business with Aaron. He had an argument with Aaron that night. But they went their separate ways. He admits he has no alibi. But he's straightening out. He's been in de-tox. With a clear head, he says he's innocent."

Monk pivoted slightly from side to side in his chair. "What brings you here?"

"You mean aside from that little deception of yours at my office?"

Monk put a hand to his cheek in an imitation of Jack Benny. "Oh that. How did you get on to me?"

"In my travels I had a conversation with a Captain Olson last night."

"Just after the *Sentinel* had come out."

"Hmm. I was getting a copy of their arrest report and he asked me if I knew someone named Monk. I told him no then he showed me your booking photo."

"I was interested in why you were getting the same back issues as I was."

"Now you know. Now I want to know what you might know that can help my client."

"I'm not sure I can, counselor. What the paper reported is more or less accurate. I was following a guy and chanced upon an attempted hit by this man with the pasty complexion."

"Which theory are you ascribing to the killer?"

"I honestly haven't made up my mind, Ms. Chacon. Can I talk with your client?"

Ms. Chacon picked up her brief case and placed it on her lap. She extracted what Monk believed were the same stapled sheets she'd been looking at earlier. She put them face up on the clean finish of his colonial desk. "That's a standard contract we provide to investigators who do work for our firm."

Monk noticed the retainer outlined on the front page. It was less than his optimum, but a hell of lot better than the money he'd already run through from Clarice. "I suppose you've petitioned the court to pick up the cost of an investigator for the defense."

Chacon smoothed out a side of her efficient hairdo. "As you're aware, the majority of court-appointed investigators are ex-policeman. Individuals with certain perspectives who are not always inclined to be as impartial, or as thorough as they should."

"And courts ain't exactly hip on picking up the tab of investigators who don't posses that outlook," Monk added from trying experiences.

"In light of these recent events, the judge agreed to my request for your assignment."

"So you believe Jones."

"I believe he should get the best defense afforded him."

"Given the current state of my finances and the twenties I keep handing out like coupons for information, I definitely have incentive."

"I was hoping you might." She put her case down again and adjusted her body in the chair. Confident but not smug.

Monk placed a hand on top of the contract. "I want to talk to Jones before I sign this."

"Fine, as long as you understand he's in bad shape, chemical dependency-wise. Though he is an articulate man."

Not knowing how to react to such a statement, Monk said, "Okay."

Chacon got out of her seat, grabbing her case in the same motion. "I've got some other errands to run today, but I'll set something up for tomorrow."

Monk offered his hand and she shook it. "I've got a notion I want to look into. I may be out and about tomorrow but you can schedule it through Delilah."

"Very good, Mr. Monk."

"Ivan."

"Fine."

He followed her out to the rotunda and placed the contract on Delilah's desk. Over the radio, he heard a press conference going on. "What's all that?" he said, pointing a thumb in the direction of the radio as Chacon left.

Delilah was reading the contract. "Grainger Wu's talking

about an incident that happened in West Hollywood last night. Seems his aide Walter Kane was in a bar that some rowdies tried to torch."

Monk listened for several moments as Wu continued talking.

"AS GOOD citizens we can't sit on the sidelines and let others carry the game. This is a fight that concerns the very future of our state, if not our country." Wu put a hand around Walter Kane's shoulder, giving him a demonstrative hug. "In this post-Cold War era, when our country faces serious economic hardships, citizens are becoming polarized around many social issues.

"As a result, there has been the rise of an increasingly violent racist backlash. Indeed, the green light was given in the Reagan-Bush years."

Wu finished up and answered several questions from the gathered members of the press. Kane shook Wu's hand, then excused himself. Ursala Brock sidled up to the senator as the press departed to file their stories.

"Look, Grainger, I think you need to be a bit more tactical on this matter."

"You mean backpedal the issue, Ursala?" Wu started to roll up the sleeves of his striped shirt.

"You know what the hell I mean. Them old crackers and New Democrats we got ain't much, but we damned sure need their votes on the military conversion bill." -

Wu smiled lazily. "And civil rights is just another special interest."

Brock looked impatient. "Sadly, for too many in the country, it is. That doesn't make it right, but it makes it real. And if we want to accomplish any part of our agenda, we need to be around for the long haul."

"Sometimes pragmatism has to give way to what's right." He went off to take care of another matter.

Brock stared after him, then disappeared into her office.

MONK SAID, "I'm heading out now, D. I've gotta look up some stuff at the *Press-Telegram*."

"What about Urbanski?"

Monk was almost to the door. "Damn." He checked his watch. "All right, I'll hang around. Do me a favor, and call your girl Ms. Scam and tell her I'd love to do her presentation in the hinterlands, but I'm too wrapped up in my current investigation."

Dryly, the woman Friday said, "I'll give your regrets and make sure she books you for something spectacular like a Rotarian banquet."

"Way cool." He made calls while waiting for the elusive Ms. Urbanski. "Gloria, Monk," he said when the line connected.

"Lover come back to me," she serenaded into her end of the receiver.

"Absolutely. Are there any particular crimes that you recall taking place in the Shores?"

"You mean something sensational like the Menendez killings?"

"No. More like was there any sort of case where the crook was caught, the evidence seemingly stacked solidly against him, but he walked anyway. It would have to be where the perpetrator was Black and the victim white."

Circuits buzzed over the line, then Traylor said, "Most of the stuff over there involving our people is the same sad story, Black on Black. Not much in the way of O. J.-mania."

"I hear you," Monk commiserated.

"But let me think about it and I'll talk with the paper's cop shop reporter if you want."

"I'd appreciate it."

"You better." She hung up on her end of the conversation.

Monk depressed the phone's plunger and dialed Kodama's number that was a direct line into her chambers. He got her internal answering service and left a brief message. Just as he replaced the receiver, his door swung inward and the woman he presumed was Mrs. Urbanski stepped inside.

She was tall, blonde, lithe and walked with an unencumbered bearing. Monk guessed she was in her mid to late forties. She wore a crinkled white swing dress with a sleeveless black silk T which displayed a set of triceps she didn't get from lifting shoe bags at the Beverly Center. On top of her head was a modified straw boater with a black sash for the headband. She extended a lavender-nailed hand to the standing Monk.

"I'm Tassia Urbanski, Mr. Monk."

"Pleased to meet you, have a seat."

She did and Monk went back to sit in his chair. "Sorry we kept missing each other. What can I do for you?"

"I believe you met my business partner who calls himself Swede." As she talked, she opened a silver cigarette case she'd retrieved from her purse.

Monk leaned across the desk to light it with the Zippo his sister had given him on a past birthday. "We had a pleasant little chat."

Her lips puckered and she blew a stream of smoke toward the ceiling. "I might mention that he bragged about his pulling a knife on you."

"Are you lovers? Was he trying to impress you?" Monk could feel his neck getting warm.

"Impress, no doubt—to get in my pants, no doubt. But lovers, not on this earth, my dear."

"I didn't tell Swede who I was," Monk remarked.

She took a deep drag on her smoke and exhaled. "My agent in the dress factory provided me with the license number of your fabulous Ford and a description. It matched the way Swede described you." She took another puff and regarded Monk through the rising haze. "Although his was not as flattering."

She was taking him down a garden path on the way to a maze. "Your agent?"

She tapped ash into the onyx tray on Monk's desk. "My apologies, I have a tendency to jump into the middle of a story. My late husband and Swede, whose real name is Alexandre Jorburg, were pals in the service. Both of them fancied themselves big wheels. After the Army, they tried a series of ventures, boiler room office product sales, rock concert promoting, even some bookie operations in Florida."

Monk wondered about her role in those activities. It must have shown on his face because she added:

"I'm Leon's—that's the late Mr. Urbanski's—third wife. I don't come into this story until he and Swede got into the clothing and accessories racket."

"Hence Swede's fake watch deal."

"Yes. At any rate, Leon died two years ago from a massive heart attack. I warned him that he smoked and drank too much and didn't get enough exercise." As if the departed husband admonished her from the beyond, she ground the cigarette out. "My background includes being a buyer for various chains, Robinsons, Macys, and so on. For Leon I helped do sales, but pretty much stayed out of the business."

"But you inherited his half of the business when he passed."

"Exactly. And therein lies my tale of torment. Over the years, Leon told me of Swede's nefarious dealings. At first, it was quite the catharsis for him. But it seems as he matured, and settled into legitimacy, he grew weary—and leery—of Swede's outlaw activities."

Monk was of a mind to pose an argument on the legitimacy of the garment trade from the viewpoint of the workers but demurred. "Now you have to deal with Swede directly."

Mrs. Urbanski placed tanned hands on her lap. On her right wrist was a silver bracelet set with a piece of turquoise veined in orange. Absently, she fingered the stone with her tapered fingers. "I've suspected he's been running a few of his extracurricular operations out of one or all of the jobber shops we own. As I indicated, I have a few employees who let me know what he's up to so my information is pretty good."

Which was not the same as proof, but he said, "How many shops would that be?"

"Three. The one you were at, one not too far from there, and another in Commerce."

"So you want me to get the lowdown on Swede and get him put away."

"I don't care if he goes to jail or not, Mr. Monk. All I care about is him becoming my ex-partner."

She let that hang between them, and for a fast moment Monk imagined she might even be suggesting Swede's permanent removal. Then she spoke again.

"I'll pay you your rate to get the goods on Swede, enough so he'll sell out his part. It's actually more like a third since he's often borrowed against it for one deal or another."

"Can you afford to buy him out?"

"I have other options."

Whatever the hell that meant. "How come Swede stays in the business now that your husband's dead?"

"Believe me, I've asked him that a time or two."

Monk had an idea but kept it to himself. He also wondered if Mrs. Urbanski hadn't been sent as Swede's goat in some elaborate con. "I assume you have proof of who you say you are, Mrs. Urbanski?"

She smiled sweetly and plucked a stuffed letter-sized envelope from her purse. "I think this will answer your questions." She placed the envelope on the desk and rose to her full height. "Why don't I give you a day or two to think about it. I've left my answering service number for you to get in contact with me."

Monk was also on his feet. "Seeing as how Swede got the best of me the other day, why'd you come here rather than someone else?"

"I asked some lawyer friends if they'd heard about you. In turn, I talked with an attorney named Parrin Teague who spoke well of your work."

Monk nodded. He'd done a couple of jobs for Teague in the past.

"Plus it seemed to me you'd have a reason to get back at Swede for—" She dropped it, letting discretion take over. "And frankly, that incident was a signal to me it was time to do something I'd been thinking about for sometime. After all, it might be me next he puts a knife to."

"You probably have something there, Mrs. Urbanski. I'll get back to you day after tomorrow."

"Very good, Mr. Monk" She tipped her hat and left the office.

Delilah came in less than thirty seconds later. "Well, well. Two good-looking woman in your office in less than an hour. What's the judge going to say about that?"

"She'll be ecstatic about my initiative." Monk was looking through the papers Tassia Urbanski had left. They included the business licenses, legal incorporations, and the lawyer of record for the umbrella firm that owned the three finishing factories. It went by the tony name of New World Rage. There was a joke in there some place but Monk refolded the papers and handed them over to Delilah.

"Make like a detective and check out the info in that paperwork, D."

"How the hell many cases you planning on juggling at the same time, Joe Mannix?" She sat down.

Monk brought her up to date. "I don't want to let my eyes get bigger than my stomach but I think I can chew on all three of these at once. Especially since two of them converge."

"And they're paying the bills. But sometimes I can't figure if you really believe the bullshit you say, or if you think that by saying it, that makes it so."

Monk was standing next to his old-fashioned coat rack and removing the houndstooth jacket Kodama had picked out for him last month. "That's funny, neither can I." He slipped on the coat over his wide-striped shirt and olive-twill cotton pants. He left his .45 locked in the closet.

"I'll probably be down at the *Press-Telegram* back issue department for the rest of the day if you need to reach me." He wrote down the number and handed it to Delilah. "If Ms. Chacon calls, she's to tell you a time when I can go visit her client. Call me over at the paper if she does. And if Dex calls, give him the number, too."

"Whatever you desire, oh master." Delilah still sat, reading through the papers that established Mrs. Urbanski's bona fides.

"Thanks, genie." Monk got back out to Long Beach and the archival den of Gloria Traylor. Since it was the lunch hour, he had to wait for her return.

"Hey, good-looking," she said upon sighting him leaning

against the wall in the hallway. Traylor was dressed in a jumpsuit with oversized brass buttons in a line from the center of her sternum to her navel.

"You see I can't stay away from you," he quipped.

"You just love me for my musty newsprint."

Monk made a sound like enjoying a good meal.

Traylor unlocked the door and they entered the darkened interior. She brought the lights to life and handed Monk a piece of paper from her desk. On it, in an unmistakable feminine script, were several brief listings and dates in parentheses.

"I asked Houston, the paper's old crime beat reporter," she began, sitting at her desk. "Those are the incidents he could remember where the victim was white and the alleged attacker was Black. And where it happened in or around the Shores. The dates are the approximate year and month the crimes happened."

She folded her hands and tapped her thumbs together. "You know there's a piece in today's *Press-Telegram* by Houston saying the sheriff and the cops on both sides of the border are working jointly on finding the Shoreline Killer."

Monk was sitting across from her, perusing the sheet she'd given him. "Yeah, I figured as much. You know, now that I give it some more thought, it might even be the mugging or robbery I'm looking for could have happened in Long Beach, or Seal Beach, or other parts around here."

"And the crook was from the Shores," she opined.

"Exactly."

"Then you have an almost impossible task. Our news reports wouldn't be so complete as to give you that kind of information on each incident. Only the law and their computers could do that." A woman in a Cardigan sweater with a pair of half-glasses suspended around her neck by a gold lamé cord entered. Traylor helped her, then returned to the desk.

"Also, how far back are you going to look?" she said.

"I'll go back three years." Monk got up. "Is there a coffee machine around here?"

Traylor gave him a mug and directions to a carafe located down the hall in a cubby hole. Monk filled the cup then returned to her department to begin his search for needles in a haystack of microfiche. So great was his dread of the tedium that lay before him, that he'd prefer to be staked out naked over a hill of angry red ants, awash in honey, with his eyelids peeled back. That or be forced to listen to an Al Gore speech. He took a deep breath and entered the chamber of doom.

CHAPTER 13

"You see," the man in the dress slacks was telling Grant, "the niggers and the greasers are undermining our Christian way of government. And they are financed and protected by Jewish-dominated organizations like the NAACP and these so-called immigration rights groups."

Grant was sitting in the neatly kept second-story office of ARM, the Aryan Resistance Movement. It was located on a serene commercial street lined with maple trees in Garden Grove, in the middle of Orange County. The man talking calmly was Earl Hooks, secretary-treasurer of the Southern California chapter of the supremacist organization, and editor of their regional newspaper.

When Grant had first entered, he had noticed a young man stuffing envelopes at a table, who had soon left and then returned. The kid was no more than twenty-two or -three, dressed in jeans and a flannel shirt buttoned to the collar. He was wearing red suspenders and his hair was cut moderately long. On the table where he worked a boom box banged out some God-awful caterwauling whose lyrics the older man couldn't make out save for an occasional, "Drive them to sea, drive the mud people to the sea."

Grant had caught the slight hand movement from Hooks

that sent the kid on his errand and he knew what that errand was—to check on Grant through the license number of the car he had parked outside. Grant realized they had seen him arrive since their office was located on the corner and afforded a good view of the intersecting streets. Fortunately, he'd established a cover. He was driving his daughter's car with changed plates and through a friend in the DMV he'd arranged for a fake name to come up on the computer. Grant felt his facade was intact.

Hooks was talking. "You see, Norman, our movement may have been set back by these years of dyke-loving, flagburning judges and lawyers always running around looking for the next poor minority to defend. And let's be frank"—the supremacist winked—"there's plenty of these supposed conservatives who talk a good game but are just as guilty of feeding at the bureaucracy trough as the socialistic Democrats."

"You mean it's really to keep the movement down," Grant reckoned.

"Exactly. Pat Buchanan is supposed to be speaking for American culture yet he dodged his duty in Vietnam by taking a deferment. See, we can't be having those kind of mixed signals. We have to steer a steady course."

"I know what you mean, Mr. Hooks."

"Call me Earl."

"Okay, Earl. I worked a long time in the sales game, traveling all over the place. Detroit, Washington D.C., New York—"

"Once good cities, cities that were the heart of this country, once-proud centers of industry that the niggers and spies have run down," Hooks amplified.

Grant nodded. "Well, like I say, I know I'm a little late in getting on the bandwagon, but now with my grand kids growing up and all, I feel I should be doing something to ensure their future."

"Do you have pictures of them?" Hooks asked, feigning innocence.

Grant pulled out the wallet his pal on the Santa Ana P.D. had helped him to prepare for his back-up story. He flipped it open, making sure the secretary-treasurer got a glimpse of the license that stated his name as "Norman Andrews." He showed Hooks a picture of a blonde Santa Ana police woman with a tow-haired girl and a brown-haired boy in a Raiders T-shirt.

"The contamination's already beginning," the ARM member dourly commented, pointing at the T-shirt.

Grant swallowed hard. "I know. Dan even has posters of that big basketball-playing buck on the wall in his bedroom. Shack something or another."

Hooks, in his mid-forties, thick but solid, shook his head from side to side, a psychoanalyst understanding his patient's troubles. "I think that's why men like you, Norman, men who've worked hard all their life, are coming to us." He leveled serious eyes on Grant. "And why the young are tired of being brow-beat by porch monkeys with PhDs and pussy-licking fembots who defend women who cut off men's penises."

"I've been reading some of Bobby Bright's stuff," Grant said. Bright, the leader of ARM, was rumored to be living in a fortified compound in Montana. He criss-crossed the country whipping up the troops and the great unwashed in the cause of white supremacy.

A former syndicated radio personality. Bright made appearances on Oprah and Sunday news shows, willing and able to debate his movement's goals and objectives. Aided by hair plug transplants, a strict diet and a tummy tuck, Bright was the Bishop Sheen of the white supremacist set.

He'd published numerous articles in the supremacist press, some of which surfaced in the mainstream. And using a small publisher north of San Francisco, Bright had put out a book of essays promoting with great exactitude the reasons, both historical and scientific, behind the greatness of the white race.

From a stack of papers and magazines, Hooks handed a recent issue of ARM's newsletter across to Grant.

"We had to go back to the printer twice on this one it was so popular." He held aloft a copy of *The Insurgent.* Grant smiled like a spoon-fed goon. On the front page was a sixty-point headline that read: "White Man's Manifesto." It was subtitled, "How We Will Take Back Our Country, House by House."

There was a bust shot of Bright set in the body of the text.

He was a dark-locked man who combed his transplanted hair straight back from a high forehead. His neck, large and muscular, like an offensive lineman's, was attached to a face of pronounced angular lines partially obscured by a full beard. Even in the grainy reproduction, the eyes suggested a willful personality.

Grant said, "Can I come to the next meeting?"

Hooks rubbed a side of his face with an open palm. "Once I check out the information you gave me. I'll let you know."

"What? I look like a cop? I'm too damn old."

"You look to be in pretty good shape if you're the age you say you are," the beefy man replied. He gave Grant another once-over. "The FBI headed by that kike has been sucking around our movement, and the Jews and jigaboos in the IRS keep threatening to take away the nonprofit status of our publications division. We have to be careful."

Grant had provided Hooks with information and phone numbers that would put him in touch with some old cronies from his days on the LAPD who would prop up his false front. "I understand your need for security." He got up, holding onto his copy of *The Insurgent* like it was holy scripture.

The other man clapped Grant on the back and handed him a brochure. On the cover was a photo of a young Chicano clothed in sagging khakis with a bandanna wrapped around his head. The title read: "The Future of America." Grant shook the other man's hand. "I appreciate you taking the time with me, Earl."

"My pleasure, Norman. I look foward to seeing you around. You'll be hearing from us."

Of that he was sure. Grant left the office and got into his daughter's car. He took the 22 freeway back into L.A. County, passing hillsides still scarred and barren from the devastating fires of recent memory. The fires before the last quake that rocked the Southland.

It had been a particularly hot and dry winter, even by Southern California standards. The fabled Santa Anas had barreled down from their mountain passes and spread the blazes from Ventura County all the way down to the Mexican border.

Some were set by humans, and others by the caprice of fate.

Yet all were subject to the unyielding laws of physics. More than two weeks of flame and heat had burned massive patches of ground where once homes and businesses, and forests and groves, had existed.

Near where Grant lived in Lake Elsinore, in Riverside County, some eight thousand acres of timberland were consumed in the Cleveland National Forest. The aging ex-cop, like many of his neighbors, had spent a night on his roof, hosing down his fire-retardant shingles. The blazing sky, a tremendous coppery orange shot through with huge funnels of black smoke, reminded him of another night long ago, when Berlin fell at the end of the war.

The then-young Oklahoman was an operative for the OSS, the Office of Strategic Services, the U.S. intelligence agency and forerunner of the CIA. Headed by the loquacious "Wild" Bill Donovan, the OSS gathered information and carried out sabotage. Grant, fluent in German—thanks to his uncle, an organizer for the Industrial Workers of the World—and just young and strong enough to think he was tough shit, had parachuted with three others behind enemy lines.

Their job was to plant ground transmitters that would confuse the radio signals of the Soviet planes, should they reach the capitol of the Reich before the Western allies did. The task was to protect U.S. interests in Germany, financial and political. The future of trans-national capitalism lay ahead. It was okay to bomb the ball bearing works in Schweinfurt or anti-aircraft placements in Regensburg but certain areas in Berlin were off-limits. That wasn't how it was explained to Grant and his colleagues at the time but years later, piecing together subsequent events, Grant arrived at that conclusion. Perhaps his post-war reasoning had been a further contribution from his Wobbly uncle.

The sky that night in 1945 took on the rich color of aged wine as the Flying Fortresses blasted emplacements on the outskirts of the city. Watching the evening light up and hearing the awful roar of the bombs exploding from his hiding place, Grant learned something about himself then. Something that came back to him while he stood on his roof, mesmerized by the glow not so far away. He loved it. Not fire like some slobbering pyromaniac, but the excitement that dangerous situations brought. The heady stuff of moving through the enemy's camp, not knowing when, or if, you'd get caught.

Like being an LAPD detective, or a private eye, like he was when he left the force in the mid-seventies. A long time ago he'd come to the disheartening revelation that it wasn't justice and great truth he was after, but the chance to make his mind and body work together as a crafty machine. The fact that he found criminal behavior abhorrent was secondary. But on his roof, in the midst of the fire, he was just an old man with a water hose in his hand, and meandering memories crowding his mind.

Eventually the maze of freeways which compose the blood system of the wicked beast that is Los Angeles carried Grant back into the city. He took the exit on Riverside Drive and stopped to purchase a bottle of Johnny Walker Black at a market on Hyperion. He drove above the area of the Silverlake Reservoir and parked at Jill Kodama's house, which commanded a view of the water.

"Dexter," she said warmly upon opening the door.

"Hey, doll," he responded, kissing her on the cheek. He ambled into the split level home and closed the door behind him. A certain smell drifted to him and he said, "Working on a new one, huh?"

"Yeah, Ivan hates it." Kodama gloated, taking the bottle of whiskey toward the kitchen. "You know where everything is."

Grant went into her study. It was comfortably furnished in an odd but workable mixture of Art Deco and Japanese functional. Along one wall was a built-in bookcase of volumes ranging from the latest John Grisham to reprints of Engels.

On an easel was a stretched canvas Kodama had prepared herself, with the beginnings of her latest oil painting. The composition had been laid out in graphite transfer and a fresh undercoat had been applied. The image depicted three people in a barge with a standing helmsman. The passengers had their heads down, forlorn looking. The boat floated along in a cavern while gaseous charges erupting from the surface of the still water. The boat's pilot bore a close resemblance to Monk.

"Damn," Grant declared.

"Here," Kodama said, handing Grant some Johnny Walker on the rocks in a heavy stout glass.

"Thanks. So what does it mean that our man here is escorting the doomed on the River Styx."

"You'll see when it's finished." She wandered off again to the sound of the doorbell. Grant could hear her greeting the painting's model.

Monk entered the study. "So what have you been up to, you old croaker sac?"

"Your mama."

"That's nice." Monk groaned at the painting. "What the hell, right?"

"Art is anything you can get away with." Kodama said, wandering off again.

"I thought that was life," Monk retorted. "I'm going to help Jill in the kitchen, then you and I can catch up after dinner."

Grant was looking at the painting again. "Sure."

The meal was a hit with everyone; southern fried chicken strips combined with a spinach, arugula and corn salad and a fresh baguette. Grant switched from whiskey to a large glass of lemonade. Kodama and Monk each had a glass of a very dry white wine. Afterward, they gathered in the study. All three had neat drafts of the Black Label and Monk was allowed to puff on a small cigarillo.

"Did you guys hear about what happened to Walter Kane the other night?" Kodama sank beside Monk on the couch.

Grant, sitting in an easy chair under a Rothko print, shook his head in the negative. "If I might be so bold, who the hell is Walter Kane?"

Monk told him and added. "I heard Grainger Wu talking about it on the radio."

The judge filled them in on the incident at the gay bar. "Someone claiming to represent the War Reich phoned a local TV station and took credit for it. The same night, there was a desecration of a Jewish cemetery, and two assaults on Latinos in Sylmar. The Reich took credit for all of these antics."

"They share some office space with ARM out in Garden Grove," Grant contributed.

"One of your police pals tell you this?" Monk took a hit on his drink.

Coyly, Grant said, "Oh I've been busy since you've been hanging out and looking through musty racks of newspapers, old son."

"You've been to their office," Kodama stated.

"Yep. They might even make me the activities director before I'm through."

Monk's eyes became slits. "Them chaps ain't for playin', Dex."

"Thanks, honey, and I'm gonna save you my 'I been at this longer than you've been eating solid food' speech." He sampled more of his Johnny Walker. "My friend on the Santa Ana P.D. told me the cops down there are definitely working the angle that the killer is coming across the Orange County line into the Shores and going back when he's done."

"How did they conclude that?" Monk asked earnestly.

"The scuttlebutt I got is from some of the guys on the anti-gang detail in the barrio in Santa Ana. They heard from some of the kids who said they spotted the white-haired man driving a red Jeep around there."

"Is the killer lining up his next target area?" Kodama wondered aloud.

"Maybe. And then there's this." Grant took out a folded paper from his inside jacket pocket. He handed it across to Kodama. It was the copy of *The Insurgent* that Hooks had given him.

Sarcastically Monk remarked, "The brilliancy of Bobby Bright."

"Who changed his name from Derek Beckworth when he started doing radio," Kodama added.

"Take a look at the want-ad section." Grant said, sitting down again.

Kodama paged through the publication. She and Monk looked through several ads for mercenaries, two for databases that provided listings of leftist and liberal organizations, and one detailing where to buy WWII-era .50-caliber machine guns complete with tripod mount. Modified not to be able to shoot, of course. Kodama pointed at a bold-faced announcement boxed in by a thick black border. It read: "To my Aryan brothers and sisters, keep the faith, your defeat on Winslow shall not go unpunished." It was unsigned.

Monk bit. "Okay, what the hell is Winslow?"

Grant explained. "It's the main street where Tri-Harbor Community College in Wilmington is located. A couple of months ago there was a dance at the gym. Afterward, some of the young folks, Black kids mostly, were hanging around out front. Now who should roll up drunk but a bunch of white kids out for a night's entertainment."

Grant gestured as he talked. "One epithet leads to another and before you know it the brothers are kicking the skins' asses."

"All of them were Reich members?" Kodama's lips compressed.

"Actually, only two of them were dues-paying War Reich members. The others were the usual disaffected white youth that Beavis, Butt-head and Howard Stern appeal to." Grant tipped his glass in a mock toast.

"I'm glad you've kept up on your pop culture," Monk joked.

Kodama surmised, "I gather news of this defeat was kept pretty quiet among the supremacist circles."

Grant nodded. "Apparently Ivan's friend Sheriff Olson took a few of the brothers and skins into custody. He was surprised when the skins didn't press charges. They paid their bail and split."

Monk added, "Yet there's this ad."

"If you're one of the ones who knows about what took place, then you know what the announcement refers to. If not, it's just one more cryptic comment in a movement full of them." Grant paused, shoving ice around in his drink with an index finger.

"And here's the exacta, Grasshopper, a lot of these young brothers were from the Shores."

"Could Bradford have been there that night?" Monk said, trying to fit the pieces in order.

"Why not," Grant conceded.

"The new unofficial theory I got from the cops across the county line is the killer might not be a War Reich member but a sympathizer," Grant said. "Or one from that night in Wilmington."

"Could be," Kodama said. "Or maybe somebody who wants to be the next Bobby Bright. Killing four Black men would make a hell of a reputation."

"You kill me, baby," Monk said.

Kodama didn't smile.

Monk placed what was left of his cigarillo in a dented brass ashtray. He retrieved the typed notes he'd gleaned from his research at the *Press-Telegram.* "I'd like you to look through these, Dex, and let me know what you think."

"What do you want to find?" Kodama asked in a demanding tone.

"Just the facts, ma'am," Monk shot back.

"Sure," she snapped.

They exchanged looks but said nothing.

Grant watched them, smiling wanly. He took another taste of his Johnny Walker, then got up. "Nothing wrong with being thorough." He placed the tumbler on the edge of the coffee table. "Well, kids, it's time for the geezer to turn in. I'll be staying at Sandy's place."

Sandy was the elder of Grant's two grown daughters. Their mother, his second ex-wife, lived in Scranton. Invariably, he never referred to the woman directly if he could avoid it. Like Monk's sister, Sandy was a teacher, but taught in a private school in Pacific Palisades, and lived in Hawthorne.

"When do you want to get cracking on these?" Grant waved the notes.

Monk replied, "Day after tomorrow. In the morning I'm going to have a talk with Ms. Chacon's client."

"Sounds like a plan." Grant kissed Kodama goodnight and left.

The judge powered up her stereo and pushed the button activating the CD player. The mournful beauty of Billie Holliday's voice bore "Strange Fruit," a song about lynching.

Mortified, the judge gaped at Monk. "I, I was playing it this morning. I didn't realize what the next song was." She made to turn it off.

"Let it play, Jill, let it play."

They sat silently through the entire song.

CHAPTER 14

The following day Monk conducted his jailhouse interview of Herbert Jones. He was in the process of undergoing withdrawal from crack and paced back and forth in the interrogation room.

"You know the routine, Monk. The sheriff didn't have to work too hard to figure me for the suspect. Ronny and I had been having an argument about an extension of . . . credit." The prisoner smiled at his euphemism.

"The people who own the Zacharias Market saw both of you minutes before having words."

Jones shook his head in the affirmative. "So I'm mad about the fact he won't spot me, and I follow him when he walks off."

"You hoped to make him see differently," Monk explored.

A shoulder nudged. "Like I said, I was hot. I don't know what the fuck I planned to do. But just because I'm an addict, doesn't mean I can be treated as if I were shit on somebody's shoe."

Monk said, "Ms. Chacon says the GSR, the gunshot residue test the sheriff conducted on your hands and clothes was negative."

"They busted me two days after what happened to Ronny.

Even dirty scum wash their hands." He finally sat across from Monk at the plain table, folding his arms tightly across himself.

Monk remarked, "For dirty scum, you're rather self-effacing."

"All kinds of people wind up on this ride, man." He continued to scratch at his arm and chest. The repeated movements began to make Monk jittery. "Look, all the law has on me is the two of us yelling at each other. I don't have shit for an alibi 'cause most of the time I'm too screwed up worrying about my next hit or hiding out from my last burglary."

Monk didn't speak for several moments, then said, "Is there anything else you can tell me about that night?"

Jones spread his hands in the air before him. "Nothing. Ronny turned me down for the second time and I split."

"But you still needed to cop," Monk said.

A street wariness halted his incessant movements. "So?"

"Then where'd you get your shit?" Monk remembered the police report Chacon had given him stated there was no dope found on Aaron's body.

"From a ho' who owed me, Monk," Jones countered indignantly. "But as my lawyer told me, her word's worthless since she's been known to lie on the stand before."

"Did you know Scatterboy Williams?" Monk asked, unfazed.

"In passing," he replied curtly, having resumed his ritual. "We weren't running buddies, but I didn't cap him either."

"Ms. Chacon tells me you've been convicted before for assault and aggravated misdemeanor. You do have a history of violence, Mr. Jones."

"So does America," Jones quipped. "Maybe the next time some fool feeling all-powerful on PCP tries to do radical surgery on my head with the jagged end of a broken bottle, I'll try to disarm him with poetry. Or better yet, I'll wait until the government puts as much into treatment on demand programs as they do for crime bills."

Monk got up. "Thanks for seeing me, Mr. Jones."

The prisoner remained seated, a faroff look in his eyes.

Monk moved for the door.

"My lawyer tells me you've seen this ofay killer working the Shores," the man at the table said.

"You heard about him in here?" Monk knocked for the guard.

Jones said, "Revolving door, man. Brothers coming in and out of here every day."

"You think he's the one that killed Aaron?"

"I'm hoping he killed Ronny, otherwise I'm fucked. 'Cause if I go down for this, even if I agree to second degree, I won't—I can't—do the time." He stopped scratching and his body seemed to draw in on itself in the chair. "You have to find him," he pleaded, "you have to find the real killer."

Monk glanced back as the door opened, then he walked away from Herbert Jones and his plight.

For the rest of the day he did paperwork, including getting the contract to Mrs. Urbanski. Based on information Delilah had verified, Monk had decided to take the assignment. Swede had played him for a chump, and he wanted to take the smirk off the asshole's tanned face with a blowtorch. So what if he took it personal? And so what if Jill was right, and his motives in the Shoreline Killer case were getting a little blurry around the edges.

He made an appointment to meet Grant the next day to start canvassing the leads he'd developed from his research at the *Press-Telegram*. After that, he went over to the donut shop. Monk was discussing the merits of the '76 Gran Fury's V8 400 versus its 360 version with Curtis the car man, while simultaneously munching a smoked turkey sandwich, when the phone rang behind the counter.

"It's Delilah," Josette said, handing him the receiver.

"Thanks. What's up?"

"Jimmy Henderson's mother just called for you. She'd like you to meet her at church this evening."

Monk suddenly felt cold but he got his note pad out. "What's the address, D?"

URSALA BROCK was smoking an unfiltered Camel. The burning thing dangled from the side of her peach-colored lips while she typed a memo on the Packard Bell set diagonally to her desk. Through the vinyl slats of her office window, the afternoon was giving way to the russet gold of sunset. There was a knock and she said, "What."

Grainger Wu entered, displaying a punitive stare at the smoking sinner. "I know, more samples from our friends over in the Carolinas and you wanted to protect me from their undue influence."

She puckered and let loose with a full stream over her computer. "Relax, boss, I don't smoke 'em in public. I wouldn't do jack to f-up your play among the constituents."

"Praise Jesus." Wu picked up a two-day-old copy of *The New York Times*, perusing it with interest. "I'm going to fly back tomorrow night. Bob says he thinks we can get a vote out of Hatter if I promise some transportation funds for his interstate mall."

Brock placed the cigarette between her fingers, waving it around like a conductor. "Grainger, Bob's yanking the short one, okay. Ain't no way Hatter, even if he is a so-called moderate Republican, gonna go his own way on this."

Wu looked up from the article he was reading. "He has before."

She pulled deep on the Camel. "How do you do it?"

"Predictions?"

"Believe. Hatter may have shown some independence, but that was only when it worked to his benefit. He's a pox carrier like the rest of his ilk."

"He has integrity, Ursala." A note of weariness lifted the senator's voice.

"You can't trust 'em, Grainger. The only way we can see daylight on getting your hate crimes package out of committee is to embarrass these schmucks. The more they show sympathy for the militia types, the more we roast them over the public fires."

"No argument." Wu put the paper back on a growing stack. "When it's necessary. But that doesn't mean we need to yank out throats every time."

"Iron fist in the velvet glove?" Brock asked disingenuously.

"The velvet touch," Grainger said, his fingertips caressing the top of her desk. "We don't always have to be on the attack, Ursala."

"Shit, we've been on the defense for the last twenty years. Stepping on a few necks to retake the high ground is okay in my rule book."

"Hold the hounds till I get back, all right?"

She made a cleaning-her-teeth sound. "I'll just be here smoking cigarettes and drinking black coffee."

"We'll jump on those folks duped in the cemetery plots on Friday when I'm back."

"Slick. Tell Bob I think he's been sniffing around Ted Kennedy's punch bowl too much."

"I'll send him your love." Wu was looking at a photo of Brock standing next to a sweating Chuck Berry at the opening of the Rock and Roll Hall of Fame, his guitar in one hand, a plaque in the other. "Will it never die?" Wu asked remorsefully.

"What?" She lit another Camel, squinting her eyes as the smoke eddied against her handsome face.

He shifted his head to dark profile as the day dimmed outside. "The need to win."

"Nothing to be ashamed about, Grainger. The headlines in history are always about the ones left standing."

"Guess that's why I wanted to get elected, huh?" A tiredness edged across his words. "See you in two, Ursala."

"Okay." Wu left and Brock went back to her memo. Finishing it, she closed the file and called up another memo she'd done earlier in the day. Brock dialed a number, activating her modem. Presently, after a series of maneuvers along the cyberways, she came to a bulletin board called Fifth Mourning. The senator's staffer typed in her online name, Lost Lamb, and was answered with swastikas cartwheeling across her screen.

There was email waiting for Brock, one message in particular she'd been hoping to get. It was from someone called Crusader, asking Lost Lamb how the struggle was going in mudville. In response to a couple of racist jokes, Brock typed "haha" and "that's one I'll use." She then downloaded her message, with a salutation to Crusader to be vigilant and to continue the struggle as our day will come.

Brock took the cigarette out of her mouth, examining it as if were an appendage whose use she suddenly realized she couldn't fathom. She tapped the escape key with a precise finality. The screen went blank, and only the glow of the dying Camel was apparent. "Winning is what it's all about, Grainger," Brock said softly as her light faded.

THE FOURSQUARE Eternal Promise Baptist Church dominated a block of single-family homes in Long Beach. Pulling into the church's parking lot, Monk watched Black, Latino and Southeast Asian kids playing street hockey along the avenue. They zoomed around like atomic particles on their Day-Glo Rollerblades, their clashing sticks cutting through the gathering quiet of evening, twisting and turning their elongated adult-child bodies in rapid motion without effort or qualm. The wonderfully arrogant ballet of youth.

Against the coming gloom, frayed palms swayed in the breeze off the ocean, and ripe dates dotted the concrete a syrupy brown. Monk got out of his car and walked toward the main entrance.

The church was a two-story building stretching back from the street all the way to the next block. It was pseudo-Romanesque, constructed of ruddy brown brick set in a basketweave pattern. The entranceway was recessed inside a vaulted archway.

Above the archway was a round stained glass panel depicting children of many colors and a woman in African dress with lengthy cornrows. The figures in the scene lay in a field of lilacs and roses, the woman reading a book to them. A lamb and a lion, in peaceful juxtaposition, also lay near them. Saffron clouds hovered over the idyllic gathering. To the left of the window, bifurcating the corner of the church, was a turret topped with a rough-hewn cross.

Monk was near the entrance when a voice came to him from the shadows.

"We'd like to have a word with you." One man now stood to his left, two to his right.

The one on his left he recognized, the other two he didn't know. But he was sure he'd seen one of them the night of the encounter with the all-white killer. "I've been trying to get a hold of you, Mr. Bradford."

"So I heard." He coughed and adjusted his horn-rimmed glasses.

"Yeah, G, what you got to do with the Shoreline Killer thang?" one of the other two demanded. He was wearing sagging DeeCee pants, a billowing blue flannel shirt, and a colorful bandanna around his head.

Monk kept his attention on Bradford. "I'm into this 'thing' because my clients have an interest in it." He didn't add that he also felt concern for Bradford's cousin, still lying in a coma in the hospital.

"That don't say shit." Blue Flannel sidled closer to him.

The third young man, a light-skinned Black kid who couldn't have been more than twenty, placed a hand on the bigger one's arm. "Be cool."

Blue Flannel shook the arm loose and got closer. The odor of malt liquor was unmistakable. "You s'pposed to be all that, huh?" His forearms flexed.

"Don't you have anything better to do than harass us senior citizens?"

Bradford stepped up. "Ajax, why don't you take a walk around the block."

"Ajax?" Monk said, surprised. "Is Agamemnon going to ride up in his Chevy Nova any minute?"

The light-skinned kid cracked up.

Ajax snorted and pointed a hand with a mammoth gold ring on it at Bradford. "Look, college boy, just 'cause you think you the next Malcolm X, don't make it you the only one that can run the show."

In a mollifying tone, Bradford answered him. "Anytime you want to be the HNIC, Ajax, you're more than welcome. I'm just your humble facilitator, my brother."

"And ain't nobody more at the roots than you, Ajax," the other one said by way of a backhand compliment.

Ajax shot back, "All you high-soundin' motherfuckahs can—"

"I'd appreciate it if you'd tone your language down, young man." The new voice belonged to an older gentleman in a plaid sport coat of questionable taste. This he wore over a faded polo shirt and double knit pants that revealed too much of his lime green socks. "I'm Reverend Tompkins. Mrs. Henderson invited Mr. Monk and you, Malik, but let's remember where we are, shall we?"

Ajax was about to go on when the reasonable one spoke again. "Why don't y'all go on up and me and Mike Tyson here will amuse ourselves with a game of chess."

"I can't think of a better recommendation," Tompkins said.

Monk walked past a brooding Ajax and the trio followed a series of flagstone steps to the reverend's office on the second floor. It was a comfortable space with old and worn, but user-friendly, furniture. On one pale green wall was a portrait of a Black Jesus, and opposite, silver-framed photos of Martin Luther King, Jr., and John Kennedy. The holy triptych of Black deliverance. The rug was an ancient Persian with some of the design rubbed off.

Mrs. Henderson was a dark-skinned woman in a full-length print dress. She sat on a cracked leather couch the texture of a dry roadbed underneath the painting of Christ. The first time he'd seen her, at the bedside of her comatose son, he hadn't noticed her appearance. Words couldn't make their way out of his mouth.

"Mr. Monk," she greeted him.

"Mrs. Henderson," was all he could manage.

Malik Bradford sat next to his aunt. "I know you've been trying to get a hold of me, Mr. Monk, but as you may know,

I've been busy. Jimmy's my cousin, and the third victim of this man they're calling the Shoreline Killer. And we know Clarice hired you to find who killed her old man. Who, it seems, was killed by the same white boy. What we'd like to know, is how much you've found out."

"I'd like to know what your theories are," Monk countered.

"I think that was clear in the article in the *Sentinel*, which I imagine you saw."

"A conspiracy between some members of the Sheriff's Department and this killer."

"Collusion, maybe," Mrs. Henderson corrected. "Could be the killer is weeding out certain elements, drug dealers and so on, whose elimination suit the interests of officials like Captain Olson."

Monk found such reasoning annoying. When the police were in the picture, Black folk were much too willing to buy into bizarro conspiracy notions.

On the other hand, it was understandable in light of many historical events: the FBI's role in undermining the '60's Black power movement, ex-LAPD Chief Gates' infatuation with the choke hold, the frequent appearance of Klan flyers in police locker rooms, the admitted racism of certain cops.

"Your son isn't a drug dealer, Mrs. Henderson," he eventually said.

An odd look flitted across her face but it departed just as quick.

"No," Bradford offered, "Jimmy's shooting seemed out of character with the rest. I mean if you consider the other ones are brothers who have records."

"A warning to you then?" Monk inquired, admitting to himself that particular spin on the case was interesting.

Bradford was glum. "I'd gotten him to help with a few things on campus." He looked doe-eyed at his aunt.

"What was it, Malik?" she said, rubbing his arm tenderly.

"There'd been an editorial in the school paper by someone from the Ayn Rand Club calling for the end to social entitlements, minority scholarships, and what not. Naturally, editorials fly back and forth. Then the Randites hold a rally, and some skins show up in support."

"There was a brawl?" Monk inquired.

"Not really. But some choice words got thrown around. Jimmy and I had a face-down with a couple of them."

"You think what happened to your cousin was payback?" Monk had a sensation of excitement, like a hunting dog getting the scent.

Bradford hesitated. "It's been on my mind." He stole a look at his aunt.

"Then you must have some idea who you're looking for," Monk commented, "the ones from campus."

"Some," was all he'd allow.

Monk was about to pursue that when Mrs. Henderson broke in.

"You looking to get more headlines for yourself?" Mrs. Henderson condemned. "Like you did with that Korean mess you were involved in."

Softly he replied, "I just want to make it right, Mrs. Henderson."

"We do think there's more to this than just some lone nut," Bradford said, ignoring Monk's emotion. "In some ways, these Shoreline killings have had a positive effect. Finally there's something, a catalyst, to help pull our people together."

"The common enemy that unites the lumpen, the workers and the intelligentsia," Monk wondered dubiously.

That got a grin out of the young man. "One can always dream."

Reverend Tompkins, who sat behind his desk listening, interjected. "I knew Scatterboy. He, ah, may not have been as straight an arrow as we'd have liked, but he was still a product of this town. What we don't want is our community becoming a freak show in the side tent between the sports and weather on the six o'clock news. We're asking you to work cooperatively with us, brother Monk, so we can continue to bring our folks forward."

Monk drew in a breath. He admired Bradford's sincerity, but he didn't want his "dirty dozen" traipsing all over the place either. "How about this. I leave the political high ground to Malik, while I—"

The door nearly came off its hinges as it swung inward and slapped violently against the wall. Ajax tumbled into the room. The other youth rushed in and took a kick at him, but Ajax rolled out of the way.

"You high yellow bitch," Ajax screamed, "I'm gonna plant my foot so far in your ass your mama's gonna taste shoe polish."

Monk was already up and trying to pull the two apart.

Bradford and Tompkins were also on their feet, helping to separate the combatants.

"What happened, Ty?" Bradford had his arm around the youth's waist.

"This punk had some more eight ball in his car so of course he goes and drinks it." Spittle flew as he rasped out his words. "Then he starts mumbling about how he should be in on this and starts to march up here."

"Fuckin' right," Ajax said, blood collecting on the side of his lower lip. "You book-learnin' chumps wouldn't have the balls to go lookin' for skins unless you'd hooked up with me and my crew." He pounded his chest with an open hand. "You might know politics, and have the great plan for the

Black race, but none of you have popped a cap on a fool, have you?" He clamped his jaw tight, weaving slightly.

Reverend Tompkins was holding onto one side of Ajax, exposing his sleeve and the watch around his wrist. Monk realized it was a Cartier.

Contemptuously, Bradford said, "I'm happy you shared that."

"I don't feel too good right now," Ajax suddenly weak, proclaimed.

Ty laughed, and Tompkins got the young tough to a trash can in the corner in time for him to get sick into it.

Off to one side, Bradford and Mrs. Henderson talked quietly with one another. She then said to Monk, "I want the man who tried to kill my baby. If you want the glory, you can have it."

"I want him too, Mrs. Henderson, believe me. He's got a debt to pay, and I intend to be the one who collects the ticket."

She seemed to weigh his words for the first time. "Why? What's your stake in this?"

His father's hand reached for him in the kitchen, the strong fingers kneading his shoulder as they pulled him toward the maw. His dad's age then was just a few years older than he was now. His old man's question hovered before him, the answer still out of reach. Monk temporarily shook loose of the memory. "We can't let this go on."

She looked at Tompkins and Bradford for their assessment.

Finally the younger man spoke. "I haven't seen any of the nazi types who were on campus that day. But our patrol spotted the killer earlier that night we ran into you and Midnight."

"You get a license plate number?" Monk asked. Over by the trash can, Ajax got sick again.

"No. We'd split into smaller units, and got the call some of the crew had spotted the red Jeep."

"You all kept in touch by cellular?" Monk inquired.

"Yes," Bradford said, "we'd keep several of our cars stationed around so that if we were to run up on him, some of us would be able to keep him in sight."

"That was good thinking. Did the man in the Jeep travel in a certain area?"

Bradford made a *Y* with his hands. "Hard to say. He was driving like he knew the Shores, but it's anybody's guess if he had Midnight specifically in mind."

"Or," Monk reflected, "any brother out that night in the same age range as the others."

"Maybe he thought it was funny to shoot a white-skinned Black man," Mrs. Henderson broke in.

"Could be." Monk turned his head to look directly at Bradford. "Were you at the dance that night at Tri-Harbor College?"

"I heard about it, but neither me or Jimmy was there that night."

Ajax groaned from the corner. He sat on the floor, his back against the wall.

Abruptly, Monk pointed a finger at the pastor. "That's quite a timepiece you got there, Reverend Tompkins. 'Course Cartier don't make 'em cheap. How'd you come by that one? Gift from a parishioner?" He smiled mischievously.

Tompkins worked on a chagrined look as all the heads in the room pivoted in his direction. Quietly he confessed, "I bought it off of Scatterboy the night he was killed. But I swear on the head of the sweet baby Jesus I didn't see anything of no ghost killer in his devil's chariot."

The reverend glanced at everyone in the room, looking like a man in a lineup. "After I bought the watch I went into the Corsair, a local tavern, where, ah, I was supposed to meet a member I've been counseling."

Mrs. Henderson placed a hand on her hip, a smirk on her face. Bradford and Ty silently guffawed at each other.

"You didn't volunteer this to the police," Monk said.

Tompkins raised his arms apologetically. "What was there to tell them? I did not see anything of him after I had my business with our dear departed brother Williams. I heard about his demise same as everyone the following day. Frankly, at the time I thought he'd met his fate at the hands of a fellow brigand he'd had a falling out with."

Monk plucked at his goatee. "Okay folks, let's see if we can't compromise here. If Bradford and the rowdy boys hold off on their night patrols, from here on in, I'll keep everyone abreast of my activities."

"Why the fuck should we do that?" Ajax had regained his vigor and was standing up, gesturing at the detective.

"Because one of you might get shot, or more likely scare the killer off."

"You've probably already done that," Bradford countered.

"Let's say that I have. But the cops are working one angle, and I'm working another. Now who's more likely to be straight up with you on this?"

Ty piped in, "But we ain't gonna sit back and have a bunch of skins running around the Shores. They can't just come here fuckin' around with us."

"We're not going to have a candlelight vigil for civil rights if the War Reich comes marching through, Monk. The time to make a stand is now," Bradford added. "This goddamn country belongs to us too, man. I don't care what Newt and his peckerwood buddies think up on Capitol Hill."

"Bat for bat, gat for gat, cuz," a pale Ajax prophesied.

"I'm talking about house meetings and town halls,"

Bradford said, rebuffing the gangbanger. "We go toe-to-toe only when we have to defend ourselves."

Ajax made a sound like air escaping a balloon.

"All right." Monk held up his hand as a sign of contrition. "Can we agree if the skins aren't around, then y'all aren't doing the night patrols? Let's not give the sheriff any excuse to jack up more brothers."

"We'll hold you accountable, Monk," Bradford promised.

"Somebody needs to." He shook hands with Bradford and Mrs. Henderson. Ty said good-bye and Ajax, back in form, gave him the nihilistic nod favored by his gangsta peers. He climbed into his Ford and made it back to his apartment in Mar Vista, tired and sleepy.

His place was in a reconditioned brick building on a block of mixed use facilities. On the ground floor was a Cuban-Chinese restaurant, a print shop, a courier service, and an auto parts store. Eighteen months ago, it was four different businesses. Eighteen months from now, it would probably be four new ones. The economy of Southern California was going through a restructuring and who knew how it would shake out. It had begun with the deindustrialization of the urban core in the '80s, displacing workers like his dad's friends, men and women who once upon a time could rely on well-paid, unionized, blue-collar work to raise a family and buy a house. But like the plains buffalo, those days were gone. They'd been put to the skewer by cowboy arbitragers, capital flight, and the bottomless greed of money manipulators out to make a fast buck by exploiting whomever, whatever, wherever.

Monk plodded up the stairs to the second floor. There was a message from his mother and one from Jill on his machine. His mom wanted him to come over for dinner on Sunday, and the judge said they needed to talk. At the moment, both seemed like Herculean tasks.

He decided his mother could wait for his yes until tomorrow. Maybe she was as curious about Odessa's young man as he was. And Jill? He felt apprehensive about their impending little talk. Was this going to be a we-need-a-little-space speech? The last few days there had been tension between them. The more he thought about their differences in earning power, the more he'd backed off in his own mind about them living together. But were there deeper issues?

Whatever, it was too much for tonight.

He got a Miller from the refrigerator, pulled off his shoes, and sat in his wing chair overlooking his portion of the city. He took a couple of sips and began to drift off. Dimly, he was aware of his hand placing the bottle on the floor.

Down the block, he heard an auto alarm go off. Then another. Maybe Midnight was stealing his way across the cities of Southern California, on his own peculiar odyssey of self-discovery. Each Alpine and Blaupunkt Midnight swiped tuned to a different station and as he ripped them from their housings, the last broken word or phrase pointed him to his next destination, until he had pieced together the whole meaningless message, the final word to complete his existential sojourn.

Monk yawned, and fell asleep in front of the window.

CHAPTER 15

The following day he and Grant began running down the possible leads he'd developed. From the onset, they knew Monk was going to get the short end of the stick. Since the cases had to fit certain parameters—a Black suspect and a white victim—it was unlikely either the victim or his kin would be eager to talk about the incident, especially to a Black man a couple of inches over six feet tall and topping the scales around 220.

The first name on his list, a woman in Seal Beach who'd been robbed at knife point and hit so hard in the head she'd required twelve stitches, slammed the door on Monk's solemn face. The clipboard he held shook with the impact. He didn't even have time to tell his story, that he was a researcher from a westside college conducting a study about people's perspectives on crime.

His second stop, at an apartment in Wilmington, went like this:

"Yeah," said a man named Tim, as he stood in the door, soda in hand, TV playing in the background.

Monk gave his spiel.

"Yeah, I used to work at a 7-Eleven, a second job, see? I work for my money rather than try to get handouts. That is until one night a couple of your cousins stopped by. One of them stuck a shotgun under my nose, and I gave them all that was in the till."

Swallowing a comeback to the man's racist comment, Monk plunged ahead, probing a little deeper with his next question.

"No, I don't think enough shit's been done to curb crime. Even with the Republicans calling the shots. Ain't hardly more cops on the beat, and they can't fry them Jehri-curled, crack-of-their-ass showin' motherfuckers fast enough for my taste." He took a sip of the soda, sweat developing on his upper lip.

Monk managed to control his voice and asked what happened the night he was robbed.

"After I did what they asked, they started shuffling out. Then all of a sudden, the one with the hog leg pivots and lets loose with a blast. That answer your goddamn question?" With that, Tim opened the door a little further, balancing his body against it. He eased his frame down into a wheelchair. Their eyes met momentarily, then the door closed.

And so it went until he met up with Grant in the evening at Continental Donuts.

"This has been an illuminating day about the intolerance of my fellow Americans," Monk quipped, pouring coffee for them into cups emblazoned with donuts interlocked in the style of Olympic rings.

Uncharacteristically, Grant didn't retort. Quietly, he added liberal amounts of milk, no sugar, to his coffee. "People aren't as bad as we think they are, Ivan. Just because they say a wrong thing, doesn't mean that same person wouldn't pull a kid out of the way of a speeding car no matter what their color."

Monk almost spilled his coffee. "I'm sorry, Dex, but you're

not going to get a lot of empathy from me on this. I know some of these people have been fucked over by criminals, but does that make me as an individual carry the burden for a minority of assholes? Especially when it's mostly other Black people Black folks usually are jacking up."

He drank too much hot coffee too quickly. It scalded his tongue and the roof of his mouth as he tried to stop from swallowing. But he did, and batted back tears.

Grant methodically stirred in his cup. "I think you're losing your perspective on this case, weed hopper."

"What the fuck am I supposed to be objective about, Dex? The old lady who I talked to today down in Belmont?" Monk began to pace as he talked. "I'm sitting there in her living room when her big corn-fed seventeen-year-old grandson comes waltzing in and says that's enough, she don't have to answer any more questions from me.

"I say why, maintaining my cool, and the kid gets in my face screamin' about some fight at school he's just had with a Black kid over what kind of music should be played at the dance. And he goes on about how you Blacks complain all the time about the whites but don't deal with our own racism. About how we apologize for crime." Monk sank into a booth. He could feel the raw trailings of skin on the roof of his mouth and it angered him further.

"Do you?" Grant finally sampled his coffee.

"You goddamn know I don't, Dex. You've never heard me make excuses for criminal behavior. But that doesn't mean I think these young brothers are genetically predisposed to crime and violence. You can't ignore the effects on the inner cities when they're stripped of resources. Or when the resources weren't there in the first place."

"But people have to take responsibility for their own actions," the older man said.

"What a goddamn insight. So what the hell did you come up with today?"

Grant let Monk change the subject. "A couple of possibles. One of them is strong. He's a relatively young white guy who joined a gun club since he was robbed last year. They caught the crook in this case."

"Why is he a possible then?"

"This chap makes his living as a special effects man."

"That's not bad, the killer was so damn white, it could be a disguise."

"Plus being in the movie business, he has access to cars, fake plates, all that."

"We should play him out."

Grant put the cup to his lips. "Absolutely. But why don't you reconnoiter this cat, and I'll take up the slack on the other leads."

Monk was going to protest but he welcomed an out. Blowing his cover was the least of his worries if he had to face more polarized sentiments. "Fine."

The older man calmly drank his coffee.

PINK SANDS was a mobile home park in the town of Belmont, a compact municipality lying between Long Beach and Seal Beach. In the past the small city had been home to first- and second-generation Armenians and Italians who were middlemen in the cottonseed oil, olive oil, apricot, walnut, fig and date trades. But Grant hadn't been there for more than a dozen years and all the homegrown wholesalers had been bought out, or driven out, by the large-scale agri-conglomerates in their ceaseless quest for greater profit and less competition.

He knocked on the door. A little more than halfway up, a wrought iron grill protected a small inset window. Over that was fixed a miniature plastic cow's skull. A female voice issued from the intercom.

"Yes, what can I do for you?"

"My name is Thomas Hillard, ma'am, we're conducting a survey about whether people think crime is down with three strikes on the books." Grant was dressed casually in a pair of creme-colored creased Dockers, a tan pair of Nunn Bush, a blue shirt with thin white strips, and a Donegal tweed bronze-hued sport coat.

What might have been a snort escaped from the intercom's speaker. "You're kidding, right?"

"No, I have my documentation," Grant enthused. They were some papers he'd asked a former forger he knew to doctor for his and Monk's cover story. "This won't take too long," he assured the voice.

"Hold on."

Momentarily the window behind the bars swung inward. "Let me see," the woman on the other side said.

Grant complied.

The larger door swung inward to a crack on double chains. Half of the face of a large, but solid woman in her late fifties could be discerned through the fissure. She was handsome with liquid green eyes and her blondish white hair was cut close but full in the back. "Mind if I see some other ID than just a bunch of papers on a clipboard?"

"Of course." Grant offered her the fake business card and a paper that supposedly detailed the nature of the study. It was on a letterhead of a famous university in the Westwood section of Los Angeles.

She examined these, then said, "If that goddamn school is doing this, then I know it's going to be some kind of liberal bullshit." She looked up from the paper to Grant's unfazed countenance. "I bet some politically correct psychologist is overseeing the project, and I bet his name ends in 'berg' or a vowel." She handed the papers back to Grant.

"I'm here to tell you, ma'am, that—"

She cut him off, "You didn't pick me by random." The face leaned closer, the mouth taking on a coarse quality. "I bet you know my husband died from injuries he got in a mugging last year."

Grant went for the gusto. "Yes, that's so. We have been combing records such as yours, Mrs. Vickers. But only so that victims, and their families, can be heard from."

She considered that, then the door was pushed toward the jamb. The chain was released and she opened the portal to let him in. "Okay, Mr. Hillard, I'll give you five minutes." She pointed a blunt finger at him. "But I damned sure want a copy of this thing when it comes out."

"Of course." Grant stepped inside. A tasteful southwestern motif marked the decor. The place was appointed in Navajo-style rugs, straight-backed chairs stained with dark varnish, unglazed thrown pots and vases, and several Georgia O'Keefe and Fritz Scholder prints framed on the walls.

Mrs. Vickers was dressed in an oversized purple top, black Spandex pants, and espadrilles. They sat at a glass table with wrought iron legs under a halogen lamp suspended from the ceiling. Grant angled his clipboard with the printed questions on it so she could take her time reading them.

"How'd you know today was my half day?" the woman asked.

"I'd been by before. I interviewed a Mr. Ramos at his job over at the tool and die on Keller." Which was the first one hundred percent true statement he'd made to her so far.

She read through the questions on his clipboard, flipped through to the second page, then shoved the thing aside. "Besides telling you that I'm still hurting from the fact the cops have never found a lead to my husband's killer, what can I say new?" There was no emotion on the surface of her delivery, just a practiced cadence that masked the deeper feeling.

Grant consulted his personal notebook, even though he knew the details he wanted to pursue. "From what we gleaned from the article in the *Press-Telegram*, it seems your husband, while in the hospital, identified his attacker as a young Black man."

"Yes, so?"

"Well, how do you and the other members of the family feel about the police and their inability to catch the killer?"

A wary twinge turned a corner of her mouth. "How do you mean?"

Grant pretended like he was still referring to his notes. "According to the article, you also have a son in his early twenties."

"He doesn't live here." The twinge returned.

The ex-cop pulled the clipboard to him. "I don't want to get into areas you don't want to discuss, Mrs. Vickers. I really do know something of what you've been through." That too was another truth.

She inspected his worn country-mile of a face, the etched lines of experience, and the slate grey eyes that hid secrets personal and political. "Alice," she said after a pause. "Would you like some coffee?"

"That'd be fine, Alice."

They talked about the incident and the days and weeks following the attack. How at first her husband seemed to be on the mend, but then inextricably wore out, all his life-force leaving him in a burst, and then he was gone. They talked about crime and how she was bitter against the assailant, but that she didn't condemn all Blacks because of it. Over the second cup, the widow pointed out it was a Black woman at work, herself the victim of a street mugging, who helped her get through the rough period.

But when Grant tried to steer the conversation toward her son, she subtly swerved it away from him. The most she'd reveal was that he was around when the father had been hurt, but was now somewhere else. He didn't push it and thanked her for her time.

She shook his hand warmly and Grant left the Pink Palms court as a light fog slid off the ocean and began to entangle itself along the land. He rendezvoused with Monk at his stakeout location on a hill overlooking Wayne Edison's house amid a series of ranch homes in Seal Beach.

"How was your day, honey?" Grant said, knowing how much Monk detested surveillance duty. He eased his form into the passenger seat of the rented sedan.

"Stunning. Subject Edison went to the union hall in West Hollywood this morning where he hung around for about an hour and a half. He then took lunch with a dyed blonde in a butt-hugging micro mini at a joint called the Narrow Margin on Oakhurst. Afterward, they went back to her place and, I presume, played hide the salami until a little past two in the afternoon."

"My, how blasé you've become," Grant needled. "Was Charles McGraw running the cafe?"

Monk ignored the comment. "After that, subject Edison drove around, eventually stopping at Aaron Records on Highland for about an hour. Then, on this side of town, he went to a hardware store that sells ammunition."

Grant filled him in on his activities. "So what do you think?"

"Shadow the widow, find out where she plays bid whist or hangs out with the girls on Fridays. And of course you just happen to run into her." Monk leered at him. "Crank up the charm, you salty dog, and see if you can't get a picture of the son."

"What about backup for your lookout on Edison?"

Monk pointed his thumb at the sound of tires crunching on the gravel laying across the shoulder of the hillock. "He's here."

Momentarily the back door of the sedan opened and a man it took Grant some time to recognize slid in behind Monk. "You remember Alphonse?"

"Oh, yeah." Grant mumbled. The last time he'd seen Alphonse it had been in a purple-hooded sweat top and the expensive Air Jordans favored by the members of the Rolling Daltons street gang. Going then by the sobriquet, "Mad-T," he was working with other gang members trying to install a truce among various chiefdoms.

"Gents, what it be?" The young man was dressed all in white: jeans, sweat shirt and tennis shoes.

Monk said to Grant, "Given brother Alphonse's daring at eluding the FBI in a previous episode—"

"And the cash you said you'd lay on me," the young man interjected.

"I thought who better to take up the slack in the wee hours."

"Your protege?" Grant inquired, not disinterestedly.

"Just hiring out for a few nights, pops," Alphonse chimed in.

Grant's head tilted toward the ceiling liner. "Pops indeed."

CHAPTER 16

"Hey, oh damn, I'm sorry, I forgot your name."

In that unmistakable gait of his, Grant got off the bar stool in the bowling alley and came over to them.

"How you doing . . . Alice, right?"

"Yes." She stuck out a hand which had turquoise and silver rings on the middle and little fingers.

He hadn't noticed the rings when he'd been at her place. Maybe she wore them only when she went out. She was dressed in jeans and a loose heavy cotton shirt. Large spangled earrings were set along the side of her rouged face.

Grant, also dressed in jeans and a worn work shirt, pumped her hand in return.

"Are you still conducting your survey?" she said.

"Finishing up in this area."

"Oh, let me introduce you to my friends."

She did and Grant saluted with the bottle of beer held in his hand. "I don't want to break up your game, but if you have time afterward, how about a cup of coffee?"

One of the women, a middle-aged looker named Connie in green eyeshadow and hair lacquered like the tail fin of a '57 Chevy Bel Air, meowed playfully.

Vickers gave her a smoldering look. "Sure. We'll be done in about an hour or so. You're welcome to stay and watch."

"Thanks."

"Thanks, my ass," the long-haired grip hissed at the assistant director.

They were standing in the middle of an abandoned building east of downtown Los Angeles, shooting a scene in a TV series about an undercover detective who solved his cases through prescience flashes from the bad guy's thoughts. It was the second day of filming in the cavernous space. Lights, cables, a dolly track and several other paraphernalia of image-making abounded.

The star was sitting in a chair, going over his lines and the guest star, a veteran actor Monk remembered from several caper films of the '70s, circled about nervously in a corner.

Monk, resplendent in soiled clothing and a tattered watchcap, milled about with other extras—actual homeless men recruited out of a shelter on Towne and Second. Two days ago he'd followed Edison down to this building. Taking a chance on being spotted, Monk had crept to the rear and, using a heavy screwdriver, pried off a wood panel tacked over a former window.

He'd sneaked inside and spied on the special effects man as he was making a rough layout of the interior. Monk had overheard Edison and the assistant director, the same one presently arguing with the grip, making small talk.

The A.D. mentioned he'd lined up some men from the Lighthouse Men's Shelter for today's filming. Monk had paid one of the men double what he would have made and took his place when the crew rounded them up shortly after seven this morning.

Their heated discussion over, the grip hitched his

equipment belt and wandered off. Edison had been busy outside but had returned and was rigging up the effects for a bazooka shell exploding. The plot of this particular episode involved a renegade Venezuelan general using ex-Salvadoran death squad members to set up rackets in Pico Union.

The TV company got its scenes, including a successful explosion replete with bursting windows and rivers of flame. Around six-thirty in the evening, the extras were paid and offered rides back to the shelter. Monk made himself scarce. The crew had parked their cars behind the building but Monk had failed to locate Edison's blue Toyota Land Cruiser.

"Shit," he blurted and ran around the corner toward the front. The men from the shelter were boarding a shuttle van like the one that had brought them that morning. Monk caught his breath as a bright red Jeep slowly glided along the street, heading in the direction of the shuttle.

Monk clawed at the small .38, the hidden hammer model, strapped to his ankle. All feeling in his heart ceased, and crazily he imagined the Shoreline Killer opening up on the van of homeless men, many of whom were Black and not yet forty.

Edison detached himself from the huddle of people as the red Jeep pulled in behind the van. The dyed blonde was at the wheel and Edison got in beside her, holding a small tool box. The vehicle got back into traffic, and took off north along Alameda, the woman's hair billowing behind her like frayed tinsel.

Monk raced across the street to the rental he'd parked in a lot before walking back to the shelter. The A.D. gaped at him as he accelerated after the red Jeep.

The car pulled into the driveway, and the lights went dead. Grant got out of the driver's side and was a little surprised that Vickers hadn't opened her door. Old-fashioned. He moved around and opened it for her.

"Want to come in for a drink?"

She stood close to him. She smelled good and Grant had to fight an urge to put his arm around her and pull her closer. Some guy with a hoarse whisper for a voice said, "Yes."

He followed her to the door, mesmerized by the deliberate swing of her ample, shapely hips. A feeling he hadn't had since the Bradley Administration ached in his gut and touched off nerves laced with nuclear current through his legs. As she put the key in the lock. Grant came up behind her, pressing his body very close, placing his hands on either side of the firm buttocks.

She reached a hand up and caressed the side of his face.

Vickers turned her head and kissed him. "I don't know about you, big fella, but I'd sure like to get you into bed right about now." Her face reddened and she amended, "I'm not a tramp, mind you. But I haven't had the pleasure of a man's company since, well—"

A melancholy overtook her as her words trailed off. Grant felt a keen disappointment. "Look, I understand, Alice, I'll just say good-night."

He made like he was going to leave then suddenly swung his legs to the left, out of the Jeep. Edison grinned elfishly at his girlfriend and stepped to the curb. A youngish Black man and an even younger girl, Southeast Asian from the look of her, stood on the street. The blonde tapped her long nails on the steering wheel to the music of a Billy Joel tape. She watched Edison and the couple as she sat in the idling Jeep.

From his vantage point in the rented car, Monk took all this in. The Black kid dipped into his sweat top's bulging pocket and produced something his hand was wrapped around. The young Asian woman was the lookout, but even from where he sat, Monk could tell she was too loaded to be very effective. Edison passed money to the Black kid, and took possession of the probable narcotic.

The special effects man got into the Jeep and the blonde popped the vehicle into gear and took off. The other couple began to saunter down the deserted industrial street, toward Monk. He remained still. The couple got closer and the Jeep came back around the far corner, heading in their direction. They heard it, stopped, and turned around. Monk got out of the car, the young woman glancing at him glassy-eyed. She plucked on her boyfriend's sleeve.

The .38 was in Monk's hand, down by his side. The Jeep kept coming. The young Black man was watching the Jeep, the woman had locked on Monk. Running up, he too was fixed on the oncoming vehicle and the right arm of Wayne Edison which had begun to extend from the Jeep. Monk brought his pistol perpendicular to his body, sucking in a small amount of air to steady his shot like his dad had taught him.

"Shoot it, baby, shoot it," Alice Vickers moaned in Grant's ear.

Grant moaned loudly and felt a hot flush as he reached a climax. "Jesus," he panted between breaths.

Vickers pressed her mouth to his as she climbed off of him, snuggling close. In the corner, a single candle threw off a soft glow.

The room itself was in direct contrast to the masculine quality of the rest of the house. It was done in soft lavenders and pastel greens with a pattern of blue and yellow cornflowers on the wallpaper. There was an armoire of some sepia wood and a large throw rug woven in a jacquard design. The curtains over the windows were imprinted in an Art

Nouveau pattern. She gazed at the ceiling, her hand lightly touching her left breast. "That was nice, thank you," she intoned.

A bit disoriented, Grant said, "No. Thank you. I think that's the first time I've used my prostate in seven years."

"I doubt that." She kissed him again, sliding her hand over his silver-haired chest and stomach. Grant's hand rubbed her buttocks and she entwined herself around his legs.

This went on until the two of them began to drift off to sleep. "I wonder how my number one son is doing," he snickered to himself.

"What?"

"Open the box real slow, dig?"

The five of them were arrayed on the darkened section of Wilmington like mismatched chess pieces, their bodies frozen against a lengthening silence. The long neck of a cargo crane jutted in black relief against the heavy gloom on a nearby lot. Monk's .38 was inches from Wayne Edison's twitching nose.

The couple who'd sold him the crack were off to one side, the young man's arm tight around the waist of the girl. She talked in a low voice to the man, and he in turn tried to comfort her, all the while keeping an eye on Monk. The blonde, wide-eyed, her chest heaving like she was trying out for the lead of Scarlett III, sat perfectly still in the Jeep's driver seat.

"What?" Edison repeated, his total focus drawn to the short barrel invading his personal space.

"I want the woman here to open the tool box you have on your lap."

As if Monk's words were suddenly translated for him, Edison gestured to the woman. "Open the box, Judith, open the goddamn thing, will you?"

Sucking in large gulps of air, she reached over, unlatched the box and pulled the lid back.

Monk growled, "Turn on the dash lights."

Judith flipped a switch and a pale arc illuminated the area under the dash. Monk stepped back, his gun pointing at the special effects man. He said, "Empty the contents out."

"What?" Edison asked.

"You got a learning disability? Empty the contents out on the sidewalk."

Edison spilled out a clatter of parts and tools that was louder than Monk had anticipated. A momentary alarm struck him as he strained his hearing, listening for anything untoward. Satisfied, he allowed himself a look at the contents. There was no gun, but there were two empty crack vials among the screwdrivers, pliers, and small gears and pulleys.

"Fuck."

His oath made them jump. The crack seller spoke up. "Hey, if you want my supply, you can have it, man."

Embarrassed, Monk looked at the gun on the end of his hand as if it were a tumor. He put it away in the pocket of his windbreaker. "I'm not here to take anything from anybody. I'm a private detective looking for the Shoreline Killer."

Edison said, "And you thought I was that guy?"

"The killer drives a red Jeep. And you were robbed at gunpoint last year and pistol whipped in Pacific Shores."

The special effects man turned to the blonde who grimaced apologetically. "I was making a buy when the dude decided to roll me. I was all for keeping it quiet, but Judith thinks I ought to have justice and calls the cops. So then, of course, I've got to make up a story to cover my ass." He fumed at her.

"Damn." Alice Vickers said, pulling on a pair of lavender panties. "I like your style, Tom."

Grant began to get angry, thinking the woman was confusing him for some other man, then remembered that was the name he'd given her. "I like you too, Alice."

She came over to him as he lay propped up in the bed, the early morning light playing through the bedroom's curtains. She bent down, and he playfully nibbled on one of her nipples. "I'll go make us some breakfast," she said. Vickers got on a terry cloth robe and left the bedroom, humming.

Grant got out of the bed and ambled into the can. He finished and came out, eyeing a walnut chiffonier set against the wall. Carefully, he pulled open its drawers. In the third one, sifting through a layer of sweaters, he came upon an ornate keepsake box inlaid with ivory. It was locked.

"Do you want some coffee?"

Grant just about had a coronary. He was relieved when he found that Vickers wasn't standing in the doorway. "Yes," he called back to her in the kitchen.

He got the box out and his Swiss army knife from his pants.

Naked, and standing next to the bedroom's doorway so he could hear if she came back, he effortlessly got the box open without leaving scratches.

Inside were personal items like rings, pins, and other knick-knacks, and a diary and several letters. The letters were all from John Vickers, with a return address in a town called Perdition in Washington state. "I'll be there in a minute," she said.

"Oh, I'll come on in the kitchen," Grant replied, as he peered through the open slits of the envelopes.

"No, no," she giggled, "I've got a little something to whet your appetite."

"All right, doll." In one of the envelopes was a Polaroid snapshot. It was a grouping of young white men, and a few women, with beer, bats and gloves in their hands. Some of the men were bare chested and everybody else wore white T-shirts. It could have been the John Deere softball team on Main Street, Anytown, U.S.A.

Except some of these All-American youths were Sieg heiling, their right arms outstretched in the nazi salute of yore. Standing next to a dark-haired woman with a ring through her nose was a tall, pasty-faced man. A sardonic smile, a week's growth of stubble, and his shock of snowy hair gave him an eerie, alluring cast. He could have been the model for a new line of men's fragrance, Aryan Winters.

Vickers was coming back and Grant rushed the box back into its drawer. He made like he was coming out of the bathroom as she entered with two cups of coffee. Her robe was open and despite, or because of, his anxiety, Grant found himself being aroused. She put the cups on top of the chiffonier and placed her hands against his body, gently shoving him against the chest of drawers. "Who are you really?" she said, gazing up into his face.

"Who I say I am," he muttered humorously.

"Shit, my late husband was in Korea." She touched one of the bullet wounds on Grant's leg. "You haven't always been a salesman like you say."

"I was in the service, too. But in the European theater in the big one." He could feel his pulse going up, giddy from lust and the fear of being discovered.

"Well, well." She took a sip of coffee and sunk to her knees in front of him. Her eyes bore into his as her head moved back and forth, making loud, boisterous sounds.

Grant exhaled in pleasure and shut his eyes. The death's-head grin of the man with the bone-white face filled his mind.

CHAPTER 17

Clarice watched her child sleeping in a baby swing on the porch of her house. She was sitting on the balustrade, gently rocking the swing with her foot. "You look tired," she said, watching Monk approach the house.

"Thinking too much," he answered, stepping onto the enclosed porch. He leaned against one of the pillars and folded his arms. Her face was still puffy on one side, and there was a discolored sash running diagonally across her cheek. "How you feeling?"

The foot stopped its motion and Clarice turned to look directly at him. "Six in one hand, half a dozen in the other."

"That's a pretty old saying for someone so young," Monk observed.

"My mom always says it." She shrugged. "Seems it's always like that for Black folks, huh? No matter what year it is. Doin' our best just to stay even, and happy when we can manage that."

Monk didn't respond but smiled at Shawndell's inert, calm form. No cares to weigh her down save eating and sleeping and getting attention from her mother. But all too soon the cruel caprice of a world not of her making and not hers to control would intrude forcefully on her existence. It would seek to tear from her the comfort of her family and plant doubt and fear in place of security and love.

Yet fear was okay, good in fact, if you could use it to hone the raw stuff tumbling out of your psyche. Use it to create the engine to plow through the landscape of the hostile environment. But for what goal?

"Is that your girlfriend?"

That made him blink. "Pardon?

"The picture of that Oriental honey in your office," Clarice elaborated.

"Yes," he said with a halting confidence.

Clarice didn't try to hide a sly lift of her mouth.

"What's that supposed to mean?" he prodded her.

"Nothing," she dodged. "So what's happening?"

"I'm going out of town for a while."

"What'd you find out?" she demanded excitedly.

"I'm not sure yet, Clarice. But it may be something."

She was up, standing close to him. "You be careful, all right?" Her hand touched his arm.

"Of course." But he didn't want to be careful. Being careful didn't ensure an even chance for a kid like Clarice or Shawndell. There was too much already in place against them. And clearing it away might take more blood and scorched earth than the sane could stand.

"Thanks, man."

"I haven't done anything yet, Clarice."

"Yes you have." She hugged him and Monk hugged her back.

CHAPTER 18

Three hours after his plane descended into the evening grayness of Portland, Monk had already passed through more seasons than L.A. saw in a year.

After landing, he'd picked up his reserved rental, checked his map, and left through a nasty gloom that was neither fog nor rain that soon gave way to a full bore storm. He got through the Columbia Gorge, the wide river on his left and high-walled cliffs rising and spearing clouds on his right. Rain beat a staccato rhythm on his windshield and the car rocked like a wobbly bassinet. Concentrating to maintain control, he was reminded of times he'd gone up California's Grapevine with the wind whipping off the Tehachapis. But at least then it wasn't raining. Now he had to worry about being blown off the road or sliding across the double-yellow into oncoming cars.

Eventually the green and grey turned imperceptibly into brown rolling hills and a placid blue sky. Past one of the huge dams that plugged the river at various intervals, Monk turned north and crossed the water into Washington State. He left Highway 97 and wound back and forth along switch-backs, got turned around once, and finally came to a tawny plateau. The plain was nearly treeless, the Columbia lost to his vision.

He descended again into another valley as a mist lifted, blowing back into the passes of the Cascades. His car passed acre upon acre of freshly tilled wheat fields. The grain was straw blonde and so evenly cut it was like looking at the top of the head of a submerged Scandinavian giant. Several rows of irrigation sprinklers maintained a steady drum of water.

A sign off to the side of the road read: PERDITION, with POP. 53,968 centered below the name. He sped past, eagerness and trepidation vying for his attention.

He came to an intersection which had a Burger King on one corner and diagonally opposite, a Rexall drug store with green shades in the windows. Overhead, the signal lights swayed lazily, suspended from electric cables where pigeons and crows perched. Monk believed the birds eyed the hood of his car greedily as he took a left and entered the city proper.

The downtown was mostly flat and long, lined with solid three- and four-story brick buildings. The main section ran between two east-west thoroughfares named after the twin summits of American civilization, Commercial and Liberty.

He rolled past several brick buildings the color of dried Tabasco lining Commercial. The air was dry and the sun shone brightly. All the rain coming over from the west side of the mountains was a distant memory.

Presently, he glided to a stop near a restaurant with a large picture window and the name, LONELY MINER, in bold dimensional script stenciled across it. Monk parked on a grade of gravel and got out of the car, stretching. Off to one side were several big rig trucks resting like sleeping mastodons.

Two white men, dressed in heavy coats and high boots,

stepped out of the restaurant. The duo walked toward a mud-caked Ford Ranger, an occupied rifle rack visible through the vehicle's rear window. The one getting behind the wheel looked at Monk, grinned and said something to his companion. They both laughed. Monk figured the twitch in his stomach was because he was edgy after his drive. He opened the door to the diner.

Inside was a buzz of plates being bused and the unmistakable din of lunchtime eaters. At the counter men wolfed down their food. Waitresses served families sitting at the tables. Monk sat at the counter next to a long-haired man wearing a T-shirt with Kurt Cobain's face on it. Beneath the dead King of Grunge's image were the words: GONE TO A BETTER SHOW. The trucker gave him a casual glance and continued devouring his Porterhouse steak and eggs.

One of the waitresses, a heavy but handsome Latina with a streak of alabaster white in her very black hair, came over and placed a cup before him. She was dressed in a faded pair of Levi's, a cotton work shirt and construction boots.

"Regular or decaf?" she asked, opening the menu flat on the counter for him to see. "You look like you haven't had your first cup."

"You got that right," he said, perusing his choices. "Make it regular, and could I have the half chicken, rice with gravy. And the soup?"

"It's split pea, pardner."

"Righteous."

She retrieved his preference and poured him a measure. "You in town to fish or hunt?"

"Neither," he said after taking a gulp. "I work for a software company and I'm scouting possible locations. We may open a service branch and interactive division in this area."

"Yeah, there's a lot of that on the other side of the mountains, but it hasn't seeped this way yet." She scrapped off some excess food into a plastic tray below the counter.

"I heard a dude in Portland say the other day their plan is to kick butt when it comes to all that Pacific Rim business. San Francisco and Seattle, look out," the trucker in the rock star's shirt contributed.

Monk raised the cup to his mouth. "Like I said, I'm just up here looking around for now." In a few minutes, his order came and he and the trucker exchanged a few tidbits of conversation that veered from computers to monster truck and tractor racing. Which his breakfast companion competed in back home in Nevada.

"How is it you picked an out-of-the-way place like Perdition to check out?" the waitress asked him, clearing away the empty plates.

"The lure of cheap land primarily," Monk said.

She rubbed the tip of her tongue briefly over her bottom lip and turned to look at the other patrons in the place. She looked back at Monk, a tightness tugging the sides of her mouth down. "Well," she said in a rushed tone, "get a good look around, pardner."

Monk asked, "Where would you recommend I get a room for a couple of days?" He kept his gaze on her. "You know, someplace where I can be comfortable."

She knew what he meant. "Oray's rooming house over on Hollis at Third."

"A boarding house, really?" he exclaimed, "complete with Aunt Bee and Gomer?"

"Pardner," she replied, resting her arm on the counter, "Juanita don't believe in three-dollar titles like Bed and Breakfast, okay? She runs a place her husband and she bought when Sly and the Family Stone were number one.

And it's a for-damn-sure rooming house." She picked up her tip and went back into the kitchen.

He left and drove around the town. According to the guide book, the city was founded in the early 1880s around wheat and timber concerns. It got its name from a wooden-legged, one-eyed, three-fingered miner named Weljkava who'd immigrated from Sweden, or Poland depending on which version of the story you heard.

He'd come to the new country to make his fortune and bought into a sawmill after finding some gold in Idaho. But his bad luck had followed him and he got his chest crushed in an accident at the mill. Dying, the man was reported to mutter "damn this perdition of my life," and the name stuck.

During the thirties, FDR's New Deal brought in planned irrigation and cheap electricity and the town diversified its economic base by raising barley, corn soybeans, alfalfa, and other such plantings that could subsist in the semi-arid region. It was also then—and he got this information from other sources—that Ira Elihu became the patriarch of the town.

Elihu was a self-styled magnate who in reality was a junior-league Rockefeller. He'd made money in the east hauling coal and aggregate (and booze in the bottom of some of those trucks). But lost a good chunk due to an avaricious appetite for flappers and the crash of the stock market. Scraping together what he could, Elihu made his way west, went bust in San Francisco, and came north, winding up in Perdition.

Unlike Weljkava, Elihu realized some measure of his dream. He did arrive in Perdition at the right time. The Roosevelt Administration had introduced massive building projects, forest regeneration, and spurred the construction of hydroelectric dams that dwarfed the pyramids. Elihu made his money not from the soil, but from what was under it—stone, gravel and sand—-the basic materials for the dams and highways that the federal government built to put the unemployed to work. Elihu became a baron of the Northwest, with views as rigid as the rock he loved.

By the time of his death in 1957 at the age of eighty-eight, Ira Elihu had the pleasure of testifying before the House UnAmerican Activities Committee that he was working double time to rid his businesses of red provocateurs. In other words: union sympathizers, uppity Blacks, back-talking Mexicans, and women who wouldn't wear skirts in his canning factory. He'd also managed to get the biggest park in town re-named after him.

Monk wound past Elihu's bronze statue. If it was true to its model, Perdition's patriarch had been a tall, stout man with lamb chop sideburns and overgrown knotty hands. The eyes were deep set and, even in metal relief, relayed a predator's ruthless nature.

A knot of white youths, male and female and some in skinhead attire, walked diagonally through the park's playground with purpose.

Monk slowed the car and waited. They passed out flyers to the three or four older white people sitting in the park and stapled several of them to a few telephone poles.

They began to walk in the direction where Monk had stopped and he got out of the car. His .45 was in a bag in the trunk but he wasn't about to get caught slipping as a troop of neo-nazis strolled by. Hostile eyes glared at him and one of them did an exaggerated version of a "pimp walk," if such a thing were possible. They laughed and sauntered past, handing out their broadsheets as they went.

Monk read one of the flyers. In a black and red motif, the message announced that Bobby Bright would be holding a rally for ARM in conjunction with the local War Reich in Perdition on the coming Saturday. A picture of the supremacist leader dominated the thing. Adopting a fire and brimstone preacher pose, he was at a podium, gesticulating and shouting to an unseen audience. Today was Tuesday.

He snatched the flyer down and folded it up. Turning, Monk watched a green and white Perdition P.D. patrol car ease up behind his rental.

A uniform, thick but solid in the middle with legs like iron cylinders, got out of the cruiser. He wrote down the rental company's name from the sticker on the rear bumper, and looked into the car. He straightened as Monk got close. "This your vehicle?"

"Yes, you can see I rented it."

"May I see the papers?"

"They're in the glove compartment."

The cop—his name tag read Anderson—centered his pale blues on Monk's hands as if they were going to leave his body and find a knife or pick a pocket. Then he shifted them in his unblinking face. "Get them, will you?" He moved his heavy body around to the passenger side, the strap still on the holster.

Monk got in the car and reached across to the glove box, the cop watching him too casually. He got the contract out and came out of the car.

He handed the folded NCR paper to the cop.

"What brings you to Perdition, Mr. Monk?"

He gave him the same story he told in the restaurant.

Anderson handed the stuff back to Monk.

"So you might be bringing some business here, huh."

"Could be."

Those unfathomable blues gave away nothing, then he

tossed off a "Be seeing you" and got back in his cruiser, driving away.

Monk started his car and headed for Oray's room and board, unclear of how to interpret his encounter.

Juanita Oray's place was a three-story nondescript wood frame house. Its saving grace was an enclosed porch that fronted it on two sides. The roof was peaked, the trim was chipped, and a tan boxer slept on the front lawn as Monk approached along the walkway.

The dog raised a lumpy head and looked at him disinterestedly. Monk found himself in a narrow foyer from which a front parlor extended on the right. An elderly Asian man in a lumberjack coat—Monk guessed him to be Chinese—was watching a soap opera on the TV. The furniture was neat, and like the house, of no particular style or era.

"May I help you?" a voice said. The owner was a lean older Black woman, of above average height, in a gray dress with matching gray hair which was pulled back from an unblemished forehead. She held a pencil in one hand and idly pointed it in Monk's direction.

"Yes, ma'am, I'd like to rent a room for about a week or so. I'd be happy to pay in advance."

"So would I." She came toward him, extending her hand. "I'm Juanita Gray, and I suppose you know this is my rooming house."

Monk introduced himself and gave her his cover story.

She seemed to be assessing the information as she bobbed the pencil's eraser up and down on the end of her thumb. "Well, Mr. Monk, Perdition is made up of many a good hard working folk. But you know, like in the big city, it's got its ups and downs."

"I understand some of the Elihu's are still around," he said conversationally.

"Yes, so?"

"They still have juice like the gent they made the statue for in the park?"

She crinkled a brow. "Why's that important to know?"

He folded his arms. "Don't you find it interesting that people with the ability to live anywhere would still stay in Perdition?"

Nonplused, she retorted, "We got 'lectricity in just last winter."

Embarrassed, Monk tried to make up ground. "I guess everybody doesn't have a fever to live in smog, crime and the bright lights of Hollywood."

"Uh-huh." She waved a hand at the dining room table in the part of the house to the left of the foyer. "Would you like some tea or juice?" There was nothing on the table, but beyond it was a swing door to the kitchen.

"Thank you, but I'll just go get my stuff then pay you."

She was already heading for the kitchen door. "That's fine."

Monk wheeled about as a young man strode through the front door. He was taller than Monk and more than a decade his junior. The younger man was a light-skinned African American and wore a black leather jacket, a mudcloth motif shirt, and jeans tattered at the knees. His hair was closely shaved to his squarish head, but there was a single braided strand in the back that extended further than the jacket's collar. An ankh earring dangled from one ear. The dog had followed him inside, suddenly energetic.

"Look at this, Mom." The young man shoved a piece of paper at the older woman. The dog sat on his foot and sneezed.

Juanita Oray opened the paper as if it were a pirate's treasure map, one hand grasping the top, the other pulling it from the bottom. "Shit," she said softly upon reading the contents. She lifted her head. "You gotta be cool about this, Orin."

For the first time, the son acknowledged Monk's presence by raising an eyebrow in his direction. "On your way to Spokane, mister?"

"I meant to come here."

Orin bent and scratched the dog under its chin and said to his mother, "What are we supposed to do? Wait and see if the mighty white Sheriff Hamm and his do-nothing men do their duty?"

"You can't stop them from having a rally." Forlornly, Juanita Oray stared at the paper again.

"Sure we can," Orin countered, rising. "As far as I'm concerned, Bright and those bastards ain't got no rights of free speech or assembly."

"Orin," she warned in the universal tone of scolding mothers.

"You sticking around for the carnival, man?" Orin gently took the paper from his mother's hand and passed it over to Monk.

"I saw them putting some up in the town park." He took the paper and placed it on the dining room table.

"Where you from?" Orin tried to ask casually.

"That's none of your business. You ain't running this rooming house." His mother put a hand on her side.

A mood shift seized the lanky youngster and he leaned over and kissed his mother on the cheek. "I'm going over to Dudley's for some grub."

"You ain't fooling no one with that act."

"I'm just hungry, Mom."

All playfulness left her voice as she spoke. "Look, Orin, I agree we need to stand up to people like Bright, but that don't mean we use their means."

"That loving your enemy stuff went out with liberals and midnight basketball." He chucked the dog on the head and the animal followed him as he walked out into the sun.

The man in the easy lounger hadn't stirred, absorbed in his program. Monk fingered the flyer, a duplicate of the one in his back pocket. "Has Bright been in Perdition long?"

"Lately, off and on for about a year now." She adjusted a sampler in a round walnut frame, her face hidden from his vision. "I grew up here, Mr. Monk. My folks came from Oklahoma in the forties to work the Kaiser shipyards down in Portland." She moved toward the swing door again.

"They lived in wartime housing in the Vanport projects." She stopped, one hand on the glass rectangle of the swing door. Her body leaned forward, as if deciding to step through the portal and somehow close off the past. She didn't move through it.

"After the war," she began, "the fathers of Portland hemmed and hawed as to what to do with all these Black workers and returning soldiers. People organized and demanded that the city Housing Authority make the Vanport Projects permanent. See the city had always resisted creating a viable expansion plan. But now with all these people, they didn't have much choice." She decided to sit in one of the cabriolet chairs at the large drop leaf table.

"Edgar Kaiser put his two bits in and brought out Robert Moses."

"*The* Robert Moses, the man who designed modern New York?" Monk asked.

"One and the same. He may have been the cat's pajamas of urban renewal back east, but folks out here criticized his plan for ignoring landmarks and old neighborhoods. Anyway, the council adopted his plan. But rebuilding didn't happen soon enough and come the Winter of'48, a dike near

Vanport gave way and washed out the shoddy projects. Displaced, my folks moved on and settled here, which was a booming city at the time."

Monk sat down also. "Was Perdition very prejudiced?"

"Not so bad. All kinds of people migrated here. It wasn't Disneyland, but it wasn't a Selma either. The town has some rough spots, especially after the timber started to run thin by the early '80s. Added to that, most of the farms have been bought up by big agribusiness concerns.

"Plus there's always been a strong fundamentalist current around here, and they kind of got their hindquarters up as the recession hit. And what with all the rising supremacist movement not too far away in Idaho, they found fertile ground for raising a new crop of haters."

Monk leaned back, taking mental notes. "So a local ARM gets started."

"Yes. But there was already skinheads. Both kinds."

"Your son Orin?"

She smiled ruefully. "Rameses as he prefers to be called among his posse."

"You tell all your guests this fascinating history?"

"I figured you ought to know. What with you being who you are and scouting for a company that could help turn this town around. It seems to me you should know what you're getting into."

Guilt made Monk involuntarily shift his eyes to the floor then back up. "I don't have the last word in the matter."

She was already up and moving. "It seems nobody Black in this country ever does."

He paid, settled in, and took a stroll around the town. He'd expected a pronounced demarcation between the racial sections of Perdition. Instead, the northern area he was in seemed older, modest in its dwellings, but mixed in its racial makeup, with whites, some Blacks, a healthy number of Latinos and a handful of Asians, if he could judge by the kids he passed wandering home from school. Closing into the downtown, he noticed some interracial couples about, several of them sporting the modified gangster style favored among the young and hip-hop.

At the southern end, the homes got larger, the lawns more spacious. He saw fewer faces of color about. The houses were built in the post-Victorian/San Francisco style, with an occasional brick-and-wood Plantation number. In the driveways, Monk observed C4 and Cabrera Porsches and 540i Beemers laced among the Marquis station wagons and even a red Jeep or two. The Jeeps caught his attention and he noted the addresses where they were parked.

He came to a house with a jockey implanted in its trim, sloping greenery. Though it had been painted over in an off-pink, some of the paint had chipped away. Flecks of dark umber, like a runaway skin disease, mottled the jockey's immobile countenance. One of the arms was outstretched but the ring that normally would have been on the end was missing. Monk wondered if the owners of the house had put the ring in the nose of a larger statue.

"Can I help you?"

He'd heard the car approach and turned his head slightly to address the deputy sitting behind the wheel. "Just enjoying the sights," he said tersely.

"You the one work for some kind of computer company?" He was already getting out of the car. It wasn't Anderson, the deputy who'd stopped him earlier. This one was shorter and wore two-toned aviator glasses. Oates was the name on his tag. He had the deceptive build of a wrestler and an affable smile was affixed to his pleasant face. "I don't mean to put you out or anything, but you being a stranger, well you just naturally stick out is all."

"Perdition isn't that small," Monk observed.

"We're just trying to be vigilant. We hear there's going to be quite a few outsiders coming to town."

"Because of the white supremacists' rally."

Oates nodded. "Don't judge this place 'cause of some kooks."

Monk didn't reply.

"Well, thanks for your time, Mr. Monk." He adjusted the hat on his head and climbed back into the cruiser. "If you have a notion I'd suggest getting over to Jenson Lake. Its been stocked recently with some Rainbow trout."

"Thanks," Monk replied.

"You bet." The car eased away.

Monk pursed his lips and continued his appraisal of the town, eventually meandering back along Hollis, the main drag in the northern end of Perdition, where the neighborhood people did their business. There was a funeral home with an overhanging roof supported by plaster Grecian columns; a restaurant called Dudley's Shack, Fine Eating a Specialty; a hardware store; a quick print establishment, a beauty parlor, and an engine rebuilding shop. Added to the mix were a bodega and a carne asada especials stand by the name of Lizardo.

But the hub of activity as the sun went down was a place called Velotis Records. It wasn't right on Hollis, but down a side alley. The record shop had a blue awning perpendicular over the entrance so that as you walked past, you could see the name in script on the side of the fabric. What drew Monk to it was spotting Juanita Oray's son standing under the awning, vigorously talking with some others.

In age and manner, they seemed to be the doppelgangers

of the crew that Malik Bradford had assembled in Pacific Shores. But this group included a number of whites and women. Some were dressed in the baggy pants look while a couple of them held to a more Rasta-like aesthetic of dreads and untrimmed beards.

One of the women, a chunky muscular white woman wearing a straining white T-shirt and leather waist jacket, had her blonde hair frizzed out with tangerine-colored tips.

Monk came up to the shop's entrance in time to catch one of the gathered vigorously jabbing a finger at Rameses.

"... When Bright gets here, I say we fuck him up. Fuck his shit up for good."

Rameses cold-eyed the kid with his baby browns and a cloister-like silence descended on the group. He remained rigid, staring straight ahead as Monk, tipping his head to the younger man, made to enter the record shop. Several of the troop were bunched in the doorway, but they parted to let him in. The door was shut on his back, and the group departed.

Several patrons browsed along the isles of the store whose inventory included the usual pop and R&B fare on tape and CD, plus a healthy collection of vinyl. In several back bins were 78s persevering in their original cardboard protectors.

Monk got wondrously lost reading through such titles as Ivory Joe Hunter on the Pacific label; Nat King Cole with Bill May and his orchestra on Capitol; and the Mills Brothers on Decca doing "You Always Hurt the One you Love."

He wanted to believe these were the ancient sounds, the calls from an uncomplicated era. It would be nice if it had been, but it was also a time of lynchings and Jim Crow. But those days were gone, right? Yeah, that's why America voted the right-wingers into office across the country. Cut them lazy bastards off welfare and give their kids to orphanages to raise 'em up right. Turn out even more Black and Brown men prepared for prison than college. Everything was just swell in the New World Darwinian Order.

Then Jimmy Henderson's respirator, rising and falling in ominous heaves, intruded on him. Maybe life was meant to be one big wheel for Black folks. A never-ending cycle of hate and fear and doubt that they pushed around and around.

Monk caught himself holding onto a brittle platter, his hands shaking, threatening to splinter the disc into countless pieces. After some effort, he focused and got back to browsing.

He found an Erskine Hawkins he'd been looking for and paid at the counter. The proprietress behind it was heavyset, of uncertain age. Her coloring was a lustrous mahogany. She chomped on an unlit thin cigar in a holder with a gold band on the end of it. The woman looked vaguely familiar to Monk, and as he made to leave, it came to him.

"You're Lonetta Thomas."

What might have been a reaction made the holder in her mouth twitch. She spoke around it, "You don't miss much, huh?"

The voice surprised him. It was like listening to a whisper in an echo chamber.

"Throat cancer, took out one of my vocal chords," she said, used to the look he gave her. "Can't be much of a singer without your pipes."

"I'm sorry," was all Monk could say.

"It's cool. Ain't nothing but life, baby. You the cat that's been looking over our town."

"Yeah, we might be setting up our interactive division here."

"You gonna bring all them kill-the-aliens computer CDs with you, ain't you?"

Monk had to laugh. “We’re not going to open up retail, Ms. Thomas. Anybody who’s got ‘Blue Yodel’ by Jimmy Rodgers on vocals and guitar, I’d stand in the doorway if the wrecker comes.”

That got her going and they exchanged a few asides on jazz and blues artists. Monk, pretending he was ready to go, asked as casually as he could. “You think there’s going to be trouble at Bobby Bright’s rally?”

She sucked in an audible amount of air. “I don’t know, mister. One way I say fine, let him have his say and the devil take the sonofabitch. But honestly, I wouldn’t mind somebody sending him and some of his kind to hell a little quicker.”

“Like Rameses and his merry bunch?”

“Worried about the business climate?” she said in her oddly compelling sotto.

“Something like that. You know I’m not just the token blood in the firm.”

She leaned her large frame across the counter, a glass top with a patchwork of business cards trapped beneath it. “Bright ain’t as big as he thinks he is. He ain’t the peckerwood’s answer to Malcolm X.”

“Malcolm broadened his agenda.”

“Well, Bobby hasn’t, and that ain’t changed since the days he was a punk around here in high school.”

Monk was about to pursue that interesting information when one of the browsers, tired of waiting, came over. She got her opening and let fly with questions about hard-to-find numbers. Monk left and walked back to Juanita’s rooming house.

The front parlor was empty but the TV was still on. At the other end of the hall was a small phone alcove with a built-in desk and overhead light. He picked up the handset and dialed

Jill's number. He hung up before completing it, and looked at the phone as if it were an alien device sent on a mission to betray him.

He wanted a drink and his woman. He'd get the first wish in a bar he'd passed on his way back. But booze would hold no answers for where he and Jill were heading. Instead, he went up to his room and lay on the bed with his clothes and shoes on. From outside, he could feel the low rumble of eighteen-wheelers as they made their way along the interstate.

CHAPTER 19

The following day Monk ate a big breakfast at Dudley's Shack. The topic of conversation was, naturally, Bobby Bright and his return to town.

"I ought to take this here leg bone and choke that redneck to death," an elderly gent in thick lenses proclaimed, sitting at a table of his peers.

"That wouldn't stop them young lions from stretchin' your sorry wrinkled ass from one tree to the next," a compatriot unkindly replied.

"Sheeit," the first man responded, "I got my cold blue Colt .44 says I'll bury some of them goose-steppers 'fore they can say 'I love you, Hitler.'"

The old fellows broke up at that one and went on to another topic.

Monk finished his stack of wheat cakes and went back to Velotis Records. He hoped but hadn't expected to catch Lonetta Thomas in this early. He returned to his room, unpacked his gun and checked it. It was an unnecessary act since he'd done that before leaving L.A., and it was unlikely it would've been touched since arriving in the Northwest. He sat on the bed, idly gazing out the window, the .45 slack in his hand.

He felt odd, like he was operating on unprocessed mental energy. All his nerves seemed to be right on the surface and it bothered him that he wasn't as detached as he liked to be on a job. He looked at the automatic and frowned at it.

On Saturday, Monk fantasized, he could stand on the periphery of the crowd gathered to hear Bright lather and foam. The supremacist leader would be going on about the mud slide and his plans for dealing with it.

Suddenly a pistol shot would disturb the air, then another, and another. In the confusion, Bright's bodyguards would try to get him to a waiting car. And that's where he'd do him, having created the diversion. Sure they'd arrest him, hell maybe the crowd would string him up on the spot.

Big deal. He'd go down in the history books, at least the real ones, as a hero of the class and race struggle. A determined brother who just wouldn't take no shit from this self-styled savior of the white race. Somebody laughed but it didn't sound like anybody he knew. Damn. Come on, Monk, check yourself before you wreck yourself. You got a killer to catch. He placed the weapon back in his suitcase, and slid the whole thing under the bed.

He washed his face with cold water for a long time and reentered Perdition's dry air. He staked out the two places where he'd run across red Jeeps. Nothing came of that and then he went to two used car lots on the off chance the killer may have traded his vehicle in for another.

The killer could have just as easily done that on the road back, but Monk doubted it. The dead-faced man would have been listening to the news which made much of the police theory that the Shores slayer was a California product.

But once back on his home turf, would he have ditched the vehicle? Monk concluded the killer wouldn't. It was his badge of honor among his kind, a roving trophy in the gallery of hate crimes.

Monk brought the car to rest near Elihu Park and got out. A matronly woman on a stroll, wearing a string of discolored pearls, glared at Monk like he was the exterminator and he hadn't gotten rid of her bug problem.

It didn't take him too long to find what he was looking for. It was in a rehabbed brick building two doors down from one of those instant lube places. The company's logo, on the roof over the service bay, was a plastic statue of a puffy mechanic in crisp overalls brandishing a gleaming grease gun, suggesting a certain kind of military precision when you brought your car in for work. The street was a few blocks northeast of the park in the beginning of what remained of Perdition's industrial zone.

War Reich's corner office didn't have a neon sign in the window flashing "We Hate Minorities," but it wasn't too hard to miss. Out in front was a rack containing several pieces of their doggerel including a recent copy of their newsletter. Monk helped himself to several samples and tried the door, but it was locked. He went around back and came upon four men in their twenties and a disemboweled '68 Camaro. A bumper sticker plastered on the back end of the trunk read: "The Original Boys in the Hood." The car's block was suspended from a hoist. One of the skins was leaning into the cavity where the engine went, working diligently.

A portable radio perched on a stepladder played a number by Bound for Glory, a skinhead rock band. One of the youths, with a bulging gut poking out of a sweat shirt too little for him, was drinking a beer. He immediately halted at the sight of Monk. Like in a cartoon, the can was frozen inches from his shocked face.

"You stopped by to sign up, darkie?" a lanky skin joked.

"No. But I was wondering if your mama was still giving out blowjobs in the back of the drive-in."

Skinny came at Monk with a heavy duty screwdriver thrust forward like a knife. Executing a move his martial-arts-trained friend Seguin had taught him, he deflected the screwdriver and hurled the man over a leg onto the ground. Casually, he kicked the man in the face as he tried to right himself.

The beer-bellied one had started toward Monk, but he was already moving in on him. The private eye got his arms around the heavier man's legs and drove him back into the fender of the Camaro. He couldn't see them, but Monk knew the other two must be working their way closer, and he wanted to get untangled from beer belly.

A fist crashed down in a spot between his shoulder blades but he was already turning and ramming his head up and into the underside of the thin one's jaw. It clapped together loudly, and Monk moved his body to the left, rotating back around and straightening up.

The one who'd been working on the car, a tallow-haired youth, brandished a long-handled socket wrench. "You best take your monkey ass out of here."

The fourth one, about twenty-two or -three with a shaved scalp and a pigtail down the back, stood off, examining the scene. Scared or just strategic?

Monk cranked it up several notches. "Why? Four against one not good enough odds for you inbred motherfuckahs? How about ten against an eight-year-old in a wheelchair?"

The heavy one again lurched forward and Monk buried a straight left into the intersection of his sternum and stomach. The younger man exhaled a gust of bad breath and sank to his knees. Monk did a roundhouse kick, connecting the side of his shoe to the side of the man's face. He went over like a busted retaining wall.

Nothing happened for several moments, time stretching and nerves compressing. A pressure was building up behind Monk's eye and he wondered if his brain were about to liquify and pour through his nose. It seemed to remain like that for a season as everyone stood immobile like trees.

A bronze two-toned four-door Lincoln Town Car came into view and pulled to a stop on the oil-stained dirt near the Camaro. A man who'd have a hard time fitting into one of Elrod's coats excavated himself from the driver's seat. He wore a short-sleeved shirt to better showcase his corded arms which were slathered in tattoos. A vermilion swastika stood out like a fresh wound on the back of one of his massive hands.

The door on the passenger side opened and another man, this one in more human proportions, also got out. He was a well-preserved individual in his late fifties, dressed in a crisp brown pin-striped suit and burgundy shirt. His face was partially obscured by huge wraparound shades. The Lincoln's back door opened and Bobby Bright stepped out. His attire was casual in worn Levi's, work boots and a multi-colored cotton shirt with the sleeves rolled up. A grain salesman making a stop on his route.

"Gentlemen," Bright said, taking in the scene. "Is there something we can help out with here?"

The massive driver moved closer to Monk, smiling with pleasure. The sensation behind his eye seemed to be spreading across the inside of his face, creating a subterranean mask whose features were a distortion of the outer shell. He had a notion to find out how hard the giant could hit, but managed enough control to remain still.

"I don't think that will be necessary, Garth." Bright spoke

with his hands clasped before him like a country preacher. "I'm sure this . . . person has finished his fun for today." The capped teeth in his head were evenly spaced and gleamed like an ad for fluoride.

Reason flooded back into Monk and he was suddenly aware of his vulnerability. How stupid it was to push things with these racists. And now it was the head supremacist who was giving him his out. Probably worried if they killed him somebody from the shop next door might see them. Or maybe not. Maybe Bright figured Monk not worth the effort. He had more important trains to run on schedule.

He almost didn't want to take it but turned and went back the way he'd come, memorizing the license number of the Lincoln. Presently, he found himself at Velotis Records.

"Hi," Lonetta Thomas greeted him. She was busy cataloging a stack of 45s in the computer.

"Hello yourself. Mind if I ask you a few more questions about Perdition?" There was a smattering of people in the shop. An olive-skinned teenaged girl with long braids worked the register.

"You're a thorough cat. You remind me of my second husband. He was my manager."

"I'm not sure how to take that."

She laughed heartily. "That's okay, he didn't either." She motioned for Monk to follow her into a office behind the counter. It contained a small desk, three padded chairs and a sparsely stocked bookcase leaning to one side. Along the walls were photographs depicting Thomas in numerous venues over the years. These were interspersed with several gold records.

"This was at the Hollywood Bowl, wasn't it?" Monk pointed at one of the shots showing a younger, slimmer Thomas on stage in front of Count Basie's band. Basie, in an open-collared suit with his omnipresent yachting cap, vigorously worked the piano's keys.

"Yep. That's got to be about twenty-five years ago." She came over and looked at the photo. "The Count, Carmen, Dinah, Little Esther, Prez, Dexter with his junkie-lidded eyes and flat crown brims, that crazy lizard-brained Miles . . ." She shook her head to ward off the tears. "All gone," she said mournfully.

"But they left something behind."

"You couldn't have been out of high school then, baby," she said, referring to the photo. Thomas tapped him playfully on the shoulder and went to sit down behind her desk. From somewhere she brought out her thin cigar and holder and inserted it in a side of her mouth. She made no effort to light it.

Monk also sat down. "You said Beckworth grew up here."

"Who? Oh, I'd forgotten that was his real name. Way I hear it from the old timers, Derek Beckworth was an average kid who played some football and ran track."

"How'd you wind up in this place?"

"After I was diagnosed with the cancer, I knew if I lived, my singing days were over. Unlike many of my peers, I wasn't ripped off by managers and record companies. Well, I was in the beginning, but we got that shit straight."

Monk nodded appreciatively.

"I was living in Oakland and got tired of all the wonderful life Cokeland had to offer. Christ. I'm sounding like Bright, ain't I? Anyway, my third husband passed, the kids had moved out, and then I heard about this store coming on the block."

"Who owned it before?"

"Kid Charlemagne, 'member him?" One side of her face raised, waiting.

Monk had to plow through some rusty doors in his mind but finally found a face to go with the name. "Yeah. Played bass with the King Cole trio for awhile, then was in Eckstine's band for a good stretch."

"Uh-huh. Seems he grew up in Portland when there was hardly no Black folks 'round here. He came back up this way to retire from the road, and because he never did like all that rain over there, he bought what used to be an electrical fixture outlet store and made the space into a record shop with classic jazz a specialty. Only he had a second of his three strokes, and his daughter got in contact with me."

Monk concentrated on a photo behind and to the left of Thomas' head. It was a rapier cut of a man draped in a light-colored zoot suit whose coattail was nearly the length of his long legs. He was wearing an incredibly broad hat and seductively hugged an upright bass as if it were a woman he'd been lusting after. Kid Charlemagne in his ascendancy.

"And what have you heard about Bright's early days?"

"Juanita is the one that knows. She used to take care of their house."

"Really."

The ex-singer idly fingered through a short stack of papers.

"Yeah, she was the housekeeper when young master Bright was lettering at Whitman High." An odd contortion pushed at her lips then her face settled back into its normal ironic cast. "You hanging around till Saturday?"

"Is this the first time ARM and the War Reich have had a rally here?"

"They tried to pull one off last year, but the NAACP, the ACLU and the Socialist Workers, or whatever they call themselves, had enough warning and brought people into town from Portland and Seattle. The skins were outnumbered ten to one."

"Why is this time different?"

"Bright and his allies. Namely that Christian fascist preacher who runs the church near Hell's Canyon. The one that says the Holocaust never happened?"

"Elmore Creed," Monk amended.

"Right. Well, this time they hired a part-time organizer to whip up the troops and kept changing the date to throw people off. Plus the fact our Sheriff Hamm is either too incompetent or too much of a sympathizer to try and ride herd on these wild-assed white boys."

Monk got up. "Thanks for your time, Lonetta."

"Sure, Mr. Ivan Monk." That odd look returned but she quickly dismissed it. "Stop back in 'fore you split, okay?"

"I promise." They shook hands and Monk found a phone booth a few blocks from her shop. He placed two long distance calls using his phone card and talked for several minutes each time. He finished and went back to the rooming house. Juanita Gray wasn't around but Mr. Khan, the elderly Asian gentleman, was in his usual spot. He waved and Monk waved, and Mr. Khan went back to the *Ricki Lake Show*.

Using the phone book, Monk found the names and addresses for the two high schools in Perdition, Whitman and Rainier. Whitman was only a few blocks away, while Rainier, if he had his geography right, was south of downtown.

It took a little doing, but Monk convinced the gate keeper at Whitman High that Intertek merely wanted to make sure the school was up to snuff. If they did build a facility, some of the management team would relocate also. The sentinel, a woman with reddish blonde hair and a squared-up body like a bookie's, judiciously reviewed Monk's card.

She dialed the number on it and Delilah, as rehearsed, answered. The woman in the school office drilled her. Monk formed the opinion that her main worry centered around how many children of Intertek employees smoked marijuana and listened to gangsta rap or heavy metal. Having satisfied her queries she enthused at Monk as she replaced the handset. "I'll get you the last few years of the state's test scores for our kids."

"Thanks. I'll wander over to the library to look around a bit and be back."

"Fine."

In the library he found copies of Richard Wright's *American Hunger* and Orwell's *Animal Farm*. It comforted him to know the place wasn't too backwards. He then found the true object of his search, the old yearbooks. As he had done over at Rainier, he worked back from Bright's age, and this time located the right volume. Figures, the dude had gone to the more mixed school. Course in those days, Whitman was probably going through a transition. The better to form his theories, Monk mused sarcastically.

Though he wasn't sure what he was going to divine, Monk stared at the black-and-white picture of senior Derek Beckworth with a cocky smile and a cowlick. Huck Finn by way of Lincoln Rockwell.

Paging through the book, he found a grainy shot of Bright tearing up yardage on the gridiron. There was even one of him and a Black kid, fellow shotputters standing side by side proudly holding up their trophies. He went back through Beckworth's earlier years but found no photo of him at an I-like-Joe-Goebbels youth rally or kicking stray dogs.

"Mr. Monk, I have your copies."

The helpful woman from the office stood over him as he

sat at the table "Nice crop of students you turn out here," he remarked, plainfaced. He closed the book.

The woman placed a sealed 9x12 envelope on the table. She tried to be sly, but made no effort to hide the curiosity on her face.

"Thanks for your help, ma'am." He made no motion to rise.

She glanced at her watch. "There's going to be a class here in a few minutes." For support, she shifted her head toward the librarian, a bear of a man wearing half-glasses quietly reading behind the front counter. If he heard her, he didn't let on.

"I'll just be a little longer."

A beat. A piercing look. Another beat. Then. "Very well." She lingered and Monk opened the book again, casually leafing through it. He heard her huff and puff away.

He quickly paged through more recent yearbooks, looking for photos of the all-white shooter, but none caught his eye. When his time was up, he left, went back to the rooming house, and got the photo Dexter had filched for him of the skinhead baseball team. He trudged back to Rainier, mad that he hadn't thought about checking for the gunner in those yearbooks.

The younger librarian at Rainier waved at him as he strolled over to the yearbook section. Once again, he took out the now-wrinkled photo. The white-faced man, when you looked closer, couldn't be more than twenty-four, twenty-six at the outside. On his second try, Monk opened the right yearbook. He'd been a point guard on the basketball team and a member of the chess and the junior Kiwanis clubs. The picture was of a taciturn young man whose hair was already showing its premature streaks. The name under the kid with the tapered square jaw was Nolan Meyer.

Monk looked back through Meyer's previous yearbooks but, as with Bright, he could find no indication that Rainier High was a hatchery for white supremacists. But he did discover that Rameses had been a sophomore in Meyer's senior year.

He quit the school, found another phone booth, and wrote down the three Meyers listed in it. Consulting his map, he located the addresses and marked them. Next stop was city hall, a substantial edifice the color of soap stone on Liberty. The mayor, he learned, was to be found in his other office.

"Howdy. I heard you've been looking our town over."

Mayor Carter Ash was a loose-limbed individual displaying a gap-toothed grin, his number twelve dogs stuffed into pointed desert boots. The curved dimensional type in his office window announced the mayor's full-time profession as Ash Concrete Coring. The letters' outlines cast oblique shadows across the yellow pine desk and the ruddy hue of the Mexican tile.

"I needed to look up some land records. Where would I find those?" Monk asked, shaking hands with the mayor. He knew where they were, but wanted to ingratiate himself with the man, maybe learn a little more about Bright.

"Well sure, that's . . ."

The mayor and Monk were simultaneously diverted by a disturbance from outside on Commercial. Some skins and some of Rameses' crew were mixing it up; shoving, pointing fingers, exchanging heated words. Rameses, and the one with the spiked hair, were in the midst of it. The back and forth business escalated and a couple of the skins produced bats and pipes.

Monk was already out the door. But there was no need to rush, most of the skins and Rameses crew weren't bloodletting, just brandishing. It was a dance of nerve and posturing between warring tribes, a ritual played out on streets from Belfast to the Gaza Strip.

Only a War Reich member, the one with the jiggling gut who he'd sparred with earlier, was upping the tempo and rushing the big woman's blind side, raising a tire iron for a home run. Happy that his aging legs still had the physical memory of his college football days, Monk the former linebacker yanked the young woman away just as the space where her head had been was invaded violently.

Blondie, taller than her assailant, stamped down on his foot in her heavy Doc Marten. Pivoting her body, she checked his follow-through blow and her hand dipped forward and across. Then Monk understood. The foot had been to hold her attacker in place. The skin doubled over, swearing and holding his face as fluid leaked from between his clutching hands.

"Thanks, cutie." She winked, one of those four-finger brass knuckle type rings favored by rap artists stradling her fist. The nameplate on the thing read: LOVE.

The yelling and pumping of fists in the air went on for a few more minutes until the clans separated, each vowing to kick the other's ass next time.

"I'm Katya." Her hand, the nameplate tucked inside her leather jacket, was out and she was breathing through her mouth.

Monk shook it and told her his name. The spiked-haired woman, a punked-out Valkyrie, had a rush in her eyes, and Monk started to get self-conscious and sick. Sex and violence were starting to have an uncomfortable association for him.

The mayor and several townspeople were out on the sidewalk and some leaned from open doorways. Ash's face was knotted in pain. Was it from concern over what his town was becoming or because his side hadn't won today? Monk filed the observation for future reference. Interestingly enough, no member of the well-staffed Perdition P.D. had shown up.

"You do all right for an old fuck," Rameses said by way of a back-handed compliment.

Monk was feeling a little light-headed but was determined to keep up appearances. Not to impress Katya he lied to himself, stealing another view of her standing there in her sweat-soaked T-shirt. "Bright's in town."

"Where'd you see him?" Katya inquired.

"At the War Reich headquarters this morning. He had a mamma jamma of a bodyguard with him."

"You see a lot for a guy who's supposed to be concerned with software and tax breaks." Rameses placed hands on his hips, mimicking his mother's body language.

"Don't I though?" Monk massaged the back of his neck and moved it side to side. He wanted to place his body, which was starting to stiffen up, under a hot shower. And he wouldn't mind a bit if Katya slowly bent down for the soap. Concentrating, he continued talking.

"There was an older fella with him. Sharp dresser. Good shape. Favored these big sort of shades." Monk held up his hand on either side of his face to indicate what he meant.

"That's Halstead," Katya offered.

Rameses daggered her and she bared teeth at him unconcerned. "He's Bright's media advisor, guru and head dick wiper."

Ash and two others Monk didn't know were coming over to them.

"Well, I'm glad no one was seriously hurt," the working stiff mayor bubbled.

"Or have your cops working up a sweat," Rameses sneered.

Ash pretended he didn't hear and said to Monk, "I want you to realize that this element is not . . ." His head jerked spastically and his hands worked for a few moments as he sought to conjure up the words.

He got back on track with, "This element is just an aberration of the hard times all of us in this region have been going through. The majority of people in this town are good enough. I know, I grew up here. We can make it into the next century if we just get a chance."

"And you two-bit acid-head miscegenationist gang-bangers are merely adding to the misery," one of the other men barked, pointing a pudgy digit in the general direction of Katya and several members of her crew.

She blew him a kiss and the multiracial skinheads hugged and celebrated one another walking away.

Ash loosened his tie. "It's a different world now." He came over to Monk, placing a reassuring hand on his upper arm. "Let me take you over to the records office. I'll buy you a cup of coffee on the way."

Monk was psyched and wanted to be doing something, connecting the dots, not listening to small town players bemoan fates they probably didn't have any control over. Particularly since he was Perdition's Trojan Horse. But he did want to talk to the man. "That'd be fine, Mr. Ash."

The other man who'd come over with the mayor, a short individual with a wandering eye, said, "So this hasn't put you off our town?"

Monk choked back a swear word and answered, "No. We have facilities in L.A., and we haven't been scared out of there yet."

Over some particularly tepid coffee in the City Hall canteen, Monk got way too much information on Perdition, its promise, and its prime location.

"I understand you went to high school with Bright?" Monk finally had to blurt out, to stem the mayor's boosterism.

"Ah, yes, yes I did," he dourly admitted. "But we took different roads after high school."

"What made him like he is, Carter?" Monk sipped like he was enjoying the taste. "Get beat up by a gang of Black guys? Some brother take his best girl?"

Ash's sallow face bleached beneath the skin. "Derek had a more than honest man's burden of problems at home. And really, who can say where any of us get our ideas." For the first time, the man wasn't talkative.

"Like what problems?" Monk tried not to sound too curious.

Ash made a thing of checking his watch. "I better get back to the office. Mayoring takes up way too much of my time, and I still got a business to run." He got off his stool. "Good to meet you, Mr. Monk. I hope you decide to come here. Believe me, this business with the skinheads will blow over."

Like cancer, Monk concluded silently. "Thanks for your time, Carter."

"Mine to give."

Afterwards, for exercise Monk walked upstairs into the section containing the birth records on the fifth floor. Forty-two minutes later Monk had the information he'd been looking for and drove over to Dudley's. He eagerly devoured three quarters of a fried chicken, a double helping of rice with gravy, two biscuits, and downed two cans of Millers.

Recharged, Monk went back to Juanita Cray's rooming house and came in just as she was lecturing her son.

"What in the living hell are you thinking with, Orin?"

"You're sweatin' it too much, Mom."

They stood apart in the far end of the dining room. Under the dissipated glow from the ceiling light, their wan expressions were in sharp contrast to their heated words.

"It's gotten beyond the point of my worries, honey." She put a hand on his broad shoulder and looked up into his face. "How far do you and Katya and the rest intend to go with this?"

"Ask him, he's the one who jumped frogish today," Rameses said, indicating Monk.

Juanita Oray pinned Monk with a look only a parent could administer to a child who constantly disappointed. "I heard something about that but figured it was just bored townspeople going on."

"One can't always be on the sidelines, ma'am."

"You look a little young for playin' out some kind of Vietnam anger," she admonished.

"By the time I had to register, the Paris Peace Talks were happening."

"So what the hell's your excuse?" she retorted.

He considered his response. Even telling the truth wouldn't answer her question. His dad's hand was reaching for him through the kitchen's half-light, the question on his whisky wet lips. What did you have to do? Beat every racist until one of them spat out the cosmic reason? The atonement for Black folks' burden?

"I'm not trying to play out some tough guy fantasy," was his feeble reply.

"But you and Orin think cracking heads is a way to deal with these fools?"

"It's part of the tactics," Rameses declared.

Exasperation made Juanita Oray's body sag. "At the expense of doing something constructive on our side?"

"You have a point." Monk nodded at them and went on

up to his room. Soon, he returned but mother and son weren't around. Mr. Kahn and another man Monk hadn't seen before were absorbed in a TV cop show Monk watched on occasion. He joined them for a few minutes as the episode unfolded. Presently, he zipped up his heavy windbreaker and went out into the chilly evening.

The rental eventually took him along an avenue tinged in washed-out blues from street lights illuminating closed-up businesses. He came to a stop and shoved the emergency brake pedal home, his breath frosting the curve of the windshield before him. It was a section of town that contained light manufacturing facilities. Monk walked past such enterprises as a rattan furniture factory, a chromeplating plant, and a taxidermy supply warehouse.

His destination was a plant at the nexus of the dead-end. It consisted of a series of tall and short cylindrical buildings whose purpose were not readily apparent to him. But as Monk got closer he could make out tall, slim cut-out lettering inscribed in an arch over a large old-fashioned iron main gate.

Thick chains snaked through the rusting bars. The name on the gate spelled out "Elihu Brewery Works." Christ, the old bastard had even tried his hand at beer making, Monk mused. Interestingly, from where he stood on the outside, the name was done backwards.

In between two towers on the abandoned lot Monk could see the contours of a large ornate Gothic Revival house which loomed behind the plant. The front of the house was the street address for the third Meyer he'd found in the phone book. The first two were a bust, but a fire engine red Jeep had been parked in the driveway of this residence earlier. He'd come around the block this time to see if there was a back way in, and to see what the plant was. The house was in the flats from which rose an assortment of low hills collectively called Paradise Hills, according to his local map. Staring up at the mansion behind the empty beer works, it came to him that inside the house, probably from his bedroom window, Elihu could've read the name right on his gate. The old man's house was built as a monument to himself and a life of making money.

"Almost missed you there, sunshine."

Monk was confronted by three skinheads walking up to him. One of them was the tallow-haired mechanic he'd encountered behind the War Reich office before. The other two were interchangeable with the ones he'd engaged in front of the mayor's office.

"Ain't no mists for you to disappear in, gorilla," the middle one said. His arms were thick, a weight lifter, and he wore an open leather vest over a sleeveless sweat shirt. His hair was long, and he talked with a slight impediment.

The other one, his hair in the style of a regimented skin, had on large boots with exposed steel toes. "You gonna give us a little sport, boy? Gonna give us a little something 'fore we do to you what them good officers in Detroit did for Malice Green?" He wet his lips with anticipation.

"I got something for you." The .45 was in Monk's hand. The one in the middle, the leader, blinked several times, his brain not accepting the image it was receiving.

"What the fuck," the quiet one said.

Big arms showed bravado. "Nigger ain't gonna do shit with that piece. Are you, nigger?" What passed for a grin made his face more ugly.

Monk placed a shot at his feet, an inch from his instep. "In case you're having trouble seeing my eyes, you better be listening to my voice, boy." He let that hang for a few heartbeats. "You better hear me when I tell you I've put a few in the hole."The gun came up even with the one in the middle's face. "And it would be my distinct pleasure to add you to the list." Monk was worried he meant it but kept the gun steady.

"No jigaboo's gonna make me back down," the one in the steel-toed boots promised.

"Then stand over here, asshole," the long-haired one snapped back.

The silent one finally spoke. "Come on, we've had as much fun as we're going to have tonight."

"Fuck that," the shaved one bellowed. "Nigger ain't shit."

Monk shifted the automatic onto him and walked forward. The youth's eyes stayed the same, but his mouth drew tight and dry.

"Uh-huh." In a vicious motion, Monk jammed the butt of the weapon against the young man's lip, splitting it open like a swollen blister. Nothing registered on his face nor in his mind as he did it.

The kid was swearing a stream of racial epithets. A weird edginess descended on everyone as the young man held a hand up to his bleeding mouth. One of them started for Monk but stopped at the sound of a Perdition police cruiser approaching from the other end of the street. Two cops were out of their car, handguns and shotguns first.

Immediately, the Remington was in Monk's back, moving him toward the wall of the brewery. The side of his face was scuffed against the brick, and Anderson, the big cop he'd run into before, was leaning his weight on the gun, clipped words coming out of him between his adrenalin rush. "Where'd you put that gun you had?"

"Kicked it, over by the curb," Monk managed in a curt reply, his mouth hot with brick dust.

"I have it." The good-natured one, Oates, ambled up with the .45 held by the barrel. "Nicely taken care of, original frame, huh?" He studied it with interest. In his other hand he held a flashlight.

Monk's face was still pressed against the wall, the big cop's shotgun burrowing a groove into his back. "Listen, I need to explain what's—"

"No need for all that, Mr. Monk." Oates said in that easygoing way of his. "We saw you assault one of these young fellas here."

"I know, I'm not that kind of guy, really. I . . . this case has been doing things inside my head." Humiliation made the words stall in his chest, made him want to hide until he was right again.

Anderson said, "What do you mean, 'case'?"

If Monk had an answer, he didn't get to it. The next thing he felt was a dull throb against the base of his neck and his face sliding down the wall.

"What the fuck you do that for?" somebody said in a high tower over his head.

"Why not? This nigger's flat nose has been sniffing all over town like he was looking for white pussy," somebody else responded.

Down on all fours, Monk's senses were rearranging themselves when a foot plowed into his rib cage. Blood collected in his mouth but suddenly there was clarity in his brain.

"I didn't tell you to get up, did I, jungle boy?" It was Oates. Good old Oates. "Stay down, dog. Ain't that what you bloods call each other these days?"

The aluminum billy club was a black streak in the indigo light and Monk blocked it with his forearm. Up on one knee, he sunk a left into Oates' breadbasket. Behind him, his eyes registered the three youths moving about. Where the hell was the bruiser, Anderson? Monk got up and hit Oates again and then his .45 was falling from the cop's limp hand.

Monk heard the Remington being chambered and he held onto Oates. The three skins appeared in front of him, the long-haired one made a move for the gun on the ground.

"No," Anderson ordered, running up, shoving the kid back with a meaty palm.

Oates got his second wind and locked his arms around Monk. It threw them both off-balance. Monk was about to hit him when something blurred the air in front of Monk's face.

The stock of the shotgun ramming into his head blunted the functioning of his brain. A curtain of velvet amethyst parted and allowed him to tumble down an aisle of fog into a sea of waiting pitch.

Lying on the ground, the crack in his head pumping crimson, he saw something funny. Then he saw the scarred end of Oates' billy club coming for his head. Then the curtain closed.

CHAPTER 20

"Goddamnit, read this."

Monk's face hurt like it'd been pulled apart by a diseased surgeon then sewn back together with burlap thread.

"Are you sure about this?"

"I asked them to confirm, they did."

"Holy jumping fuck."

Something crashed onto something else and there was breaking and smaller pieces spilled all over the place. Monk tried to roll over but it took too much effort and hurt too bad. He opened an eye. That hurt less. A statuesque woman grinned at him. She wore bikini pants and a tank top barely containing breasts the size of New Hampshire. She was leaning across the hood of a clean '65 Mustang rag top. The keys were in her hand. Bless you Lord, he'd gone to glory.

"Hey, asshole, you awake?"

Asshole didn't feel like answering.

"You better let the doctor see him."

"Fuck that."

"Yeah? What're you gonna do when somebody calls over here looking for him?"

"Tell them we arrested him for assault and resisting."

"Like that's going to stick."

"It better stick, Anderson," the other voice threatened. Then it said to Monk, "Get your big ass up so I can take a look at you."

Monk didn't move.

"Look here, I'm Sheriff Hamm, Mr. Private Eye. You beat up one of my deputies last night. You got some serious charges to answer for."

Monk said in a tired voice that reminded him of his grandmother. "So do you, Hamm."

That got the right kind of response, nothing. After a stretch, in a more tempered tone, "What's your reason for being here?"

Monk got the other eye open. The photo taped to the ceiling of his cell had been ripped from a car magazine. "Oates attacked me. Anderson is a witness."

"You resisted arrest."

"Is that right, Anderson?" Monk got onto his side, nausea welling inside his mouth. "We'll see when I file my report."

Anderson combed one of his big hands through his widow-peaked hair. His blues shifted from Monk to a point somewhere over the injured man's shoulder. Another deputy sat quietly in a chair.

Hamm was a tall man with a solid build. He had a clipped salt-and-pepper beard and clear hazel eyes set in a traveled face. In one hand was the fax he'd received. Monk knew it was from the Bureau of Consumer Affairs in California. They'd run the numbers on his gun and his fingerprints.

"Now look, Monk," the sheriff began, shaking the fax, "you also attacked some of our citizens."

"They make a complaint?"

Silence, then Hamm replied tersely, "It doesn't matter, my deputies witnessed the act."

Pain came between Monk and a witty response. The door to the office opened and Oates came in. He stopped, assessed the scene, and strode over to Hamm. He talked in a low voice with him, and allowed a couple of head nods at Monk.

Hamm calmly folded the fax and turned back to the cell. "Your plane came into Portland. The feds have their district office there. Is that who you're working for?"

"You figure it out, Hamm," he bluffed.

"I should have put a choke hold on you last night," Oates said sharply. He inclined his head at Anderson who gave him a frosted stare. Oates spoke to Hamm. "Let's take him over to Spokane so there's no chance of him yakking to the media."

"You and Bryce could take him," Hamm said evenly, calculating his next moves.

"Yeah," Oates said, not trying to hide his glee.

Monk's teeth set on edge as another bout of nausea tossed his stomach. Fear started in on him, and all he could do was look at Anderson who averted his eyes.

"But we still have to know who he was working for, what he's doing around here," Hamm said, talking as much to himself as to his men.

"There's nothing in his room except his clothes, his license and his wallet. He's got a photo in it of a swell-looking chink. I say we take him out on one of the switchbacks. I imagine the mountain air will help him remember." Oates all but salivated.

Monk tried to stand but couldn't figure out how to make his legs work. Falling back onto the cot, he said, "Fuck you, small change."

Oates came up and leaned on the bars. "Come on out and play Mr. Monk," he taunted.

The door opened again and Rameses, Katya and three others poured in.

"Kick him loose, man." Katya got in Hamm's face.

"Get the fuck out of this office," the sheriff ordered.

Oates, Anderson and Bryce started to move until Rameses cut them off with, "Shit's gonna blow if you fuck with us, man."

"You mongrels ought to spend your time more constructively. Like trying to guess who your daddies are." Oates contemptuously chortled.

"I know it's hard for you, Oat-dick, but think you can count past four?" Katya winked at Monk.

Bryce pulled back the window blinds as Rameses leveled one of his long arms, pointing toward the street. "Hey, come over here."

Hamm looked out and swore. All sorts of media trucks were driving along Liberty.

Rameses said, "Want us to have a little press conference?"

THE CREW got Monk to a clinic shortly thereafter. They took an X-ray of his head and the doctor was pleased to discover that the cartilage hadn't been disturbed. The nose bone wasn't broken, merely cracked. He also had a slight concussion, swelling over one eye, and a hairline crack along the left cheek bone. Plus two of his ribs were bruised and one of his kidneys was enlarged from the pounding he'd taken.

Rameses insisted Monk not stay overnight in the place. The youth leader got the prescription for his antiinflammation medicine and pain killers. He rode in the car with Rameses, Katya, and another youth. The quartet stopped at a drug store to get Monk's medicine and some cold paks. Resting in the car, he got another look at what, besides the media's arrival, was upsetting the sheriff.

Milling about town were several large groups of skinheads of numerous hues and shapes. Added to that were various other types more readily classified in the gangbanger category.

"How long have you been organizing this?" Monk asked.

"Some of us started out as wiggers," Katya answered. She saw the blank look on Monk face and explained. "You know, white niggers, those who dress and act like they're African American. The gangsta style, home," she said, slipping into an effortless Black inflection.

"Started hangin' with some of the homeys in high school," the other one in the car began. He was a tall Latino, about twenty-two, with nut-brown skin who called himself Juke. "My folks settled in Idaho, you know, sponsored by a church group to leave Guatemala. The old lady was involved in some shit." He let that settle in before continuing.

"But Mark Fuhrman's new home state wasn't hittin' it, ya know? We soon got over this way, just kicking it on the positive tip. Ain't gonna have them white boys runnin' us ragged here."

Silently, everybody acknowledged Juke's political analysis.

"But it ain't like we all joined hands and sung 'Kumbaya,'" Rameses informed Monk, rounding a corner where Dudley's stood. "You had the Blacks and Latinos going after each other and then ganging up on the Asians."

"Is Bright the common enemy everyone needs?" They hit a pothole and Monk's eyes teared up.

"Certainly helps," Katya said. To their left, a group of supremacist skinheads were coming along the sidewalk, and Rameses slowed the car. But the skins, who must have come from out of town, suddenly realized which part of Perdition they were in, and changed direction for downtown. Rameses and Katya grinned at one another, then he drove the nondescript Aspen on to his mother's rooming house.

"You remember the original 'Outer Limits' with Robert Culp?" Katya asked no one in particular.

"Which one? He was in a few of them," Monk remarked.

"The one where they're sitting around a table, drawing their names from a bowl."

"'Architects of Fear,'" Monk and Juke said simultaneously.

The passengers laughed and Katya continued. "So these scientists are going to take one of their own and make him into a monster."

"Thus pulling people together," Monk finished, images of the episode flickering through his subconscious.

Rameses pulled in to the driveway. "Before they were the War Reich, they were just a ragtag group of metalheads with angst and nothing to do but swill beer and go over to Spokane every once in a while and ambush a queer."

Juke and Katya helped Monk get out of the car and up the steps of the old well-kept house. The young woman had a muscular arm around Monk's waist and squeezed him playfully as they went along.

Rameses went on with his local history. "But that was before Bright and ARM made the scene. It was in '87 these supremacists and some right-wing Christian types have a big confab in Hayden Lake, Idaho and decide to concentrate on youth organizing. From that groups like the War Reich came about."

"The following year we could start to see the results in high school," Katya said. "Flyers started appearing denouncing interracial dating. Then the Reich tried to get recognized as a campus club and that helped bring some of us together."

They reached the screen door. Through it, the omnipresent sound of the TV greeted them. "Look, what I said the other day," Monk started, addressing Rameses. "I've been acting like I've been sniffing glue or something. But it takes a good old-fashioned ass-whuppin' to remind one that solving this kind of problem isn't done by meeting fists with fists. I mean, I believe in self-defense, but you've also got to take this beyond street action."

Rameses looked at his two companions. "Okay, grandpa."

"Fuck y'all, and help me to my rocking chair."

"Get your rest, big daddy." Katya said, patting him on the butt.

Monk creaked up to bed.

CHAPTER 21

Monk slept the remainder of the day and woke to a gentle knock on the door to his room. "Come in." He tried to get on his side, but took the path of least resistance and stayed on his back. It was like when he overdid a workout, and the muscles got so tight you couldn't move without pain.

The door opened inward slightly and Juanita Oray's handsome face filled the space. "I didn't wake you earlier, but you had a call from a woman named Jill Kodama."

"Oh yeah?"

"Yes," she stammered, "I'm afraid I told her more than maybe you wanted her to know."

What? That he was flirting with Katya? Panic pushed words out of him breathlessly. "How do you mean, Mrs. Oray?"

"I told her you were upstairs resting and she said she found that odd, considering. Then I didn't want her to think you had gotten sick or something so I—"

"Don't sweat it, Mrs. Oray."

The older woman entered the room, her alert eyes glittering. "So you're a private eye."

"A battered one, yes." Monk rubbed a hand over his unshaven face and suddenly felt very hungry. He managed to prop himself against the headboard of the bed's polished maple.

"You might be interested to know there's all kinds of press people prowling around town since right before sundown."

"We saw them this morning. Bread and circuses," Monk glumly concluded.

"How's that again?" Juanita Oray took a seat near the bed, placing her hands in her lap.

"The show they're all expecting on Saturday."

"It seems it's going to be the largest rally Bobby Bright's pulled off yet."

"I understand you tended house for his folks when he was in high school."

She lifted a hand and moved an imaginary object with it in a small motion. "His folks were decent people. His father owned a lumber yard and his mother sold a little real estate now and then."

"Something traumatic happen to him then?"

"To make him like he is now?" She inclined part of her body like doing an impression of a giant question mark. "Not that I can recall. He was like any kid then."

"Popular?"

"Not particularly, but not the loner type like Oswald or something."

"Any of his friends still in town?" Monk moved and became acutely aware of how sore his kidney was.

"A few. He and Carter Ash used to hang around together back then. Car nuts, you know. Bobby, or Derek in those days, had some kind of car he'd hot-rodded. It was a purple Dodge something or another I think."

"He was into sports too, I understand."

"That's true. I believe he was disappointed when he didn't get a football scholarship to a Pac Ten school."

That was two things he had in common with Bright. One more, and they'd both be holding hands and singing "Day-O" over hot rum toddies. "Rameses played hoop in high school," Monk safely guessed.

She beamed with a mother's pride. "Varsity in his second year, got scouted by a couple of back east schools too. But he was already more into reading DuBois and Angela Davis than memorizing game books. He took classes locally, but lost interest in that too." There was little admiration in her voice then.

"Last couple of years Orin's been working over at the Firestone out on the interstate. But he keeps reading and at least he's working with some of these less together young folks, giving them direction."

"But you'd be happy if he found his."

"You have children, Ivan?"

"No, but lately I've thought more about having them."

"Parenthood has its moments," Juanita Gray said.

"Are there any of Bright's old girlfriends around?"

Guardedly, she said, "No, there aren't."

"Aren't around?"

"Not really."

It seemed to Monk there was more there but he wasn't sure of the angle to take to get to it.

"Mrs. Oray," Monk wheedled.

Her frame straightened. "It was a different situation, then."

"What kind of situation?"

"Youthful miscalculations." With that she abruptly made to quit the room but added. "I'll be back with your dinner in an hour or so."

"I'm sorry about leading people on with that story about scouting for a company."

Juanita Oray chewed on the inside of her mouth. "Well, the way everybody on our side of town figure it, Mr. Monk, you must be here for something to do with these supremacists. And that can only be a blessing, can't it?"

Monk wondered if any deity did indeed oversee the doings of private eyes. And if one such being did exist, surely he or she in their patented trench coat had a sardonic wit only another god would appreciate. He spent the next forty minutes going over in his head what he'd learned and how he might go at Mrs. Oray again with what she meant about "youthful miscalculations." No astounding plan emerged. He got up to use the can.

He passed a trickle of blood but the intern at the clinic said not to be worried unless it continued on the third day. Presently, he ate a hot meal of roast beef, mashed potatoes and steamed Chinese broccoli. Full and sleepy, he took the tray downstairs and returned it to the kitchen. He got a glass of water from the kitchen and went to use the phone in the alcove.

"Hey," he said after the line connected.

"Ivan, what the hell is going on?"

Monk brought Kodama up to date.

"You want me to get ahold of the Legal Aid office down in Portland? If they're not already doing it, they could probably send up some observers for the bash on Saturday. And I mean that jokingly. And you might need to talk to them in case the good sheriff gives you some lip."

"That'd be solid." The two of them let a little silence slip away then Monk spoke again. "I'm glad you called. I did call you, but I didn't leave a message. I was still mad. Mad because I'm not sure what's happening to us."

She didn't speak for a time then said. "Since you've been gone, I've been thinking about . . . things. When you're around I sometimes feel you take our relationship for granted. Good ol' Jill always there for you."

"And when I'm gone?" he asked tentatively.

"Come home soon, baby."

Monk clucked his tongue. "You're too tough."

"I'm not going to waste time with be careful and all that bullshit. I know you will be, up to a point. But I also know justice isn't always so easily obtained."

"The things you say, counselor," Monk joked. "I love you, Jill. I probably do assume too much. But that doesn't mean I can't learn."

"Yeah, right."

Monk whispered a lascivious reply and he and the judge did their version of trying out for an X-rated record until he had to ring off or figure out how to crawl through the receiver. He got up and gasped. His back was locked as if it were in a steel brace and the bones under his left eye pulsated. He put a hand out on the wall to steady himself, and it took a few moments to gather his strength. "Too much phone sex," he mumbled to himself.

Finally, he began to make his way up the stairs. Monk heard the front door open and was terrified he couldn't swing around with anything approaching swiftness. It had to be Bright and his big grinning goombah come to polish the kitchen linoleum with his head.

"Continental Dick."

"That was Op," Monk corrected, agonizingly turning his body. Katya stood in the doorway dressed in faded black jeans torn in both knees, a loose fitting plaid shirt, and her motorcycle jacket. "What brings you around here?"

"Just making sure you were safe. I know you ain't up to speed just yet." She came over to the foot of the stairs.

"I'll be all right."

"Sheriff's got your gun, Ivan Monk." She pulled back her leather jacket, displaying a pistol in its rig beneath. She took the automatic out and walked up the stairs, holding it by the barrel. "Come on, I'll show you how to shoot it."

She walked past him and Monk, his temples warming up, followed her. In his room she sat on the bed, placing the gun beside her. He remained standing.

"Use this model before?" She hitched a thumb in the weapon's direction.

Monk picked it up, examining it. On the inlaid rubberized grip was a familiar round stamp of a double wing stylized eagle. "Ruger P90, isn't it?"

"Yep. Closest thing we had to your ancient ACP 1911 model." She took off her jacket, revealing the fact that the top two buttons of her shirt were undone.

The healthy curvature of her breasts momentarily flustered Monk. "How many guns do y'all have?"

"How many you think Bright and his boys have?" She leaned back on the bed. "Don't worry, son. Some us may be strapped on Saturday, but we won't throw down unless those assholes start the shit. But we're gonna make sure this ain't no Greensboro."

She was referring to the incident in the South where the members of a communist splinter group had, essentially, issued a challenge to the local Klan and hate groups. Sure enough, the day of the supremacist rally, the progressives mounted a counter-rally. Only the crackers didn't need much provocation and promptly murdered four members of the organization in an ambush. An all-white jury exonerated the killers.

Monk considered responding but concluded it would only be hypocritical. "I got one for you," he said, placing the gun on the nightstand. "Who is Nolan Meyer?" Outside, he could hear little sounds hitting the window like the steady tapping of cat's paws. A drizzle had started.

She snorted. "He's the big cheese of the bully boys. How do you know him?"

"Did you know him at Rainier High?"

She sat up again. "Sure did. He was a junior when I was a freshman."

"And he's the son of Elsa Meyer, the daughter of Ira Elihu."

She took a pint of Southerbys out of her jacket pocket. "That's right. Why? Is he the reason you came to town?" She broke the seal and poured a dose into a glass on the nightstand.

"In due time, Honey West, in due time."

She made a snicking sound with her tongue against her teeth and handed the glass to Monk. She stood close to Monk and touched the bottle against the glass in his hand. "Skol, baby." She took a swig.

Monk also took a drink, against the advice from the clinic and his own good sense. Keenly aware of the young woman's allure, he was torturing himself by fantasizing about quenching his real thirst with the nectar of sex. "Look, Katya, aside from the fact I got enough years on you to be your much older brother—"

She didn't let him finish. Her arms were around his neck and her body, powerful and full, was against his, her lips and tongue probing his mouth. Reluctantly, Monk eventually pulled away. "Can't we just be friends?"

"Tease," she said, sitting in the bed again.

"Anyway, what about you and Rameses?"

"We're comrades, Monk. We tried the other bit but it didn't shake out, dig?"

"Dug. What else can you tell me about my boy Nolan?"

"I remember in his senior year he drew some flack for a presentation in speech class. Touting the line that the Holocaust never happened, you know? It split the faculty because of the free speech aspect." She took another pop on the bottle then, putting the cap back on, placed it at the foot of the bed.

"Was he ever involved with any violence during this time?"

"No, I mean nothing beyond the usual harassing of interracial couples at dances or him and his crowd making fun of Jesse Jackson, blasting quotas, the whole shtick. But even then his hair was turning white and it sort gave him a kind of mystique. He cultivated a certain attitude on campus."

"This would be about the time that Bright was starting to get national attention," Monk absently reflected, sipping his scotch.

"Yeah. The summer he graduated Bright came back through here and it was Nolan and some of the others who then organized a local War Reich chapter."

"Do you think Nolan is jealous of Bright's notoriety?"

"Hey, I don't call him up and inquire." She squinted at him. "What's the angle, Coffin Ed?"

"I'm getting there. I've noticed a few plaques around town not only thanking her old man, but Elsa Meyer herself, for her philanthropy and so forth. The clinic you guys took me to has one in the waiting room."

She uncapped the whisky, took another nip, and slanted her head at him.

"And did mother dear put a little money in the coffers of her darling's home for wayward psychos?"

"It is alleged she gives money on the regular to the War Reich." Katya drank some more.

"Well, well."

Katya put the bottle on the nightstand and got up again.

"Since you won't let me ravage you. I'm not staying around here playing Della Street to your Mason. I'm outta here."

"Keep out of the rain, Katya."

She had her hand of the door knob. "It's gonna fall on everybody, Ivan. Sooner or later."

CHAPTER 22

Somewhere a steam calliope played, and a juggler, his fingers bleeding from Victor Jara's guitar strings, kept in synchronous orbit the mummified heads of Augusto Pinochet, Papa Doc, and Le Pen. The event was staged by Federico Fellini while Rudolf Hess and A. Philip Randolph went best two out of three in the ring to see who would be the keynote speaker. It was Vegas rules, so the end of a round wouldn't save you if you were decked on the canvas. Swifty Lazar asked Ida B. Wells and D. W. Griffith to work the crowd for after-party invitees.

Canopies were provided by I. G. Farben and the shrimp dill sandwiches had been shipped in on dry ice courtesy of the National Front. Leonard Jeffries and Margaret Thatcher exchanged suggestive peeks while they parked the cars. The booze came in off the docks of Marseilles driven by Lucky Luciano in a straight eight flatbed. Sister Souljah and Vladimir Zhirinovsky provided color commentary while tossing a grenade back and forth. In a side tent, Nguyen Giap debated economics while playing Monopoly with Joseph Mobutu. Baruch Goldstein and Colin Ferguson, both wearing their Brooklyn Dodger caps, took care of the security. Cornel West sent Enoch Powell and a few Khmer Rouge out to hunt down some beef hotlinks, and to bring back the proper red wine. Bertold Brecht and Ruben Salazar took notes, and Frida Kahlo sketched with urgency.

Monk banished the scenario from his mind and came up behind a gathering of townspeople. Bright's rally was taking place in Elihu Park. There was a portable bandstand and a miked podium set near the statue of the deceased patriarch.

At various places along the perimeter, and lining the bandstand, were a number of skinheads doing security. Milling about or setting up tables to sell their paraphernalia of bile were neo-nazis in German military uniforms replete with swastika arm bands, Aryan Nationalists, some Klan in their off-white and grey silks and, Monk gathered from their placards, Christian Identity types, tax resisters, and a few militia followers.

On the south side of the park, across the street and behind a soon-to-be-useless police barricade, a growing throng of racially diverse skins, punks, wiggers, taggers, revolutionaries, and gangbangers gathered. Monk thought he recognized several Rolling Daltons from L.A. and Oakland.

News crews and journalists weaved in and around the activity like worker ants with broken antennas. They were receiving blurred signals and didn't know where to be when. Hamm and his deputies stood to one side. Oates stood next to the sheriff, and pointed at Monk when he saw him. Anderson paced back and forth in tight, controlled circles.

Presently, state police cars came rolling off the interstate and Hamm, cursing, ran over to greet the Captain who got out of the lead cruiser. Monk was pleased. That was the result of one of his calls which had been to Grant.

People on both sides of the ideological and geographical line were shaking their signs and hefting bullhorns. Monk had never been in war, at least not one Uncle Sam recognized, but he knew this was how it felt, sitting in the foxhole or bombed-out house waiting for the next mortar to drop, the next round of incoming fire. Monk hadn't been this apprehensive or excited in a long time.

Perdition was a bottle of gas and somebody, before the day was through, was just liable to stick a lit rag in it.

The Lincoln Town Car peeled off the east side of the street and came onto the grass next to the bandstand. Bright, and the other two Monk had seen with him the day before, got out. And one other passenger, Nolan Meyer.

Monk held back, rather than follow his first inclination and edge close to the stage to keep an eye on Meyer. He didn't want Meyer to think he was keying on him. But assuming Meyer and Bright already knew he was a PI up from L.A., why did Meyer show up? Well, why not? What proof did Monk have? And, he gravely surmised, maybe they figured Monk wouldn't be returning to Los Angeles anyway.

Reverend Creed kicked the rally off with an invocation. He was a fervent white supremacist theologian who espoused, among other bizarre ideas, that Blacks were the product of mating between apes and aliens.

Then Meyer came to the podium and began the festivities in earnest. "Proud white members of the race gifted by God, as section leader of the western states War Reich, it is my pleasure to welcome you to this gathering that dares to speak for white rights in Zionist Occupied America. Indeed my friends, these coming months will be the time of the great pendulum. Will it swing this way or that?" his arms demonstrating his words. "The dawn is coming, and we're going to see if it'll light the way to ballots or bullets."

Applause went up from the crowd and Monk wondered if anybody realized Meyer stole his last line from one of Malcolm X's speeches.

Meyer had an orator's skill and knew the correct places in his presentation to modulate his voice; where to add emphasis and where to be soft-spoken. His icy features stretched over his calm death's-head face added to his ability to arrest the crowd's attention.

Along the street, the state cops had formed a loose wall between the supremacists and the anti-racists. Some of them hefted their banners, and made occasional bursts into their megaphones in an effort to disrupt the skinheads. But the bulk of them were also paying attention to a counter-rally. Monk could see Rameses up on a raised platform, talking and gesturing with his hands passionately.

It went on like that for an hour and a half, each crowd pretending to ignore the other. The sky had started out a pale blue but was turning a slate grey by the time Bobby Bright came to the mike accompanied by a chorus of Sieg heils. Monk kept an eye on Meyer and, from where he stood, he could see him sitting rigidly in a folding chair next to the podium.

"We must fight for the soul of America," Bright said, surveying his audience with his arms outstretched. "Block by block, house by house, we must take our culture back, my friends."

"And send the niggers home with tight shoes on and fried chicken in their knapsacks," somebody yelled from the audience. A round of laughter went up. From over Monk's shoulder, somebody retorted. "You inbred motherfuckers ain't taking nothing house by house 'cause you can't count that high." That produced a series of guffaws on the multiracial side. Several beer cans and rocks sailed from the park and a couple of the state cops gripped the handles of their batons tighter.

Name calling went back and forth and suddenly there

were two distinct sets of youths facing one another down the middle of the street, a thin stream of busy state cops in tan the only thing separating the two groups. More name calling escalated to shoving.

Monk's stomach tightened and he weighed his chances of reaching Meyer should an all-out melee ensue. But even if he could, what would he do then? Half a dozen skins would be on him like white, literally, on rice and beat the living shit out of him. Or maybe Meyer would recognize him from that night in Wilmington and blast him on the spot. Either way, crowding the man wouldn't produce any desired results.

Bright had remained calm and from the stage was encouraging his people to return to the park. A few more tense minutes of unblinking eyes and free flowing epithets, and the racists drifted back to their event.

Bright smoothly went back into his speech while sweat beaded on the foreheads of the state cops. Hamm and his deputies were also on the line, and more than once Monk caught Oates staring at him malevolently.

The time seemed to compress as Bright's speech continued. Beer drinking began on both sides of the police line, but the authorities made no moves to halt it. There was even the unmistakable aroma of weed wafting about—again on both sides. Like a spectator watching fish swim in an aquarium, Monk noted the physical characteristics of the gathered. He became fascinated with how they moved, with their body language, all the while calculating how he'd keep up with Meyer after the rally.

"I'm pleased to announce that we have broken ground on 250 acres near Bayview, Idaho. This will be our training facility, our study center, our data base, our sanctuary against these mongrel hordes." Bright pointed to an artist's rendering which had been propped up on an easel. From where he stood. Monk couldn't make out the details save for a piece of architecture which rose on one side of the compound. It was a cylinder spiraling like the Tower of Babel with a stylized cross at the apex.

Cheers and whoops of delight went up from the increasingly unruly skins. Monk spotted Katya and angled close to her.

"I'm going to try something later this evening, Katya."

She leveled a serious look on him. "Like trying to snatch Meyer?"

Monk shook his head vigorously. "Nothing that goddamn crazy." Some of the skins started a chant and they both turned nervous glances in that direction. "Does Meyer live in that big mansion on the other side of the beer plant?"

She nodded in the affirmative. "Yep, he lives with his mother. And check this out, home fries, I know a way to get in there and it ain't the front door."

Monk flashed on a half-formed image. An indistinct Polaroid seen through a haze. It was the last thing his brain had registered as Oates was clubbing him into unconsciousness. The three skins entering a dark maw under that odd light of the dead end street. "Can you show me?"

Katya pulled on his hand grasping her upper arm. "I wish you were this excited when I came over last night. Sure"—she chuckled heartily—"if we're all in one piece by tonight. I'll show you."

They set a tentative time and Monk made his way across the street, stopping at a wall of skinheads who tried to obliterate him with their glares. Bright was winding up with a pitch to the crowd to give what they could to realizing the fascist dream of the facility in Bayview. The damned thing was called the Waffen Lair.

"How much you plan to contribute to the Waffle Shack?" Monk asked one of the snarling goons.

No reaction. He moved off, after assuring himself that Meyer was still on the stage. Eventually, after the pitch and mini-concert from an Oy band calling itself Hammer Blow, the rally began to dissipate. The sky finally let go and the rain came down. Not in a rush, but fat heavy droplets like a wound intermittently bleeding.

Evening in Perdition was like being in a frontier town where anarchy and the law coexisted but had little relationship with one another. The racist skinheads were everywhere and so too were their antithesis. Fist fights and skirmishes broke out on Hollis, in front of the mayor's business on Commercial Street, and more than one window got itself shattered. Monk roamed around like a UN observer without a mission.

Hamm was forced to quell fights if only to maintain some semblance of competence, the presence of the state police forcing him into action. Out on the interstate, a carload of skins in a big-wheel utility truck were shot at by a sniper. Someone set fire to Velotis Records, but Monk and some others quickly put that out. Rameses placed guards on the establishment.

By ten, the rain had started its steady rhythm on several skinheads passed out in the park under trees from too much liquor. Some skins tried to break into the bank and the state cops arrested them, placing them in one of several Black Mariahs that had been brought into town after sundown. A few gangbangers charged into the Lonely Miner and overturned tables and chairs until Anderson and a couple of deputies arrived to drive them off. They left behind a spray-painted tag that read: "Crackers ain't worth the peanut butter they're spread with." A gas station was set alight and amazingly the tanks didn't blow before the fire department arrived to extinguish it.

A young man naked to the torso with long red hair astride a Harley began racing around calling for Armageddon. It was unclear whose side he was on.

Low-intensity warfare was waged back and forth throughout the town. At ten-thirty, Ash got on Perdition's local radio station to announce the National Guard would be arriving by midnight. Over the airwaves, several rounds of gunfire could be heard punctuating his statement.

Meanwhile, Monk made to keep his appointment.

"Say, ain't you the one who got smart with me earlier?" The youth was drunk, and the button fly of his jeans was undone. The woman standing next to him was stylish in grunge attire and there was a piece of rebar limp in her right hand.

"How can you tell?" she slurred. That busted both of them up.

"The only thing you people know to do in this town is fight. Go find a kitten to torture." Monk walked forward along the street. From not too far away he could hear "People Get Ready" by the Impressions blasting into the brutal night.

"Nigger lips," the woman growled, haphazardly bringing the section of metal up.

Monk stepped under the drunken swing and snatched the bar from her hand. He threw the bar away and trotted off to meet Katya.

"The Guard rolled in off the highway 'bout fifteen minutes ago." She was leaning on the south wall of the plant, her hands behind her back.

What with her big frame, orange-tipped blonde hair and tom jeans, under the soft glare of the blue lights, Monk imagined Katya as a war angel stranded on Earth. "Yeah, on my way over I noticed some of the skins driving out of town."

She pointed at the outline of the large house beyond the grounds of the once-thriving enterprise. "I came this way from the other side, the front of the house. It's actually on a rise and there's a dead-end street at the bottom. There's a set of stairs cut into the hill. I saw Bright's Lincoln parked in front."

"Show me how to get to it from here, then I want you to split."

"You care about me, Ivan?"

"Like a sister."

Deadpan, "You believe in incest?"

At night the door was virtually imperceptible from the solid face of the high metal wall. Even in the day, you might pass by it since it had no handle or visible hinges. The wall itself was composed of sheeting of various sizes riveted into place. The door that Katya swung open was made to mimic that motif.

"How'd you know about this?"

"When Nolan was in high school, he used to brag about this secret entrance. Some of us followed him once to watch him go through it."

Monk looked in on a darkened chamber which apparently ran inside the wall, the length of the factory. "Old man Elihu must have built it to sneak out from reporters or creditors."

"Rumor has it he had a few mistresses and they came in this way. He had a separate bedroom," Katya amended.

Down at the other end of the block, a column of flaxen-colored flame spiraled upwards, tickling the moon. Yet there was now a quiet which seemed to have reasserted itself on the town. Monk touched Katya's shoulder. "Thanks, doll."

"Be cool, baby." She kissed him on the cheek and they

hugged. "Take this, huh?" She handed him a pen flashlight and took off.

There were two light fixtures with drawstrings embedded in the ceiling of the passageway. At the end was a wooden door with a ring in it. Cautiously, Monk pulled on the ring. To his relief, the barrier gave way silently on well-oiled hinges. On the other side of the door was an expansive backyard that included a large flower garden, trees, and the shadowed bulk of a gazebo.

There was ground lighting and Monk could make out various sprays of white marguerites, jade plants, and hyacinths. The landscape contained other shrubs and a copse of ghostly birch trees. Monk waited in the doorway for more than a minute. Then another. When no dog or creature came sniffing, he walked into the yard.

The house had a screened back porch and, off to the right, another door. Probably the maid's quarters. Probably where old man Elihu conducted his extra-maritals. To the left of the mansion, hidden by a growth of overhanging vines, was a walkway. Monk followed it around the side of the house and found himself under a lighted window. Drawing close, the sound of muffled voices could be discerned.

The window had slats over it, so Monk pressed his ear to the pane. Agitated voices grumbled on the other side. He couldn't discern the nature of the discussion so he moved back. Monk was almost spotted as two voices came out the back door. He bent low and pressed against the side of the porch trying to make out the dark shapes. It was getting cold so he cupped his hand over his mouth to cover the clouds of condensation his breath formed.

He could see through the screen's filigree two red dots as cigarettes were lit. Monk chanced to sneak closer to them, the shrubbery of the place serving as cover.

"Why's he pushing him on this?" one of them asked the other.

"Maybe he thinks he has better ideas," his companion responded.

Smoke drifted into the evening for awhile, then one of them spoke again. "Could be he wants to be top dog."

"Yeah. Which way would you go if it got to that?"

More smoke. "I'm not sure."

The finished cigarettes were extinguished and the two ambled back inside. Monk stepped around one of several Adirondack chairs onto the back porch, listening. He tried the knob on the back door and, as he'd hoped, it was unlocked. He took two breaths and entered.

The door let onto a service porch, damn near the size of Monk's living room. Off to his left was a door ajar to servants' quarters redone as a guest room. The kitchen itself was cavernous and well-appointed with an array of iron pots and steel pans in overhead racks, spacious ash-blonde-faced cabinets and blue-green pavers for flooring. The swing door that led beyond the kitchen was closed, and Monk went to it.

Picturing himself as an overgrown bat, he sent his hearing out like sonar to decipher the sounds in the other parts of the house. He could hear footfalls and the clinking of ice in glasses. But it was too hard to figure out what the voices were saying.

His left hand pushed on the door slowly, deliberately, the Ruger was in his right. He got it open a hair's breadth and looked in on a darkened hallway. At the other end was a warm light and he could hear Bright talking.

"Don't think I'm stupid, Nolan. I know what the fuck you've been trying to do."

"I'm helping the white worker, Bobby. The little guy who

gets up every morning and goes to the job and gets grief from bull-dykes and Harvard-educated beaners."

"You're advancing your own goddamn agenda."

"And you're not?"

Monk pushed the door further until a creak of the hinge caused a constriction in his throat. The Ruger came up beside his face, ready to be extended shooting range fashion. Print some paper, as the saying goes. Fortunately, Bright and Nolan were trying to talk over each other and had smothered his blunder.

His eyes had became adjusted to the darkened hall and at the end of it he could make out the partial outline of the stair's banister leading to the second level. Only there was no way he was going to reach it without being spotted. He closed the kitchen door and considered his options. The objective was simple. Get into Meyer's room and either find the guns he'd used, or find something else that would tie him to the murders.

Well, he could hide somewhere in the back and hope everybody went out later, but that seemed unlikely. Besides, where was Elsa Meyer? Out of town? Upstairs asleep? Reading a book? Monk had an idea and turned, walking back the way he had come. Sure enough, there were back stairs meant for the help to use. He took off his tennis shoes and, tying the laces together, put them around his neck. Crablike, he clambered up the carpeted stairs using his hands and feet so as to cut down the noise.

Monk reached the second landing. Light shone under a closed door down the way. He had to cross to that side of the house without exposing himself by walking next to the upstairs railing. He put the shoes in a linen closet and, using the penlight from Katya, he peered into a room next to the closet. It was a bathroom and, going through it, he came into a sun room with flower print curtains. There was an exquisitely redone padded rocking chair, a low rise Eileen Gray sofa, a roll-top desk, and a bookcase containing volumes with cracked spines. Off in a corner was an antique sewing machine which reminded Monk of his business with Mrs. Urbanski.

A door opened and Monk switched the pen light off, glad he had it pointed upwards and had closed the doors. Feet padded along the hall and the light in the bathroom snapped on. Monk waited behind the big couch which faced the doorway to the bathroom.

Minutes eased by and Monk remained as still as a painting. The toilet was flushed and water from the sink flowed. The door to the room he was in opened. A whiff of perfume trailed in, and Monk was sure it was the mother. He could just see the headlines now, "Crazed Black Man Shoots Leading Perdition Citizen and Benefactor. Bobby Bright for President." The feet came into the room, paused, then the light went out again.

A relieved Monk got up and crept to the hall door, listening. He checked in the bathroom and found that its hall door was also open. He waited and listened some more then went across the tiles in his stocking feet. Down below, he could hear some more words as the front door opened and slammed. Momentarily, somebody came up the stairs and, without knocking, entered the room where the band of light was under the door.

Presently the door opened again, and Meyer came out, went down the hall, then to his left and into a room, flipping the lights on. Monk, crouching low in the dark recesses of the bathroom, took it all in. After several moments, Meyer came back into the hall and this time knocked at the door with the band of light.

It opened and a woman in a short robe appeared, leaning on the jamb. The hair was piled high on her head and the legs below the short hemline were taut, shapely. Her profile was in the light and Monk surmised she was older than her legs would lead you to believe. She held a glass of some golden liquid in one hand, which had rings on three fingers, and had the thumb of her other hand hooked in the robe's sash.

"Where you going? Is the trouble over in town?"

"Pretty much. I just have to check on a few things, Elsa."

"Everything all right?" She playfully tugged on one of his belt loops.

"On schedule."

"What about this Black hawkshaw Hamm said is up here?"

"I saw him at the rally, but I don't think he's going to be a problem." He said it unemotionally, but his words were like a surgeon gutting a fish. Methodical and deadly.

His mother spoke again. "See you when you get back. Guess I'll keep myself busy with the book I just opened."

They kissed on the mouth quickly and Meyer descended the stairs, his mother drinking and watching him as he went. She left her door ajar as the front door closed again.

Monk straightened up in the bathroom, processing the scene he'd witnessed. Not sure of how to interpret it, he quietly made his way along the hall. He stopped inches from the mother's door, holding his hand out as if it each finger had eyes. Nothing. Monk strained his hearing but nothing—no movement, humming, turning of pages that could he detect. A minute. A minute and a half.

Praying that speed would make him invisible, he danced past the crack of the door, then halted on the other side. His heart was going so fast he was sure he was going to have a stroke. But there was no scream, no pounding of bare feet across the lush carpet. He moved on past the bend in the hall, on into Nolan Meyer's room. Monk took another chance and eased the door shut when he entered. He turned the knob so the beveled latch was all the way in and slowly pressed the portal closed, allowing the latch out into its slot quietly.

His light revealed a large room which was more of a studio apartment than a simple bedroom. In the front part were chairs, a couch, a large desk, two filing cabinets, and a modernistic desk where it was obvious Meyer did his paperwork. A 486 SX computer was on the desk, and a laser printer rested on a side stand.

The room itself was divided by a curtained arch, with the bed and dresser in that part of the space. Grazing the beam over a low set of book shelves, Monk saw copies of such works as the supremacist near-future novel *The Turner Diaries, The Bell Curve,* a Newt Gingrich tome, and *Clausewitz on War.*

The file cabinets were locked and Monk wasn't about to force them open. He knew he couldn't be thorough about his search. And he hoped he would hear the front door or Elsa Meyer's bedroom door if either opened.

On the desk were bills the War Reich had incurred pulling off today's rally, other miscellany, and a sketch of a flyer intended for distribution to high school teens. But a search of the closet, under the bed and in the drawers of the dresser didn't yield anything of value. No guns, no incriminating personal diary.

In a letter caddie there were opened envelopes with messages from Bright and from several chapter heads of ARM and the War Reich from across the country. Just for kicks, Monk copied down the names and addresses on his steno pad. There was one letter from California that mentioned the Pacific Shores killings but the writer was going on about if the authorities caught the killer, they ought to start a defense fund for the guy. A wink and nod to Meyer? That wouldn't stand up in court. As if tainted evidence obtained from his illegal entry would be admissible.

After another twenty minutes of fruitless endeavor, Monk was ready to quit the room and the warm and cuddly racist household. He'd go with what he had to the Legal Aid contact Jill had given him and see if they could get some action. At the least, leak the information to the press and hope a brushfire of inquiry lit under Meyer and his War Reich. Maybe char Bright's tail in the process.

Monk's body calcified at the now-familiar sound of the front door opening and closing. He shut his fight off. The gun was back in his hand, and he stood alongside the door, ready to slug Meyer if he entered. Mom too if necessary. Run like a bastard and hope to get away before being identified.

Attuned to the quiet, Monk could hear the soft clomp, clomp up the stairs, and another door opening, then giggling and music underneath.

"Well," he heard Elsa Meyer say.

Monk couldn't make out the response and stood immobile for a minute, but he couldn't tell what was going on. Shit. He did his bit with the lock and eased the door open a sliver. The door to the mother's room was now wide open and light spilled out into the hall. He could hear mumbling and the rustling of clothes.

Hell, he couldn't go back that way. He was also getting nauseous again, and his kidneys began to ache. His stomach started to knot, and he shut the door to Nolan Meyer's room, desperate for another way out.

He went to one of the windows and, pulling back the

drawn shade, looked out on the roof. Monk was seriously considering that route when he chanced to look down at the wastebasket beneath the window, set against the wall. The familiar red striping of the phone bill caught his attention. He took it out of the trash and uncrumpled the sheets.

Scanning it, Monk made out a man's laughter approaching. He jammed the bill in his back pocket, unlatched and slid the window open, and went out on the roof. From the outside he carefully closed the window.

He flattened his body on the wet shingles. Down below, the street was empty, an unnatural calm holding. Off somewhere, there was shouting and the rumble of heavy machinery.

The shade was down over his exit window but a sudden aurora of light spread around it. There were sounds of rummaging around and, briefly, a distorted silhouette of a couple which slipped from view like melting butter. Monk crept backwards, his feet coming to a rain gutter. Deftly, like a spider, he got his body around and looked over the edge. He was above the pathway. And then he remembered his damn shoes were in the linen closet. Now the music—Gershwin?— was turned up, and he heard throaty laughter in the room.

Monk clambered slowly like a backwards crab along the multiple tiered roof with its intersecting triangular parts. Wet and apprehensive, he finally got in position over the porch and eased his body to the ground. The damp concrete instantly soaked the bottom of his socks and inspired him to go to the front rather than around back across cold mushy earth.

Parked in front at the curb was the Camaro he'd seen the War Reich members working on the other day. The red Jeep was not around. Monk jogged over to the vehicle, tried the door, but it was locked. He wrote the license number down and scurried back to the side of the house at the sound of another approaching vehicle.

Maybe it was how Ahab felt upon finally cornering the great whale, the object of his fear and loss. The moment that crystallizes the long search. Knowing it would take only one more thrust of the spear, one more twist of the harpoon to end the existence of the creature obsessing his life. Monk watched the red Jeep driven by Nolan Meyer roll down the street.

He hadn't realized it, but the gun was back in his fist, the veins on the back of his hand pronounced from the pressure of his grip. One shot to the head. The authorities would write it off as one more anonymous incident in a violent day. Sure, they'd probably hassle Rameses, but they couldn't make him for the hit. If he worked it right, he could even make it look like Bright had done the deed.

With Meyer gone, the comatose Jimmy Henderson, tubes running in and out of his emaciated body, would no longer rise to point an accusing finger at Monk in his dreams. Clarice would have satisfaction. And maybe some of the debt to his dad would be paid.

The Jeep slowed and pulled into the driveway, its lights briefly illuminating the moist blades of the lawn, the droplets glowling brightly as if sprayed with glycerin. Monk crouched down, his eyes registering the young white-haired man getting out of his vehicle, getting something out of the back end. The composition handle of the gun was warm against his palm as if it too were responding to the acceleration of his senses.

Meyer was carrying a briefcase. It was almost too easy. The fates must want this. The young War Reich leader stared at the Camaro for a long moment, pivoted, and walked to the house, keys in his free hand. He got to the door, his back to the street, head down as he concentrated on getting the lock sprung. Bap. Bap.

The door stuck slightly, swelling from the day's moisture. Monk pressed the barrel of the gun against his own forehead. But its coolness didn't ease the heat in his brain. Meyer entered the house and Monk tried to think normally. He straightened up and headed back to Oray's rooming house.

Monk's poplin jacket was nasty and clammy from his jaunt on the roof. His feet were freezing in wet socks and he took them off and threw them away. He hadn't gotten too far when a patrol of National Guardsmen in Humvees stopped him.

"Is there a problem, sir?" the officious Huck Finn of a sergeant asked him.

"I got pushed around by some skins. They took my shoes and socks," he lied.

"Do you have any ID?" the Guardsman asked nicely.

Monk produced his driver's license and gave them his cover story, hoping none of them were locals in possession of the truth.

"How come you were out this late?" the sergeant inquired, holding onto his license.

"I'd been over in Port Cascade most of the day. By the time I got back, the riot was going on and I got caught up in it." Monk wove a tale about being forcibly stopped by skins in another car and the harassing they'd given him. With no radios or VCRs tucked under his arm, his shaky story carried him through. The accommodating sergeant offered Monk a ride back to the rooming house. Actually, insisted on it as he was sure they wanted to know if that part of his story was true.

On the way back, Monk could see the state cops and

Guard had got things under control. He saw the part-time soldiers patrolling the town, placing blankets on passed-out skins and hip-hoppers. Big Brother with a smile.

Nearing Juanita's, Monk noticed a car of four skins parked up the block. They were just sitting there talking and smoking while their radio played low. They had a good view of the front. The Humvee slowed, and the car, a Bondoed '77 Grand Prix with mismatched tires, started and drove off. Monk was sure they'd been waiting for him.

The sergeant verified who Monk was with a harried-looking Juanita Oray, who went along with the Intertek front. Rameses and a few of his crew were camped out in the front room, looking angelic for the Guard.

After they left. Monk thanked Mrs. Oray and took a hot bath to thaw out his feet and fell asleep while soaking his tired body, the Ruger on the bath mat beside the tub.

A single gunshot in the early morning woke him, terrified, from his light sleep, certain his psychic emanations had manifested themselves inside Meyer's house.

CHAPTER 23

The number rang three times, on the fourth, an answering machine took over and announced its message. Monk hung up before the beep. He checked the number on the bill he'd filched from Meyer's wastebasket, and dialed it again. Same message. Thoughtfully, he replaced the receiver. He made a notation beside the 213 area code and got up from the phone in the alcove.

He'd identified most of the numbers on the bill outside of the area code he was in now but this last one was unexpected. Several of them seemed to belong to other supremacists and one was to the ARM national headquarters in Iowa. Bright's voice was on a machine for that one.

Rameses, Katya and Juke came into the house. There was a large bandage taped along the Latino kid's cheek and chin.

"What'd you find out last night?" Rameses demanded.

"Riddle me this, hombre," Monk countered, "who is the tallow-haired guy who drives a duel carb, Hedman headers '68 Camaro with racing slicks."

Katya was about to respond but Rameses stopped her with, "You first."

"Let's go upstairs." They did and Monk told them why he'd come to town. From the bottom of the clothes hamper in the bathroom, he extracted the photocopies of the news clips he'd brought along. The three read them in silence.

"What would be Nolan's purpose for doing these killings?" Rameses asked.

Katya twisted her mouth and said. "Is Meyer doing this on Bright's orders?"

"I considered that, but from the way it sounded last night, it seems he and Bright are contending for the throne of the most high racist," Monk said.

"Yet you're sure he's the Shoreline Killer?" Juke asked.

"If he ain't, then somebody's built an awfully intricate frame." Monk rubbed his stubbled face, the possibility of such a scenario making him irritable.

Rameses added, "Let's assume Nolan Meyer must have some logic, some rationale to this. It has to fit into his plans." Monk put his hands in his pockets, assembling the sections in his mind. "All right. He's setting up Bright somehow."

"Maybe blame the killings on him to get him out of the way," Katya theorized.

"There's something to that," Rameses concurred.

The other two shook their heads in agreement. Juke said, "So that's gotta be it. Meyer must be arranging things to move against Bright when the time is right."

"And the Camaro?" Monk asked again.

Juke looked at the others and lifted his shoulders. "It belongs to John Vickers."

"Okay," he said, not elaborating.

"Don't be sly, slick," Katya joked.

Monk bugged his eyes at her and got the Ruger from beneath the mattress. He handed it back to her. "I want to thank you cats for your help. And I hope you continue to organize against these dimestore fascists. Peacefully."

"Where you headin', Lone Ranger?" Katya asked.

"Back to Los Angeles."

"What about Meyer?"

"The chickens might just come home to roost," Monk allowed.

A collective "What the fuck?" went up from the assembled.

Later, Monk went downstairs with his bag. Juanita Oray was sitting in the front room listening to the radio report about last night's riot, a broom in her hands, a dustpan at her feet and a trash can nearby. He hadn't noticed before, but two of the house's large front windows had been busted out.

"At least five people got themselves shot up pretty bad last night, one of them might not make it. The law made at least forty arrests." She turned the set off and took a taste from the coffee at her elbow. "On the positive side, with all the media around town, Sheriff Hamm is squirming like the pinhead insect he is."

Monk placed the bag on the floor and sat down. "Before I settle up, mind if I ask you something?"

She stirred the coffee. "Go ahead."

"You know why I'm here."

"Solve some murders in L.A. Pretty much the opinion of folks around town was from day one you couldn't be who you said you was."

"So much for the James Bond bit. I believe this thing is going to end where it started."

"Most of our journeys do," she said sagely.

"So I'm told, Juanita." He leaned forward. "Don't you think that anything we can use against these supremacists we should use?"

"Are we to be as vicious as they are?"

"A little ruthlessness is necessary at times," Monk conceded.

"That's like being a little bit pregnant. But what I know is . . . gossipy." Her finger traced the rim of her cup.

"But you know something." He showed her the note he'd made next to one of the numbers on the purloined phone bill. He explained what the place was.

"They just answer the phone and tell you that?" she said doubtfully.

"I made an early call to a research service I've used on occasion. Using their access to data banks of unlisted reverse phone books, they provided me with the owner of the number in the 202 area code."

"Amazing things, computers," Mrs. Oray remarked sincerely.

"Information is the key to power."

Her lips compressed. "I get the hint."

"GIVE ME back my gun or the next thing you'll be wearing a uniform for is parking cars."

Hamm and Oates were on their feet, the deputy had his hand on the butt of his bolstered revolver. "Get the fuck out of here, Monk," the sheriff warned.

Oates made a move to clear his weapon as Monk remained still. "Go ahead, asshole, do it. I've already had a long talk with my attorney in Los Angeles." Which was truth of a sort. Only the subject of the return of his .45 hadn't come up in his sexy talk with Kodama.

Hamm placed a hand on Oates. "What are you saying, Monk?"

"There are no complaints against me, Sheriff," he said contemptuously.

"You're not licensed to carry in Washington State, Mr. Monk." Oates' face broke into his practiced affable grin, the hand not far from the holster.

"You didn't let me finish, moron. I told my lawyer all about a little dickweed cop who attacked me and how I'm all set to press charges. I've got medical reports from the clinic and I've already struck up a swell friendship with a few of the reporters who were around town."

In one of the cells behind the cops, two skinheads were snoring, sleeping off their drunk. In another, a Black kid with a handkerchief tied around his head watched with interest. Hamm looked down at his badge as if it were a spider crawling up his chest. "If I give you back your piece, you'll leave town?"

"I'm already gone."

Oates got excited. "Shit, Bert, don't let this wise-ass—"

"Shut up," Hamm said, cutting him off. He went to a locked cabinet, opened it, and handed Monk his gun.

The magazine and the chamber were empty, but otherwise it seemed to be intact. Monk placed the gun in a large manila envelope and started for the door.

"I'll see you around, Monk," Oates hissed.

"You just make sure nothing happens to that kid in your jail, Hamm." He turned his head sideways. "Try to do your job for once." Anderson came through the door, noting the small package in Monk's hand. The private eye stepped past him and out onto the street.

In the morning sun Perdition didn't look too much worse for wear. There were National Guardsmen stationed around, but they mostly joked amongst themselves or sat on benches or upturned milk crates. Their M-16s leaning against their legs as if they were a new form of fashion statement.

Behind a detachment of them were two trailers. One for the white racists that had been arrested, the other for the multi-racial prisoners. Each trailer was beige.

There were buildings with busted-out windows and walls

with gaping holes. Some stores had been looted, and several had been set fire to. An appliance store had a running refrigerator propped against the still-locked expanding metal grill. Somehow, it had been positioned that way and its doors taken off to allow the removal of its contents from the street. On the shelves were several unopened beer cans, a pitcher of what looked like Margarita mix, and three long-stemmed glasses.

Walking past Ira Elihu's statue in the park, Monk saw where the old boy's lips had been spray-painted a sunset orange and a pair of boxers were draped over his head. Curious, Monk drew near the War Reich's store front but only found a scorched front entrance, remnants of a Molotov cocktail scattered at its base.

Around back there were no cars and he tried the rear door. It was locked but he wasn't going to chance his second burglary in less than twenty-four hours. He got back to his car and drove over to Velotis Records. Juke and another young man were hanging around front.

Worried, Monk asked, "Is Lonetta all right?"

"She's fine, man," Juke assured him. "She just asked us to keep an eye on her place while she went into Spokane. Some radio station wanted to interview her about what's been going on."

"Y'all be cool." Monk shook the young man's hand.

"*A luta continua.*" Juke raised his fist half way in the air and shook it as Monk walked away waving.

Monk had already said goodbye to Rameses, his mother, and Katya. He went by the Elihu mansion but the red Jeep, as he expected, was gone. In an upper window, a curtain was pulled back but the house held no more mazes for him to traverse. There was nothing left holding him in Perdition. He guided the rental back onto the highway. In the tape deck, Monk inserted a Frank Morgan cassette, “A Lonesome Thing.”

Morgan’s alto seared bold notes in a continuum Monk’s mind wandered in for awhile. The road stretched out as the introspective sax man wove his blissful tapestry. It would be soon enough for the music to stop.

CHAPTER 24

An hour before dawn, sheriff Olson has sent through a contingent of bomb-sniffing dogs. Twin metal detectors were erected at the church entrances. Along with a number of deputies and several Metropolitan Transit Authority cops, there was a detachment of LAPD personnel assigned through Harbor Division. Their ranks also included four of the plainclothes detectives who had been working the Shoreline Killer detail. One of them was Lt. Marasco Seguin on loan from Wilshire.

He finished giving directions to three uniforms and rounded a pillar in the spacious vestibule of the Foursquare Eternal Glory Baptist Church in Long Beach. Absentmindedly, he undid his two-button Avery Lucas coat as he walked between one set of metal detectors into the open air. He craved a cigarette which meant he was nervous.

Time to center yourself, man. Draw down on the kung fu you'd learned in the service. Move all the energy down the center, be in the middle of it so you know which way to jump when the truck comes barreling out of the side roads. Be like the raindrop falling from the bamboo shoot. Be all you can fucking be. A thin smile lifted the corners of his drooping mustache.

Cars were already starting to crowd the big parking lot for available spaces. Members of the church's men's auxiliary had been pressed into service and they began to ferry cars around the block to the lot of the Smart and Final which Reverend Tompkins had the use of. Seguin scanned the people piling out and remained immobile as they filed past him.

A trilling of the metal detector made a muscle in his neck twitch and Seguin swung about, wary. But it had been triggered by the ostentatious brooch in an elderly Black woman's hat and she got it back after one of the female deputies had looked it over.

Pulling in front of the church was a Lexus the sheen of malachite with Senator Grainger Wu at the wheel. Walter Kane and Ursala Brock got out of the car with Wu. A second car let out the state cops assigned to the senator.

"Lieutenant," Wu said, extending a hand. "I believe we have a mutual friend."

"If I'm not mistaken, the good judge is coming today," Seguin said, shaking the hand of the man he voted for.

"Well, I certainly appreciate the pressure you and your fellow officers have been under to catch this killer."

"Thank you. Would you mind calling my house and telling my wife that?"

Wu laughed genuinely. "See you inside, Lieutenant Seguin."

Kane nodded at the cop and Brock stared straight ahead, seemingly unwilling to break her concentration. A uniform showed the trio around to the side and the secured entrance to the room behind the choir section, the state cops trailing behind like temple eunuchs.

Coming across the street were at least twenty-five young men and women led by Malik Bradford. Some of them gave

Seguin an insolent once-over as the group sauntered into the church. He lingered on the steps under the vaulted entrance for a few moments, then went around the other side of the church.

About twenty minutes after the appointed start time people had filled the lower pews and the balcony of the main portion of the church. Another 350 or so had been seated on padded folding chairs in the adjoining multi-purpose center. There was a widescreen video monitor set up and the audience was afforded a clear view and sound by massive JVC speakers as Reverend Tompkins delivered his opening remarks.

"Friends, brothers and sisters, if God puts a period on it, it's not for me to replace it with a question mark."

The reverend's opening line got some audible chuckles from the assembled. "By that I mean, we are all here on this earth for a purpose, but it surely seems there are those who don't, as my daddy used to say, know mess from Shinola." He paused for effect. "And you know my old sharecropper daddy didn't say 'mess.'"

Tompkins was batting a thousand and Seguin, as had been prearranged, moved into the pantry of the kitchen beyond another door. Built-in open-faced cabinets were lined with clean, crisp shelf paper and stocked with enough canned goods and jarred preserves to wait out World War III. Leading from the storage area was a large functional kitchen of the industrial variety. It was outfitted in stainless steel counters and drawers all burnished to a starship sheen with two stoves that had eight burners each.

Ursala Brock entered from the far door and spotted the LAPD detective. Seguin perceived a change in her demeanor. Was this woman put off by cops or was it something else? The door opened again and one of the state cops came in, followed by the tall one, Walter Kane. Seconds afterward, Wu also came in, munching on a handful of peanuts.

Seguin joined them.

"I asked you all here to get your opinion on the possibility of a national health plan," Wu said jocularly.

As one, the five pressed forward, Seguin in the lead. The group had just passed a metal side door with a push bar which let onto the parking lot. The door's mechanism clicked and it swung outward.

"That goddamn thing's supposed to be locked," Seguin whispered, his hand wavering close to his gun.

Several reporters flooded through the open door, their laminated IDs loose about their necks like cheap pearls.

"Senator Wu, do you think your proposed legislation on hate crimes has a chance of getting out of committee?"

"Senator, what is your take on this supremacist center that Bobby Bright is going to open?"

"Just one question, Senator, don't you think your recent comments about what you say is the lack of resolve by Congress to curtail the militia movement will make enemies in the wrong quarters?"

Kane was trying to urge Wu forward but he patted his aide's shoulder and slowed down to respond to a few of the questions. As he did, there was a sudden commotion from behind the gathered journalists. Bodies were jostled and shoved as if a running back were trying to bowl his way through from the outside.

"Hey, hey, ho, ho, chink has gotta go," one of the new voices said. "Back to nipland where his rice-eatin' daddy and GI dick-suckin' mama came from."

Seguin glumly concluded there was no use arguing with the shouter about his mismatch of derogative adjectives.

As if they'd been teleported, several skinheads were now

pushing their way in, chanting, finger pointing and a few brandishing their clever signs.

Seguin tugged on Wu's arm, urging him forward. At the same time, the state cop and Kane tried to form a barrier between the senator and the vociferous skins, who, at the moment, were engaged in vigorous repartee with the reporters.

A body went down and others got entangled and all of a sudden the doorway was a jumble of arms and legs and shouting. Against his best intentions, Seguin felt his body being pressed back into the pantry and he had to shoulder someone hard to reinsert himself into the middle where Wu was.

Kane and Brock were trying to help Wu along when a sound like a wooden ruler slapping against a desk top went off. He'd been brought up attending Catholic Sunday school on the east side. The seasoned detective knew what the real source of the retort was. "Shots," he hollered.

A bolt of fear thundered through the mob and Seguin locked onto Wu, getting his wiry frame over the man. The plainclothes cop forced him to the ground. The state cop barked orders into a mike on the underside of his lapel. One of the skinheads was looking around with a confused expression, a small animal with its leg caught in a trap. The crowd began to point at him.

"He did it, he shot Wu," a woman reporter yelled, aiming her mobile mike at the man like the Book of Judgment.

Somebody else swore and two youths—one was Bradford—detached themselves from the bunch and tackled the young skin. "I got it, I got it, he's got a gun, goddamnit."

Seguin moved off and ran into a skin who he decked without a beat by a sideways blow to the temple. The state cop was also moving and the two of them with Bradford dragged the kid in and shut the door. They hauled the young man to his feet.

Seguin appraised the scene even as he did so. Several of the reporters were still about and three or four other skins who looked a little surprised. "All you fuckheads are under arrest," he informed them, emphasizing his point with his nine-millimeter.

The state cop had managed to wedge a chair under the push bar, freezing the door. He too had his gun trained on the young racists.

They complied and the reporters moved back, scribbling away or chattering into tape recorders. Bradford and the young man with him also stood back, arms lank at their sides, their eyes taking in everything. Kane looked shaken but Brock and Wu, who seemed to be unhurt, remained still.

"Hey man, I don't—"

"Shut up," Seguin said to the young man someone said had pulled the trigger. "You're under arrest for the attempted murder of United States Senator Grainger Wu." He informed him of his rights, and made him sit on the floor, his hands in bracelets.

"There it is, there's his gun," Brock said, pointing at it on the scrubbed linoleum. Instinctively, she bent down to retrieve it.

"Don't do that," Seguin warned, using a tone he reserved for his youngest daughter. "You must know better than that."

The state cop had handcuffed two of the skins lying stomach down on the ground. Seguin tossed him his other pair of cuffs and edged toward the weapon. It looked like a Charter Arms and was a .38 dull-plated revolver with a textured grip and taped trigger.

"Want my pen?" one of the reporters said to Seguin, offering him a thin ball point.

Seguin almost smiled. "We don't put those things down the barrel. It might screw up the insides." But he did take it and moved people back from the gun. More cops and others were trying to jam into the kitchen through the doorway he'd entered. Seguin picked up the gun by the checkered grip with two fingers—prints couldn't be deposited on the uneven surface anyway—and marked its location with the ball point on the floor.

"Why'd you want to kill the Senator?" One of the reporters was quizzing the fingered gunman. He was a husky skinhead in red suspenders, shiny boots and a sweat-stained Guns 'N' Roses T-shirt.

His chest was rising and falling rapidly and he looked to his other fellows for help. "I, shit, I, hey, that Black bitch shoved the piece in my hand." He indicated Brock with his head.

"Fuck you," the communications director snarled and lunged at him, kicking.

A deputy got between them and Wu got an arm around Brock. Sheriff Olson bowled into the kitchen. "Just what the fuck's going on around here?"

"I'll leave that to you law enforcement personnel to figure out," Wu began, wiping his forehead with his hand. "I'm going to make my presentation."

Seguin said, "Look, Senator—"

"You say this is the man who took a shot at me, fine. It's his type that I'm here to speak about."

Reverend Tompkins clasped Wu around the shoulders and walked with him out of the kitchen.

A STUDIOUS-LOOKING young man with modish-length hair in a buttoned-down broadcloth shirt and creased poplin trousers strolled along the sidewalk and came to his car, a blue Acura, under the shade of a big maple. He got his key in the lock and felt the tickle along his rib cage.

"You got to give it up," the harsh voice said from behind him.

"If you want the car, take it," the collegiate-looking man replied, holding up his hands.

"Aren't you wondering how it was your arm got bumped just when you were making the shot, Vickers?"

He turned and stared open-mouthed into the placid face of Ivan Monk.

From the next block, they could hear a round of applause erupt from the Foursquare Eternal Glory Baptist Church.

CHAPTER 25

"You two-faced bastard." Alice Vickers' arm jerked and Monk grabbed her roughly by the wrist. The styrofoam cup of hot coffee she meant to toss into Grant's face was upset. The contents spilled across the desk, dribbling onto the floor. Nobody went for a napkin.

Grant stood before her as she sat perpendicular to the table, her back pressed against the wall. Just above that was the one-way glass which looked in on the interrogation room. Inside, her son sat, his head resting on the room's scarred table. A tin ashtray filled with crushed butts smoldered before him.

"I'm sorry, Alice," Grant said. "But it wasn't me that tried to murder a man yesterday."

"I hope the devil fucks you in hell, old man." Hate and betrayal were evident in her red-rimmed eyes as she fixed them on Grant.

He stuffed his hands in his pockets, turned away, and went to lean against the wall on the far side of the table.

Seguin looked at Monk then spoke. "Here it is, Mrs. Vickers. We can place John at the scene, we can establish motive, and we have a confirmed test from the residue analysis which means he'd fired a gun recently."

"He'd been out to the range, I told you that," she answered defiantly. "I don't care what this ape says." She didn't look at him but she meant Monk.

"We talked to the range master there. We made it clear if he didn't tell the truth, losing his license to operate would be the least of his worries." Seguin waited, letting the import of his words sink in.

Alice Vickers blew air out of her mouth and turned to view her son behind the glass. He looked straight ahead at a point only he could see. She said, "What's the deal? What do you want me to convince him to do?"

"Tell us what he knows about Nolan Meyer's involvement with the Shoreline killings and who ordered him to assassinate Senator Wu." Seguin sat on the edge of the table.

"Gee, I'm glad it's not much," she spat sarcastically.

"In return," Seguin went on, "I'll recommend that he get immunity from prosecution for attempted murder and conspiracy to murder."

"You guarantee that?" the mother asked in a concerned tone.

"I'm not saying the feds will okay it. I'm just saying as far as the LAPD is concerned, we'd look on his cooperation as benefiting the resolution of this matter."

Alice Vickers slumped in the chair, her hand propping up her head as if it were about to detach itself from her neck and roll off down the hall. "He's gotta have better than that. He's got to be relocated so, so—"

"I'll see what the feds will agree to," Seguin promised.

Grant and Monk walked out of the precinct as the Vickers waited for the arrival of the public defender and the answer from the FBI.

"How do you feel?" Monk asked Grant, clamping a hand on his shoulder.

"It's not the first time I let somebody down," he answered noncommittally.

Monk studied him. "You really felt something for her."

Grant turned on him, angry. "Does that surprise you, Ivan? Am I supposed to be some kind of social security James Bond who screws chicks for information then kicks them from moving cars when the case is over? Am I supposed to be as hard as you work at?"

Stung, Monk couldn't think of anything to say. He lowered his gaze.

Grant made motions with his hands. "Jesus, Ivan. When I saw that damn photo in her bedroom I knew I should have bailed then. But you get my age, telling yourself it's okay you've been divorced twice and only one of your two daughters will have anything to do with you. And you rationalize, telling yourself she'll be okay with this, she'll see her son has done wrong and what you're doing is really helping him. Meanwhile, I kept going to her bed every night. Not even telling her my real name."

"You're the one that drilled it into me about detachment, Dex," Monk said lamely, feeling the hurt from his old friend's words.

Grant stopped. They had wandered to his Buick on the visitor's lot. He unlocked the trunk of the vintage deuce and a quarter and handed a hefty file folder to Monk. "This is the stuff I got on Swede. It oughta make your client happy."

Monk had all but forgotten about Urbanski and her problem. "Thanks." He was trying mightily for consoling words. "Dex, if you hadn't been at her place three nights ago, we wouldn't have known Vickers was in town when he came over to see her. And how he'd changed his appearance."

Grant shrugged then trained his battleship greys on Monk. “How’d you figure they’d make the hit at the church?”

Monk winked at Grant. “I had a good teacher.”

CHAPTER 26

Off the kitchen, a faucet dripped intermittently. A dog barked not too far away and, overhead, a small engine prop job rambled through the dry afternoon air. A cone of sunlight broke the somber plane of the Navajo-style rug as the front door swung inward.

The man stepped quickly into the house, shutting the door silently as he did. He crossed the living room in long strides and continued into the dining room with purpose. Sitting there at the glass table was another darkened figure. This man was backlit against the translucent white curtains in front of the big sliding glass door.

The intruder halted, his eyes adjusting to the muted interior. He could now discern the other presence and he placed his feet apart, the weight put forward so as to put some power behind either flight or fight.

"How's it hangin', Nolan? I hear the feds paid a call on the mansion up north but you weren't home. Raided the Reich's headquarters up there and down here, no clue. Even rounded up a buck-toothed girlfriend of yours, still no dice."

Meyer's lips barely parted. "But you knew I'd come back here. Even Vickers didn't know that."

Monk filled him in gladly. "Grant and I got permission

to toss this place after the cops pulled their stakeout off after two weeks. He'd learned earlier from the neighbors around here they'd seen a man matching your description around here about a month before."

"You found the two pistols and money I hid, just in case," Meyer said.

Monk didn't respond. But he'd concluded Meyer had hidden the items either for a getaway, or to further implicate Bright, or maybe Vickers on Bright's orders, as the Shoreline Killer.

Meyer said, "Come by yourself?"

"Just you and me, sugar pie." Monk got up from the table, pushing the chair back with his sole as he did.

Meyer got closer, squaring his shoulders and rolling his head as a boxer might before the first round. "You got that sell-out motherfucker Vickers to give me up."

"And your boyfriend?"

Meyer laughed hollowly. "Sorry, hot dog, it's only Bobby who likes the chocolate speedway action." Meyer unloaded a punch so quick it caught Monk off-guard even though he was braced for it. He staggered back and tried to counter with a jab but Meyer was in motion, bringing his left up and level while twisting his torso. The blow tagged Monk on the side of his face and for a moment he had a hard time focusing.

Meyer's hand was reaching beneath the tail of his knit shirt. Monk willed his body into motion but not in time. The gun was out, releasing a round.

The glass table top seizured into myriad segments, its irregular chunks littering the floor. Monk, who had ducked underneath it, had a hold of one of its legs and was twisting the bulk of it around and up as he stood.

He caught Meyer in the upper legs and the supremacist

cursed from the impact. A carved wooden bowl which had been the table's centerpiece was within grasp and Monk flung it and the glass it now contained. Meyer knocked it away but the diversion allowed Monk the opportunity to push the frame forward, forcing Meyer back.

Bleeding from his hands and several cuts along his arm, Monk got around the upset iron frame. Ignoring the pain, he closed the gap between him and the white-haired killer, shards of glass crunching and splintering beneath his shoes as he trampled around. The gun—Monk wasn't sure what kind it was save that it was a semiauto—was rotating into position but Monk had his .45 in his hand and did a back swing with it.

He knocked his against Meyer's weapon, a shot going wild from the other's muzzle. Monk clubbed at Meyer's head but the killer dived to the left, Monk right after him. The two went over a low, small piece of furniture with magazines on it, their bodies clumping along the floor as if they were drunk bears who'd forgotten their circus routine.

Meyer tried to get to his feet, and at the same time get untangled to bring his gun into play. Monk's was on the floor, out of reach. But he was aware of a piece of glass just to the side. He grabbed it, thereby giving Meyer a chance to get his gun hand free. As he sought to let off a round into Monk's sweating face, the private eye buried the triangle of glass in Meyer's thigh.

"Nigger shit," he screamed.

Monk blocked the arm with the gun on the end of it with his forearm. Simultaneously, he crawled, reaching out, getting both hands around the gun, yanking it from Meyer's hand.

"I got your nigger shit, white boy," Monk bellowed, digging the gun into Meyer's cheek.

"You ain't got the balls, mudboy." Meyer's death's-head leered at him in the dim light, taunting him in its absolute whiteness. "You pride yourself on thinking like a white man, don't you, Monk? You head-scratching coon."

Straddling the killer, Monk distantly heard someone else click the hammer back on the piece, some other hand was probing the pistol deep into the side of the skull face. It wouldn't be like in Perdition. He'd kill him with cold fury and eat a big dinner afterwards.

But all too quick there was a painful sensation as Meyer buried a shard in the arm with the gun at the end of it. Meyer bucked and dislodged him.

Meyer kicked him, the tip of his foot connecting with the underside of Monk's jaw. He reeled, rearing back on his haunches. He went over on his backside, splayed across the nice bleached wood of Alice Vicker's floor.

Light again invaded the room and Meyer was vaulting through the open front door. Monk gulped air like a vacuum cleaner, got up, and sped after him. They ran around the mobile homes on their stanchions among the sparkling concrete court of the Pink Sands lot. They rushed across lawns of verdant green astro turf and past a free-standing sculpture of giant aqua-blue whooping cranes in a concrete pond.

Monk took a shot, missing the fleeing killer as he made it around the corner of a house designed in a western motif. The bullet took a chunk out of a wagon wheel half buried in the flower garden. He churned his trudging legs as fast as he could and cursed himself for not jogging more often with Jill.

Meyer was in front of him, both of them whipping down a narrow passageway between two homes. Monk raised the weapon—it was a hefty Browning P-35—and it occurred to him it might not look too swell on the record if he missed again and sent some pensioner watching "The Young and the Restless" to soap opera heaven.

He got to the end of the passageway and ditched the gun in a recycling bin. Meyer was heading down a side street of the court. Monk's arm hurt like hell but he couldn't stop.

An elderly man in a threadbare robe and slippers was trimming alligator weeds out of an equally threadbare garden. He was livid as first the white-faced man, then Monk, charged through the meager plot of withered tomatoes and bug-eaten lettuce.

"Bastards, I'm calling the law on you ruffians," the retiree said, shaking a pair of clippers.

Meyer got to a waist-high gate that led to a pool and Jacuzzi. He went up and over, Monk closing the distance between them. Two older woman had been sitting at the edge of the pool dangling their toes in the water. They screamed and waddled away.

Monk's prey snatched open a small shed where a net on a pole and miscellaneous yard tools were stored. He swung a push broom at Monk who was moving as fast he could.

The edge of the thing caught him in the side and something began to cramp inside his body. The broom came crashing down on his head, momentarily disorienting him.

Meyer jabbed at Monk's gut, but he grabbed the handle and twisted. It snapped and Monk used his section to counter thrust at Meyer, who was throwing punches. The splintered end of the handle dug into the fleshy part on the underside of Meyer's armpit. Blood thick as ketchup coated the end of the handle as Monk withdrew it.

"Goddamn you," the supremacist huffed. Blood leaked into his shirt and a few drops descended onto the pristine tiles.

Monk missed with a right but connected with a left to Meyer's body. Then another short jab to the lower body again, causing the other man more anguish. "Come on, Meyer, give me what you got."

"You fucked up everything, Monk." Meyer brought a foot up and into Monk's chest, driving him back.

He followed with a fist that rocked Monk, but all his nerves were firing and the synapses in his brain were jagged and alive like a junkie on a rash of amphetamines. Monk kicked the other man's shin with the steel-toed boot he was wearing.

Meyer grimaced again and took a few steps back, gaining space between them.

"There's nowhere to run, Meyer," Monk contended, sucking in gallons of air. "You're made solid for doing the Shoreline killings to set Bright up. You heard about what happened to Vickers' father from your big-legged mama." Monk smiled sadistically.

"Shut up, shut your filthy mouth." Meyer had stopped backing up.

"What is it, Nolan? You don't like your mom's choice of boyfriends? Or is it something else?"

Underneath the flaccid quality of Meyer's face an unhealthy gray began to creep into his complexion.

"You did the murders to implicate Bright and get him out of your way so you could be the number one boy." Monk shook the broom handle at him accusingly. "Maybe you also wanted to show your mother who's the real man, huh Meyer?"

A dead voice said. "Vickers tell you that?"

Monk was moving closer to him. "You might say pillow talk helped put your dick in the vise, boy. Seems your old lady mentioned to her other lover, Vickers, what you'd been up to." He could reach Meyer in one move now.

Meyer's body shook and he extended a rigid arm and finger. "You're not bringing my—" and he hesitated for just a moment, as if searching for the proper adjective, "mother into this, you degenerate snoop."

"Look who's talking."

Meyer yelled something incoherent and launched himself at Monk. The two collided like bucking rams. Meyer got his hands around Monk's neck and squeezed with a fanatic's resolution. His pupils were pin pricks in his head. Monk leveraged an elbow and drove it into Meyer's Adam's apple. But he didn't let go. Rather than try to pry him loose, Monk grabbed him close and went down, he on top of Meyer. The pair slammed onto the redwood decking of the jacuzzi, Meyer taking the brunt of the fall.

The force of the impact loosened his hands and Monk got free, rolling off. A yellow-and-pea-green finger painting did itself inside of Monk's head as he got on all fours, hacking. Spittle and a bad taste gathered in his mouth. Where was Meyer? He looked up and saw the other man running away. No, he wasn't trying to escape, he had a purpose in mind.

There was a barbecue grill tucked in a corner of the pool area. A brick had been placed behind the trailing leg to steady it. Meyer had it and was wielding it in a slashing motion back and forth, advancing on Monk. "Come on, nigger, come on and dance." His nose was bleeding and he limped slightly.

"Sure," Monk hissed.

Meyer brought the brick across in a vicious arc that would have split Monk's head open like a ripe grapefruit had it registered. But he went low and came up inside the swing. Monk brought a knee up and got it in Meyer's stomach.

But the other man engaged the brick again in a downward

swipe which crashed into Monk's deltoid and a portion of his upper left shoulder.

"Shit," Monk blared, shock and a throbbing pain beginning to set in.

Meyer was raising the brick again but Monk grabbed the man's wrist, temporarily halting the blow. Weakness lanced through his injured arm and it took all his will to put any strength into it. Then he shifted his body, toppling them both into the small pool.

Monk got Meyer back against the rim of the tub. The brick was still in his hand and he attempted to club Monk again. "I'm going to kill you, nigger boy."

"Not today. This is one Black hide you ain't tacking to the wall, Meyer."

Head down, arms over it for protection, the brick tore off a piece of Monk's hand but he bulled headlong in the water, slamming into Meyer. He brought his head up, butting the other man under the chin. Monk got his hands around Meyer's throat, but the left had lost a lot of sensation.

Meyer cackled, knocking away the hand. He hit the other man in the lower body with a fist and used the brick again. But Monk had turned, most of the blow landing on his upper back.

The water was turning carmine and Monk laced his fingers together, batting Meyer alongside his head. The skin on his right hand hung like streamers. But he clamped it on Meyer's face and dug his fingers in like an excavator. He shoved, forcing the man under. Using him for leverage, Monk got out of the tub, encircling his arm around Meyer's neck, hauling him back up.

Red water poured from Meyer's mouth. "Monk," he bleated.

Gripping the edge of the jacuzzi with his left hand, Monk

pulled up with his right arm across the dead-faced killer's carotid artery, a variation on the LAPD's once-infamous choke hold. Monk planted his left hand against the back of Meyer's neck. It was a technique which shut off the supply of blood to the brain. And one in which the ex-LAPD Chief Daryl Gates said caused the death of more Black suspects because they didn't have normal physiology. Monk laughed a sick, salacious burst at the irony. Do whatever it takes, he raged. Do whatever it takes. Meyer beat at Monk's forearm with the brick but his desire for the other man's death made the pulping his limb was taking insignificant. Meyer let go of the brick and he got both his hands on Monk's arm in an effort to pull it off. But a lust had possessed Monk and he jerked up, getting his knee into the other man's back.

"Monk," Meyer rattled, fear in his voice, "let—" But the rest was lost in approaching death.

"It's your turn in the box today, Nolan."

Hoarsely, Meyer got out, "Please." Impotently, his fists beat at Monk's arm and face. Then they dropped to his sides.

Monk continued the pressure, cutting off the words, trying to cut off the hate he'd built up. Meyer twitched a little, but was rapidly losing energy. "What's wrong, Nolan? Black cat got your tongue?"

A primal gurgle and spittle the consistency of syrup issued from the dying man onto his front. The last gasp this side of the grave. His legs had ceased thrashing, and his hands were now completely lifeless. Meyer's head lolled forward like a patient injected with too much sedative.

Strobe light images of Jimmy Henderson's chest rising and falling, rising and falling, showed themselves on the back of Monk's brain. Anonymous Black life that Meyer was willing to snuff out to accomplish his own ends. Life worth no more to him than the thought that went into lighting a cigarette. Or extinguishing it.

It was so easy. At worst they'd charge him with justifiable homicide. His friends would testify to his good record and his past accomplishments. He was an asset to the community, not this scumbag supremacist he was killing. All his friends would understand.

Yeah. Through the electric haze fevering his thoughts Monk saw his mother, then Jill, then his dad, standing in the yard, laughing that big laugh of his as his young son caught a pass he'd just thrown him. His hands holding onto the George Halas-autographed football from the Rams as he ran into his dad's muscular arms. He had his father's build and the old man's arm was ending someone's life. Something that deserved it.

His head hurt and he felt like passing out. The arm which was now throbbing and useless came away from Meyer's neck. With his other one he brought the inert figure out of the still water.

He dropped Meyer on his chest, and fell back on the deck, spent. Too beat and too ambivalent to do anything else. Meyer could live or die, and he didn't have an opinion one way or the other.

Eventually the other man began to cough, spit up gore and fluid. Monk felt neither elated nor cheated. He could conjure up no emotion. But that didn't bother him either.

CHAPTER 27

A '70s number was playing on the spike's stereo when Jill Kodama walked into the bar: "Everybody Plays the Fool" by the Main Ingredient.

"Nice legs, sweetie," one of the queens said flatteringly to her as she went past. "You must tell me how you do it." Another one at the table raised a glass of wine to Kodama who smiled back at them. She joined Walter Kane on a stool next to his lean form. A tumbler full of rough pieces of ice and brown liquor, a bowl of pretzels, and a folded section of the late edition of the *Times* were on the bar in front of him. Half of Nolan Meyer's battered face was visible in the article about his capture. The piece had run in the early edition, too.

"Hey," he said, chewing on a pretzel.

"Could I have a gin and tonic?" Jill said to the bartender. "Long day, huh?"

"Mmmm." Kane took a swallow, making a face as he did so. "It's gonna get longer, ain't it?"

"I suppose." Her gin arrived and she dug for money in her handbag.

"Let me get it, Jill," Kane said, putting his hand on her arm. He handed a ten across. "Reporters were all over the office today like friggin' cucarachas," he continued, picking up the thread of their conversation.

"Meyer's a tough mother, he ain't said squat so far." Kodama took a sample of her drink.

"How do you know?" Kane asked, assessing their reflections in the mirror tucked behind the tiers of whiskeys, bourbons and liqueurs. Offerings to the muse of bottled wisdom.

"I heard it straight from someone I know in the D.A.'s office. Meyer has refused to speak and won't take any food down at Parker Center. His only statement was he considered himself a prisoner of war in Zionist Occupied America."

"Good for him," Kane sarcastically jibed. He took another sip. "Would you like an appetizer?" He turned his handsome face toward her, showing teeth like a model in a suit ad. His pencil mustache glistened with alcoholic sweat. "The grilled shark sticks with artichoke palms are very vogue."

"Why don't you tell me about it, Walter?" Kodama tried her gin.

"I think the shark's yummy."

"I'm not here to play," Kodama warned.

The pretzels on their way to Kane's mouth stopped on the ridge of his lip. "How do you mean, Jill?" he said with too much innocence.

"Ivan put it together, playboy. It started with some numbers Meyer called from his house in Perdition. Including an electronic bulletin board he subscribed to."

Kane threw back his head, raking his hair with his supple fingers. "Since I know your stud isn't on the fav list with most branches of law enforcement. I'm willing to bet he obtained that information illegally." He dumped the pretzels in his mouth and chewed with vigor.

"I wouldn't know, we're not having this conversation. But

we learned from Ursala she'd gotten onto this particular board by pretending to be a supremacist."

"How charmingly risqué." Kane chuckled.

"To keep up on them," Kodama shot back. "Seems she stumbled into an ongoing conversation with someone calling himself 'Crusader,' who'd suggested he'd done more than just talk about the problem."

"Interesting," Kane retorted blandly.

"Seems she also confided in you about this. That from what 'Crusader' said, he might be the Shoreline Killer." Kodama studied her friend for several moments. "One of the numbers on the bill was the line into that bulletin board. Was he, Walter? Was 'Crusader' Nolan Meyer? Was that how you first made contact?"

He bunched his shoulders, munching more pretzels.

"I also understand one of the numbers was to your inner line."

"A crank call," Kane said, probing a finger inside his cheek for pretzel residue.

"Maybe. Only the other number of interest Meyer had was to the Mattachine Association in Washington, D.C."

"So he's coming out of the closet. I knew those skinheads were hiding something by being so aggressively homophobic," Kane said triumphantly.

Kodama considered her cocktail but didn't try it again. She'd lost her taste for the stuff. "The operating theory is that Meyer was gathering background dirt on Bobby Bright. Who, for practical reasons, has had to hide his sexual preference from the supremacist movement."

"That hunk of yours get that information over the phone, huh?"

"Of course not, dear heart. But he's got the eyewitness testimony of a woman who knew Bright when he was a teenager and had seen more than one time his bringing 'friends' over to study up in his room."

A faraway look glazed Kane's eyes. "That was such a nowhere time for me. I was a high school jock, and I loved to go to the funny car races with my dad. But he didn't take me much. He wasn't around much after he and my mother went their separate ways. She was a woman who thought sex would be a parachute, but she still fell into ruin." His voice halted, whatever was in his head seemed too much for him to articulate. Kane had more of his drink.

"The Mattachine Association is a national lobbying and advocacy organization for lesbian and gay rights," Kodama said rhetorically. "Anyone can call their main office in D.C. and obtain a number for contacting a particular local chapter. When the FBI searched Elsa Meyer's mansion, they found the newsletters which had been sent to her son."

Kane waited.

"They were from the Palm Springs chapter. Which is also where Bright had recently rented a house under the name of Edmond Wilde. That name was in the last issue of the chapter newsletter as a recent member."

"But—" Kane began.

"But Dexter, that is Dexter Grant," Kodama interjected, "Ivan's old boss, found out about the alias and told Ivan when he'd called him from Perdition. Dexter heard Bright moved around the country using various names for security reasons. Our friend, Lt. Marasco Seguin, got Ivan in on the sly to see what the seizure by the FBI had produced."

"One thing always leads to another, don't it?" Kane remarked. After a pause, and after he'd taken another swallow of his drink, Kane spoke again. "Meyer called me up once after I'd gotten this plan rolling with him wanting to know if Bright and I were lovers. Can you believe the gall?"

"Were you?" Kodama asked seriously.

Kane guffawed. "Oh Jesus, I may be a schemer, darling, but I haven't lost my good taste."

Something was welling in the back of her throat. "Walter, why did you arrange the murder of your friend Grainger Wu? One of the last good ones to make it to Capitol Hill." She'd tried to sound detached, but disgust was rapidly overtaking her objectivity.

Kane rubbed a hand over one side of his taut face. "So you all thought there was some connection to me and Bright? That we were having a tryst?" He gazed at her from behind his hand, still held against half his face, laughing softly.

Her right hand trembled on the bar, and she brought it down onto her lap. Kodama spoke. "After establishing that Bright was a member of the Mattachine Association, Ivan, me, and Dex discussed it. None of us was sure what it meant. But when the venue for Grainger's speaking engagement changed, we put our money on you."

"Honored." Kane bowed his head slightly. "You must have talked to Grainger and he told you I was the one who convinced him to make it Tompkins' church."

"The funny thing is that Grainger did think that was a good idea, talking about the need for support of his legislation in the area where the Shoreline Killer had struck. Very symbolic," Kodama admitted. "And very goddamn sick."

Kane contemplated his image behind the bottles again and said nothing.

Kodama continued. "Ivan thought it was significant for another reason. If it was going to be at the Shrine Auditorium as planned, he knew they had their own security force who'd be covering all the exits. The sudden change of location might mean something was going to happen."

Kane ventured, "That's not much to go on."

"Ivan had Dex shadowing you since finding out you were the one who suggested the change."

"Really. Are you wearing a wire, cutie?" His lip curled back melodramatically.

She put her arms out at ninety degrees. "Search me."

"Alas, it would afford me no pleasure," Kane demurred.

Kodama placed both her hands on the edge of the bar as if to steady herself. "Dexter saw you step outside the kitchen door of the church. That was the morning of the afternoon of the event. That must be when you jammed the lock somehow."

Kane drained his glass, then rolled the empty tumbler between his hands. "Unless your old friend has Kryptonian vision, even with binoculars all he could say for certain was he saw the senator's chief aide doing his job." He leaned into her, "making sure everything was cool."

She wouldn't give him the satisfaction of recoiling. "Why, Walter?"

Kane reached across Kodama and started on her drink. "You know how all these right-wing assholes love to glom onto certain incidents? Creating rallying cries for them and their hateful buddies. These yahoos are still fetishizing over the supremacist shoot-out at Ruby Ridge, and making heroes out of a maniac like Koresh from the Waco debacle.

"So Randy Weaver gets three mil and change from the FBI for the death of his wife and son. But where was the compensation for Fred Hampton and Mark Clark? Slaughtered in their sleep by the law during the government's war on the Black Panthers." He glared at her, daring her to refute his indignation.

Kodama said humbly, "The state of Illinois settled, eventually."

"But no Panther got a chance to tell his side of the story

to a Senate sub-committee complete with TV cameras while choking back tears and earning sympathy."

"I know the system is racist," Kodama answered defensively.

"And where was the outrage from the politicians when the children of MOVE died? No more in command of their own fate than the children of Waco were. You know why, Jill. They were Black, they were extremist on the left, therefore no purchase, no succor can be found for them among the agendas of the demagogues stalking the hallways of Washington."

His serpentine logic crawled into her head, and it bothered her. "There are other examples, Walter. Like when the nazis burned the Reichstag in 1934, blaming the communists so as to aid in the consolidation of Hitler's power."

Kane replied, "When you get down to it, the left and the right have employed similar tactics over the decades in numerous countries."

"And Grainger would become a martyr. His sacrifice writ large as a catalyst to bring people together, Walter? For what, so you can lead us to the mountain top?"

Kane drank, the ice clinking in his glass making a loud noise.

Kodama pressed on, getting it all out was the only way she could maintain equilibrium. "Grainger told me, about six months ago you went to a meeting of other gay rights activists in New York. The conference was sponsored by the Mattachine Association."

"Networking, discussing strategies to use against the religious right, and so forth. All very kosher considering my . . . frame of reference."

Kodama stared with a stranger's eyes at him. "Is that where you heard about Bright being gay?"

"An old rumor, love."

"But it must have been substantiated there. Something happened to get you to conceive this bizarre idea."

"How about getting our ass kicked all the time?" Kane snarled. "Shit, laws of average say there's gotta be a few other prominent white supremacists who have fantasies of getting it up the rear by Stallone."

"Why didn't Bright get outed?" Kodama asked, a hotness on her breath.

"Though they stole the name, this incarnation of the Mattachines, unlike in the fifties, aren't lefties. Being a liberal doesn't make you gay, as being conservative doesn't make you straight. It's in the genes, baby.

"The Association's got Log Cabin Republicans to in-your-face Jesse Helms Act-Up members on the board. Their creed is respect for the gay lifestyle. Outing someone, even a Bobby Bright, isn't their thing," Kane said with melancholy.

Kodama would not allow herself to feel empathy for him. "You're a foul, self-important bastard, Walter."

He moved his mouth silently, as if talking were an unknown practice. "You ever hear of man called Isaac Kaufman from the fifties? During the witch hunts?"

Kodama, wanting to understand, searched through the past then said. "Yes, the psychoanalyst to the Hollywood Communist Party members and fellow travelers. He convinced some of his patients to rat before HUAC because it would resolve their inner conflicts. And it's alleged he even told McCarthy's bully boys confidential information he'd learned from his sessions."

"And his rationale?" Kane asked, knowing she knew.

"Advance the class struggle," she replied wearily. "By ridding the Party of a bunch of armchair revolutionaries and cocktail-circuit Bolsheviks, the core that remained would be that much stronger. Those remaining would constitute a hardened vanguard."

"And the fear and hysteria that was whipped up would polarize the masses, thus heightening the contradictions, comrade." Kane emptied his glass, looking over the rim past the walls of the bar. "The worse it gets, the more one is forged." It was as if he were reciting scripture.

"So Grainger dies at the hands of a white supremacist," Kodama said. "His hate crimes legislation, which is never going to get out of committee, would pass. Public sentiment would carry it. But there's no way to control all the fallout."

"Politics is about taking chances," he chimed. "Momentum is very important.

"That's very Machiavellian of you," Kodama commented ruefully.

"I like to think somebody like Ralph Reed would appreciate it, dear." Kane gripped her arm. "Look at what's taking place in Italy, France, Germany, Bosnia for God's sake. Fascism and racism and homophobia and anti-Semitism ain't dead, it's breeding, Jill. We don't have time for piss-ant reformist measures. We have to be as ruthless as our enemies."

"And Bright went along with this?" She removed his hand.

Kane licked his lips. "Let's pretend, you and I. Let's pretend someone could convince our conflicted supremacist there was somebody like him on the other side. Only this person's gayness was open, his supremacy was closeted."

"And Bright rationalizes his homosexuality in the Roman fashion. Making love to a man was the ultimate expression of his manliness, therefore his whiteness," Kodama finished.

"There you go." Kane finished the gin.

"No, Walter. What about striving for the higher ground? What about vision and compassion? We can do better."

"In Never-Never Land," he sneered.

She backhanded him with enough force to rock him on his stool. Several of the queens put hands to their mouths in a theatrical manner.

"Harder, baby."

A cunning look seized Kane. "Let's pretend our avatar sets Meyer in motion, too. Behind Bobby's back, of course. The younger man has the respect of the more violence-prone members like the War Reich. He was the one always pushing for more direct action, more confrontations with a society he didn't acknowledge." An envy lit him from within.

"It wasn't hard, Meyer'd publicly accused Bright of being too much in love with the cameras and talk show circuit. He was looking for a way to bring the faggot down."

"And I bet you're the one who confirmed it for him about Bright being gay," Kodama observed icily.

"Chaos from within, an emboldened movement slicing parts of the enemy away from without."

"And what kind of victory would such a poisoned movement sprout?" Kodama demanded.

Kane broke a pretzel neatly in two. "That's a question the ones left standing have the luxury to answer."

Kodama rose, leveling a finger at her one-time friend. "Maybe there's no evidence to be put against you, Walter, but I'll make sure everyone knows what you did."

"That would be slander, your honor."

"Sue me." She walked toward the exit.

Kane called out. "You'll just be building my reputation, Jill. I'll get all kinds of offers to run presidential campaigns."

On the stereo "Smiling Faces" by the Dramatics played.

CHAPTER 28

Bobby Bright disappeared, *Hard Copy*, *Inside Edition*, *A Current Affair*, and even *Unsolved Mysteries* did variations on Bright and the theme of the making of a gay skinhead. Juanita Oray didn't allow herself to be interviewed for any of these shows. But there were others who were more than willing. For the right price.

There was one show with a skinhead, his face obscured via pixelation, who said he was gay and knew of many others who were gay in the white supremacist movement. There was another with a woman who'd been Bright's babysitter and told of the horrifying incident of Bright touching the private parts of his male cousin. It was pointed out later they both had been five at the time and taking a bath together.

On one tabloid program members of a skinhead rock band debated drag queens. It ended in a brawl, the hostess got a concussion, but the show topped the week in ratings. Howard Stern hosted the babes of white supremacy contest on one of his pay-per-view specials. The woman with the daggers tattooed on each areola and her pubic hair shaved in the shape of a swastika won.

There was even an open invitation from one of the tabloid

shows to Bright for him to do an interview from underground. They offered to pay him $100,000. But some pointed out that in addition to his being outed, maybe the fact that a federal conspiracy to commit murder warrant hung over him might be another reason he wasn't going to take up the offer.

Monk returned to Perdition at the request of Rameses and Katya. They'd asked him back to provide public testimony on a hearing they'd pushed Ash and the city council to hold on the growing threat of the supremacist's movement.

"Hey, isn't that—?" Monk asked Katya, standing with Rameses and some of the others on a street corner after the hearing.

Solemnly, she said, "Yes, that's her."

"Damn," Monk replied, shocked.

"Both of her loves are gone, Monk." Rameses intoned softly.

"Damn." Monk looked at Elsa Meyer as she crossed the street in front of them.

"She just wanders about town, stopping to buy groceries and such, but that's about it," Juke added, looking at the retreating figure.

"Look boys, let's not forget she financed the War Reich as much for her son as to keep the town from being united. She's still a big landowner around here and has fought community development on our side of the tracks for years," Katya reminded them. "With few businesses getting loans in our part of town, the skinhead shit on top of the usual bank redlining, everybody had to shop downtown where the stores that rented from her are."

"Granted, Katya, still it's a shame," Monk commented.

"Methinks friend Monk cries crocodile tears," Rameses said.

Monk was going to respond but Juke interrupted.

"Here, you can be one of our first contributors." Juke handed him an envelope with something printed on the front.

Monk read it. "Really?" he said, looking at Rameses.

Katya responded, "Hamm's up for reelection this year. We think with everything that's happened, we've got a good chance. At least we'll raise the issues."

"Hell yes." On the top of a car, Monk wrote out a check and put it in the envelope. It was printed with the message, "Contributions to the Orin M. Oray for Sheriff Campaign."

ELSA MEYER walked back to her big, empty Gothic Revival mansion. She climbed the darkened stairway to the second floor. At the top, she momentarily paused, looking at the apartment her son had occupied. She lowered her head and marched into her room, leaving the door open.

At an easy chair facing the window with the curtains pulled back, next to a table with a half-empty bottle of Chablis on it and a lead crystal glass, she sat down. Clad in a shapeless, long-hemmed dour dress, her hair now all white, her face like leather dried in the sun, Elsa Meyer poured herself a measure.

She raised the wine to her mouth, her lips barely touching the glass. Something had caused her eyes to wander, the focus lost behind them. The glass slipped from her hand. It struck the Belgian carpet and the stem broke away from the body, the contents eddying onto the thick rug, soaking into the surface. Elsa Meyer stared at it, watching it disappear. A solitary tear ran down her cheek.

IT TURNED out at the very moment Ronny Aaron was killed, Nolan Meyer was the in-studio guest of the local War

Reich on their cable access show out of Tustin. Herbert Gaylord Jones finally admitted his guilt. He'd been clean and sober for a month.

"THANKS, MR. Detective." Clarice bounced her daughter on her slim hip. She offered him a sealed envelope.

Monk made a deferential motion with his good arm, the busted one in bandages and a sling. "Keep it for Shawndell, Clarice." It was that awkward time, the resolution of the puzzle which was supposed to bring satisfaction. But the dead did not rise, and the grieving kept on missing them. Clarice kissed him on the cheek.

Garcetti, the D.A., was going to ask for special circumstances concerning Meyer, making him eligible for the gas chamber. That wouldn't make the future any brighter for the struggling teenage mother, but it seemed the feeble best the current stock of no-butter-more-prisons politicians on both sides of aisle could offer in these waning days of the American empire. While the cellular phone set jockeyed for position to catch the rising wave of Chinese capitalism on their Sharper Image brand surfboards.

SWEDE WAS forced to sell his part of the garment finishing businesses. In return, the information on him wouldn't get in the hands of the IRS, and he was not to bother Mrs. Urbanski. Subsequently, she sold the business to some cheerful folks who promptly cut wages and increased the workload.

Somebody delivered an informative package to the local Union of Needle Trades Industrial and Textile Employees, and they promptly waged an organizing campaign.

MONK, OVER time, convinced himself the hate was stamped down, buried under the layers of the cool observer he sought to maintain. Yet like a chronic heart condition, he knew it would come back. No doctor could cure it, no treatment was strong enough.

And Jimmy Henderson still lay in a coma, an innocent who'd become a totem of his failure. And in true modern fashion, his family was fighting the insurance company to keep him alive on the machines.

"OKAY, BUT you have to wash your hairs out of the sink when you trim your goatee," Kodama admonished him.

Monk was wrestling with a crate of his LPs, placing it alongside her couch in the den. "Yes, dear."

"Be cute," she said.

"I'll try." Monk went out to retrieve another box of his stuff.

The judge never did finish her painting.

ACKNOWLEDGMENTS

Bob Coe is the first, and will remain the best book editor I'll ever have. His on-point observations and guerilla fighter's discipline for verisimilitude in content and form has shaped this work into something much better than it was.

Naturally, its shortcomings are all mine.

The research and topical material published by People Against Racist Terror, the Center for Democratic Renewal, R.A.S.H. (Red and Anarchist Skinheads) Update from the Center for Contemporary Activities, the Southern Poverty Law Center and the Anti-Defamation League were not only great stores of information, but demonstrated how common folk of various races working together can combat the rise of hate groups.

And though we weren't drinking buddies, the late Gordon DeMarco is responsible for my further forays into the world of Ivan Monk. For that I am grateful. I hope you found Harry Lime, man.

Lastly, this is being written on the day after Ross Thomas's death. It meant something to me that we shared a panel once, and had both worked for unions in our time. He signed my copy of his *Seersucker Whipsaw*, "... to a fellow porkchopper." Mr. Thomas, you'll always have game.

Continue reading for a preview of the next Ivan Monk Mystery

BAD NIGHT IS FALLING

PROLOGUE

Burning The Darkness Down

Efraín Cruzado's first sensations were of opening his eyes and coughing roughly. He awoke next to Rosanna with a vicious dry hack ratcheting from his body. Damn, he reflected sleepily, maybe he should get over to the all-night Sav-on over on Alvarado. Suddenly Rosanna too was coughing, and Cruzado realized their bedroom was far stuffier than usual.

"What's happening? Put on the lights," his wife said groggily, rousing herself from her slumber.

It came to him in the same moment he got to his feet. "Fire, Rosanna, there's a fire in our place." He tried to sound calm, he didn't want her getting panicked as he clawed along the wall for the light switch through the invading soot. His eyes began to cloud from fear and smoke.

The light from the fixture in the ceiling had a weird, otherworldly effect, illuminating the moist, oily fog rolling through their bedroom. Cruzado was already out the door heading for the girls' room. Behind him, he could hear Rosanna loudly coughing and stumbling about, her idea the same as his.

In the hall he bumped into a hurtling body and Cruzado crazily imagined that it was one of those *mayate* bastards, one of those Blacks, who'd surely set the fire. Or, goddamn him, maybe it wasn't them. Maybe it was the others. Damn this hopeless city, and goddamn these Rancho Tajauta Housing Projects.

"Efraín, Efraín," his sister, Karla, exclaimed, latching onto his arm, "I can't see anything. Where are the children?"

He grabbed her shoulder and gently but forcefully pushed her to the right. "Stay still. Rosanna is coming this way, and I want you to hold onto her," he said in Spanish, moving to his left. The door to the girls' bedroom was hot and he knew what that meant, but what could he do? A father can't ignore his responsibilities.

He got the door open, the heat from the room literally sucking the breath out of him. He rocked back, sagging down against the far wall as the fire's fury overpowered him. A blur loomed before him and Cruzado, an agnostic, knew it was an archangel come to collect his children.

But the time for sweet music was not just yet. He could hear their wails. The girls, the girls had to be saved.

"Karla, please," he heard Rosanna plead.

He found some air but it hurt to take it in. His lungs were singed like meat on an open spit but he had to get up, he had to do something.

One side of the girls' room was a dance of glowing saffron and Cruzado could hear Olga screaming in that particular wail of hers. Normally the sound got on his nerves, but now it was a beacon guiding him in a savage terrain.

"I'm coming, *mija*, Daddy's coming," Cruzado promised. He was up, shuffling forward, his chest feeling as if an electric blanket were wrapped around his insides. He got to the girls' doorway, dazed, tired. Rosanna emerged from the burning whiteness eating away at their home and encroaching on their bodies. Olga was in her mother's arms, Lola had her arms wrapped around the woman's legs.

"Take them out, I'll get Marisa," Cruzado blared.

Her dead stare cut him off. "There's no need to go back in," she said gravely.

Cold iron poured over his knees and it was all Cruzado could do not to faint. He watched the tears silently travel the length of his wife's face, and he put his hand on her shoulder. "Mother," he said with a sick realization.

"I'll get the girls out." Rosanna clutched Olga tightly.

A whoosh of flame shot at them as if driven by a jet engine. The girls screamed and Cruzado beat at his arm, which was now on fire. "Yes, out, get them out into the yard," he desperately repeated. "I've got to see about Mama."

Karla had stumbled over. "I'll go with you."

"No." He pushed her and his wife toward the front. "You two must take care of the girls."

Smoke undulated behind the father. He'd stopped the fire on his arm, but the limb radiated a tremendous pain that intensified as he tried to moved it. "Mother," he called out, turning around and moving off. He was swallowed up by the mass of gray. "Mother," he called out as he found his way toward the small room off the service porch.

He could hear nothing as he got to the room. The door was closed and cool to the touch. Cruzado nervously twisted the knob and snatched the door open. More smoke, gray and glistening with malicious intent, came at him. He didn't bother to call her name as he bent down to her bed. She was warm, but she wouldn't be going anywhere in this world any longer.

The virulent pall congealed around him, gagging him and gorging into his watery eyes. Then it ebbed and parted to briefly reveal the carved rosemary wood cross he'd tacked over her bed. The cross for Christina.

Cruzado got up. The room was suddenly lit by a jagged

flame that was billowing across the worn linoleum. A flame eating its way to where he stood. From somewhere he could hear the neighbors' voices and hoped that meant the rest of his family was safe. He removed one of his mother's blankets and wrapped it around himself. Since he wasn't sure what he believed in after this life, he assumed God would find it awfully hypocritical for him to start praying for deliverance now. He got the blanket about him as best he could, took a last look at his mother, and plunged into the fire.

ONE

Antar Absalla was not one who enjoyed having a finger poking at him. And he was particularly not fond of Mrs. Reyisa Limón, twice widowed. He was therefore hard-pressed to hold his tongue as the older woman hooked her talon at his face as she reprimanded him.

"Where were your security people, Mr. Absalla?" she demanded for the fourth time since the meeting had begun a long hour ago.

Absalla mentally centered himself before speaking. "At those hours of the morning," he began with a forced calm, "there is a thinner crew than during peak time. This was a financial decision that your tenants' association made, Mrs. Limón. As you'd be aware if you'd reread the minutes from past board meetings." He managed not to smirk.

"You don't need to remind me of the procedures of Robert's Rules, Mr. Absalla," she leveled. "It's your performance that's in question here."

"I don't think that's quite the case, Reyisa," Henry Cady, the president of the tenants' association, responded. The aging Black man did that little self-effacing clearing of his throat and adjusted his black horn-rimmed glasses. "We've convened this emergency meeting to see what we need to do to make sure something like this horrible thing doesn't happen again."

Several heads around the square conference table indicated agreement.

Mrs. Limón leaned back in her seat, the chair creaking under her commanding size. The woman made a slight gesture, a slice of her palm like the drop of an axe. "I'm not saying we aren't. I am saying we hired a twenty-four-hour security force who are supposed to be ensuring the safety of our residents."

"And the Ra-Falcons were on the scene in less than three minutes," Absalla pointed out. "My team was helping put out the fire before the fire department got here. And two of them were taken to the hospital for smoke inhalation after trying to enter the premises to get free Mr. Cruzado." Indignation made his face warm but Absalla was determined not to lose his temper, and thus play into the scheme of this tormentor who sat across from him.

"You do have a point," Juan Carlos Higuerra said. "I think if we can discuss this so we can better the patrols, we can get something accomplished."

Limón fixed a gaze to seize hearts on Higuerra, silently damning him for his usual conciliatory approach. "We must also talk about how we're going to deal with this vicious gang element."

"The Ra-Falcons security are not the police," Cady asserted.

"But"—the long finger went to work again—"Absalla does employ those he admits are ex-gang members. They can find out who killed the Cruzados. If they don't know already."

"I've asked my people what they've heard, and no one knew about any rumor to harm the Cruzados. And of course we will continue to ask around to see if we can find out anything." Then he used his index finger on Limón.

"Yes, some of the Ra-Falcons used to be gang members," Absalla continued. "They come from these impoverished neighborhoods. They are also young men and women who have decided to turn their lives around, and give something back. This is not so-called, it is a fact. None of my crew are criminals. They wouldn't be on the patrol if they weren't disciplined and dedicated."

"Some of them used to be Scalp Hunters though, right?" Mrs. Graves, who'd been quiet until now, asked.

"Yes," Absalla answered. "Just as some of them used to be members of one or more of the Rolling Daltons set or the Del Nines."

Mrs. Limón leaned forward again, her heavy breasts expanding against the edge of the table. "What's important is that everybody around the Rancho says it was the Scalp Hunters who firebombed the Cruzados' apartment. The little bastards set the fire off in the girls' room. They broke the window and shoved their . . ."—she paused, searching for the word—"Molotov right in there between the bars." Her sunken face testified to the cruelty of the crime.

"How do you know that?" Cady inquired.

"It's common knowledge," she barked.

"I don't mean the rumor about who set the fire," Cady clarified. "I mean how do you know where the device went off less than two days after the incident."

"I have friends on the fire commission," she said proudly.

She bestowed on Absalla a sidelong glance, which seemed to imply she also had friends on other commissions—like the one that oversaw the police department. He felt like backhanding her.

"I've already sat down with my sergeants to figure out how

we can change our patrols to best cover the complex during the off-hours. But I'm afraid it's difficult without putting more people on staff."

Limón snickered but didn't say anything.

Cady said, "We're under the knife on this, Mr. Absalla. As you know, the owners of this property will soon be allowed by the Housing and Urban Development Department to place the Rancho on the private market. To counter that, we have to have a two-thirds majority of the families organized to agree to buy the property for themselves. If the residents vote to incorporate as a limited-equity cooperative, we can qualify for federal grants and loans to do so."

Cady removed his glasses. "I don't need to tell anyone here, the conservatives who control Congress are looking for any excuse not to allow those grants to be issued. These murders must be cleared up if we are to have a chance at realizing something for ourselves."

"I know we need results," Absalla said sincerely.

"Not to mention your contract comes up around the same time as the grant application," Limón needlessly reminded him. "And if the murderers of the Cruzados remain free, let alone if more horrible things happen to other Latino families, this body will take that as a sign we may need to do things differently."

"Blacks get attacked too," one of the African-Americans interjected.

"Nobody's saying different," Mrs. Limón blurted.

Trying to ease the tension, Cady said, "Let's stay together, people. This whole body must examine and discuss the facts. We have to set the example for the rest of the Rancho." He looked directly at Mrs. Limón. Surprisingly, she bestowed a deferential smile on him without displaying any of her usual combativeness.

Absalla promised to submit a revised patrol plan to the tenants' association by the end of the week. Leaving the multipurpose center, Absalla noted not for the first time the tranquility it was possible to find walking around the projects. Sure, all the cinder block buildings, lying squat and heavy and uninteresting-looking against L.A.'s lethal air, wouldn't be on the cover of *Architectural Digest* anytime soon. And yes, the taupe-colored apartments were in bad need of paint, having last seen a fresh coat sometime during the middle of the Bradley Administration.

But many of the residents took pride in keeping their plots neat, their stoops swept clean. Arrow shirts and prim little girls' dresses hung nonchalantly from clotheslines, and several dogs romped around, wagging their tails, their brown eyes gleaming with playfulness.

As he turned a corner on the row of apartments along Biddy Mason Lane, Absalla spotted several young Black men lounging against the fender of a lowered '73 Monte Carlo, the front raised on jack stands. Despite himself, he instantly categorized the youth. Due, he reasoned as he confidently strolled past, to the blaring boom box at their feet and the ubiquitous forty-ouncer being passed around.

He purposefully slowed down. "You young brothers ought to put as much time into cracking a book as you do standing around bullshitting and drinking that piss."

One of the young men was tall with elongated muscles like an NBA pick. His shirt was unbuttoned, displaying a torso adorned with three California Youth Authority-type tattoos. He bowed slightly. "*A-Salam-aleikum*," he said, chuckling, and the others also dipped their heads.

"Got some pigs' feet if you want one, Minister Absalla," another one piped in.

The security chief didn't even bother to shake his head as

he moved on. The offices of the Ra-Falcons were located on the second floor of the building housing the laundry rooms. It was a structure on the southwest end of the complex, some distance from the old, defunct Southern Pacific tracks that cleaved diagonally through the Rancho.

Originally, when the place was built in the waning days of FDR's New Deal years, the Rancho, located near the central city, was envisioned as an experiment in planned multiracial living. The Taj, as the old-timers called the place, along with public housing places like Nickerson Gardens and Imperial Courts farther south in Watts, had also been part of that vision. They were all part of a plan that was drafted by the progressives who'd burrowed their way into the local Housing Authority. It was an objective endorsed by the bipartisan reform forces at work in the city in those days.

But those people, and that dream of institutions playing a role in the engineering of racial harmony, had both long since been discarded like so many old bottles.

Absalla's reflections ended as he arrived at the Ra-Falcons' office. On its steel door was a colorful decal, which displayed a stylized profile of a falcon's head with a golden ankh prominent in the center of its ebon orb. Encircling the head was a border containing various African and Egyptian symbols of the warrior and the harvest.

Before he could grasp the knob, the door swung inward to allow a man with sergeant's stripes on his shirt's bicep and another man, a corporal, into the passageway.

"Brothers," Absalla greeted the two.

The sergeant, Eddie Waters, said, "Boss man, how'd it go at the meeting?"

"We got to get on this bad, Eddie," Absalla said, zeroing them both with a stern look.

"I know," Keith 2X, the other one, answered. "There's already been a retaliation."

Absalla didn't want to seem out of the loop in front of his crew, but he hadn't heard and so was forced to ask. "What happened? I've been so busy with the tenants' association that I didn't catch this."

"Old Mrs. Ketchum and her sister got a nasty note tacked to their door last night," Waters said. "The note said something about how the Blacks at the Rancho bring down the place, and how maybe somebody's going to do something about it."

"Their apartment's near the Cruzados'," Absalla said. "I guess they didn't see who left the note."

"No, but it's a sure thing them Los Domingos did it," Keith 2X replied.

"We're on our way to check it out, and maybe get a little sumptin' sumptin' on them punk-asses," Waters added with enthusiasm.

"Don't be no provocateurs, you hear," Absalla warned them. "Just confirm it if you can, understand?"

"We ain't scared of them *mojados*," Waters spat with bravado.

"Restraint, Black man, remember," Absalla retorted.

"It's cool," Waters said, and the two started to leave. "Oh yeah, there's an ese in there to see you." He grinned.

"Who?"

"Surprise." Waters tapped 2X on the shoulder, and the two departed.

The Ra-Falcons' office was one large room with two feeder rooms off that. A third area had been a walk-in utility closet, but the door had been removed. It now served as residence for a fax and a small refrigerator.

The larger area contained a black vinyl couch trimmed in

ash wood with matching chairs scattered about. Several other chairs and desks, spanning various eras and tastes, were also present.

Hunched over the phone at the main desk was a woman who also had sergeant's stripes on the sleeve of her dark blue uniform, LaToyce Blaine. She made small circles with her free hand as she talked, her vermillion nails flashing like dry blood on shark's teeth.

"Hold on," she said to whoever she was talking to. "Five-0 in there to see you," she whispered to Absalla.

The security chief didn't break stride as he went into one of the lesser rooms that served as his inner office. He came upon a Latino, who he made to be a Chicano, dressed in an olive green gabardine suit. He wore a bronze-hued tie, offset by a dark green shirt.

The cop, who'd been looking at a mounted photo of Absalla leading a contingent at the Million Man March, turned to greet him. "I'm Lieutenant Marasco Seguin," the man with the drooping mustache said. He handed Absalla a card.

On the card's left corner was a raised-relief image of a detective's shield in silver. Superimposed over that was a gold banner proclaiming his rank in blue lettering, City Hall in gold, and below that a bar in gold with his badge number in blue. The card stated that Seguin worked out of Wilshire Division on Pico.

Absalla put the card on his desk and stood looking at the clean-decked cop. "Look, Lieutenant, a couple of detectives from Newton have already been all over me about this Cruzado mess." He let his annoyance show. "'Sides, aren't you out of your division?"

Seguin scratched at his chin. "This is an investigation the brass wants solved, with haste. I'm temporarily reassigned, and in charge of Fitzhugh and Zaneski's investigation."

Absalla was tempted to tell Seguin he'd found Zaneski particularly funky to deal with, but he wasn't sure this Chicano would empathize with a Black man's plight. He moved behind his desk and they both sat down.

"Why is this murder so important to the LAPD?" Absalla asked.

"It's a little unusual even for the Rancho to have a triple homicide in one night." He paused a beat, and as he went on, a sour look contorted his face. "Especially when one of them was a little child."

"And the city wants the turnover of the Rancho and other public housing units to go through," Absalla observed. "No more matching funds the county is obligated to pony up if there's no federal program. The cost savings must look real good to the county supervisors what with the budget shortfalls we always have."

"Sometimes interests collide, Mr. Absalla," Seguin countered. "Some of your employees have records, don't they?"

"You know they do. I've asked all of them if they know anything, and they say they don't. These young folk who are the Ra-Falcons have demonstrated time and again they are no longer following the life, Lieutenant."

He put his hand flat on the desk like a distended creature. "I vouch for each and every one of them." His gaze didn't move off Seguin.

The cop said nothing and Absalla continued. "And it's still anyone's guess on who did the firebombing. I heard that Cruzado may have been mixed up in some kind of trouble back in his hometown in Mexico. That's why he came up here."

"I'd like copies of everybody's personnel record, Mr. Absalla."

"I don't think so without a court order."

"This isn't about you against the blue-eyed devil, man. This is about finding the guilty."

"A ten-year-old Black boy named Troy was gunned down three months ago in what we gleefully call a cycle-by. Where was your special assignment then?" Absalla demanded.

"Sometimes it takes the deaths of one too many innocents to make things happen."

The right kind of innocents. "Uh-huh."

"I'll have the court order in the morning, Mr. Absalla." Seguin stood up, unconsciously fingering his tie. "I want to repeat that the department is looking for a slam dunk on this. Cooperation can go a long way."

"I'll bear that in mind."

"Please do."

Seguin left and Absalla sat looking intently out the grilled window at a cracked concrete walkway and one of those plastic tricycles designed to look like a rocket sled. After some moments, he got up and went back into the outer room.

Blaine was busy filling out her patrol report from last night. An oldies soul station played softly on the radio near her.

"Who was that brother you mentioned to me?" Absalla asked, moving about the room like a panther in search of meat.

The sergeant's braided head tilted toward the ceiling. "Ah, Pope or something like that."

"And he's a private detective?"

The young woman shook her braids. "I think so. At least, he helped a girlfriend of my friend whose boyfriend was shot to death."

He didn't bother to follow that trail. "Get his number, will you?"

"What you up to, Antar?"

"About not being put in a trick bag." With that the stocky, shaved-headed Muslim went back into his office, closing the door tightly against what he could feel was a mother of a storm gathering.

Other Titles in the Soho Crime Series

STEPHANIE BARRON
(Jane Austen's England)
Jane and the Twelve Days of Christmas
Jane and the Waterloo Map
Jane and the Year Without a Summer
Jane and the Final Mystery

F.H. BATACAN
(Philippines)
Smaller and Smaller Circles

JAMES R. BENN
(World War II Europe)
Billy Boyle
The First Wave
Blood Alone
Evil for Evil
Rag & Bone
A Mortal Terror
Death's Door
A Blind Goddess
The Rest Is Silence
The White Ghost
Blue Madonna
The Devouring
Solemn Graves
When Hell Struck Twelve
The Red Horse
Road of Bones
From the Shadows
Proud Sorrows
The Phantom Patrol

The Refusal Camp: Stories

KATE BEUTNER
(Massachusetts)
Killingly

CARA BLACK
(Paris, France)
Murder in the Marais
Murder in Belleville

CARA BLACK CONT.
Murder in the Sentier
Murder in the Bastille
Murder in Clichy
Murder in Montmartre
Murder on the Ile Saint-Louis
Murder in the Rue de Paradis
Murder in the Latin Quarter
Murder in the Palais Royal
Murder in Passy
Murder at the Lanterne Rouge
Murder Below Montparnasse
Murder in Pigalle
Murder on the Champ de Mars
Murder on the Quai
Murder in Saint-Germain
Murder on the Left Bank
Murder in Bel-Air
Murder at the Porte de Versailles
Murder at la Villette

Three Hours in Paris
Night Flight to Paris

HENRY CHANG
(Chinatown)
Chinatown Beat
Year of the Dog
Red Jade
Death Money
Lucky

BARBARA CLEVERLY
(England)
The Last Kashmiri Rose
Strange Images of Death
The Blood Royal
Not My Blood
A Spider in the Cup
Enter Pale Death
Diana's Altar

Fall of Angels
Invitation to Die

COLIN COTTERILL
(Laos)
The Coroner's Lunch
Thirty-Three Teeth
Disco for the Departed
Anarchy and Old Dogs
Curse of the Pogo Stick
The Merry Misogynist
Love Songs from a Shallow Grave
Slash and Burn
The Woman Who Wouldn't Die
Six and a Half Deadly Sins
I Shot the Buddha
The Rat Catchers' Olympics
Don't Eat Me
The Second Biggest Nothing
The Delightful Life of a Suicide Pilot

The Motion Picture Teller

ELI CRANOR
(Arkansas)
Don't Know Tough
Ozark Dogs
Broiler

MARIA ROSA CUTRUFELLI
(Italy)
Tina, Mafia Soldier

GARRY DISHER
(Australia)
The Dragon Man
Kittyhawk Down
Snapshot
Chain of Evidence
Blood Moon
Whispering Death
Signal Loss

Wyatt
Port Vila Blues
Fallout

Under the Cold Bright Lights

TERESA DOVALPAGE
(Cuba)
Death Comes in through the Kitchen
Queen of Bones
Death under the Perseids
Last Seen in Havana
Death of a Telenovela Star (A Novella)

DAVID DOWNING
(World War II Germany)
Zoo Station
Silesian Station
Stettin Station
Potsdam Station
Lehrter Station
Masaryk Station
Wedding Station
Union Station

(World War I)
Jack of Spies
One Man's Flag
Lenin's Roller Coaster
The Dark Clouds Shining
Diary of a Dead Man on Leave

RAMONA EMERSON
(Navajo Nation)
Shutter

NICOLÁS FERRARO
(Argentina)
Cruz
My Favorite Scar

AGNETE FRIIS
(Denmark)
What My Body Remembers
The Summer of Ellen

TIMOTHY HALLINAN
(Thailand)
The Fear Artist
For the Dead
The Hot Countries

TIMOTHY HALLINAN CONT.
Fools' River
Street Music

(Los Angeles)
Crashed
Little Elvises
The Fame Thief
Herbie's Game
King Maybe
Fields Where They Lay
Nighttown
Rock of Ages

METTE IVIE HARRISON
(Mormon Utah)
The Bishop's Wife
His Right Hand
For Time and All Eternities
Not of This Fold
The Prodigal Daughter

MICK HERRON
(England)
Slow Horses
Dead Lions
The List (A Novella)
Real Tigers
Spook Street
London Rules
The Marylebone Drop (A Novella)
Joe Country
The Catch (A Novella)
Slough House
Bad Actors

Down Cemetery Road
The Last Voice You Hear
Why We Die
Smoke and Whispers

Reconstruction
Nobody Walks
This Is What Happened
Dolphin Junction: Stories
The Secret Hours

NAOMI HIRAHARA
(Japantown)
Clark and Division
Evergreen

STEPHEN MACK JONES
(Detroit)
August Snow
Lives Laid Away
Dead of Winter
Deus X

LENE KAABERBØL & AGNETE FRIIS
(Denmark)
The Boy in the Suitcase
Invisible Murder
Death of a Nightingale
The Considerate Killer

MARTIN LIMÓN
(South Korea)
Jade Lady Burning
Slicky Boys
Buddha's Money
The Door to Bitterness
The Wandering Ghost
G.I. Bones
Mr. Kill
The Joy Brigade
Nightmare Range
The Iron Sickle
The Ville Rat
Ping-Pong Heart
The Nine-Tailed Fox
The Line
GI Confidential
War Women

ED LIN
(Taiwan)
Ghost Month
Incensed
99 Ways to Die
Death Doesn't Forget

PETER LOVESEY
(England)
The Circle
The Headhunters
False Inspector Dew
Rough Cider
On the Edge
The Reaper

(Bath, England)
The Last Detective
Diamond Solitaire
The Summons
Bloodhounds
Upon a Dark Night
The Vault
Diamond Dust
The House Sitter
The Secret Hangman
Skeleton Hill
Stagestruck
Cop to Corpse
The Tooth Tattoo
The Stone Wife
Down Among the Dead Men
Another One Goes Tonight
Beau Death
Killing with Confetti
The Finisher
Diamond and the Eye
Showstopper

(London, England)
Wobble to Death
The Detective Wore Silk Drawers
Abracadaver
Mad Hatter's Holiday
The Tick of Death
A Case of Spirits
Swing, Swing Together
Waxwork

Bertie and the Tinman
Bertie and the Seven Bodies
Bertie and the Crime of Passion

SUJATA MASSEY
(1920s Bombay)
The Widows of Malabar Hill
The Satapur Moonstone
The Bombay Prince
The Mistress of Bhatia House

FRANCINE MATHEWS
(Nantucket)
Death in the Off-Season
Death in Rough Water
Death in a Mood Indigo
Death in a Cold Hard Light
Death on Nantucket
Death on Tuckernuck
Death on a Winter Stroll

SEICHŌ MATSUMOTO
(Japan)
Inspector Imanishi Investigates

CHRIS McKINNEY
(Post Apocalyptic Future)
Midnight, Water City
Eventide, Water City
Sunset, Water City

PHILIP MILLER
(North Britain)
The Goldenacre
The Hollow Tree

FUMINORI NAKAMURA
(Japan)
The Thief
Evil and the Mask
Last Winter, We Parted
The Kingdom
The Boy in the Earth
Cult X
My Annihilation
The Rope Artist

STUART NEVILLE
(Northern Ireland)
The Ghosts of Belfast
Collusion

STUART NEVILLECONT.
Stolen Souls
The Final Silence
Those We Left Behind

So Say the Fallen

The Traveller & Other Stories
House of Ashes

(Dublin)
Ratlines

GARY PHILLIPS
(Los Angeles)
One-Shot Harry
Ash Dark as Night

Violent Spring
Perdition, U.S.A.
Bad Night Is Falling
Only the Wicked

SCOTT PHILLIPS
(Western US)
Cottonwood
The Devil Raises His Own

That Left Turn at Albuquerque

KWEI QUARTEY
(Ghana)
Murder at Cape Three Points
Gold of Our Fathers
Death by His Grace

The Missing American
Sleep Well, My Lady
Last Seen in Lapaz
The Whitewashed Tombs

QIU XIAOLONG
(China)
Death of a Red Heroine
A Loyal Character Dancer
When Red Is Black

NILIMA RAO
(1910s Fiji)
A Disappearance in Fiji

MARCIE R. RENDON
(Minnesota's Red River Valley)
Murder on the Red River
Girl Gone Missing
Sinister Graves

JAMES SALLIS
(New Orleans)
The Long-Legged Fly
Moth
Black Hornet
Eye of the Cricket
Bluebottle
Ghost of a Flea

Sarah Jane

MICHAEL SEARS
(Queens, New York)
Tower of Babel

JOHN STRALEY
(Sitka, Alaska)
The Woman Who Married a Bear
The Curious Eat Themselves
The Music of What Happens
Death and the Language of Happiness
The Angels Will Not Care
Cold Water Burning
Baby's First Felony
So Far and Good

(Cold Storage, Alaska)
The Big Both Ways
Cold Storage, Alaska
What Is Time to a Pig?
Blown by the Same Wind

LEONIE SWANN
(England)
The Sunset Years of Agnes Sharp
Agnes Sharp and the Trip of a Lifetime

KAORU TAKAMURA
(Japan)
Lady Joker

AKIMITSU TAKAGI
(Japan)
The Tattoo Murder Case
Honeymoon to Nowhere
The Informer

CAMILLA TRINCHIERI
(Tuscany)
Murder in Chianti
The Bitter Taste of Murder
Murder on the Vine
The Road to Murder

HELENE TURSTEN
(Sweden)
Detective Inspector Huss
The Torso
The Glass Devil
Night Rounds
The Golden Calf
The Fire Dance
The Beige Man
The Treacherous Net
Who Watcheth
Protected by the Shadows

Hunting Game
Winter Grave
Snowdrift

An Elderly Lady Is Up to No Good
An Elderly Lady Must Not Be Crossed

ILARIA TUTI
(Italy)
Flowers over the Inferno
The Sleeping Nymph
Daughter of Ashes

JANWILLEM VAN DE WETERING
(Holland)
Outsider in Amsterdam
Tumbleweed
The Corpse on the Dike
Death of a Hawker
The Japanese Corpse
The Blond Baboon
The Maine Massacre
The Mind-Murders
The Streetbird
The Rattle-Rat
Hard Rain
Just a Corpse at Twilight
Hollow-Eyed Angel
The Perfidious Parrot
The Sergeant's Cat: Collected Stories

JACQUELINE WINSPEAR
(Wartime England)
Maisie Dobbs
Birds of a Feather
The Comfort of Ghosts